The Cross
and the Dragon

The Cross
and the Dragon

by

Kim Rendfeld

Fireship Press
www.FireshipPress.com

The Cross and the Dragon - Copyright © 2012 by Kim Rendfeld

ISBN-13: 978-1-61179-227-0 (paperback)
978-1-61179-228-7 (e-book)

BISAC Subject Headings:
FIC014000 / FICTION / Historical
FIC027050 / FICTION / Romance / Historical
FIC000000 / FICTION / General

Cover design by Christine Horner

Cover art: *Enid and Geraint*, 1907, by Rowland Wheelwright (1870-1955)

Address all correspondence to:
Fireship Press, LLC
P.O. Box 68412
Tucson, AZ 85737
Or visit our website at:
www.FireshipPress.com

1.0

For my husband, Randy.

Acknowledgments

I could not have re-created life in eighth-century Europe without the work of scholars who translated primary sources from medieval Latin and analyzed them. My library includes Einhard's *The Life of Charlemagne* translated by Evelyn Scherabon Firchow and Edwin H. Zeydel; *Carolingian Chronicles*, which includes the Royal Frankish Annals and Nithard's Histories, translated by Bernard Walter Scholz with Barbara Rogers; P.D. King's *Charlemagne: Translated Sources*, and Pierre Riché's *Daily Life in the World of Charlemagne*. (Historical novelist's disclaimer: any mistakes are mine and mine alone.)

But there is more to writing a novel than research. The Lafayette (Indiana) Novel Group assisted me with storytelling through their insightful critiques. I owe Mary Ellen Freel, Roberta Gellis, Laura Havran, Robin Morehouse, and Mary Ann Nester more than I can ever say.

I would also like to thank the crew at Fireship Press for investing and believing in *The Cross and the Dragon*. Special thanks go to my editor, Jessica Knauss, for her enthusiasm and helpful suggestions in giving this novel its final polish. I wish her all the best in her new venture.

I could not have done this project without my family's steadfast support of my creative endeavors, especially my husband, Randy. He has been unfailing as I spent hours holed up in my office, staring at the computer screen, my mind miles and centuries away. He even made sure I got fed as I worked on revisions.

Chapter 1

Late August 773
King Charles's assembly in Geneva

Alda wished she did not loathe the man her brother wanted her to marry.

She glanced at Count Ganelon of Dormagen, sitting to her left at dinner. When she had met him two months before at Drachenhaus, her home many leagues to the north, she had thought him the handsomest man in Francia. Muscular, with broad shoulders and well-formed legs, he had a face that could have been chiseled from marble, topped by a cap of pale blond hair. In the castle's great hall, his silver medallions gleamed in the light from the walnut-oil lamps and midday sun.

A movement caught Alda's eye. A cupbearer, head down and shoulders hunched, shuffled toward Ganelon. No older than ten winters, the boy was stick thin and clothed in rags.

How can anyone so mistreat his servants? she thought, wincing.

His face a mosaic of bruises, the boy sipped from the cup and placed it in front of Ganelon. Alda looked away, disgusted with Ganelon and still seething over this morning's argument with her brother, Count Alfihar of Drachenhaus. Alfihar had ignored her protests, insisting that she did not need to like Ganelon to marry him. No, she didn't, she admitted to herself, but she wanted to be able to suffer her husband's company.

She turned her head toward the roasted venison, steaming in front of her on the slab of stale bread that served as a plate. Enticed by the aroma, she tore into the meat with her eating knife.

Ganelon sneered. "I never would have guessed a frail-looking girl like you would have such an appetite."

Alda's pale cheeks flushed. She wished she could think of a cutting reply. Any mention of her weight vexed her. She had tried to make herself plump, but no matter how much she ate, she could not add to her hips or breasts. Finally, her words came out in a grumble. "Obviously, I am not frail."

"You are lucky anyone would wish to marry you. You are so thin you look like a peasant in disguise. Even that servant beside you has more flesh than you."

The heat of a blush spread over Alda's face and down her neck. Veronica, her servant and companion, had a fuller figure, but no man with manners would point it out. Why would Ganelon insult her? Baring her teeth, Alda stabbed the meat, wishing it could be Ganelon's face.

To her right, Veronica nudged Alda. "A pity God blessed Count Ganelon with good looks instead of a good brain," she whispered. "Most men flatter women they want to marry."

Alda covered her mouth to suppress a giggle.

"Why do you allow your servants to eat with you?" Ganelon asked contemptuously.

"Her name is Veronica." Alda's forest green eyes flashed. "She is my foster sister and my dearest friend."

Laying aside her knife, Alda squeezed Veronica's hand under the table. How could Ganelon say such a thing about the young woman whose mother had nursed both of them?

"My servants stay away from the table," Ganelon said. "I cannot bear to watch them eat like beasts."

"Perhaps you should give them more food," Alda snapped. Her gaze fell to the jeweled hilt of his eating knife. "My brother says you can afford it."

"That is not your concern," he retorted.

Alda's nostrils flared. She did not know how she was going to endure Ganelon through dinner, let alone the rest of her life. She gazed to her right. Alfihar was dining five paces away with their uncles and the man she wanted, Prince Hruodland, heir to the March of Brittany and King Charles's kinsman.

Hruodland's features were plainer than Ganelon's but still pleasing. At perhaps twenty-one winters, slightly older than Alfihar, Hruodland was a tall man with the warrior's build that came from wearing armor and wielding a sword. He had dark brown, almost black, piercing eyes, a long nose, a square jaw, and dark hair that fell to his shoulders. She smiled as she remembered meeting him in the castle's courtyard yesterday morning and later talking with him long into the night.

Veronica's whisper broke into her thoughts. "Stop gawking at Hruodland! It will provoke Count Ganelon."

Alda's lips drew into a thin line, but she followed Veronica's advice and turned her head. This meal was difficult enough without Ganelon's jealousy. Glancing at Ganelon, she shuddered. His icy blue eyes were full of malice.

Other guests chatted and laughed, while the musicians played and sang. But dinner continued in silence between Alda and Ganelon. Alda was glad when the meal was finished and guests started to rise from the benches. As Alda got up and stepped over the bench, she saw Alfihar and their uncles from Bonn, Bishop Leonhard and Count Beringar, stand. In animated conversation, they walked to the stone hearth and sat on a bench, their backs to her. Watching Hruodland leave the table, Alda heard a cough and looked down.

Ganelon's scrawny servant was staring at the slab of bread upon which her meat and vegetables had rested. Now it was empty save for the gristle and bone. The child gazed up at Alda. He had the look of a dog begging for food.

"Poor child," Alda murmured. She reached toward the table and handed the servant the bread.

A meaty hand grabbed her right arm and yanked her a half turn, causing her to stumble. Ganelon was standing over her. Alda struggled to pull away, but his grip was like a hunter's snare.

"That is my servant!" he shouted, his breath a hot blast reeking of wine. "You have no right to defy me."

"Release me!" Alda cried.

Ganelon raised his right hand, preparing already to claim his marital right to beat her.

Mother of God, save me. Alda clutched her dragon amulet with her free hand.

A shadow fell across Ganelon. Hruodland rushed forward, seized Ganelon's raised arm and shoved him away. Ganelon let go of Alda's arm and staggered back a few steps. Hruodland placed his tall frame between them.

"Who do you think you are?" Ganelon snarled at Hruodland. "You have no right to interfere."

He is the answer to my prayer. Alda's pulse pounded in her dry throat. Standing on her toes, she watched Ganelon over Hruodland's shoulder. She rubbed her arm, too shocked to speak.

"Alda is my friend." Hruodland's baritone was on the edge of fury. "I will protect my friends."

"God gives a man the right, no, the duty, to discipline his wife," Ganelon yelled.

Anger gave Alda her voice. "I am not your wife."

From the corner of her eye, Alda saw Alfihar, Leonhard, and Beringar hurry toward them.

"Why are you quarrelling?" Leonhard calmly asked.

"This viper, he stuck himself into a matter of discipline between me and Alda," Ganelon spat.

"Discipline?" Alda blurted. "You were about to beat me for giving bread to a starving child. I hate you, Ganelon! You have no rights or duties over me. God has not joined us, and He never will!"

The men stared, speechless, at Alda. Alda covered her mouth, unable to believe her own outburst.

Leonhard rushed to Alda and put his arm around her shoulders. "Come with me, Alda. You have had too much wine and need to rest."

As Leonhard led Alda through the great hall, she looked over her shoulder.

"Hruodland, Ganelon," Alfihar said, raking his fingers through his light brown hair, "this must be a misunderstanding. Let us have some wine."

Hruodland and Ganelon glared at each other, like two dogs raising the fur behind their necks, growling and baring their teeth.

"I am well, Uncle," Alda murmured, turning her head toward him. "I had only a few sips from the cup."

"I know," he muttered. "I am trying to protect you. You surely were not in earnest."

"I meant every word. If you wish to protect me, persuade Alfihar to negotiate with another suitor. My brother will not listen to me."

She drew her sleeve past her elbow. Ganelon's grasp had left bruises on her pale skin.

"No one has ever touched me that way," she told Leonhard. She felt hot. Her face was flushed. "My father would never allow it. My father would end negotiations with a man like Ganelon."

Leonhard and Alda both looked back.

"Alfihar, forbid your sister from speaking with Hruodland," Ganelon bellowed. "He is trying to steal what is rightfully mine."

"She is not yours yet," Hruodland growled, his dark eyes narrowing, "and if you hurt her, I swear by God and all His Saints that you will taste my sword."

Alda gasped. "I must go back. I can't let Hruodland risk himself in a fight."

"You will do no such thing," Leonhard said quietly and firmly, pulling her closer. "Your presence will only make matters worse. It's only words, my dearling."

Something in Hruodland's voice told Alda he was not speaking idly. Joy and worry washed through her. He would challenge Ganelon to protect her! She tried to twist and go to Hruodland, but Leonhard's hold on her was strong.

"Niece, I said no," he muttered.

Alda looked back again.

Ganelon drew his muscular frame closer to Hruodland. "Alda belongs to me, not you!"

"You have no right to touch her!" Hruodland's spine was arrow straight.

"Uncle," Alda whispered, "it is not mere talk."

But broad-shouldered Beringar clapped his massive hands on Ganelon's and Hruodland's shoulders and slowly pushed the two men apart. "We should not fight among ourselves. His Holiness will need all of us to fight the enemy." His deep voice matched his hulking build and boomed throughout the hall.

"I will gladly use my sword to send the Lombards to hell." Ganelon's icy eyes bored into Hruodland.

"We are crossing the Alps to save Rome," Hruodland retorted, "not forever condemn the Lombards."

"We should be fighting the Saxons instead," Alfihar grumbled. "The moment they learn we're far away, those oath breakers will start burning churches again."

"But we have no choice," Hruodland replied. "Not even gold will lure Desiderius away from Rome."

See, Alfihar? Alda thought. *I told you the Lombard king is mad.*

"Son of a whore's filthy sow!" Alfihar said. "Still bitter that King Charles divorced his worthless daughter."

Ganelon chuckled.

Scowling, Hruodland looked about. "Don't let Grandmother Bertrada hear that. She hoped the marriage would bring peace."

Ganelon snorted in derision.

Beringar glowered at Alfihar and Ganelon. "The queen mother is not alone. She did everything she could, but peace with the Lombards is difficult, almost as difficult as peace between King Charles and his brother, God rest his soul."

"I'm surprised the peace between Uncle Charles and Uncle Carloman lasted as long as it did," Hruodland said. "Uncle Carloman was petty and jealous and not a good king."

Alda looked forward, glad they were no longer talking about her. "Alfihar is going to rebuke me for causing this quarrel," she said in a low voice.

Leonhard turned away from the group of men and led Alda toward the door that opened to the garden. Lingering at the doorway, she listened to the men again. Calling Desiderius all sorts of vile names, they were rehashing how the Lombard king tried to divide Francia and force Pope Hadrian to anoint Carloman's toddling sons, giving his young widow, Gerberga, the power to rule as regent.

"One might think..." Leonhard's voice trailed off, then he shook his head.

"One might think what?" Alda asked

"Nothing," Leonhard said. "Hruodland seems fond of you."

"He is a good friend. If it were not for him, Ganelon would have struck me. He has no right to do that, not yet, has he?"

"No, Niece, Ganelon has no right. Negotiations have barely started."

"How long will they take?"

"Weeks at least, probably months, maybe even years. Or, God willing, they fail altogether." He frowned. "I told Alfihar not to choose Ganelon. But you know how pig-headed your brother is, and with Beringar, it is doubly so. Neither admits to mistakes. When will you see fifteen years?"

Alda thought for a moment. "Next summer."

"Church law will be on your side then. The nuptials will require your consent."

Alda shivered despite the warmth of the day, praying it wouldn't come to that. Although Alfihar had never hit her before, her refusal to marry Ganelon might anger him enough to beat her, a punishment for her willfulness and the embarrassment she would cause the family. Or he could disown her and leave her without an inheritance, despite their late father's wishes. Then what would she do?

For a moment, Alda and Leonhard walked in silence through the garden just past its summer peak. The thyme and sage released their scents as Alda's skirts brushed past them.

Leonhard relaxed his hold on Alda's shoulder. "Promise me you will not seek Hruodland out."

"I enjoy Hruodland's company," she protested. "I have no reason to stay away from him."

"Do you not have eyes to see what happened in the hall?"

"Ganelon was going to beat me for an act of charity. Is that the man you want to be my husband?"

"You know I don't," Leonhard said impatiently, "but Alfihar and Beringar do. I will do my best to dissuade them, but if I fail, you must not inspire Ganelon's jealousy."

"I will not marry Ganelon," Alda said, a tremor in her voice. "I will join the convent on Nonnenwerth first!"

"With that crazed abbess?" Leonhard whispered. "That would be worse than marrying Ganelon."

"It can't be."

Alda heard someone approaching them from behind. Gritting her teeth, she wondered if it was Alfihar coming out to scold her. The tread was solid and heavy like a man's, but no, it was not Alfihar's footsteps. Her eyes widened. Was it Ganelon? Was that rat going to finish what he had started?

Her throat constricting, Alda looked up to Leonhard.

Her uncle glanced behind them. "We should talk to him," he said. "He will follow us if we walk away."

"I've had more than my fill of Ganelon today."

"It isn't Ganelon. It's Hruodland."

"Hruodland?" Alda beamed. She turned suddenly, her long ash blond hair flaring.

It was Hruodland! He quickened his pace when Alda faced him, and she lifted her skirts slightly so she could rush to meet him.

"Alda!" Leonhard's voice carried a warning, one she dared not disobey, not if he was to speak on her behalf against Ganelon.

She let her skirts fall and waited for Hruodland to come to her.

"Alda," Hruodland said anxiously, "did that cur hurt you?"

Alda's long sleeves now covered the bruises. How she wanted to show them to Hruodland and have him fight Ganelon and disfigure that hateful face. But Leonhard shook his head almost imperceptibly, telling her what she already knew. It would be wrong to draw Hruodland into a fight that was not his. She clasped her hands in front of her.

"I am well." She opened her mouth, but for a moment, no words came out. "I don't know how to thank you."

"It was nothing," Hruodland said. "I only wish I had stopped him earlier."

Leonhard cleared his throat. "Did Count Ganelon see you come out here, Prince Hruodland?"

"Why should I care what he sees? He was going to the assembly with Alfihar."

"Because I don't want your presence to send Count Ganelon into a jealous rage," Leonhard said. "It would be Lady Alda who suffers for it."

"I don't care how jealous that monster is," Alda snapped. "I refuse to marry him!"

"Alda," Leonhard said evenly, "this is no time to be willful."

Alda frowned, but she held her tongue, afraid Leonhard would change his mind if she contradicted him again in public.

"Now that you have seen my niece is well, Prince Hruodland, I must ask that you refrain from seeking her out again."

"Bishop Leonhard, why would your family negotiate with a man who would hurt Alda? Your family can do better than Ganelon of Dormagen."

"My brother, my nephew, and I will determine whom Lady Alda marries," Leonhard said coldly.

Alda looked down, her lower lip trembling. Although the marriage negotiations were not Hruodland's concern, she hated the way Leonhard was speaking to Hruodland, but she felt helpless.

She looked up when Hruodland touched her shoulder. "We are still friends," he said gently. "If you need my aid, send a message to the March of Brittany."

Alda nodded. This was his farewell, and there was nothing he or she could do about it. She feared if she spoke now she would burst into tears.

Chapter 2

Soft footsteps interrupted the conversation. Recognizing the rhythm of Veronica's walk, Alda felt her heart lighten slightly. She, Hruodland, and Leonhard turned toward the sound.

Veronica bowed, her dark braids almost sweeping the ground. "Prince Hruodland, Bishop Leonhard," she said, "my master, Count Alfihar of Drachenhaus, sent me to tell you that the assembly will start soon."

"Prince Hruodland and I must go inside," Leonhard said. "Alda, as long as you are quiet, you can listen to the discussion."

"I need air," Alda mumbled.

Before her confrontation with Ganelon, she had wanted to listen to the men making plans for war, but now she dreaded facing Alfihar again. She had no desire to hear him scold her for what she had said to Ganelon. Nor did she wish to see the ice-eyed, pale-haired count of Dormagen.

Choking back her frustration, Alda watched Hruodland and Leonhard return to the hall. Hruodland hesitated at the door and then turned toward her. The pain in his dark eyes pierced her.

No longer able to hold back the tears, Alda whirled around and fled further into the garden. Veronica ran after her.

In the shade of a yew hedge, Alda leaned over, hands on her knees, bracing herself against the sobs that rocked her body. She would never run to him when he came home from war and throw her arms around his neck. She would never know the feel of his embrace or the taste of his lips. He was lost to her, and all she could have was an occasional rumor from a passing merchant.

"I wish I knew some words to comfort you," Veronica said, stroking Alda's back.

"Hruodland wants me. I know he does. Why can't Alfihar see that?"

"Affection has nothing to do with marriage, especially marriage of the royal family. And the rumor is that Hruodland's father wants him to marry the daughter of the Breton duke. No count's sister can compete with that, even if the Breton were as ugly as a toad and you were as fair as the sun."

"But why must Alfihar insist on marrying me to a man I despise?"

"I hear Count Ganelon is wealthy."

"Oh, he drips with wealth and spares no expense on himself. A pity he won't use his treasure to care for his household. Why can't Alfihar see the obvious?" Alda wiped the tears from her cheeks.

"Your brother is a good man, but blinded by pride."

* * * * *

As the afternoon wore on, Alda grew more resentful of Ganelon. He had won. On the journey to Geneva with their soldiers, he had jeered at her interest in warfare, and now she was in the courtyard near the women's quarters, embroidering a skirt with Veronica.

"God curse Ganelon," Alda said between clenched teeth. "Because of him, we are here instead of listening to the plans for war."

"Why not go inside, then?" Veronica asked. "You cannot avoid Alfihar forever."

"I am in no hurry for his tirade. I did nothing wrong."

Veronica quickly looked down as if she were concentrating on a complicated stitch.

Again, Alda's curiosity about the plans for war gnawed at her. Laying down her embroidery, Alda gazed at the mountains, most of them steel gray and austere, some snow-capped, all cutting into the sky, more formidable than any fortress. *How will they ever cross them?*

"If only Father were here," Alda mused, picking up the needle again. "He would find me a lord who knows how to respect a lady, at least a man who knows it's rude to tell a woman she's too thin, even if it is true."

"I've been thinking about what he said at dinner," Veronica said. "It's like when your mother points out the defects in a merchant's wares to make him lower the price."

"God's wounds, you're right! I expected haggling over the bride price and dowry but not insults. What is Ganelon thinking? That I will run to my brother and beg him to lower the bride price because I'm too ugly for any man to want me?"

"I told you God did not bless Ganelon with a good brain." Veronica giggled.

"Or a good heart." Alda twisted a thread. "What if Uncle Leonhard cannot sway Alfihar? If I marry Ganelon, could I send a message to the Church or anyone else? I would be at Ganelon's mercy, and he has no mercy. I fear him, Veronica."

"I know," Veronica said softly.

"It's more than that. Either this marriage will cost me my life, or I will become a murderer."

Veronica dropped her needle. "Alda, you don't mean that. He cannot..." She shook her head. "You don't have a murderous heart."

"I do mean it. He could make my heart as black as his."

Alda managed five more stitches before letting her needlework fall to her lap. Staring at the door to the great hall, she fidgeted. She could almost see Alfihar's flushed face, could almost feel his hands shaking her shoulders.

She glanced at the mountains, then the door. Setting her embroidery aside, she started to pace. She stopped and gazed at the door, tapping her finger to her lips. She could almost hear the noblemen arguing about Lombardy.

She narrowed her eyes. Veronica was right. Alfihar was going to scold her anyway. She might as well listen to the debate.

"Maybe I can sneak in without anyone noticing me," she muttered.

"Do you want me to put away our embroidery?" Veronica asked, already gathering needles and threads.

Nodding, Alda strode to the door and peeked inside. Bright with the light from the windows, lamps, and fire, the hall was spacious, especially now that the planks of the trestle tables and benches had been stacked against the walls. The nobles had gathered twenty-five paces to her right. Their voices echoed, forming a jumble of words.

Slipping inside, she crept toward the crowd. At the front of the room was a dais, where the king and queen sat on thrones. Even without his crown, Charles, the hero who had united Francia, would look like a king. A towering man in his mid-twenties, his torso and neck were massive with muscle. Round-faced, he had a long nose and large, bright eyes.

Charles's queen, Hildegard, a Swabian from an important family, was magnificent next to her husband. A year older than Alda, she was great with her second child and wore a vermillion gown that flattered her figure. Embroidered with gold thread, the gown lay over a purple fine linen tunic and matched her silk veil, secured with gold pins and topped by a crown, glittering with the rest of her finery.

See those jewels, Alfihar? Alda thought. *See those clothes? King Charles treats his wife like the high-born lady she is. Choose a man like that for me.*

When she reached the back of the crowd, Alda stood on her toes and craned her neck. Just off the dais and to the king's right, Queen Mother Bertrada, grim-faced, sat stiffly in an ornate chair. Tall and well past forty winters, she covered her hair with a black silk widow's veil secured by a silver and sapphire circlet. Beside her, a nurse sat on a stool and held the sleeping baby Prince Karl, the son of Charles and Hildegard. Prince Pepin, Charles's four-winter-old stoop-shouldered son by his first wife, a Frankish noblewoman, played with silver warriors at his nurse's feet. Near the children, two clerks with wax tablets and styluses listened intently to the conversation.

Hruodland and the king's uncle Bernard, a rugged warrior who had seen forty winters, stood just behind Bertrada, facing the king. Alda's gaze lingered on Hruodland. His sky blue tunic fit snugly on his torso and fell to his knees, showing off powerful calves in red silk leggings secured with dark blue bands of cloth. How she wished she could be closer! She scanned the crowd. Ganelon's pale head was in the front row near her brother and uncles.

Alda glanced over her shoulder. The door to the outside, her escape from Ganelon, was twenty paces away. At the sound of Hruodland's voice, she turned toward the dais.

"We should split the army in two," he said. "We can move faster through the mountains."

"If we move as one," Ganelon argued, a sneer in his voice, "we would overwhelm the Lombards."

"We can't overwhelm them if we're stuck in the Alps," Hruodland retorted.

"Lord Bernard," King Charles said in a tenor voice, "what say you?"

"We could more easily move our men if we do as Hruodland says," Bernard said, his voice raspy. "And we can confound Desiderius if we invade by two routes. I can take my men through the Great Saint Bernard Pass, you lead your followers through Mount Cenis, and we reunite where the paths meet in a valley."

"And what say you, my lady mother?"

"Split the army," Bertrada answered, her chin jutting. "With this foe, you will need every advantage. The Lombards are strong sons of whores in fortified cities. They will not surrender easily."

"My lady queen mother," Hildegard said smoothly, "if God wills it, we cannot fail. The Lombards closed the roads to keep the pope's envoy from us, but the Good Lord delivered him to us by sea. Surely, He will protect our men."

Charles laid his hand over his wife's and smiled at her. *You see, Alfihar?* Alda thought. *That is what I am talking about, a man who not only respects his wife but is fond of her.*

"Then we will hold Masses and litanies asking the Good Lord for His favor," Bertrada said. "I will see to it personally."

"My lady queen and my lady queen mother are wise," Charles said. "Let us do as Lord Bernard says. We will leave tomorrow after prime. We have no time to waste."

Even as the crowd dispersed and men filed past her, Alda stayed rooted to the mosaic floor, feeling as if she had been punched in the chest. She clutched her iron dragon amulet, hoping to draw strength from its oval stone, a fragment of Drachenfels Mountain near her home. *Tomorrow! They are leaving tomorrow!*

Her need to speak to Alfihar shoved aside her fear of his scolding. She approached her brother, weaving her way through the crowd. After she took a few steps, Alfihar turned and saw her. The annoyance on his face softened. He nodded to his uncles and said something to Ganelon, then made his way toward her.

"What troubles you?" he asked.

"The war in Lombardy." She grabbed Alfihar's hand.

"You are always this way before I go to war. Do not worry. I will be home in a few months." He patted her hand.

Alda gave him a tremulous smile. *That's what Father said the spring before he was killed.* "Promise me you will keep your dragon amulet with you at all times."

"I promise. And you wear yours as well."

"Yes, Alfihar. I will pray for you."

"I know." Alfihar kissed her forehead. "Tell the servants to pack for both of us. You must leave for home tomorrow."

"Very well," Alda murmured.

For a moment, neither spoke. Then Alfihar frowned and his features hardened. Alda's eyes widened. Not only was he about to scold her: he was going to humiliate her in public!

"I do not wish for us to part in anger," he said in a low, stern voice, "but I must say this. I am your brother, and it is your duty to obey me."

Alda nodded. She refused to allow Ganelon to turn what might be her last conversation with Alfihar into harsh words. She would not quarrel with her brother this time, but their argument was far from over.

* * * * *

At the evening meal, Alda sat beside Alfihar. Beringar's deep laugh drew her attention. His receding hairline of sandy locks was one of the few signs he was past his prime. But two decades of wearing armor had made Beringar's shoulders and chest as broad as the trunk of an old tree and his arms like thick branches. Beside Beringar was his younger, thinner brother, Leonhard. In white robes, Leonhard had the look of a scholar: pale skin, clerical tonsure, bright gray eyes, and hands like those a woodcarver would create for Jesus — long, clean fingers, square at the tips.

Her gaze then fell on Ganelon. He was looking her up and down as if he were appraising a horse. Alda, unnerved, shifted in her seat.

Heaven forbid that I be destined to be his wife. Maybe the war will claim him, she thought, feeling a twinge of shame at wishing for a countryman's death. Then, she felt a flush of anger. Already his evil was preying on her!

She looked toward Hruodland, now seated five paces away with his younger brother, Gerard, who was preparing for the priesthood. Alda's melancholy deepened. After the war in Lombardy, he would return to the March of Brittany, many leagues west of her home. She would pray for Hruodland to survive the battles, even though she had one certainty. *I shall never see him again.*

Chapter 3

Late September 773
Drachenhaus on the Rhine, south of Bonn

During the evening meal in the great hall, Alda's gaze fell on the tapestries recounting Siegfried's deeds in reds, greens, and yellows, brilliant even by firelight. She realized how much she had missed Drachenhaus, built with stone from Drachenfels Mountain across the Rhine, where Siegfried had slain the dragon centuries ago and bathed in its blood for invulnerability. The mountain's rock carried that magic, and Alda felt it envelop her.

When servants brought in stews, soups, roasted pork, and bread, the aromas from the food blended with the wood smoke from the fire, lemon balm rubbed on the wooden tables and benches, and the fresh mint and thyme strewn on the stone floor. Alda stared at Alfihar's empty chair at the head of the table. Where was her brother tonight? Was he shivering near a fire with their uncles and Hruodland? Were they exhausted from their trek up peaks so high and sharp they cut into the sky, dwarfing the mountain on which her home sat? She shuddered. After the warriors' struggle with the Alps' steep paths and trackless ridges, a well-armed and well-armored enemy awaited them.

Her mother's voice interrupted her thoughts. "I am getting old," Theodelinda said.

Alda gazed quizzically at her mother. Theodelinda had seen almost forty winters, and care had etched lines around her mouth and gray eyes. Yet her mother possessed a strength that belied her short stature, slenderness, and age.

Theodelinda rubbed the small of her back. "I no longer have the vigor to watch over both the house and the affairs of the count. I need you to watch over the house while I oversee the farms and settle quarrels among the peasants. You will have a household of your own soon."

Alda exchanged a glance with Veronica sitting a few paces away. Veronica raised her eyebrows.

"Thank you, Mother," Alda replied. "I promise to care for this house. I shall be worthy of holding the keys."

"It heartens me to hear it," her mother said.

Theodelinda loosened her girdle and slid off the ring with the keys. She gave them one last look before handing them to Alda. Alda cupped the keys in her hand. At this moment, they were more precious than the rings on her fingers.

Over the next few days, Alda found running a household more difficult than she had expected. The servants readily obeyed all her mother's commands, but when Alda gave an order, they stopped working as soon as she left the room.

How does Mother rule them? Alda wondered.

She had to prove that she was a grown woman and could run a household by herself. Alda refused to seek help from her mother, who would again tell her she was only a child, but she suspected the servants knew that as well.

"This is the third time I have told you to clean the hearth," Alda scolded a maidservant in the hall.

The maid gave Alda a defiant look.

"Have her whipped," Alda heard her mother say behind her. "Alda, if you do not discipline them, they will take advantage of you."

Alda stood still.

"Alda!"

Alda marched toward the servant and delivered a slap that carried all of her frustration. The maid froze and stared at Alda. Alda raised her hand again. Flinching, the maid immediately grabbed the broom and swept in quick strokes. Alda turned to go to the kitchen and plan dinner.

"Alda, you need to watch over that servant," her mother said. "She has already proven her laziness."

Alda faced the servant. "I am going to the kitchen." She pointed to the hearth. "That had better be spotless when I return, or you will receive more than a slap across the face. Understood?"

Her cheek still red, the servant nodded.

Alda turned to her mother. "If you want me to watch over this house, you must let me do so. You need not hover over me."

"The servant refused to do her work," Theodelinda replied. "She did it only when you disciplined her."

"The lesson is learned." Alda threw up her hands. "I must get to the kitchen or else you will ask why dinner has not been made." She added only half to herself, "I shall be eager for my own house."

"How can you be so ungrateful? When I came here, I was younger than you are now, and no one had taught me anything about caring for a house. I was completely lost. I am trying to teach you to be mistress of Ganelon's house."

"Mother," Alda said in a tone that sounded like a rebuke. "Please." Her tone then softened. "Please tell Alfihar to negotiate a betrothal with another man. Perhaps he will heed you."

"Daughter," Theodelinda said, exasperated, "Alfihar warned me of this in his letter. I had the clerk read it to me several times. Ganelon has much wealth. He has much to offer to the clan."

"Listen to me," Alda pleaded. "There must be another suitor who can make a good offer to our family. Like Hruodland of the March of Brittany."

"Hruodland of the March of Brittany?" Theodelinda blinked back her surprise. "You truly expect a match with the king's kinsman?"

"A generous dowry could lure him to us."

"The river has brought us riches, but Hruodland's family will want him to marry a princess or the daughter of a duke, not the sister of a count."

Alda frowned. Her mother was right, but she was not about to admit it. "Alfihar should choose someone other than Ganelon."

"I understand why you would be uneasy about marriage," Theodelinda said gently. "I was anxious when I married your father. I had known him only a few days. But once we were better acquainted, we became quite fond of each other."

"Ganelon bears no semblance to Father." Alda clenched her fists.

"No man, not even Prince Hruodland, is ever going to spoil you as your father did."

The room had become too quiet. Alda turned toward the servant, who had stopped sweeping and was eavesdropping on the conversation.

"What did I tell you?" Alda raised her hand. "What is said between me and my mother is not your concern. If I have to warn you one more time, you *will* be whipped."

The servant hurriedly resumed her sweeping.

"You're learning, Daughter. Now listen to me, you are fortunate to attract Ganelon. He is wealthy, and you yourself have said he is a fine looking man."

"If I could judge him on his looks alone, yes, I would be happy," Alda snapped. "Whole songs could be created about his fine, blond hair, his pale blue eyes, and his muscled legs, but I am not talking about his looks. I am talking about his heart. His heart is black, black and shriveled as..." She looked around and pointed to a burned, twisted piece of wood. "...this spent log in the hearth."

"Daughter, you have known him but a few weeks. Perhaps you are mistaken."

"Mother," Alda said as if she were explaining something to a slow child, "he was about to beat me for giving bread to one of his servants. If I marry him, what is to stop him from killing me?"

"It's your fancy," Theodelinda muttered, shaking her head.

"Father would have believed me," Alda cried, her face flushing. "Father would have never chosen him. Of that, I am certain."

* * * * *

The autumn and winter passed with no word from Alfihar, not even a message on the occasional merchant boat that visited them. The empty chair at the head of the table seemed emptier during the Feasts of the Nativity and the Resurrection. When the time for spring planting approached, Alda and Theodelinda climbed to the top of the tower. Swollen with spring rains, the Rhine swirled through the mountains, blanketed in shades of green. Peasants were leading livestock to the pastures, where shoots emerged through last winter's dead grass. Yet many fields were still brown, save for a few weeds.

Gazing upstream, Theodelinda sighed and wrung her hands as if she could see past the Rhineland mountains, past the Alps to the tents where her son and brothers had spent the winter, huddled around fires amid the snow.

"They had provisions for only a few months," Theodelinda said.

"They are resourceful." Alda laid her hand on her mother's shoulder. "They can hunt."

Neither spoke of her worry of the Saxons. The merchants had told them the devil-worshiping brutes were burning churches and advancing west, just as Alfihar had predicted. The Saxons had not crossed the Rhine, but Drachenhaus's defenses were in place. A wall higher than two men ringed the castle. Only one guarded gate allowed visitors to enter.

Land beyond the castle was vulnerable: the thatched, wooden houses in the village, the guarded mill by the river, the fields where crops would be planted, the pasture with its livestock, and the vineyards. This piece of civilization had clawed out a space from the forest, which smothered both banks of the river and the mountains. Alda's gaze wandered to Nonnenwerth, the Rhine island where the Sisters of the Sacred Blood lived. Their tenants were also taking animals out to graze.

If Leonhard failed to sway Alfihar to end negotiations with Ganelon, could the abbey on this island be her refuge? Alda sometimes envied the Sisters of the Sacred Blood — to have a life where all a woman had to do was pray when the bell rang.

"Damned Lombards," Theodelinda spat. "When your father led freemen to war, they did not stay away this long. Why did our king need one man from each free house?"

"We need a large army to save Rome," Alda said.

"God curse those Lombards for keeping our men away during spring planting!"

"What shall we do, Mother?"

"I am not going to let these people starve." Theodelinda's eyes darkened to the color of storm clouds. "We will use whatever means necessary."

They descended from the tower, and Theodelinda sent for the village priest and what was left of Alfihar's tribunal — old men whose sons had gone to Lombardy.

"Alda, you will join us," Theodelinda said. "I hope this will never happen in Dormagen, but you should learn in case it does."

Alda nodded. Feeding themselves was far more important right now than arguing yet again about Ganelon as they had all winter.

Chapter 4

After hours of discussion, Theodelinda, Alda, the priest, and the peasants on the tribunal came up with a plan. When the fields were dry enough for the hoe, Theodelinda suspended all judgments and taxation. Every peasant and every castle servant worked in the fields every day of the week, even the Sabbath.

"The Lord needs His fighting men in Lombardy," the priest said in Frankish during his homily at each sunrise Mass, "but we still must do His work here, and His work for us is spring planting. Allowing our children to starve is a greater sin than working on the Sabbath, and the dowager countess is giving alms to the Church on behalf of all of us. God will show His mercy."

Hearing their own words echoed, Theodelinda and Alda nodded from the front row. Alda glanced over her shoulder and saw relief on the peasants' faces.

* * * * *

A month later, Alda was at the top of the tower admiring the fields, bright green with vegetables and shoots of spring wheat, rye, and oats.

"My lady," asked the guard, a pockmarked young man, "is all well?"

"Oh, yes, two cooks were squabbling over..." She rolled her eyes. "Not important. I just need a moment of quiet."

"I see something that will please you more." Grinning, he pointed to the river.

A merchant barge, its square sail unfurled, was approaching them. Laden with barrels and chests, the wooden craft was large enough to take up two-thirds of the great hall. Alda gasped, then rushed down the stairs. The horn's call drowned out her clattering footsteps.

Lifting her skirts, she raced to the great hall, where Theodelinda was barking orders to guards and servants to get packhorses and carts, invite the merchant to the castle, and carry his wares. As servants rushed about, Alda quickly inspected the room. A glance at the hearth assured her its glowing hot coals would suffice in the warmth of the day. The thyme and mint strewn on the floor would last a few more days.

Theodelinda sent the cupbearer for wine, while Alda ordered a maidservant to fetch rolls and cakes. The two ladies took their places in ornate chairs the servants had placed near the hearth.

"Remember," Theodelinda warned in a low voice, "don't be too eager."

"I know," Alda replied. "If the merchant has cloth, point out a loose thread. And argue if he says our potters' bowls are flawed."

"Be pleasant, though. We need to buy salt."

"I hope he has cinnamon and nutmeg."

Mother and daughter were still whispering about what to trade when the merchant, a short, well-dressed young man, entered the hall and bowed to them. Theodelinda invited him to sit on a stool and refresh himself.

"Do you have tidings of my son, Count Alfihar, or my brothers, Count Beringar and Bishop Leonhard of Bonn?" It was the same question Theodelinda asked every merchant who came to Drachenhaus.

"Any news of Hruodland of the March of Brittany?" Alda added.

"Daughter, you should be asking about Ganelon of Dormagen."

Alda glared at her mother but held her tongue about Ganelon. She did not want to be sent upstairs to the solar, away from the bargaining and the gossip.

"I know nothing of any of the men you speak of," the merchant said, tugging at his collar.

"Do you have news of the royal family?" Alda asked. "We heard Queen Hildegard and the princes followed King Charles into Italy, and that the queen mother went to Aachen. But we've heard naught of the child Queen Hildegard was carrying."

"The queen bore a girl this past winter, but the child lived only three months." The merchant's shoulders sagged.

"God rest her soul," Alda murmured. Bowing her head, she made the sign of the cross. Every family she knew had lost babies, but the news never ceased to sadden her.

"It's God's will." Theodelinda laid her hand over Alda's. "I will have our priest dedicate tomorrow's prime Mass to the princess. The rest of the royal family, are they well?"

"Yes, Countess. Did you know Gerberga and her sons surrendered in Verona?" he asked excitedly.

With wide eyes, Alda and Theodelinda shook their heads. "I thought our army was holding siege at Pavia, where Desiderius is hiding like the rat he is," Alda said.

"This is the first we've heard about the king's sister-by-marriage," Theodelinda added, leaning forward. "Please, have some more wine."

"Lady Alda, you are correct," the merchant said, taking a drink. "Our army has had an enormous camp outside Pavia's walls since autumn, but Gerberga and her sons fled to Verona with Desiderius's son. Our king and some of his men gave chase. The Lombard prince escaped, but Gerberga did not resist."

"Where are they now?" Alda asked.

"I know not."

"And Desiderius is still in Pavia?" Theodelinda asked.

"Yes. Our king even spent the Feast of the Resurrection in Rome and prayed for the Lord's aid. Yet the siege continues, and the Lombard king refuses to surrender."

"Damned Lombards!" Alda said. "The queen mother was right. They are strong, stubborn sons of whores."

* * * * *

Spring days lengthened and became warmer, the grain in the fields grew tall and rippled with the wind, and still no word from

Alfihar. It was the height of summer, with the hay cut and drying in the fallow fields, when a messenger arrived at Drachenhaus with a rolled parchment bearing Alfihar's seal.

He is alive, Alda thought. Until this moment, she and her mother had not known.

"Saints be praised," Theodelinda murmured, wiping her tears with her hand.

"Saints be praised," Alda echoed, leaning against her mother's shoulder. Her throat fluttering, Alda watched the clerk read the message.

His eyes scanning the text, the clerk smiled and translated into Frankish, "Alfihar, count of Drachenhaus by the grace of God and Charles, king of the Franks and Lombards and patrician of Rome, to our beloved mother, Dowager Countess Theodelinda: We send loving greetings in the name of our Lord to you and through you, to our dearling sister. We and our uncles are well. God has granted us victory in Lombardy. Rome is secure. Desiderius has been sent to the cloister. We will return within a week's time with Beringar, count of Bonn; Leonhard, bishop of Bonn; Our Lord King Charles; and a company of many."

* * * * *

While the rest of the household rushed to prepare the castle for guests a few days later, Alda and Veronica were embroidering falconry gloves for Alfihar. Servants were rubbing linseed oil and lemon balm into the castle's furniture and the altar of the chapel attached to the manor, scrubbing the floors and baths, and hauling water to the bathhouse. Theodelinda had planned a feast and ordered servants to take inventory of flour, honey, and spices; clean the stables; pull weeds in the garden; and cut off spent blooms. Alda thought it was odd for everyone to be scurrying about while she passed the time with needlework.

"Was I a good mistress of this house?" she asked Veronica.

"Yes, the house ran smoothly, once you became accustomed to giving orders."

"Why was my mother so hasty to take back the keys? The clerk had barely finished reading Alfihar's message when she held out her hand and said, 'Alda, you will not need those anymore.'" Alda imitated the gesture and her mother's commanding tone.

"She is the dowager countess, Alda," Veronica said, not taking her eyes off her embroidery. "You knew you could not keep the keys forever."

"But without so much as a 'thank you.'"

"You didn't need to throw them at her. You almost spat when you said, 'Here are the keys, Mother.'" Veronica looked up. "You were a good mistress of the house, and you will soon be a good mistress of, uh..."

Alda picked up the needle but then turned toward the window.

"I wonder what has become of Ganelon," she said half to herself. "Alfihar's message made no mention of him."

"I assume the count of Dormagen will be with your brother, if he survived the battles," Veronica replied, making another stitch.

Alda lifted the needle, then laid her hand on her lap. A cold, heavy fear sank into her chest. What if Alfihar and Ganelon had negotiated dowry and bride price?

Again, Alda picked up Alfihar's glove. After embroidering two stitches in the dragon's wing, she put the glove down again and looked toward the window.

"Do you think Alfihar will marry Empty Head soon?" Alda asked.

"Shh!" Veronica giggled. "Lady Gundrada might find out you call her that."

"She cares nothing for affairs of the realm. She told me so while we were in Koblenz. We will be suffering a fool when she and Alfihar are..."

Two notes from the horn at the tower vibrated through the solar. For a moment, all noise seemed to stop. The guards sounded two notes only when they saw an invasion or the return of the men from the battlefront.

Alda caught her breath. "Veronica, was it..."

Veronica nodded.

"Saints be praised!" Alda shouted, raising both fists overhead.

Setting aside barely stitched embroidery, Alda and Veronica left the solar, arm in arm, their heels striking the oaken floor. They headed for the tower and ran up the stairs.

* * * * *

Alda knew her questions would be answered soon. Was Alfihar whole? What had happened to that beast who called himself Ganelon?

A breeze from the Rhine played with her hair as she stood at the top of the tower. She had expected these notes from the horn. The host of men was traveling on the road near the Rhine, the same road she and Alfihar had taken south almost a year ago.

The guard at the tower showed Alda what he saw. Soldiers, on horseback, in horse, ox and mule carts, on foot, emerged from the forest's thick, green canopy. Alda saw Nonnenwerth's sisters and tenants, as small as ants from this height, empty the church, the fields, and their homes to greet their men. A handful of the abbey's tenants dragged boats to the bank of the river to ferry their men home.

The soldiers were in the clearing, just beyond the wheat fields. The gate to the fortress ground open. Peasants dropped their hoes in the fields and came up the mountain to the chapel to meet their kinsmen.

Panting from her climb up the stairs, Theodelinda joined Alda. When the guard showed the dowager countess what he saw, Theodelinda let out a shriek and embraced Alda.

Theodelinda, Alda, and Veronica hurried down the narrow stairways, their shoes scuffling on the steps. They ran outside to the steps of the chapel, whose bell clanged overhead.

The villagers cheered to see Theodelinda and Alda. Crowding the courtyard, they were murmuring and gossiping. Alda could feel the excitement and worry of the families: They would see their sons or husbands or brothers or fathers — if they lived.

"He is almost here," Theodelinda squealed.

The villagers raised their voices when the royal couple and their guards came through the gate on horseback, hooves clattering against the hard ground. Alda was smiling, cheering, clapping.

King Charles wore an iron crown and a gold belt with a sword hilt to match. A bejeweled and plump Queen Hildegard rode beside her husband. Five-winter-old Prince Pepin rode a pony while toddling Prince Karl was carried in a horse-drawn portable cradle.

Mounted noblemen, some of the king's courtiers among them, entered the courtyard next. Alda scanned the crowd and let out a breath when she beheld Alfihar. He looked the same. He still had both eyes and both feet. Like the other horses, his stallion was dirty and needed to be fed but easily carried his master and the armor that had been rolled and secured behind the saddle. The stubble on Alfihar's chin matched his light brown hair.

Alda beamed to see her uncles, Beringar and Leonhard. Her smile faded when her gaze rested on the man she hoped not to see: Ganelon. *There he is. The war did not claim him.*

Her eyes were then drawn to two noblemen who were not from this part of the kingdom — actually, one nobleman, a tall, dark-haired man on a black stallion. Alda felt a pang near her heart. *Hruodland!*

"Veronica," Alda whispered, "yonder, near Alfihar, do you see?"

Veronica gasped. "Yes."

"Could it be? Am I dreaming?" she said in a daze.

"Not unless we are both asleep," Veronica whispered back.

"I thought I would never see him again."

"What is he doing here? His home is leagues and leagues away."

A wave of cheers drowned out conversation. Servants and commoners were following the noblemen in horse and ox carts and on foot. Alda instinctively moved closer to her mother. Soldiers crowded the courtyard.

Splatters of dried blood, mud, and manure stained their clothes, and on some men, bloodstains formed brown circles on their leggings. Some of the men in the ox carts had their arms or legs in splints. Others were missing fingers or hands. Some of the horses had scars on their legs and necks.

Villagers pushed past each other to meet their kinsmen in the army. The soldiers kissed their wives, hugged their mothers and fathers, picked up their children. Most families smiled and laughed and looked at each other in wonder. Some could barely speak. Others were talking all at once. Some children cried in the arms of the strange men who were their fathers. A couple of mothers and wives wept for a lost eye or hand. A few mothers and wives kept searching the crowd until a friend of their family shook his head. They wailed, sobbed, and fainted as the friend held them.

Alfihar guided his horse toward Alda and Theodelinda. He raised his hunting horn, carved from bone, to his lips and blew. The crowd fell silent.

"We have arrived at the House of the Dragon," Alfihar called, "where we will have a great feast to celebrate our triumph. Your hostesses are my mother, Countess Theodelinda, and my sister, Lady Alda. Be merry!"

Alda had barely heard Alfihar. Her attention was drawn to Hruodland. Their eyes met for a moment. Hruodland smiled. Alda swallowed and smiled back. Veronica nudged Alda to follow her mother's lead. With Theodelinda, she approached the king and bowed.

"We are honored, my lord king, to have a guest of such greatness," Theodelinda said.

The dowager countess described the baths and the clean clothes that awaited them. She signaled the stable hands to attend to the horses and ordered her servants to attend to the noblemen's needs.

Alfihar dismounted and handed the reins to a groom. He approached Theodelinda and Alda and embraced his mother, then his sister.

"Oh, how I have yearned to see home!" he roared.

Alda again watched Hruodland. He dismounted from his stallion and gave the reins to his servant. He pushed his hair away from his eyes. Like the other noblemen, he was dirty and unshaven. As he spoke in Roman, that strange tongue from the western part of Francia, she picked out the name of his brother, Gerard, but nothing else.

Alfihar, his arms now around both his mother and his sister, called to him. "Hruodland!"

"Hruodland," Alda whispered.

Chapter 5

other, Alda, I have brought a friend," Alfihar said. "Prince Hruodland, this is my mother. Of course, you remember my sister."

Hruodland's dark eyes pierced Alda. Her knees weakened. Her heart pounded. Her mouth went dry.

"My greetings," he said in a baritone as musical as any singer's. Hruodland bent to kiss Theodelinda's hand, then Alda's.

Alda thought she would faint.

"Mother, I must talk to you," Alfihar said, leading Theodelinda away, his arm around her shoulders.

Alda saw Ganelon halfway across the courtyard making his way toward her. She held her dragon amulet, desperately thinking for a way to avoid him without fleeing outright.

"Count Ganelon," Leonhard called cordially.

Puzzled Leonhard did not tell Hruodland to leave her, Alda watched Ganelon turn toward her uncle.

"My nephew has fine hounds for hunting," Leonhard said. He dismounted and handed the reins to a servant. "Come, let me show you the kennels."

"What is she doing with my enemy?" Ganelon snarled, pointing at Hruodland and Alda.

Alda's eyes widened as she noticed Hruodland's hand clenching into a fist. Now, she had to get the two of them away from each other, despite what Leonhard had said about staying away from Hruodland. God had granted her fondest wish — to see Hruodland again, and the last thing she wanted was for him to be hurt in a fight.

"Our enemies are the Lombards and the Saxons," Leonhard chided. He strolled toward Ganelon. "We have conquered one and will subdue the other."

"*He* is still my blood enemy," Ganelon replied.

"But we are all Franks," Leonhard said calmly.

While Ganelon and Leonhard argued, Alda's mind raced. With Ganelon's back turned, she could escape and be alone with Hruodland. But first, she had to think of an errand for Veronica.

"Veronica," Alda said quickly, "was our embroidery put away? Could you see to it?"

"Of course," Veronica muttered and walked toward the manor.

With Ganelon's back still turned, Alda gathered from snatches of their conversation that Leonhard and Ganelon's argument had turned to religious matters. Alda suppressed a smile. Ganelon would be occupied for a long time with her literate uncle, who knew much of the Bible and books of the saints by memory. The pale-haired count of Dormagen would be fortunate to have time for a bath before dinner.

Hruodland was scowling as he looked toward Ganelon. The hostility at Geneva had not dissipated.

"Hruodland, would you like to see our lands from the tower?" Alda asked, already grabbing his arm and leading him as quickly as she could away from the group.

"Yes, certainly." His scowl disappeared into laughter.

Alda told herself not to look back at Ganelon. At the entrance to the tower, Alda realized Hruodland might think of her as bold. *He may have ideas about me that a man should not have of a Christian lady. Then again... can I not have a little pleasure before my sentence to purgatory with Ganelon?*

Alda walked slowly, trying to be graceful, trying to unlearn her walk, heavy on the heel, halfway between marching and running. She glanced at him from the corner of her eye. To her relief, he was still smiling.

"How long will you stay with us?" Alda asked.

34

"A few days," he replied. "Enough time to rest our animals and bake some bread."

While they climbed the stairs, his right sleeve slipped, revealing a jagged, scarlet scar.

"The wound on your arm," she asked tentatively, "does it cause you pain?"

"Oh, this? It's nothing. The Lombard who delivered that blow was twice your size. And with Durendal," he said, patting his sword, "I finished him with one swift stroke."

"Oh my," Alda said admiringly.

She and Hruodland reached the top of the tower and approached the waist-high wall on the side overlooking the river.

"Do you not have a guard posted here?" Hruodland asked.

"Yes," Alda answered. "He must have gone downstairs to join the others." She smiled. She was alone with Hruodland.

"This view is well worth the climb." Hruodland rested his elbows on the wall and leaned forward.

Alda leaned beside him, facing the river. "My father had it built high so he could see merchant boats. If anyone tries to invade, they cannot take us by surprise." She frowned. *Why did I say that? Trade and war are a man's domain.* Then she became angry with herself. *Ganelon has poisoned my mind already. I never cared if a man thought I was meek or bold before. Why should I care now?*

"Does something trouble you?" Hruodland asked. He shifted his weight and touched her shoulder.

"Perhaps I should not talk of trade or war," she mumbled.

"Why not? It is good when a woman understands such things." His arm swept toward the river, the mountains, and the forest. "This is a welcome sight after the war. And so are you."

Alda felt the heat of a blush spread over her cheeks and neck.

They stepped back from the wall and faced each other. Hruodland took half a step closer. She did the same. His face wore the look of a man reuniting with his sweetheart.

"It is good to see our men home again," she said.

"Yes, it is good to be back in Francia," he said with a smile. "We would have come home sooner, if not for the willfulness of the Lombard king." Hruodland shook his head. "He could have spared his own people much suffering. It was a sad sight when he finally did surrender." He winced. "The women and children were starving and sick. Think of the beggars outside the church, a whole city of them."

Now it was Alda's turn to wince. She had seen the ragged, diseased beggars on the church steps in the cities she visited on the way to Geneva. The beggars, desperate for a miracle to heal their twisted legs and pus-filled sores, had come to pray to the relics of the saint housed within the church, whether it was in Worms or Strasbourg or Besançon.

"What kind of a monster would do such a thing to his own people?" Hruodland spat. "He deserves to be in the cloister. It is an act of mercy on Uncle Charles's part."

King Charles, Alda thought. Although she had heard Hruodland call the king such a familiar name before, she still found it difficult to fathom. "The iron crown our king wears, I have never seen it before," she said.

"He wears it well, doesn't he? It's the iron crown of the Lombards. Good for ceremony, but he tells me it is quite heavy. Now that the people have seen our triumph, it will rest in the treasury until we come to the next town."

"I am so glad to see you again. With the March of Brittany so far away..." Her voice trailed off. "What brings you here?"

"Um, I was curious about Alfihar's home. You and he both spoke so much of it. And, of course, the mountain across the river. Which one is the place where Siegfried slew the dragon?"

They turned toward the river, and Alda pointed to Drachenfels, where the long-ago hero had slain the monster and bathed in its blood to make himself invulnerable. With her free hand, she touched the beige, oval Drachenfels stone in her amulet, a gift from her father.

Hruodland touched her shoulder. They turned toward each other again and stepped closer. They were in an embrace. Alda could feel Hruodland's breath. She closed her eyes, anticipating the next moment. They heard footsteps on the stairs. They opened their eyes, looked at each other, and moved apart, watching the stairwell.

It was Veronica. "Alda, your mother is asking for you. You will find her in the kitchen. If you follow me, Prince Hruodland, I will show you to the hall, where you can prepare for a bath."

Hruodland followed Veronica. Alda walked, almost marched, to the kitchen, a small building just behind the manor. Despite the open windows and door, smoke filled the kitchen and stung Alda's eyes and nose. In the massive stone hearth, drops of water boiling in an iron cauldron escaped over the rim and hissed when they hit the flames. Skinned and dressed calves and lambs were suspended from chains to roast at the back of the hearth, while plucked ducks and geese hung on hooks on the hearth's periphery with shoulders of swine. The aroma of white and rye bread wafted to Alda's nostrils as the baker used a long-handled wooden paddle to remove loaves from the wide oven, built into the stone back wall, its white-hot ashes in a lower chamber. Cooks chopped shallots and carrots, their knives clunking against wooden tables.

"Alda, we have a special guest," Theodelinda said over the noise. She handed Alda a few sprigs of fresh mint. "You should look your best at dinner."

"I have no wish to look my best for Gan…" A pop from the hearth cut her off.

"I have no time for a quarrel," Theodelinda said in her mother tone, a tone that still stopped all arguments.

Alda stormed out of the kitchen. Grinding the mint with her teeth, she marched back to the manor and climbed the stairs to the solar, where the afternoon sun shone through arched windows on an embroidered tapestry of the Virgin and her Child. The solar was spacious enough to accommodate two curtained beds for the count's family, cots and pallets along the wall for maidservants, looms, chests for clothes and sheets and drying cloths, chests for jewelry, a basin and its stand, a few stools, and a small table for the night candle, combs, ribbons, and clay bottles of perfumes and lotions.

Hearing footsteps on the stairs, Alda turned toward the sound. When Veronica entered the solar, Alda offered her a sprig of mint and opened the chest, releasing the bittersweet scent of wormwood, and picked through the shifts and large-sleeved gowns. She decided on a robin's-egg-blue gown embroidered with dark red and yellow threads.

After Alda removed her jewelry, she picked up her rose oil and her clean clothes. She and Veronica descended the stairs and walked to the women's side of the bathhouse.

The bathhouse was a wooden structure just outside the manor. Slaves had dug four holes in the earth, each big enough for ten people, and had lined the holes and the floor with stone and clay. Slits in the walls allowed some light. Usually, servants lit tallow candles on bath day, but Theodelinda had ordered them to use the beeswax candles for the royal family. A fire burned in the warming room, heating the cauldron of water. Servants had dumped the river water into the cold baths and the water from the cauldrons into the hot baths. A partition of warped wood separated the women from the men.

Alda and Veronica hung their clean clothes on pegs in the warming room. They stripped, unbraided their hair, cut lavender, rosemary, and chamomile hanging from the rafters, and stepped into the room with the baths.

With her maid beside her, Queen Hildegard relaxed in the hot bath, smelling of lavender. In a nearby tub, Prince Karl was bathed by his nurse.

Alda saw flickers of light from the men's side and heard splashing. They were singing ribald tunes — "Out there a fool, in here a maid." Alda could distinguish the voice of Alfihar, Hruodland, and the king among the others. Veronica dipped a bowl in the hot bath and crushed chamomile into it. Alda and Veronica threw lavender and rosemary into the water. The scent flooded the room as they slipped into the bath.

"It is good to see you again, my lady queen," Alda said. "You look well."

"I feel well, other than some morning sickness."

"You are with child again?" Alda asked breathlessly.

Hildegard smiled and nodded.

"How wonderful!"

"It's a blessing," the queen said. She leaned forward so her maid could wash her back. "And you, Lady Alda, do you have a betrothed?"

"My brother was negotiating with him, then the war took him away."

The nurse finished with the prince and took him to the warming room. Following them with her eyes, Alda spied her mother entering the bathhouse.

"Who is the man?" the queen asked.

"Ganelon of Dormagen."

"You are the one. Oh, Good Lord." The queen frowned and made the sign of the cross. "Do not consent to nuptials with him. He is a cruel man."

"Forgive the intrusion, my lady queen," Theodelinda said, stepping into the bath with her maid. "But why do you say this to my daughter?"

Theodelinda's servant added rosemary to the water. Its scent blended with the lavender.

"Ganelon would be a bad match for your daughter and worse for your clan," the queen replied. "Very few men can abide him. I cannot abide him."

"Why?" Theodelinda asked.

"He pretends to have morals, but he shows no respect for God's commandments — 'You shall not covet another's man wife.' During our siege at Pavia, he sought favors from Karl's nurse and sent little gifts — ribbons, cakes, and the like. She had no desire for him, and nothing she said could sway him. I myself heard her say, 'I cannot betray my husband.' And his response? 'What I am asking is not betrayal. It would not produce a child.'"

Alda winced. Not at the thought of Ganelon seeking the attention of other women. Other women would be a relief. Besides, a man's sins were a matter between him and his confessor, not his wife. What made Alda wince was how he twisted divine commandments as he had when he had been about to beat her in Geneva.

"There is more," the queen said. "The nurse continued to refuse him, and her refusal only seemed to increase his ardor. She was greatly troubled. I do not know what she feared more — Ganelon's attention or a beating from her husband because he would think she was untrue. I became vexed, and I myself told him, 'Let her be. The whores who travel with us will do whatever favor you ask.'"

"And how did he respond?" Alda asked.

"He bowed and said, 'As you wish, my queen.' I thought the matter was settled. And what happens but two days later?" Her fists hit the water. "He was standing over the nurse and rebuking her for my words. As soon as I yelled at him to leave her alone, he slunk away. Even so, I'd had enough of him and went to my husband."

Alda suppressed a smile at the thought of the queen, who had seen perhaps sixteen winters, marching to the king. It did not matter if he was in the middle of war plans or a hunt. Alda knew from the queen's manner that she could command her husband's attention anytime.

"Only after I told my husband did Ganelon give us peace," the queen said, her shoulders relaxing. "No woman should be bound to a beast like that, Countess. Surely, there are men who can offer your clan better."

The prince's nurse came in and said the toddler was asking for his mother.

"Children," she muttered. "Well, I am finished here. Come," she said to her maid.

Still vexed with her mother, Alda said nothing as Theodelinda and her servant hurried their toilette and left the bath. Alda watched as the maid combed her mother's long gray-streaked blond hair and helped her mother dress in her best clothes, an embroidered dark green gown over a dandelion yellow tunic, paired with a black silk veil.

"Alda, do not forget about the rose oil," Theodelinda called over her shoulder.

"Mother," she chided, "I am not a child."

Theodelinda shook her head and left the bathhouse.

Veronica dipped her fingers in the lavender water and sprinkled it on Alda's forehead. Alda gave Veronica a puzzled look.

"Lavender water on the forehead preserves chastity," Veronica said.

"Why are you worried about my chastity?"

"I saw you and Hruodland in the tower."

Alda blushed. "We did nothing. We simply talked."

"He was interested in more than conversation. I could tell by the look in his eyes. Be careful with him. Men do not desire unchaste wives."

Alda shrugged and shook her head. As she relaxed in the steam and lavender, she imagined Hruodland naked on the other side of the wall.

"Perhaps, my mother should not have told you those stories when we were so young," Veronica said. "I think you believe them. Do not let your fondness for him blind you."

"I am not given to fancy," Alda said, looking at the partition, wishing she could see Hruodland through it. "I simply want a husband who will not beat me to death. Or starve me."

"Do not anger Count Ganelon."

"I could more easily change the flow of the Rhine. I shall do anything to stop negotiations. I am not yet his wife."

She looked at the partition again. The man she wanted was on the other side. Veronica grabbed her arm.

"Banish that from your thoughts," Veronica scolded. "These men have lain with dozens of women. Lying with you will make the one you desire think you are not virtuous."

"Virtue has nothing to do with marriage. As long as I have my wealth, they will court me, even if I were the wickedest woman on earth. As long as I am not with child, who would find out?"

They realized the voices on the other side of the partition had become quiet.

"They'd check the sheets," Veronica whispered. She raised her voice. "Alda, you should not joke about such things."

Veronica emerged from the bath. Alda bowed her head while her servant poured the bowl with chamomile rinse to lighten her hair. Alda rose from the warm bath and took a dip in the cold bath that smelled of mint before she followed Veronica to the warming room.

Alda and Veronica dried themselves, hung the linen drying cloths on pegs and threw on their shifts. Alda sat on a stool and spread her dripping hair over her shoulders. It almost touched the floor. Veronica parted Alda's hair and dragged the comb through the dark blond strands, picking out an occasional louse and throwing it into the fire.

"I could lose my heart to Hruodland," Alda mused.

"That is my fear," Veronica said.

* * * * *

After Alda donned her jewelry in the solar, she and Veronica descended the stairs and entered the hall. The evening sun lit the hall and illuminated an embroidered tapestry of Siegfried standing in triumph over the slain dragon. Alda could hear the peasants celebrating in the courtyard, enjoying the old ox and bread Theodelinda had given them.

Inside the castle hall, the scent of lemon balm mingled with the smell of fresh rushes on the floor. Lit beeswax candles stood on the table, even though the day lasted long this time of year.

The hearth had a few glowing embers, just enough to keep the fire alive. The room was warm even without the flames. Musicians, both the king's and Alfihar's, sat in a corner, their hands caressing their flutes and the strings of their zithers while drummers tapped sticks against taut cattle skins.

In addition to bathing, the noblemen had shaved and donned clean clothes, borrowed from Drachenhaus. Beringar wore Drachenhaus's largest tunic, and it still stretched across his broad chest and arms. He was speaking with Ganelon, who had found time for a bath and a shave. The borrowed clothes were a bit too short, but they flattered Ganelon's muscular body. *Why can't his heart match the fairness of his face?* Alda thought.

Alda distinguished the king, who was wearing his own clothes. Nothing in Drachenhaus could have fit his towering, hulking frame so well. As Hruodland had said, the king no longer wore the iron crown. With his arm around Queen Hildegard's shoulders, he was chatting with Leonhard and Alfihar.

Alda scanned the rest of the crowd. She saw Hruodland standing by a window and talking to his brother. Gerard, a lanky young man perhaps a year older than Alda, wore white cleric's robes and had his dark hair closely cropped.

But Alda's attention was drawn to Hruodland. He wore a scarlet tunic the same shade as the bands of cloth that held his clean, blue leggings.

And she could understand why Veronica worried about her chastity.

Chapter 6

ruodland stretched and enjoyed the breeze from the Rhine drifting through the narrow, arched window. He ran his fingers through his still damp hair, glad to be clean. The discomfort of a borrowed linen tunic a little tight in the shoulders was minor.

Spying Alda at the foot of the stairs, Hruodland forgot what he and his brother were talking about. He admired how her blue gown flattered her figure and how her long ash-blond hair hung in waves. Their eyes met. Her eyes were as green as the trees near the Rhine, as if the trees blended together to create them.

"Hruodland?" Gerard asked.

"Yes?" he said, blinking. "I shall speak with you later. Go practice your Frankish."

Alda was walking toward Hruodland. They met in the middle of the room. Inhaling the scent of the lavender and roses, he beheld her for a few moments, speechless.

"Be seated by me at the meal," Alda whispered.

"I do not think your betrothed..." Calling Ganelon her betrothed was like sticking his hand in a pile of dung, but he had to know her sentiment.

"He is not my betrothed. Not yet," she added. "I did not take the vow, and the war, thankfully, took him away. And now he has returned."

"You ought to be happy," he said, wondering how far to take this matter. "God has shown His mercy."

"God has shown His mercy to a wicked man. There are some who wish that the Lord would..." She bit her lip. "...have called Ganelon to be with Him."

Hruodland leaned to whisper in her ear, "So do his men, except they would not expect him to be with God."

Alda's smile suddenly disappeared. Her hand flew to her dragon amulet. Following her wide-eyed stare, Hruodland beheld Ganelon, who wore the look of dog about to fight for a choice bone. Hruodland looked his rival up and down. The same size and experience in battles, they would be equals in a fight. When Hruodland's gaze slid to Alda, the back of his neck tightened. That son of a whore's cur would tear her to pieces.

"Why are you speaking with this man?" Ganelon demanded.

"This is my house. I can speak to whomever I please." Alda's voice was defiant, almost masking the tremor in her voice. Almost.

"You avoid me but tempt Hruodland," he said sharply. "Is this the way to treat your betrothed?"

"I am not your betrothed," she snapped, stamping her foot.

"When I have you, I shall tame you," Ganelon spat.

"I am not yours to tame," she cried.

"Hruodland, I thought you were stronger than this. So brave on the battlefield. To succumb to a mere girl."

"Do not attempt to flatter me," Hruodland said coldly. "Or use false praise. The Lombard who gave me this..." He pushed back the sleeve to show his scar. "...was a skilled warrior. I do not seek out and slay the youth who has barely learned to hold a sword and then boast about it. Nor do I threaten women."

Hruodland stepped between Ganelon and Alda and crossed his arms. His dark eyes burned into Ganelon's. *Strike me, Ganelon. I dare you.*

Ganelon looked from Hruodland to Alda and back to Hruodland. He shrank back, muttering, "I will have my claim to her."

"We shall see if you will have a claim to her," Hruodland said to Ganelon. His voice stayed even. He stepped away from Ganelon and put his arm around Alda's shoulders. "In the meantime, I will protect my friend from harm, no matter what guise it takes."

* * * * *

To Alda's relief, the music stopped for a moment, and Theodelinda called the guests to eat. While the guests took their seats, the flutes and zithers again wove joyous melodies. Glad to see Alfihar in his ornate chair at the head of the table, Alda sat next to Hruodland and five seats away from Ganelon. As servants brought in stews, roasts, vegetables, and countless other dishes for the first course, Alda savored the wine and found herself drinking more than usual. She chatted and laughed with Hruodland and ignored Ganelon's stares. She expected her mother to ask to speak to her alone and berate her for treating Ganelon so poorly.

But Theodelinda seemed too busy to notice. She was talking and laughing, pleased with the guests' compliments on the feast. After a while, Alda stopped watching her mother, and it felt like she and Hruodland were the only two people in the world.

The feast continued with hours of humorous stories and gossip. In the fading daylight, crumbs of bread and cakes littered the table. Alda gave bones and gristle to the servants who took care of the dogs.

The dowager countess rose from her seat. "My lord king," she said, "the House of the Dragon would like to present you with gifts."

Servants showed the king two casks of wine, incense, a bolt of silk, a bolt of linen, and a large, highly wrought, gold cross.

"We are grateful," said the king. "In return, we will present gifts to your house."

The king gave Alfihar two cups from which he had drunk, silver candlesticks for the chapel, and a tapestry of the ascension of Mary, Mother of God.

While Theodelinda watched the servants put the gifts away for safekeeping, Alfihar beckoned the guests to sit by the hearth. Musicians played the introduction to the first of many songs about Siegfried.

Alda watched Ganelon through sidelong glances. As she saw him rise from the table and leave the hall in the direction of the privies, she had an idea. She leaned toward Hruodland and whispered, "Would you like to see the garden before night falls?"

He nodded, and they walked outside. They passed servants hurrying between the kitchen and hall. It was a cool evening. The garden was quiet except for the festivities near the chapel, where the commoners laughed, sang, and danced. The celebration blended with the call of frogs near the river. Alda's eyes adjusted to the near dark. The purple light softened everything and made it appear celestial. A fire pit near the chapel cast an orange glow.

Wine muddled Alda's mind and heart. Even with the dragon amulet and the cross to protect her, she was tempting demons and spirits of the dead. The white-silver moonlight seemed to keep the spirits at bay. Hruodland and Alda brushed past silver-green sage gone to seed and sweet-scented lavender.

Alda was not sure why she had suggested they come out here, except that it was a beautiful night and she wanted to share it with Hruodland.

But things will be worse with Ganelon when we return to the hall. Alda looked over her shoulder. No Ganelon. "Perhaps we should go inside," she said.

"Why?" Hruodland asked. "We just came out here."

"I have caused much discord."

"What do you mean?"

"Between you and Ganelon," Alda murmured, hating even to mention his name.

Hruodland laughed. Alda looked up, startled.

"There is nothing you could do to cause discord between me and Ganelon," he said. "The blood feud between our two families started before you were born, before I was born."

"Oh? What happened?"

They stopped walking and looked out toward the Rhine, a silvery purple in the moonlight. "You know my mother grew up in Grandfather Pepin's palaces," he said.

King Pepin, our present king's father, Alda reminded herself. *Shall I ever become accustomed to his manner of referring to the royal family?* Alda nodded for Hruodland to continue.

"She was my grandfather's niece, but he raised her as his own daughter after both her parents died, or so my nurse told me. And when she was a marriageable age, my mother was betrothed to the count of Dormagen."

"Ganelon?" Alda asked. "But he is your age."

Hruodland laughed and placed his arm around her shoulders. "Ganelon's father."

"Oh. Did Ganelon's sire resemble the son?" Alda's arm slid around his waist.

"Perhaps. But my mother ruined the arrangement. Shall I tell you how?" he asked with a sly look.

Alda nodded eagerly.

"She was carrying another man's child," he said. "Me."

"How bold," she said, putting her free hand to her lips.

"My nurse always described my mother as willful and proud."

Alda looked down, remembering how Alfihar had called her willful when she had protested an arrangement with Ganelon.

"She wanted to marry my father," Hruodland continued. "When she lay with him, she knew nothing of the negotiations with the count of Dormagen until she was betrothed to him. I was already in her belly.

"So the count of Dormagen broke off the betrothal. He claimed he did not want an unchaste wife." Hruodland shook his head. "He would not have cared if my mother was not a virgin. Her wealth and royal blood would have more than compensated for her lack of virtue. It was me, the child who was not his. She would not consent to the nuptials unless the count of Dormagen vowed to allow me to stay with her."

Hruodland stared at the mountains, which had become a green-blue-gray. "How I wish she had lived beyond my birth!"

Alda embraced Hruodland. "She loved you."

He stroked her hair. "And she was fond of my father. Even with the threats of us being sent to the cloister, she refused to name him. So he confessed."

"He confessed?" Alda gasped. "He could have been put to death!"

"He had a great affection for my mother, and he was willing to risk his life to restore her honor."

"How brave!"

"My nurse told me that my mother pleaded for his life. It might have been the only time she ever showed humility. Grandfather Pepin was moved to spare my father's life, but he tripled the bride price and ordered him to marry my mother."

"I am glad your mother got to marry a man of her choosing," Alda said.

"Most women like this story." Hruodland smiled. "Most men who hear it are horrified that a woman subverted the will of her guardian."

"And you?"

Hruodland pushed his hair from his eyes and looked up at the stars that were starting to appear. "My mother..." He paused. "My mother is and will always be a mystery to me. What I wish most of all is that I had a true memory of her."

"Do you have a betrothed waiting for you?" Alda blurted, emboldened by wine.

"No. No betrothed. Not even a start of negotiations, saints be praised. Simply a scheme of my father and Grandmother Bertrada."

Queen Mother Bertrada, Alda thought, arching an eyebrow.

"My father, actually Grandmother Bertrada, wants me to marry the daughter of the Breton duke," Hruodland explained. "I heard the clerk read her message assuring my father of the Bretons' loyalty. As if the Bretons understand such a thing. The marriage would be for naught, just as it was for Uncle Charles and the Lombard." He gave her a sidelong look. "Do you know what a Breton virgin is?"

Alda shook her head, smiling.

"A sister who can outrun her brother."

Alda tried to look appalled, but a giggle broke through her lips. Hruodland was laughing with her.

"I do not know Grandmother's logic to bind me with such a savage," he said, shaking his head. "I do not know why my father would consent to it. He did not marry a girl who sleeps in the woods like a wild beast. Father told me I could arrange not to see her often, but once is too many times."

"At least, you could have concubines," Alda said. "A man is forgiven for that. A woman is not forgiven for having a lover, no matter how unhappy she is. I cannot abide Ganelon."

She looked toward the hall, afraid Ganelon might come out, more afraid of him than the demons that might be lurking in the forest outside the garden wall or the bats flying over the Rhine, afraid she might have to explain herself, what was she doing with this man? She looked back toward Hruodland. "He would not want to marry me without my dowry. All I can do is refuse my consent and pray for a miracle."

"What if Alfihar saw why you loathe Ganelon — if in fact he begins to dislike Ganelon himself — and decided that you should marry a different man?" His voice had a tone of urgency, as if her answer would change everything.

"A different man would be better," Alda said, "especially if he was like you." She looked down. "But I have no say in the matter. I trust Alfihar to pick someone who would make a good alliance, if not a good husband. Perhaps, I should not have listened to those stories about princes and maidens. They are only stories."

"Yes, only stories," he murmured.

"Would you marry a maiden your heart desires?" Alda searched his face for an answer.

"I am not given to fancy," he said.

It stung Alda to hear her own words used in such a way. She looked away.

"My heart might happen to desire a maiden I married for her fortune and her connections," he said, stroking her back. "There is one maiden my heart and head want."

"Any woman who married you would be happy," she said, turning toward him. "You will make a good husband. You deserve a good wife."

Hruodland pulled her toward him and kissed her. She felt a hot thrill where his hands caressed her. She ran her fingers through his hair and ran her other hand up and down his strong back. In the silver light, they pulled away a little and gazed into each other's eyes. Then Hruodland looked up. Alda followed suit. Bats sailed overhead.

"We should go inside," he said softly. "We are tempting the creatures of the night."

Alda nodded. Hruodland held her hand as they walked toward the house. The arched windows glowed with the light of candles and torches. The songs of the frogs mixed with the zither, the voice of the singer, and the laughter near the chapel.

"What if the girl had been fond of the man for some time?" Alda asked. "What if she told her brother, I mean her guardian, that there is only one man she will consent to marry? Of course, she would not mention affection to her guardian because he will think that she is blinded, that she is an infatuated, weak girl given to humors. She knows by now that what she desires is not important to him. But the man she wants to marry would be in her heart as she extols on his virtues, his wealth, his family, his friendship to her brother, his bravery on the battlefield. What do you think?"

"She would be very bold," he said, smiling. "But the man would like that. She would do this when she is sober?"

"Of course. She wishes for her brother to take her seriously, not think she is in some drunken fancy. She is earnest."

"So is he, the man who wants to marry her."

This cannot be real, Alda thought. *I must be in a dream to be this happy.*

When they entered the manor, Alda could see only the moonlit garden outside the open windows and the people in the bubble of light from a recently stoked fire in the hearth. The queen, the nurses, and children had retired, but most of the men, along with Theodelinda and Veronica, were listening to the song. The musicians stood on the edge of the firelight and sang about Siegfried. They were on Alda's favorite part, where Siegfried lay in a trench, ready to kill the dragon.

Alda knew the story from memory: Siegfried had one chance, and if the blow was not fatal, the dragon would spray him with venom. She looked out the window toward the moonlit mountain across the river. *That is where it happened,* she thought, as she had thought thousands of times. She could feel the magic of the stone on her bosom.

Alda did not need light to find her way around Drachenhaus. She guided Hruodland to the hearth. Alfihar passed the cup to her.

Ganelon scowled. "Where have you been?" he asked her, his voice sharp.

"In the garden," she replied, trying to sound calm.

"With him?" Ganelon pointed his chin toward Hruodland.

"This is my house. I can go wherever I please, with whomever I please," Alda said defiantly, passing the cup to Hruodland.

"You are fortunate I will marry you despite your infidelity," he said. She watched his right hand, the one that would bloody her and break her bones if they married. It twitched. "When you are my wife, I will make you virtuous."

Or dead, Alda thought.

Hruodland squared his shoulders as if he were about to challenge Ganelon again. To Alda's left, her mother wore a stern expression, staring at Alfihar. Veronica sat up straight.

"Ganelon," Alfihar barked, "I shall not have you talk to my sister this way. You will address her with respect. We are an honorable family."

It stunned Alda so much she could not speak. She had expected Alfihar to rebuke her for her boldness and try to soothe Ganelon.

Alfihar drained the cup in one swallow. The cupbearer ran to the wine cellar to refill it. Alda's uncles scowled at Ganelon.

"I meant no insult to the family," Ganelon stammered.

"An insult to one of us, especially one of our women, is an insult to us all," Alfihar snapped. "My sister is an honest maiden. And I, we, shall defend our honor."

Ganelon opened his mouth as if to say something and then shut it. He looked fearfully from Alfihar to Hruodland.

"Alfihar, say the word," Hruodland growled, "and I will give him the beating he deserves for this insult."

"Stop it, all of you," Theodelinda said in her mother tone. "Hruodland, Ganelon, I will not have you pursue your blood feud in here."

How does Mother know about the blood feud? Alda thought. *Of course, she heard it from the merchants' gossip.*

Everyone fell silent and listened to the musician sing of Siegfried's deeds. But Alda was distracted by Hruodland and Ganelon. They glared at each other as if at any moment one would leap from his seat and strike the other.

Theodelinda cleared her throat. "My lord king, our forest has much game, should you desire a hunt."

"We have wild goats, stags, monstrous boars, and a few bears," Alfihar added. He pointed to the wall nearest the hearth, where a pair of antlers resembling large branches were mounted. "Those are from a stag I slew."

"It will be a welcome diversion while the army's stores are replenished," the king said.

Alda, too, welcomed a hunt. Drachenhaus had not had a good chase since she and Alfihar had left for Geneva. During the winter, the huntsmen had brought in hares or a doe, but Alda longed to hear the hounds baying at their prey and feel the horse carrying her into the forest at a gallop. The gleam in Alfihar's eyes told Alda he felt the same longing.

As the cupbearer made trip after trip to the wine cellar, the nobles turned their attention to the musicians. The singer began another song, recounting Siegfried's loves and heroic deeds. Guests started nodding sleepily while the fire burned down to embers. The musicians ended their song at Siegfried's murder in the city of Worms, upstream of Drachenhaus. The bells at Nonnenwerth and Drachenhaus rang to announce matins, the sixth hour of night.

Alda looked around the hearth. To her relief, Ganelon had fallen asleep on the bench. The king stretched and yawned.

"I should retire," he said.

"My lord king, your beds have been assembled in the solar, where your queen and children already sleep," said Theodelinda. She picked up a candle. "I shall show you the way. Alda, Veronica, you should retire as well. You need to rest for tomorrow's hunt."

Alda looked to Alfihar, although she knew he usually would not go against their mother's will. Alfihar drained the cup and shook the shoulder of the slumbering cupbearer.

"Fetch more wine," he said. He looked toward Theodelinda. "Let her stay, Mother. I shall send her to the solar soon."

"Very well," Theodelinda said to Alda's surprise.

Theodelinda looked almost too tired to stand, let alone to argue. Veronica was slumping and nodding off.

"Veronica, you should retire as well," Alda said.

Veronica straightened and looked from Alda to Hruodland and back to Alda in silent protest. "Alda," she said weakly. "Perhaps..."

"You are falling asleep. Go to the solar," Alda ordered.

Veronica joined Theodelinda, but she looked over her shoulder at Alda and Hruodland several times before climbing the stairs.

As the musicians played Psalms, the nobles dropped off one by one. Alfihar finally fell asleep on the bench. One of the musicians looked toward Alda. She nodded her permission for him to stop.

Realizing she and Hruodland were the only nobles still awake, Alda got an idea. *If I were carrying another man's child, Hruodland's child, Ganelon would no longer want my hand.* She looked from Ganelon to Hruodland. *Yes, it just might work. It's worth the risk.*

"I am too weary to climb the stairs tonight," she said. "The servants have set up a few pallets in the hall."

It was mostly true. She wanted to sleep.

"Yes," he said, with a mischievous grin, "it is late."

He picked up one of the candles and helped her to her feet. She leaned on his arm, realizing she truly could not stand without his support. She reminded herself not to drink so much wine ever again. Even with the help of his arm, she staggered. They found a pallet. Another pallet was close by.

"Perhaps you should be seated," he told her.

Alda sat on the pallet. She could barely keep her chin up. "With all these men here, I would feel safer if you were close," she mumbled.

As Alda watched Hruodland lift his pallet, her eyelids felt heavy, too heavy to keep open. *Just for a few minutes,* she thought, closing her eyes and falling over.

* * * * *

Hruodland looked around, hoping they were the only two awake. He smiled with anticipation and then worried. *Why is she so eager? Is she truly a virgin?* he wondered. *What if her kin discovers us?*

Hruodland looked toward Alda. She was asleep. He gently placed his pallet close to hers and sat across from her.

"Alda," he whispered, shaking her shoulder. "Alda?" He dared not raise his voice and risk waking the others. She did not stir. He felt as if someone had thrown a bucket of cold, muddy river water on him.

"If you wish to seduce me, you must be awake," he pleaded.

In the candlelight, he admired her pale face and the curves of her hips and breasts. She was not plump, not like other counts' daughters, but he could tell by the way she walked and ate that she was healthy.

He stroked her cheek and lips. Still, she did not stir.

Too much wine. He shook his head. *Now what do I do?*

Hruodland felt unsteady himself after traveling all day and drinking so much wine that night. Even if he could carry her up the stairs, he did not think he could find his way to the stairs with only the light of a low fire, a few candles, and the moon streaming through the windows. And since he was not lord of this castle, he did not know how the women would react to his entering the solar unannounced.

Hruodland yawned and set the candle on the floor. He, too, wanted sleep. He lifted Alda and laid her on the pallet. She moved a little but remained asleep.

Perhaps in a couple of hours, I can wake her, and she can join the women upstairs.

He pulled off his boots, lay on the pallet beside her, and blew out the candle. He reached toward her. His hand found her thigh. He stroked her, hoping one last time to revive her. No response.

"I will know you," he promised. Yet he did not know how to interpret her eagerness to lie with him. *Is she simply enthusiastic? Or would she be hungry for any man, especially while I am away at war?*

He had never coupled with a virgin, only whores who followed the army, whores in the cities—and Judith of Bordeaux, a countess in his uncle's court who complained that her husband was too old and infirm to fulfill his marital duties. *Why did I let myself be seduced by that? Of course, she is pretty and plump. Any excuse to lie with her would have worked. But Judith was lust. Alda is...*

He stopped himself short, afraid to finish the thought. His hand rested on Alda's hip. He grimaced at the thought of Alda becoming anything like Judith, and not just because the children might not be his.

Even if you are a virgin, Alda, will you remain true? He stared into the dark until sleep finally overtook him.

Chapter 7

A sharp whisper startled Alda awake. Her eyelids felt heavy, and her head felt as if it would split. She opened her eyes just enough to see Veronica holding a tallow candle, silhouetted against an open window, where the first gray-white rays of daylight broke the horizon of the dark sky. Despite the pain, Alda turned her head and saw Hruodland on the pallet close to hers. The candlelight flickered over his scarlet tunic.

"Have you lost your wits?" Veronica hissed. "What have you done? If anyone finds out... It's time for Mass. You must make your toilette upstairs. I pray you are not with child."

Alda sat up, her left hand on her belly. She grimaced, fighting back a wave of nausea. She made the sign of the cross then clamped her hand over the nail of pain above her right eye.

"Alda!" Veronica whispered. "Come quickly, before someone sees you. Do you want everyone to find out?"

Alda scrunched her eyes shut and bowed her head. "There is nothing to find out," she murmured. "Unfortunately."

"What do you mean, 'unfortunately'? Are you trying to inflame Ganelon's jealousy even more?"

They both heard a moan. Alda opened her eyes again and looked toward the sound, despite the candle's searing light. Hruodland rolled on his back, covering his eyes with his arm.

"Hruodland? Are you well?" Alda asked, her own voice ragged.

"Take the light away," he barked.

Veronica tried to shield the light with her fingers.

Hruodland sat up. His face was pale. He looked about and took in his surroundings. "Is it morning?" he asked.

"It is almost prime," Veronica replied, straightening. "I must take my lady to the solar."

Hruodland nodded and made the sign of the cross. He hunched over, leaned on his elbows, and held his temples.

"Hruodland?" Alda asked.

Hruodland looked up and watched her rise. He steadied himself as he stood.

"I meant what I said last night," Alda said, her tone of voice as much a question as a statement.

He pulled her close and kissed her tenderly. Alda wanted to linger in the kiss. "So did I."

* * * * *

Following Veronica upstairs to the solar, she tried not to think of the pounding in her head. She realized she still wore her jewelry and boots. In the solar, the royal family finished dressing and descended the stairs. Alda discovered her mother was already awake and dressed.

"Alda, what happened?" Theodelinda asked.

Veronica looked at Alda wide-eyed.

"I fell asleep in the hall," Alda mumbled, her hand again on her forehead as if she were trying to keep that spot from bursting.

"I knew you should have retired when I did," Theodelinda said, shaking her head. "Alfihar should have heeded me. Are you well, Daughter?"

"Yes," Alda whimpered, fighting back another wave of nausea.

"You are not," Theodelinda said. "I can see it in your face. Do not drink so much wine."

Alda winced at the harshness of her mother's voice.

"My poor girl," Theodelinda sighed. "You should rest after Mass."

"But the hunt..." Alda pleaded.

"I shall have Veronica wake you in time to change clothes."

Alda nodded, too ill to say anything more. In the dawn's light, her gaze fell on the tapestry of the Virgin and her Child, which always brought her comfort. Dazed, she made the sign of the cross and then washed her face with water in a clay basin and smoothed her hair and the wrinkles in her dress.

"Time to leave," Theodelinda said.

Veronica held the candle and led the way down the stairs. Theodelinda and Alda followed.

Many of the men had slept on the floor and on benches. A few had made it to the cots and pallets. Alda noticed Ganelon was among the sleepers, but Hruodland, his brother, and her uncles were not.

"I cannot rouse the count," a servant told Theodelinda.

"When is that boy going to learn?" Scowling, Theodelinda marched up to Alfihar and called his name shrilly. "Do you realize this makes you look like a sluggard?"

Alda grimaced at the tone of her mother's voice and clamped her hand above her eye. Alfihar did not stir. Alda envied his ability to sleep through such a noise.

"Come," Theodelinda snapped.

As they walked, Alda's own footsteps crashed inside her head. When they entered the chapel redolent with incense, Alda noticed some of the peasants had slept here after last night's celebrations.

The bell rung by the priest clanged overhead. Usually, Alda welcomed the call to Mass and thoughts of heaven. Today, she braced herself against the sound slamming in her mind. The now-awake peasants cradled their heads and rocked. The first red-gold rays of the sun slipped through the chapel's narrow windows and made the Crucifixion mural on the west wall seem especially bloody.

Alda stood next to her mother. A few paces away, Hruodland stood with the royal family. The village priest descended from the bell tower. Bishop Leonhard walked to the altar and opened the Mass with "*Dominus vobiscum.*"

"*Et cum spiritu tuo,*" Alda chanted in reply with the rest of the worshipers. She didn't know what the Latin chants meant, only that they were the language of the Church, beautiful and mysterious. Alda could tell Leonhard, too, was miserable. His face was pale and sweaty. *He always has put duty above comfort.*

Alda snuck a glance at Hruodland. Their eyes met. Alda thought she saw, in the corner of her eye, that her mother was smiling. But when she turned, Theodelinda was looking at Leonhard. *Was Mother watching me and Hruodland?* Alda wondered, following the Mass.

As worshipers left the chapel after Mass, Alda whispered to her mother, "I must speak to Uncle Leonhard." She walked away before her mother had a chance to reply.

When she approached Leonhard, he suggested they stroll through the garden. "The air might help us both," he said.

Alda nodded. The sunlight outside the chapel was bright gold, painting a sheen on the green mountains and giving the muddy river jewels of light. On any other morning, the light would have been a tonic for sleepy eyes. But this morning, Alda shielded her eyes and reminded herself to never again drink so much wine.

"I need your aid," Alda said.

"Anything."

"Hruodland of the March of Brittany, he wants to marry me!" Alda grabbed both his hands.

"Wonderful. This would be a good match. We can give his family wealth. He can give us royal blood. Speak to your brother once he awakens."

"Alfihar will not heed me," she said, pouting. "The last time I told him I would not marry Ganelon, he called me willful."

"Speak to your brother. It is his decision."

"Will you speak to him for me?" Alda pleaded. "He might listen to you."

"He needs to hear this news from you," Leonhard said calmly.

"You said you would help me." Alda put her hands on her hips.

"I will speak in favor of the match," he replied, touching her shoulder, "but you must speak to your brother first."

Alda flinched as the pain in her head worsened.

"Are you well?" Leonhard asked.

Alda shook her head.

"You need rest," Leonhard said. He took Alda's arm and led her toward the manor. "And then speak to your brother."

* * * * *

58

Alda slept in the solar until midmorning. Her headache had cleared, but she still felt nauseous. Still wearing last night's dress, she rose from her pallet and descended the stairs. If Alfihar was awake, she had a little time to speak to him before she dressed for the hunt.

She found Alfihar sitting at a table in the hall. Hruodland was sleeping on a cot, while Ganelon still slumbered on a bench near the hearth. Her uncles and Hruodland's brother were chatting in a corner. Alda could tell her brother was sick from too much wine.

"Fetch some mint," Alda ordered a nearby servant, knowing the mint would settle their bellies. The servant scurried toward the garden.

"Alfihar," she said, "I must speak to you."

"Now?" he asked, looking down, his hands holding his temples. "Can it wait?"

"Now," she said firmly. "I have waited long enough."

He straightened and grabbed the cupbearer by the elbow. "Fetch some wine, and don't tarry."

The cupbearer grabbed a cup and ran to the cellar.

"I shall not marry Ganelon," Alda said deliberately.

"We have talked about this before..."

The servant returned with the mint. Alda gave half the sprigs to Alfihar.

"Listen," she said, tearing off a mint leaf with her teeth and pointing the stalk at her brother. "There is only one man I shall consent to marry. Hear me? One."

"Who would that be?" he asked wearily. He stuffed the sprig into his mouth.

"Hruodland of the March of Brittany. He has much wealth and..."

The cupbearer returned with a full cup and drank a sip. Alfihar took the cup and slapped the cupbearer. "You tarried!"

"He did not tarry," Alda said irritably while Alfihar downed a couple of gulps of wine. "You did not need to discipline him. And you are fortunate Mother did not see this. She would have..."

"Hold your tongue!" Alfihar slammed down the half-empty cup.

"I will not." She winced and shook her head. *This is going all wrong.* "About Hruodland..." she said softly.

"I already know his virtues," he said, waving her silent. "Hruodland is a good friend and a good ally. Are you certain?"

The question startled Alda. She had expected him to say Hruodland would never marry the sister of a count on the Rhine, despite the family's wealth, and to insist that she marry Ganelon.

"Alda? Did you hear me? Are you certain?" Alfihar repeated.

"Yes," she managed to reply.

"Good."

That is all? No argument? "You... you give your word you will negotiate with Hruodland?" she stammered.

"I give you my word," he said. "I swear by the dragon's blood. Swear to me that you will consent to marry Hruodland?"

"By the dragon's blood," Alda replied, her hand on both the cross and the dragon amulet.

"It is near terce," Alfihar said, "and the king will want us to be prompt. You should change clothes."

"As should you."

"You are like Mother. If you see her, tell her I shall be in the solar shortly, and yes, I know not to be tardy for a hunt when the king is our guest."

Alda let out a giggle, and Alfihar smiled. She rose from the table and spotted Veronica talking with maidservants. Alda called to her foster sister to help her dress and braid her hair.

When they entered the solar, Alda and Veronica went straight to their chests, Alda threw open the lid and eagerly dragged out her hunting clothes, which included a bright green dress for riding.

"I am glad to see you have recovered," Veronica said.

Alda still felt a little sick, but she was not about to allow that to get between her and a hunt. She removed her rings so that they wouldn't impede her grip on the javelin.

"I have the best news," Alda said excitedly. "Alfihar has agreed to negotiate with Hruodland for my hand."

Before Veronica could reply, they heard familiar steps hurrying up the stairs. Alda put her finger to her mouth and whispered, "Not a word. I haven't told Mother." *How shall I tell her?*

Now was not the time.

* * * * *

While Alfihar was changing clothes, Alda went to the courtyard and found other nobles watching the preparations for the hunt. Grooms led saddled horses. The huntsmen and dog trainers leashed the hounds, already leaping and barking and wagging their tails. Servants gave the nobles their swords and handed arrows and spears to their men.

As the terce bells rang and all the nobles cleared the hall, the murmur of eagerness rose. Alfihar walked through the crowd to mount his stallion and held his horn overhead. The crowd quieted. "Let the hunt begin," he shouted.

Alda and the other nobles mounted their horses. Everyone was eager for this hunt. Prince Pepin rode beside his father. Servants helped Queen Hildegard onto her mount, although she would simply watch from afar as the party drew closer to their prey.

Alda heard the king say to his eldest son, "When the boar or stag appears, join your mother."

"But Father..." the five-winter-old boy started to whine.

"You must protect her and your unborn sibling."

"Oh," the boy replied, straightening his shoulders as much as his curved spine would allow.

Remaining at the castle because of his age, toddling Prince Karl wailed, stomped his feet, and threw himself on the ground.

"But, child," the nurse pleaded, "a hunt is too dangerous for you."

When the gate ground open, the baying of the dogs almost drowned out Karl's cries. The dogs strained at their leashes and dragged their handlers down the mountain path.

Alda scanned the crowd, looking for Hruodland, but could not find him. Nor could she see his brother or her uncles. How odd for her uncles to miss a hunt — they enjoyed the sport more than she did. *Where are they?* she wondered. *What are they doing?*

* * * * *

"We are here to negotiate a marriage pact, aren't we?" Leonhard asked.

That is what Hruodland had presumed when Leonhard had asked him and Gerard to stay behind at the last minute. He studied Alda's champions. Her uncle Beringar was a good warrior who had slain many foes, but he was not one to keep track of how much cattle or how many horses or jewels Drachenhaus possessed. Leonhard, on the other hand, would know. In negotiations, Hruodland believed Leonhard would be the more formidable adversary. Like Beringar, Hruodland was skilled in battle, not negotiations for trade. Hruodland needed Gerard's intellect.

Hruodland swallowed a mouthful of wine. It felt as if the whole world hung on his answer. He had wanted to wait to start negotiations. He thought he would know Alda better on their second meeting and instead found himself asking more questions, especially of her virtue. *Did she lie and tell them I have lain with her?* Aloud, he asked, "What has Alda told you?"

"She said you want to marry her," Leonhard replied, "and Alfihar has asked us to start negotiations on his behalf. Answer my question: do you or do you not intend to make my niece your wife?"

Saints be praised, they don't know what I had almost done with her. "Yes," Hruodland said, "I wish to start negotiations. But why isn't Alfihar here?"

"A count cannot miss a hunt on his own land," Beringar answered.

Hruodland frowned. Beringar and Leonhard were withholding something from him. Hruodland was indoors during a hunt, and judging from the baying of the hounds, it was a good chase. He wished he could be riding through the forest right now instead of being confined to the hall. By the look on Beringar's and Leonhard's faces, they wished for the same thing.

"Why are we missing a hunt?" Hruodland asked.

Leonhard cleared his throat. "With everyone otherwise occupied, it is a good time to start negotiations."

Hruodland was not satisfied. Ganelon was still on the hunt, and when the men had prepared for the hunt in the hall, Ganelon had acted as if nothing had changed.

"Does Ganelon know our families are negotiating?" Hruodland asked.

Beringar and Leonhard looked at each other. Leonhard answered, "We must protect our niece's interests. If we cannot reach an agreement with you, we will pursue a pact with another suitor."

"Ganelon?" Hruodland growled. He felt Gerard's elbow in his ribs.

Beringar and Leonhard looked at each other again. "Perhaps," Beringar said.

Hruodland felt a knot in his belly. "But Alfihar told me you did not favor a union with Ganelon."

"If we cannot reach an agreement with you," Leonhard said, "Alda's marriage is not your concern. At this moment, we believe you have the best offer for our family. But until we reach an agreement, it's best for Alda if we keep these negotiations secret. We do not wish to anger other suitors."

Hruodland slammed his fist on the table, causing the cup to shake. He didn't care how angry negotiations would make Ganelon. How could they force Alda to marry that brute?

"Calm yourself, Hruodland," Gerard muttered in Roman. "It's a ploy to make you more generous with the bride price." Gerard raised his voice and said in Frankish that was still not perfect. "Before we start, I need speak to brother in private."

"Beringar and I also must have a discussion," Leonhard said.

Hruodland and Gerard walked across the hall to a corner near a window.

"What is it?" Hruodland asked irritably in Roman. "These negotiations will take long enough without your delay."

"And we are missing a hunt because of it," Gerard added petulantly in his mother tongue. "Are you certain of this? You know it will anger our father and the queen mother."

Hruodland stared out at the garden, remembering the drunken, bold young woman who took him there last night. He had thought the ideal wife was meek and obedient. Alda was untame, yet he could not stop thinking about her. He wanted to hold her, to run his hands along her curves, to know her intimately. But Gerard would need a better explanation than Hruodland's sentiments.

Hruodland touched the wall. "See this?" he said. "It is stone. This family must have great wealth, and once our father sees the riches we have brought to our family, his anger will be assuaged."

"That is possible. But the queen mother?"

"I hate to disappoint her, but Uncle Charles told me this morning that I should not marry the Breton only to please Grandmother. It was the reason he married the Lombard, and that marriage was a disaster. He said a union with a wealthy, well-connected family would be better and has his blessing."

"If you are going to wed Alda," Gerard said, "we should negotiate a generous dowry. Your royal blood will help us bargain."

"That, and the fact that neither Alda nor Alfihar wants a union with the count of Dormagen."

* * * * *

Hruodland remembered how Alfihar had frowned when they both had overheard the queen complain to her husband about Ganelon during the siege of Pavia. The king summoned Ganelon immediately.

"You will keep your distance from my queen, my children, and their nurses," the king yelled, the veins in his thick neck bulging. "I shall have your head if you break this commandment."

As soon as Ganelon left, Leonhard turned to Alfihar and said, "I told you Ganelon would make a bad brother. The only reason the king showed him mercy is that he needs Ganelon's men. Anyone can see the great affection the king has for his queen. Ganelon is a brute. Only a blind man or a fool would fail to see it. Swallow your pride and choose a different husband for Alda."

After dark, Alfihar and Hruodland sat by one of the campfires. Neither could sleep. Hruodland gazed at Pavia's walls and wondered when the siege would end. He turned to Alfihar, who was staring into the flames.

"Does something trouble you?" Hruodland asked.

"Did you hear my uncle when he spoke of Ganelon?" Alfihar asked, passing a wineskin to Hruodland.

"I could not help but hear it." He took a drink and gave the wineskin back to Alfihar.

"I was negotiating Alda's marriage pact with Ganelon before the war. I thought his lands would compensate for his faults." Alfihar shook his head. "But after what happened today, I..." He hesitated. "I see it is a bad arrangement, and so does Uncle Beringar. Ganelon is out of favor with the king, and Uncle Leonhard would never forgive me if Ganelon and Alda were wed."

"With her dowry, Alda would make a good wife to any man," Hruodland said.

"Perhaps you should marry her," Alfihar joked.

Hruodland thought for a moment before replying, "Perhaps, I should. We would make good brothers."

"You are earnest? You would marry Alda? Why didn't you say anything to me in Geneva? And what about the Breton your family wants you to marry?"

"I shall *not* marry a Breton. As for Alda, I had spoken with her but for one night. The next morning, word spread through the palace that you were negotiating with Ganelon. I believed my cause was hopeless."

"Your cause is not hopeless now, with both my uncles opposed to a union with Ganelon." Alfihar lowered his voice. "In truth, Ganelon is vexing me. The way he keeps asking about Drachenhaus's riches — not only Alda's dowry, but how often merchants visit and what tolls we collect and how many servants we have — you would think he would have a claim to my inheritance as well as Alda's."

Hruodland raised his eyebrows. *That's why Ganelon wants Alda! If Alfihar died childless, her sons would inherit Drachenhaus.* "I would like to speak to Alda again," Hruodland said aloud, "to be certain if a union between us is God's will."

"After Pavia falls, accompany me to Drachenhaus. You will see that we can afford a generous dowry, and if it is your will, she will be your wife."

* * * * *

Faint barks from the woods near Drachenhaus brought Hruodland back to the matter now at hand: negotiating his bride price and Alda's dowry.

He and Gerard spoke of what to request from Alda's family. Hruodland looked toward Alda's uncles, who were speaking intently, most likely about the same subject. They all sat down again at a small table. Hruodland was glad to have Gerard on his side. He dared not admit it, but he could never have negotiated a marriage pact on his own.

As Hruodland heard the baying of hounds again, he longed to ride swiftly on a steed, chasing his prey, and he wondered what beast the nobles were hunting.

Chapter 8

Alda watched the dog trainers release the hounds from their leashes. Almost every grown dog in Drachenhaus was set loose for the hunt — greyhounds, wolfhounds, boarhounds, bloodhounds, staghounds, and mastiffs.

At the head of the hunting party were King Charles, Alfihar, Theodelinda, Alda, and Ganelon. Alda stayed near her brother and away from Ganelon, but as the dogs' barking became louder and more enthusiastic, Alda forgot about the icy-eyed count of Dormagen.

The nobles urged the horses to a trot to keep up with the hounds as the dogs ran through the forest, noses to the ground. They bounded through a thicket and a chorus of barks resounded through the woods. To Alda's delight, she saw scratches in the earth among the paw prints.

"A boar!" a huntsman bellowed. "The hounds have found a boar."

The dogs panted and wagged their tails before they started running again. Alda and Alfihar and the others urged their horses to follow. Alda was heedless of the leaves and twigs and dirt that stirred and landed on her dress and in her hair. A small branch caught on one of Alda's braids and tugged at it. Alda felt her braid become undone as she kept riding. Even with her hair flapping against her face and neck, she focused her attention on the chase.

Behind her, she heard the heavy thud of a horse falling, followed by a man's shouts. The obscenities he uttered let Alda know he would be fine and that his servants would attend to him.

Now the dogs were in a frenzy, and the nobles were just as excited. Alda caught a glimpse of the beast in a clearing, and already she could tell it was larger than any boar she had seen before.

"Pepin," the king called to his son, "tend to your mother. Do not let the beast near her."

The boy drew his wooden sword and rode to the queen, who was already lagging.

The rest of the hunting party drew closer to the boar. The beast was a giant among its kind, bigger than any of its best-fed cousins in Drachenhaus's swine yard. Its black bristles stood on end, and Alda saw the fire in its eyes. This monster was going to fight to the death.

Alda and Theodelinda called for javelins, and Alfihar and Ganelon dismounted and called for their arrows. The king dismounted and drew his sword.

In a cacophony of barks, the dogs surrounded the boar. It snorted and bared its tusks. It charged and gored a large bloodhound, throwing the dog as if it had been made of rags and then did the same to three other hounds.

Alfihar let loose an arrow and shot the boar in the shoulder. The beast shrieked when the feathered shaft pierced its shoulder, but still it gutted another dog, one of the finest greyhounds, as it turned toward Alfihar. Alda grabbed her dragon as she used her knees to steady her horse. With her other hand, she tightened her grip on the javelin and raised it.

Alfihar let fly another arrow, again landing in the boar's shoulder. The blow only enraged the boar even more.

The boar charged Alfihar. Screaming, Alda let go of her dragon and hurled her javelin. A second javelin, this one from her mother, flew with hers, and both landed in the beast's back. The boar staggered. A hound ran between Alfihar and the boar, barking, growling, and baring its fangs. The boar paused to gore that hound, which let out a loud wail as it collapsed.

The king raised his sword, gave a battle cry, and ran straight toward the beast. With one swift stroke, he landed the sword in the boar's neck. Blood gushed on the king and the forest floor. The boar fell while the king leapt back.

The king blew his hunting horn and called to his huntsmen. "Carry this beast back to the castle and have it roasted. Preserve his tusks as trophies of our victory."

Alda looked sadly at the dogs the boar had slain. "They were good hounds," she whispered, brushing aside a strand of hair.

She watched the surviving hounds gather around the boar, wagging their tails. The huntsmen slashed open the boar's belly and then stood back so the hounds could eat the innards.

The dog trainers fetched carts to take the slain dogs back to the castle, where they would be buried with honor in shallow graves. Already, carrion birds were circling.

Alda noticed one man had his arm set in a sling and another was limping and needed help to mount his horse. She was relieved their injuries seemed to be the worst — no one had been crippled or killed.

Something besides the dogs' deaths troubled Alda. She had seen dogs die in a hunt before and mourned them, but knew that hounds lived for the hunt. A dog's death in a hunt was like a warrior's fall in battle — an honorable death. No, something else about the hunt gnawed at her mind. She recalled everything that had happened today. The hunt seemed normal, but she could not shake a feeling that something was amiss, even as the hunting party returned to the castle.

* * * * *

When Alda dismounted in the courtyard, she brushed off the bits of leaves and twigs clinging to her hunting clothes and sweaty skin. She needed to wash and have Veronica unbraid her hair. She and the other women rushed inside and up the stairs to the solar, where maidservants were filling basins with water.

Shedding their hunting clothes, now dirty and stained with sweat, Theodelinda and Alda talked with the queen about the hunt. Alda splashed water on herself, rubbed her skin with a drying cloth, and plunked down on a stool. Veronica gave her a clay bottle. Alda lifted the stopper, sniffed, and smiled: rose oil. She stroked the perfume behind her ears, wanting to make herself irresistible to Hruodland. Why did he and her uncles stay in the hall during the hunt? Could they be negotiating?

After the women donned fresh clothes and had their hair combed — all the while recounting the hunt, they descended the stairs to the hall. Alda's eyes were drawn to Hruodland, and his smile reassured her of his affection. Still, she would not feel at ease until the betrothal. The real celebration would be the nuptials, when Alda and Hruodland would make their vows before God on the chapel steps.

As they had done last night, Alda and Hruodland walked toward each other. Suddenly, she felt a tight grip at her elbow. Digging its fingers into her flesh, the hand spun her around face-to-face with Ganelon and his wine-stinking, hot breath.

"Women should not have such enthusiasm for a hunt," he sneered.

Now Alda knew what had been troubling her since the end of the hunt. "Why didn't you come to my brother's aid when the boar was charging at him?" she spat. "Everyone else tried to help, but you did not shoot a single arrow."

"Do not question my hunting prowess," he growled. "I am destined to be your master."

He seized her other arm and crushed her against his body. His kiss stifled her scream. She struggled to free herself, but he was too strong.

Chapter 9

Ganelon!" Alda heard Alfihar roar behind her. "Unhand my sister at once!"

Ganelon released Alda. She stumbled back and noticed Hruodland was at her side. He looked at Alda, then Ganelon. As if his hands had a will of their own, they clenched into fists, and the right fist slammed into Ganelon's jaw. Ganelon punched Hruodland in the gut.

A circle formed around the men as fists smacked into flesh. Alda screamed when she saw a flash of iron. Ganelon had drawn his eating knife and was lunging at Hruodland. Hruodland leapt back and drew his own knife as Ganelon's slashed the air.

"Stop it! Both of you!" Alda shrieked, clutching her dragon amulet with both hands.

Alda felt her mother's hand on her elbow pulling her away from the fray, while Beringar, Alfihar, Gerard, King Charles himself, and others wrestled both men to the ground.

"There are women and children in here!" Alfihar bellowed. "Do you want harm to come to them?"

Alda faced her mother, quickly thinking of reasons for her outburst: *What was I to do? Let them fight like tomcats?*

Theodelinda's stern face softened when she met daughter's eyes. Alda's gaze fell to her boots.

"Mother, I..." she sputtered. "I did not intend..."

"I know, Daughter."

Alda looked up and saw the men pulling Hruodland and Ganelon to their feet. Even with Beringar's and the king's strength, it took three men each to drag them away from each other — and keep them apart.

"Mother..." Alda wanted to say so much. That she would not marry Ganelon. That she wanted to marry Hruodland. But she did not know where or how to begin.

"Hush," Theodelinda soothed. "If you wish for a man to listen to you, you cannot give yourself up to fits of humor." She smiled grimly. "Not that it matters in this case. It is nearly impossible to keep those two from fighting. Their enmity runs long and deep."

"Dung-eating son of a whore's rat-tailed cur!" Hruodland yelled.

"Go revel in the muck with the other worms!"

"Is that the best you can think of, you..." Hruodland let out a stream of obscenities.

"Hruodland does not have to repeat himself," Alda murmured to her mother, suppressing a giggle.

"Men," Theodelinda muttered. "When they have become quiet, I need you to be a hostess."

Alda nodded, puzzled by her mother's manner but too weary to argue or question her further. She drew back the sleeve on the arm that Ganelon had first grabbed and beheld bruises left by his fingers. Theodelinda gasped, but anger revived Alda.

"Do you still favor a union between me and Ganelon?" she hissed. "He has no right to do this. If he does this to me now, think of what he will do to me if we are wed. I shall not marry him, Mother!"

"No, you will not," Theodelinda said calmly, keeping her voice low.

"What?"

"Hush! I said I do not favor a union between you and Ganelon, not since Alfihar told me of Prince Hruodland's interest in you."

"You knew?" Alda stammered, closing her eyes, trying to absorb this information.

"That is what he wished to discuss with me yesterday immediately after he came home. Do you think there is any business in Drachenhaus that I would not know about?" she asked.

"Do you think Alfihar or your uncles would know what we can offer as a dowry or what to request in a bride price? Do you think I would leave everything to them?"

"Why? Why didn't you tell me?"

"I intended to, but you seemed to charm Hruodland better when you thought you were destined for Ganelon. For once, your willfulness worked in this family's favor."

"Perhaps, we should tell Ganelon," Alda mused.

"You will do no such thing," Theodelinda said in her mother tone.

"What I tell him does not matter. I told him months ago that God will never join us, yet he is still seeking my hand. But Alfihar should tell him. It is not right to let Ganelon think he has hope of a union with me." *And I wish to be rid of him.*

"Have I taught you nothing of negotiations? If Hruodland thinks another suitor is seeking your hand, he will be more generous with his bride price."

"But Hruodland and Alfihar are friends," Alda protested.

"Nevertheless, marriage is a pact, not unlike trade with the merchants. One cannot be too eager, or all is lost."

Alda looked at her bruises again. She was glad Ganelon had done this when Alfihar was watching. She clenched her teeth, more determined than ever to seduce Hruodland and carry his son in her belly.

* * * * *

When Hruodland and Ganelon finally tired of shouting, Alda and her mother returned to the group. Among the nobles and royal family, Alda saw Ganelon and Hruodland sitting as far apart as they could. Veronica was chatting with one of the king's menservants. Despite herself, Alda smiled when she saw the bruise on Ganelon's jaw. Ganelon looked up at her and the baneful expression in his icy eyes caused her to shudder. His look said he would beat her, kick her, stomp on her, make her beg for mercy, make her long for the days when she received only bruises.

She looked at Hruodland, who was talking with her brother. He smiled at her, and that smile beckoned her. As she passed Ganelon, he muttered, "You will pay for this."

Alda swallowed to hold back the bile and the insults she wanted to throw at him. She wanted to scratch him, kick him, pummel him with her fists, and that desire made her despise him more. She looked at Hruodland again. *Better if he thinks I am meek,* she told herself as she walked toward him. She wondered how best to lure him to one of the pallets when darkness fell and make him think that lying with her was his idea.

Before Alda could think of a plan, one of the cooks ran into the hall and whispered something to the dowager countess. Theodelinda nodded and announced the servants would set the table and bring the first course.

* * * * *

Dinner was lively, but no more blows were exchanged. Theodelinda had seated Hruodland and Ganelon as far from each other as possible.

After dinner, the guests again took seats by the hearth. Ganelon sat beside Alda. She jumped up and walked away, not caring how it appeared. She was never going to be that close to Ganelon again.

Ganelon shifted in his seat as if he was about to pursue her. But then he looked at Alfihar. Alfihar glared at him, and Ganelon settled back on the bench.

Hruodland approached Alda and put his arm around her shoulders. As much as she longed for the feel of his hand, Alda stepped away from him. He looked hurt.

"Hruodland, I don't want there to be another fight," Alda pleaded.

"I'm not afraid of Ganelon," Hruodland said, stepping closer to her. "If he ever lays a hand on you again, I will break his arm. No man will treat my wife in such a manner, I promise. I would fight a dragon and walk through fire before any harm came to you."

While the musicians and the singer recounted the revenge of Siegfried's widow, sunlight stretched the shadows, then darkness crept into the hall. With everyone else distracted, Alda's body tingled with desire as she tried to think of a way to get Hruodland to one of the pallets in the shadows. Her reverie was shattered when her mother called her name. Never before had Theodelinda's voice sounded so shrill to Alda's ears.

"It is time for sleep," her mother said.

Alda looked to her brother, already nodding off. "Yes, Alda," Alfihar murmured. "It's late."

"But I am not sleepy," Alda protested.

Theodelinda frowned at her daughter. Alda pouted. Her desire to lie with Hruodland was overwhelming, but she sighed and obeyed her mother. *He must not think me willful*, she thought. Other women, including the queen and Veronica, took their leave and retired for the night.

Alda glanced over her shoulder one last time. She admired Hruodland's muscular form in the firelight. *Tomorrow is another night. I will know you. I will have your child.*

* * * * *

Two weeks passed as Alfihar and Hruodland negotiated bride price and dowry. Alda wished more than ever that Alfihar would tell Ganelon that she would never be his bride. Ganelon's stares were becoming more hateful by the day.

Alda and Hruodland talked each night by the hearth, but she could never manage to be alone with him. Just when the opportunity might present itself, Veronica suddenly had a question that needed to be answered, or her mother said it was time to retire to the solar.

One morning, Ganelon came into the kitchen, where Theodelinda and Alda were planning dinner.

"The king has given me leave to return to Dormagen," he said, "but I have unfinished business here."

No, you don't, Alda wanted to say. But she held her tongue and looked at her mother.

"I am merely the count's mother." Theodelinda shrugged. "You must speak with him. He is master of the house."

"It seems as if your son is avoiding me," Ganelon said. "He is always speaking with Hruodland and his kin — in low voices."

"Ganelon, are you blind?" Alda blurted.

"Child, hold your tongue," Theodelinda said in her mother tone.

"What does she mean?" Ganelon asked Theodelinda.

"She means you should speak to the master of the house, don't you, child?"

"I am not a child," Alda yelled, stamping her foot. "I have seen fifteen winters, I shall be married soon, and I do not need you to speak for me."

"Act like a grown woman, and I will treat you as such," Theodelinda retorted.

"I marvel at how you can suffer such insolence, Countess," Ganelon interjected.

"Insolence?" Theodelinda snapped. "You are calling my daughter insolent? I will tell you what I will not suffer — a union between my daughter and the likes of you. As we speak, my son and Prince Hruodland are negotiating the bride price and dowry."

"What? But she is promised to me!" Ganelon shouted, stepping closer to Theodelinda.

Alda whispered to Veronica, "Fetch Alfihar. Ganelon will not notice you." *Sweet Mary, do not let Ganelon hurt my mother,* Alda prayed, clutching her dragon.

As Veronica slipped out the door, Theodelinda picked up the nearest object, a large, bloody knife on the butcher block and gestured with it.

"Is there a bride price? Is there a dowry?" she asked sarcastically. "And when did you and my daughter exchange vows?"

Ganelon stared at the knife and would not take his eyes off it even as Alda called to him.

"I told you I would never consent to a union with you," she said sharply. *Please, Alfihar, hurry!*

"You *will* consent," he growled, his right hand twitching.

"Nothing will make me consent," Alda cried, trying to distract him from her mother.

"Nothing?" Ganelon asked. "Not a beating? Not starvation?"

"No one treats *my* daughter in such a manner," Theodelinda snarled. "No one."

"It is my right as..."

Suddenly, Alfihar burst through the kitchen door, with Hruodland and their kin at his heels.

"Ganelon, if any harm befalls my mother or my sister, you will answer to me," Alfihar roared.

"And me," Hruodland added.

"Is it true?" Ganelon asked Alfihar, still watching the knife Theodelinda held. "Have you been negotiating a marriage pact between your family and his?"

"Step outside the kitchen," Alfihar barked, grabbing Ganelon by the collar. "Leave our womenfolk in peace."

As Alfihar dragged Ganelon out, Veronica slipped in. The door closed. Theodelinda looked at the knife and dropped it back on the butcher block. For a moment, the three women clung to each other.

"We should see how my brother fares," Alda whispered.

Theodelinda nodded and waved for them to come to the window and watch what the men were doing.

* * * * *

"You have not answered my question," Ganelon snapped. He pulled himself out of Alfihar's grasp.

"Yes," Alfihar said, "we have been negotiating. Alda and Hruodland have been betrothed since my clerk wrote the pact for the bride price and dowry this morning."

At the kitchen window, Alda put her hand to her mouth and wept. Veronica looked at her, astonished by the news. Theodelinda put her arm around Alda's shoulders and pulled her daughter toward her.

"Betrothed?" Ganelon sputtered. "Betrothed? But she is mine."

"I made no promise," Alfihar said, his chin raised, his back straight. "We were simply negotiating. Hruodland made a better offer."

Ganelon gave Hruodland a murderous stare. "You are just like your father," he spat. "Stealing what does not belong to you."

"I stole nothing," Hruodland shot back. "She is my wife by right. If the idea of theft will not leave your head willingly, I can break your skull and let it out."

Ganelon looked at the men who surrounded him — Hruodland, Alfihar, Gerard, Alfihar's uncles. "I will take my cause to the king."

"Ganelon," Hruodland called, "settle this here. With me. Now. If you truly believe yourself ill used, challenge me to a duel, or are you man enough?"

Ganelon paused for a moment and then kept walking toward the hall.

"Just as I suspected." Hruodland spat on the ground.

The door to the kitchen opened, and Alda, Theodelinda, and Veronica spilled out. Alda rushed into Hruodland's arms.

"Hruodland, why did you challenge him to a duel?" she cried. "He might have hurt you."

Hruodland stood back for a moment and held her tear-streaked face in his hands. "Him? Hurt me?" He laughed. "I have faced warriors twice his size."

Leonhard cleared his throat. "We should go to the hall. No doubt he is stating his case to the king."

The party followed Ganelon. As Leonhard had predicted, Ganelon stood before Charles. "...and Your Excellence, Lady Alda was promised to me."

"I was not," Alda interjected from the security of Hruodland's arms.

"Lady Alda, allow Count Ganelon to state his case," said the king.

Alda seethed as Ganelon again said that she should be his bride. She bit her lip to prevent vile words from spilling out. To her right, Alfihar clenched and unclenched his fists.

"Count Alfihar, what have you to say?" Charles asked, his voice calm.

"My sister and Count Ganelon were not betrothed," Alfihar replied in clipped tones. "We never had a pact. Your nephew had a far better offer for my family."

"My lord king, if I may speak on my family's behalf," Leonhard said, his voice as calm as Charles's, "Alda has seen fifteen years and has reached the age in which a marriage requires her consent."

"He is lying," Ganelon yelled. "He is her uncle."

"Ask any of the learned men who travel with you, my lord king."

The king's archchaplain, who had overheard the conversation, interrupted, "The bishop of Bonn speaks correctly, Your Excellence. A woman of Lady Alda's years must consent to a union between herself and any suitor."

"What I am saying," Leonhard stated, "is that Alda would never have given her consent to a union with Ganelon."

"Lady Alda, does your uncle speak the truth?" Charles asked.

"Yes," she said, glad to finally speak. "I never would have taken any vow to be united with that man. I would have joined the cloister on Nonnenwerth first."

"You would have joined my cousin Radegunde's strict cloister before marrying the count of Dormagen?"

"Yes," Alda said without hesitation.

"If the bride will not give her consent, there is nothing we or the Church can do," the king said, folding his hands under his chin.

"But you are the king!" Ganelon protested.

"We, too, are bound by Church law," the king said, gesturing toward his archchaplain. "Fulrad said this marriage depends on the consent of the bride. While the bishop of Bonn has an interest in whom Lady Alda marries, Fulrad has no stake in this matter. Our judgment is this: the betrothal between Lord Hruodland and Lady Alda is valid."

Mouth agape, Ganelon stared at the people about him. His baneful gaze fell on Hruodland and Alda. Alda trembled in Hruodland's arms.

Hruodland remained steady. As the nobles step aside, he handed Alda to Alfihar and stepped into the clear space they had made. He pushed back the sleeve to reveal the scar from the Lombard and crossed his arms.

"Well, Ganelon, what will you do?" He made no attempt to mask his contempt.

"I shall leave this den of wolves," Ganelon said through clenched teeth. He turned his hate-filled gaze to Alda. "And you, strumpet, you are worthless to any man without your dowry."

"No one insults my wife," Hruodland shouted.

He lunged at Ganelon and punched him in the gut. Ganelon returned the blow before a dozen guards separated the two. Alda leaned against Alfihar as Hruodland and Ganelon shouted new obscenities at each other.

When their curses were finally spent, Ganelon called to his servants. "We are leaving post-haste," he barked. "Anyone who tarries will be flogged."

Ganelon's servants, bone-thin and clothed in rags, hurried to do their master's bidding. Ganelon went out of his way in Alda's direction. Hruodland raced toward Ganelon.

"I will be avenged," Ganelon muttered. He turned on his heel and left.

Hruodland rushed to Alda. "What did the cur say?"

"He said he will be avenged." Alda shuddered.

"Is that all? He has always said such things." Hruodland shrugged. "Alfihar, why did you send the guards to separate us?"

"The same reason as before," Alfihar replied. "If the blows between you and Ganelon led to a brawl, the women and children would be hurt."

"Yes. You must protect the women and children."

"A betrothal calls for a celebration," Theodelinda called out as if to distract her guests from the servants hurrying to pack Ganelon's possessions. "We shall feast on the fattest calves."

Alda watched Ganelon's servants. *No more of Ganelon's hateful eyes,* she thought. *No more of that twitching hand. He is leaving. Gone, gone, gone from my life.* The thought was intoxicating. It made her giddy, so giddy that she could not stop giggling.

"What amuses you so?" Hruodland asked.

"I am so glad, so glad that you are my betrothed." *And not him.* Her giddiness was tempered by his parting words to her: *I will be avenged.* She wondered what form his vengeance would take.

Chapter 10

Alda sat next to Hruodland at the betrothal feast. He placed his hand on her thigh, and she felt a thrill. She looked at him, eager to be alone with him, to know him intimately.

Then her mother called to her. "I must speak with you in private."

Alda winced. She looked at Hruodland longingly and kissed him before accompanying her mother to a corner of the hall.

"What is it?" Alda asked, vexed.

"Do you think I am blind? Anyone can see your desire. You are not to lie with him before your nuptials."

"What?" Alda said sharply. "He is my husband. I have every right to lie with him."

"After we have the nuptials, you can meet with him all you wish."

"It is not a sin to meet with my husband."

"Sin has nothing to do with it. Hruodland has yet to deliver the bride price."

"Hruodland is a good man." Alda bristled.

"But he must get the bride price from his father, who knows nothing of this arrangement. And if his father does not deliver, we must still be able to negotiate with another suitor. We would be better able to negotiate if we can tell them you are still chaste."

"No one would believe us."

"They would believe us more if there is no baby," Theodelinda retorted.

"But I want him now. I have waited so long."

"You will have to wait longer." Theodelinda's face was stern.

"How long?"

"I do not know. The March of Brittany is far away. It may be a year."

"A year!" Alda was about to protest. Instead, she bit her lip. *No use to argue.* "Very well, mother," she lied.

Alda returned to Hruodland and asked to speak with him privately in a corner of the hall. She related the conversion she had with her mother. She was glad to see Hruodland straighten his spine and narrow his eyes.

"Your brother said nothing about waiting," Hruodland snapped. "You are mine now. Not your mother's. I will go speak to your brother at once."

Alda touched Hruodland's shoulder. "Hruodland, wait. I have a better idea." She whispered in his ear.

"But we have no reason for secrecy," Hruodland said. "We are betrothed. And what if I engender you with a child?"

"Exactly," Alda said, her eyes shining. "If I were carrying an heir in my belly, your father would gladly pay the bride price."

"But my father might doubt the child is mine. Not that I would," he hastily added.

"Show him the sheets where we have lain. It will prove I have known no other man."

* * * * *

When the lauds bells marked the ninth hour of night, Alda lay still in the bed, listening for the slightest sound. She heard only her mother's soft breathing beside her and few snores in the solar. Using the light of the thick night candle, she searched the room with her eyes. Because the night was warm, the curtains on the beds had been left open. Alfihar slumbered in a bed three paces away, while Charles slept with Hildegard. Near the royal couple,

Princes Pepin and Karl shared a bed with their nurses. Throughout the room, maids slept on pallets and cots.

Carefully, Alda slid back her sheet. She rose, naked, and put on a tunic that reached her ankles, then took a slender tallow candle and held it to the night candle. If someone did see her, she would say she was on her way to the privy.

She crept down the stairs to the hall and headed for the pallets where Hruodland said he would be sleeping. By the light of glowing embers in the hearth, she saw several noblemen had fallen asleep on the benches and floor, which felt cool against her bare feet.

She found Hruodland on two pallets pushed together. He opened his eyes when the candlelight fell upon him. He smiled and sat up. The sheet fell away to reveal his bare, scarred chest. Despite herself, Alda gasped.

"Those scars," she blurted. "Do they cause you pain?"

"These? They are simply the marks of a warrior." He patted the empty side of the pallet.

As Alda set aside the candle and sat next to him, she stared at the scars and touched one on his shoulder. "But there are so many."

"I have seen many battles," he replied casually.

His hand found the hem of her garment, and he slowly raised it to her thighs. She wriggled to get the garment past her hips and helped him take it off. He gazed at her.

"You are so lovely," he whispered.

He drew back the sheet. Alda's hand flew to her heart. Her eyes grew wide. "Hruodland!"

His arms encircled her, and he drew her down beside him into a kiss. She tasted his lips hungrily. She felt a thrill wherever his hands strayed. She had felt desire like this ever since she had become a woman two years ago. Hruodland's presence heightened this longing, this ache that had a will all its own, this hunger that demanded satiation.

"Oh, yes," she sighed. "Oh yes. Know me. Make me your wife."

And he did.

Afterward, Alda rested her head against his bare shoulder, his arms encircling her.

"I wish I did not have to return to the solar," she sighed.

"Stay here," he said. "We are betrothed. Let them know we consummated our marriage."

"You do not know my mother. She would give me no peace if she found out."

"But if you conceived..."

"She will find out then." She kissed him and sat up.

"Alda, wait," Hruodland said. He turned and rummaged through the pile of clothes near his pallet. "I have a gift for you."

He slipped a gold ring studded with rubies onto her trembling finger.

"It is beautiful," she whispered. "I shall always treasure it."

She rose, feeling giddy. She looked longingly at him one last time over her shoulder. He rested on his elbow, grinning dreamily at her. *How wonderful to know him.*

* * * * *

Descending the stairs with the other women just before sunrise prayers, Alda was shocked by what she saw. She had expected Hruodland's tender smile and, near his pallet, the folded sheet she would arrange to be packed with his possessions. Instead, she was greeted with rumpled linens — and Hruodland's dark eyes were burning through her.

"Mother, Hruodland and I will join you at Mass in a moment," Alda said, hoping to sound calm. The other women's faces mirrored Alda's confusion, but they made their way to the chapel. Alda approached Hruodland and whispered, "What troubles you? Why is the sheet not folded?"

"There is no blood on the sheet," he hissed.

"That... that is impossible," she stammered. "I have known no other man."

"Then, why is there no blood?" he growled.

Alda lifted the top sheet and gasped. There was evidence they had lain together, but no blood, not one drop. She let it slip from her fingers. "I don't know why there isn't any blood," she said, her voice shaking. "But I swear by the Mother of God that I was a virgin until I knew you last night."

Will he repudiate me for unchastity? she wondered. *What if I am with child? Will the baby grow up fatherless?*

84

She felt a familiar trickle between her legs and cursed under her breath. "Hruodland, I must return to the solar," she said abruptly. "I will join you in the chapel."

She ran up the stairs without further explanation. In the solar, she confirmed what she already knew: her womanly courses had started. She laughed at the irony. *If I had but waited a day, there would have been more than enough blood.*

* * * * *

At Mass, Hruodland stole glances at his betrothed, standing beside him. All color had left her face. Wincing, she placed her hand over her belly, where a child would grow.

Questions kept repeating themselves in his mind. Why was there no blood? She had acted as he expected a virgin to act. She had felt as a virgin ought to feel.

Was she with child by another man? Hruodland frowned. He would not acknowledge a child who wasn't his. But how could he be certain?

What do I do now? If I go to Alfihar, he will know I lay with her before the nuptials. Was that her scheme all along? But then why would she tell me to save the sheet? Who is this woman I married?

More than anything else, he wanted to believe her. He wanted to believe he was the only man who would ever know her. *She did swear by the Mother of God, but how can I ignore the evidence?*

He glanced at her again. She flinched like a soldier who had just been stabbed. His pity tempered his anger. How he wished she did not have this power over him. "Are you well?" he asked.

"It is my monthly courses," she murmured, with a blush.

"Oh," Hruodland said, looking down, relieved that any question of paternity was moot.

"I must rest for a couple of hours after Mass," she said apologetically.

Hruodland nodded. He had no wish to discuss a woman's monthly courses any further. He had overheard more than enough such conversations among women before.

* * * * *

"What have I done?" Alda cried out. Wearing only a shift and flux rags, she was curled on her bed.

"Do you want to me to fetch some wine?" Veronica asked, placing Alda's clothes in the chest.

"Why didn't I bleed last night?" Alda wailed.

"Alda, what are you speaking of?"

"I knew him last night." Her throat tightened as panic overwhelmed her.

"Hruodland? You are betrothed."

"But there wasn't any blood on the sheets," Alda whispered. Alda thrashed on the bed, anything to rid herself of the pain in her belly. *Why did Eve have to bite into the apple?*

"It wasn't the first time," Veronica said.

Alda stopped her thrashing. "It was the first time," she insisted.

"But how could there be no blood?"

"I don't know. What shall I do?"

Veronica responded with a blank look. They heard footsteps on stairs leading up to the solar and immediately fell silent. Alda knew it was her mother and drew the sheet over her head.

"How do you fare, Daughter?" Theodelinda asked.

Alda moaned as another spasm of pain coursed through her belly. She heard her mother's footsteps approach the bed and felt her mother pull back the sheet and stroke her hair.

"I remember feeling thus during my womanly courses when I was your age," she said gently. "It will pass."

Alda moaned again, wishing her mother would leave.

"I noticed you are wearing a new ring," Theodelinda said. "Who gave it to you?"

"Hruodland," Alda said, her voice barely audible.

"Is it a morning gift?" Theodelinda asked, her voice as sharp as a thorn.

Alda's eyes opened wide. She hesitated, trying to decide whether to tell her mother the truth.

"It is a morning gift!" Theodelinda snapped.

Alda drew her knees to her chest. "Mother, I am in pain. Quarrel with me later."

"An apt punishment for disobedience," Theodelinda spat. "I hope God curses you with a child as willful as you are. Child, why?"

"I told you: he is my husband. At least now he is."

"What do you mean, 'at least now'? He is betrothed to you, and he has known you."

"I fear he will repudiate me."

"Why?" Theodelinda put her hands on her hips.

"I did not bleed," Alda mumbled.

Theodelinda laughed harshly. Alda and Veronica gaped at her.

"Not all women bleed," Theodelinda said, shaking her head. "And that will not excuse him from the betrothal. If he dares to make such a claim, he will answer to your brother — and Alfihar will challenge him to a duel, unlike that spineless fool who just left."

"Mother, do not tell Alfihar," Alda pleaded. "I could not bear to lose either of them."

"Alfihar is not to know, not yet. He would only make this worse. But if Hruodland refuses the nuptials," Theodelinda said gravely, "Alfihar will have no other choice."

Alda burst into tears.

Chapter 11

As soon as the Mass had ended, worshipers emptied the chapel, but Hruodland stood with his arms crossed in prayer and wondered what to do about Alda. He did not move even while the village priest put away the Host and the cup. Finished, the priest waved to the only two people inside: Hruodland and his brother.

"Hruodland, the Mass has finished," Gerard said in Roman.

Hruodland nodded but did not look up.

"What troubles you?" Gerard asked.

"I knew her last night, but she did not bleed," he said as if he were someplace else.

"You lay with Alda?"

Hruodland nodded.

"And you are concerned because there is no blood on the sheets, even though her family did not want you to meet with her before the nuptials."

"How did you know?" Hruodland asked, detecting a note of sarcasm in Gerard's voice.

"If they wanted you to meet with her, they would not have sent her to the solar and you to the hall. So she did not bleed." Gerard shrugged. "Did you expect a woman to be true?"

The Cross and the Dragon

"I expected *her* to be true. She told me she had known no other man."

"In the eyes of the Church, she still belongs to her family. In the eyes of the Church, her sins are not your concern."

"She is my wife," Hruodland growled. "She is mine. I thought I married a virgin."

"Is she trying to pass off a bastard as yours?"

"She said her womanly courses started this morning."

"There is no bastard to worry about. Why does this trouble you? Is she cold?"

"She was eager for my touch, quite eager. She came to me." Hruodland smiled at the memory of her sighs and moans of pleasure.

"That is worth more than her virginity. Hruodland, women are incapable of virtue. God created them so frail." He gestured to the mural of the serpent tempting Eve with the apple. "The first woman ever created was thus.

"Alda is a good wife, as good as a woman is capable of being. If I had such a bride..." Gerard paused for a moment. "You know, I should be encouraging you to repudiate her and follow our father's plan for you."

"I shall do no such thing. That Breton is a savage. Alda is a good woman, and..."

The single call of a horn interrupted their conversation.

* * * * *

Propped on pillows in her bed, Alda was sipping wine, desperately hoping it would dull the pain, when she heard the call of the horn. *Merchants*, Alda thought as she set aside the cup and threw back the sheet. Alda tried to ignore the pain in her belly, which was as easy as ignoring a knife twisting there.

"Alda, are you well?" Veronica asked.

"Merchants," Alda said, as if it were a chant in a spell, an incantation to help her ignore the stabbing in her womb. "Help me dress. I must speak to Hruodland."

Raising her eyebrows, Veronica obeyed.

Alda looked out the window and saw guards and servants leading packhorses toward the river. She rushed downstairs with

90

Veronica at her heels. She had to find Hruodland. Under her breath, she prayed, "*Ave Maria, gratia plena,*" hoping the Latin words would please the Mother of God enough to make Hruodland listen to her.

After asking several servants, she found Hruodland and Gerard on the steps of the chapel, where the nuptials would be. *If there are nuptials. Mother of God, please let there be nuptials. Please don't let there be a duel.* She ran up the steps. "One note," she said, panting. "Merchants."

"Merchants?"

"The bride price," Alda said, searching his face. "You can buy the goods for the bride price, if it is your will. Is it your will?" She held her breath for his answer.

"We are betrothed," he said. He reached for her hand and squeezed it.

Alda wept. *Thank you, thank you, thank you, Mother of God.*

Hruodland wrapped his arms around her and kissed her. She clung to him.

Gerard cleared his throat. "I will get the document of the bride price."

"I will need my jeweled scabbard, too," Hruodland said.

Gerard strolled toward the manor. Hruodland led Alda down the steps.

"Why would Gerard have the document in his possession?" Alda asked. She saw her mother walk into the courtyard.

"He can read well," Hruodland replied. "Hold these chains." He took off the gold and silver he wore around his neck.

"Why?" Alda asked, holding out her hand.

"I need something to trade with the merchants."

"Is that why you asked your brother to fetch the jeweled scabbard?"

Hruodland nodded. He had taken off all the gold and silver chains except for the gold chain upon which his cross hung.

"How will you protect your sword?" Alda asked.

"I have a leather scabbard," he said, with a shrug. "Once we return home, I can buy a fine scabbard for Durendal."

His sword, Alda reminded herself. *Why do men always name their swords?*

Gerard returned with a rolled parchment and the scabbard. He said something to Hruodland in Roman. Hruodland replied in the same language.

Alda bit her lip to stop herself from rebuking them for speaking in a foreign tongue as if she was an interloper. She felt fortunate that Hruodland would exchange vows with her despite the lack of evidence of her virginity. She ran her hand over the emeralds and rubies in the gold scabbard.

"I should not tell you this — it is your bride price — but do not settle for anything less than a breeding horse and a colt for that scabbard," she said. "It is worth at least that much."

"How you know bride price include breeding horses?" Gerard asked in stilted Frankish.

"My family is always seeking horses."

Alda guessed the merchant and his slaves were ascending the mountain now, with the merchant's horses and the laden packhorses from Drachenhaus.

"The merchant will not wish to trade now," Alda said. "Mother no doubt will invite him to the table. I must go greet them."

As she rushed toward the merchant, she tried to still the voice in the back of her mind, whispering that even the scabbard and chains might not be enough for the bride price.

* * * * *

After the meal, Hruodland, with Gerard in tow, spoke to the king in the hall. "Uncle, I need aid to purchase the bride price from the merchants," he said.

"Why not ask your father to provide the bride price?" Charles asked irritably.

"It will take the remainder of the summer to return home," Hruodland replied. "Then I must convince my father to forget Grandmother's scheme to marry me to a Breton..."

"The Bretons understand a show of force better than matrimony," Charles said.

"And if I tarry in paying the bride price, Alfihar might think I have broken my word. And I will have the enmity of another family and lose Alda's dowry."

In his mind, Hruodland went over the dowry: cattle and swine, six cups each of clay and gold, many clay bowls, plates and jugs, otter and marten furs, ten bolts of linen of white, blue, gold, and green, the same amount of wool, two bolts of silk, salt to last through winter, several tapestries, two chests laden with gold coins, and another chest full of jewels. Alda also would take Veronica and other servants, pallets, linens, clothing, her horse, many hunting dogs, a falcon, and a Bible with illuminations.

"Let us not lose that dowry or the family's loyalty," Charles said. "What is the bride price?"

Gerard unrolled the parchment and read: "A pair of breeding horses and incense to last a year."

The king sent for Queen Hildegard, the guardian of his treasury, and they all ascended the stairs to the tower where Alfihar stored his most precious possessions. Two guards stood outside the thick, wooden door, but it was already open.

Alda's voice floated to Hruodland's ears. "Our potters are the best in all Francia and the cleverest. Look at how they shaped these pitchers like pigs. Their workmanship is flawless."

Gerard touched Hruodland's sleeve and whispered in Roman, "If you are bent on defying our father's will, you would be hard pressed to find a better wife than Alda."

A good wife who can negotiate with merchants and care for a house, Hruodland thought. *A good wife who is eager for me. But perhaps not an honest one.*

Hildegard gestured for the men to follow her inside. In the light from a single parchment-covered window, Hruodland made out the chests lining the walls and the shelves filled with pottery and jars of rare spices. Bolts of cloth and leather stood in the corner. Alda stopped midsentence, and she and her mother turned toward the newcomers.

"Pardon the intrusion," Hruodland said. "I wish to buy wares from the merchant, enough for the bride price."

At the mention of the bride price, Theodelinda's look of vexation was replaced by a broad smile. "After my daughter's betrothed has finished his trade, I would still be interested in your wares. Come, Alda. Let us leave the men to their business."

"Good luck," Alda mouthed, following her mother.

* * * * *

"Speak Roman?" Hruodland asked the merchant in Roman. He wanted Gerard to understand every word.

"Of course," the merchant replied in Roman. "My trade takes me all over the world."

The three of them stood in the stables, a shingle-roofed timber structure where the merchant had brought his horses. Tall and sleek, they were fine steeds, so fine that Hruodland could imagine himself astride one of them, charging into a hunt. He revealed the jeweled scabbard and asked about the animals' price.

"You said you wish to purchase enough for a bride price?" the merchant asked. "I have never done such a thing, but I am pleased to aid in the union of two good families. Where did you say your home was?"

"The March of Brittany," Gerard piped up. "Our father is the prefect."

Hruodland glared at Gerard. The merchant's prying irritated him. As far as Hruodland was concerned, where they were from was none of the merchant's business.

"I have traded in the March of Brittany. You must be the sons of Milo," the merchant said. "You must be Hruodland, and are you Gerard?"

"Yes," Gerard said brightly.

Hruodland's vexation deepened. He realized why Alfihar left the merchants to his mother and sister. All this was nothing but idle gossip.

"Let us return to the matter at hand," Hruodland said abruptly. "Two horses for this scabbard."

"One horse," the merchant said.

"Two horses," Hruodland countered. *I must keep my wits about me.*

"But look at the jewels in the scabbard," Gerard cut in. "It must be worth at least two horses and their saddles and bridles."

"It is a well-made scabbard," the merchant said. "I would give a colt for most of them, yet this sheath is a better quality. But look at this stallion. See how his coat gleams? He is healthy and ready to engender foals."

Negotiations continued in this fashion. Hruodland could barely tolerate the tedium as the sun slipped toward the horizon. He would have left immediately if he did not wish to exchange vows with Alda soon and take her home. Shadows lengthened as Hruodland and the merchant returned to the hall and debated how many coins and how many of his gold and silver chains would buy incense. The last red gold rays of the sun found Hruodland without his chains and many of Charles's coins, but he had the bride price.

* * * * *

The morning of the nuptials came seven days after the merchant boat left for the next county, shortly after the prefect of Koblenz and his family arrived with Alfihar's betrothed, Gundrada. Alda wore her best dress, a deep blue gown embroidered with gold thread. She donned her favorite jewelry: the ruby and gold ring Hruodland had given her, a sapphire girdle, her cross and dragon, and several bracelets. Alda dabbed rose oil behind her ears. Its fragrance blended with the scent of violet and lavender water from the baths two days ago. Alda's hair hung free in waves.

Theodelinda's eyes welled up as she beheld her daughter. Veronica started weeping, and Alda could not contain herself. For a moment, the three women stood in the solar and could not stop crying.

Alfihar called from the foot of the stairs: "The guests are waiting."

Alda wiped her eyes and swallowed. The women descended the stairs.

Alfihar, dressed in his best tunic and silk leggings, met Alda at the foot of the stairs, kissed her on the forehead, and took her arm, giving her strength to be steady through the ceremony.

In his free hand, Alfihar held a rolled parchment, which listed Alda's dowry. He led her to the steps outside the chapel, where Hruodland waited. The peasants, soldiers, servants, the royal family, Gerard, Beringar, the family from Koblenz, all gathered outside. Bishop Leonhard stood at the top of the steps.

Hruodland gave Alfihar the rolled parchment that listed the bride price. Alfihar handed Alda to Hruodland along with the parchment that listed Alda's dowry. Hruodland passed the document to Gerard, then Alda placed her hands in Hruodland's.

"The bride price and dowry have been exchanged," Leonhard said. "Now let the bridegroom and bride make their vows."

Hruodland squeezed her hands. "I, Hruodland of the March of Brittany, swear by God and His Merciful Mother, that I shall have you, Alda of Drachenhaus, to be my wedded wife, that I shall honor you and protect you and keep you in sickness and in health, and forsaking all others, keep only unto you, so long as we both shall live."

Alda smiled and spoke the words that Leonhard told her to say, an oath that would forever bind her to her betrothed: "I, Alda of Drachenhaus, swear by God and His Merciful Mother that I shall have you, Hruodland of the March of Brittany, as my wedded husband, that I shall obey you and serve you, honor you and keep you in sickness and in health, and forsaking all others, keep only unto you, so long as we both shall live."

"May God bless this marriage," Leonhard said. He raised his arms and prayed in Latin.

After Leonhard's benediction, the king ordered his servants to give beer and rye bread to the commoners as a form of alms on behalf of the bride and groom. Alfihar led the nobles back to the hall for a wedding feast.

Alda leaned against Hruodland's shoulder, not quite believing this all was happening. She thought she overheard Alfihar say to Gundrada, "Our nuptials will be just as joyous."

As they entered the hall, musicians started by playing Psalms. A cupbearer fetched wine, and the nobles took their seats. Servants paraded in with the first course of soups, stews, roasted pigs and geese, bread, and vegetables. By the time the evening sun slanted through the windows, the songs had become bawdy, the nobles emptied dozens of cups, the meat was nothing more than bones, and the candles melted to nubs.

Hruodland nudged Alda and whispered in her ear. Alda smiled and nodded, and Hruodland helped her to her feet. The other nobles followed the newlyweds up the stairs to the solar. Hruodland and Alda undressed while the nobles watched, clapping and cheering.

"Good thing that sword didn't get any lower," one drunken man slurred.

"You wish you had as many scars."

"Alfihar, don't you feed her?" the drunk continued.

Alda's cheeks burned as she dove between the sheets of the bed. She tempered the urge to shout, "We have already seen each other naked." She wished the lot of them would go away.

"I did not get a good look at her so I could warn Hruodland. Look, she is blushing," the drunk said, laughing.

Hruodland joined his wife in the bed and stroked her back. "My eyes are fine," Hruodland retorted, "and I got a good look at her. Of course, you have had so much wine tonight, you cannot please a woman if you wanted."

Nobles laughed and slapped their thighs. Alda gave a pleading look to her uncle.

"That is enough," Leonhard said. "We have all had a chance to see the bride and bridegroom. Do they accept each other?"

"Yes," Hruodland and Alda said together.

The crowd watched as Leonhard blessed the couple, then all of them left the newlyweds alone and went back downstairs to continue their merrymaking.

Hruodland touched Alda's bare shoulder. "We are one in the eyes of God now," he said, pulling her into an embrace.

"Yes," Alda sighed, savoring his touch.

As Alda and Hruodland lay with each other again, she was glad the merrymaking downstairs was too loud for the guests to hear her shrieks of delight.

Afterward, Hruodland gazed at Alda's right hand, which rested on his chest.

"You are still wearing my morning gift," he said dreamily.

"I always wear it," Alda purred.

"Good," Hruodland said. "Never take it off."

Alda fell asleep in Hruodland's arms, glad that no one would care now if they were found together in the morning. She woke as lauds bells rang. In the light of a night candle, she again beheld his body, a warrior's body, muscular, scarred. She lightly ran her finger on a scar on his shoulder. *How many battles has he seen?*

She looked at his face. His eyes were still closed, but they seemed to follow something. He awoke with a gasp. He gazed around him. His face had a look of terror.

"Hruodland?" Alda asked. "What troubles you?"

Hruodland's features relaxed when he heard Alda's voice. "It is nothing. Only a dream," he murmured. His eyes rested on hers, and he smiled. He kissed her. "Make me forget."

"Yes," she whispered, wrapping her arms and legs around him, satisfying their hunger and forgetting about the journey that lay ahead.

Chapter 12

The farewells at Drachenhaus a week later were tearful. Even Alfihar could barely keep his composure. Servants had packed and loaded into ox carts the linens Alda had sewn since childhood, the chest with her clothes and sheets, her chest of jewels, and some pallets along with her dowry. It was as if every trace of her existence was being removed from Drachenhaus. She did not know when she would see her home, her mother, or her brother again. Tears blurred her vision.

The royal family led the procession, trailed by the aristocracy of counts and bishops — including Hruodland, Alda, Alda's uncles, and Gerard — all mounted on horses. Alda rode alongside Hruodland, astride his stallion. Veronica rode pillion with a huntsman.

Before they descended the mountain path, Alda looked over her shoulder one last time. Alfihar had his arm around their mother's shoulders. Alda waved and faced forward so that she would not start weeping again. At the foot of the mountain, soldiers, servants, the warriors' doxies, and carts drawn by packhorses, mules, and oxen followed the nobility.

Sunlight peeked though the canopy of beech, maple, and oak leaves. Alda laid her hand on her dragon amulet and cross and realized how much she had come to love this forest and its smell of pine and spruce. She saw squirrels chase each other on a beech tree and listened to the birdsong.

"What troubles you?" Hruodland asked Alda.

"This is my home." Alda managed a smile. "This forest is familiar to me."

"We have forests in the March of Brittany. They, too, are fine grounds for hunting. Why, the boar I slew there was twice, no three times, the size of this stallion." He patted the horse he was riding.

Alda giggled. "You must have had pork for a week. What are the woods in the March of Brittany like?"

"Those woods are dense with beech and oak and full of boars and bears. I have heard more wolves howl at night there, but we have fine wolfhounds to keep us safe."

They passed through the village of stick and mud houses with thatched roofs that could be washed away if the river so chose. Now, the river rested quietly between the mountains and cliffs, content to lie between patchwork quilts of green, run the mill, and carry the boats on its broad back, bringing trade and prosperity. The peasants of the Drachenhaus village stood to watch the procession leave.

I know these people, Alda thought. *Among them, I am a ruler, the green-eyed lady of the dragon's blood. And now, what lies before me? What will I become?*

As the travelers entered the forest, King Charles pointed to Drachenfels across the river. "See that mountain yonder," he said to his wife and sons. "That is where Siegfried slew the dragon."

"Was it a big dragon?" asked Prince Pepin.

"Gigantic." Hruodland grinned. "With teeth as long and sharp as daggers and venom so poisonous, a single drop would kill even the strongest of warriors."

"But the dragon is long dead," interjected Pepin's nurse from the cart behind them. "He cannot harm anyone now, so there is nothing to fear."

"Why would I be afraid?" the boy said, squaring his shoulders as much as his spine would allow. "Why, I would take my sword." He pulled out the wooden sword that sat at his hip. "And thrust it through the dragon's heart, just like Siegfried."

Poor child, Alda thought, *he never will be a warrior.*

The road cut a thin, ragged ribbon through the forest, as if the trees begrudged even that space. The pines and oaks created their own light and shade. Some grew so tall that Alda could not see the tops, so wide that she could not wrap her arms around them. Beeches drank the drops of sunlight under the oaks. Willows on the riverbank let their branches droop into the water. Sparrows flitted among the branches.

They traveled until the sky was a violet blue and then made camp for the night among the roots of the trees alongside the road. The travelers stood while the king's archchaplain led the vespers Mass.

Men chopped saplings and pushed rotting logs away so they could pitch tents and lay blankets on the ground. The forest canopy blotted out the stars and moon. As the wolves howled, frogs and insects called, and mosquitoes bit despite the pennyroyal oil, Alda told herself not to be afraid of ghosts or demons. Several fires burned, and men kept watch. She held her amulet and remembered the protection of the dragon's blood.

After they ate an evening meal of bread and salted pork, Hruodland stroked Alda's thigh. "Shall we retire?" he asked with a wink.

Alda nodded enthusiastically. They shared a pallet in a tent but did not sleep.

* * * * *

After two days on the road, the travelers reached the town of Bonn in the late afternoon, and the homecoming scene from Drachenhaus repeated itself. Hugs, kisses, laughter, and tears as families were reunited, wails from those who were not. Bishop Leonhard offered his hospitality, baths, and another feast.

Leonhard and Beringar settled into their homes, and the king's army spent three days replenishing their supplies before leaving for Cologne. After three days' journey by foot, ox cart, and horse, they reached the vast, crowded city, one of only a few places with a bridge across the Rhine. Cologne was also the end of their journey as a large group. Counts took their men home to cities to the north, west, and east. Hruodland and Alda traveled west with Charles and his retinue to Aachen.

"You will like Aachen, Lady Alda," Queen Hildegard said. "Its baths are pools fed by hot springs."

"And it has the finest hunting grounds," Hruodland added.

When Alda entered the courtyard four days later, the villa did not disappoint. The roses and small trees were vibrant against the manor's stone walls, solid as any castle. As Alda dismounted and stared at her surroundings, she overheard the king tell Hruodland, "Once the Saxons are pacified, I will make this place magnificent."

It already is magnificent, Alda thought, walking arm-in-arm with Hruodland toward the entrance to the hall. A woman among the nobles who came to greet them caught Alda's attention. She appeared to be in her twenties and wore a bright blue veil and a matching, close-fitting gown that flattered her plump figure. And she was watching Hruodland intently.

"Who is she?" Alda asked.

Hruodland blinked as if he was startled. "Did you say something, dearling?"

"That woman across the way, watching you, who is she?"

The woman in blue smiled at Hruodland and beckoned him.

He waved to her with his free hand. "Judith of Bordeaux."

"Why is she watching you so?" Alda asked. "Did you meet with her?"

"My sins are not your concern," Hruodland snapped, letting go of Alda's arm. They stopped walking while everyone else passed by.

"You did meet with her," Alda said sharply.

"Hold your tongue," he barked. "As long as I do my duty as a husband, anything I do outside our marriage is not your concern."

"A duty?" Alda said, anger and jealousy making her voice shrill. "Is that all I am to you, a duty? You have been more than a duty to me! Don't you know how much I care about you? Perhaps, too much. It pains me that another woman has known you as I have known you."

Hruodland placed his finger under her chin and raised it. His eyes met hers. "Wife, you may not ask me about other women. That is between me and my confessor."

"Very well," Alda said coldly. "I will remember. Then, my sins, too, are not your concern."

"What?" Hruodland raised his hand and drew it back.

Her body tensing, Alda clutched her dragon. *Mother of God, he's going to beat me!*

But Hruodland's eyes widened a little, and he let his hand fall to his side. "I am your lord. You took a vow to obey and serve me."

"And you took a vow to honor me — and forsake all others," Alda retorted.

"But it is different for women. When you carry a baby in your belly, I must be certain that it is my child."

They stared at each other. Alda's hands rested on her hips. Hruodland's arms were crossed. After a moment, his scowl disappeared, and he started laughing.

"What amuses you so?" Alda asked. It sounded like an accusation.

"We are quarreling about a woman I would tell you to avoid, a woman who means nothing to me."

"Nothing?"

"You are my wife. You are the one I chose to join with before God. You are the one I want to be the mother of my children. You are the one I would walk through fire for. Do you think I would walk through fire for her?"

To Alda, his words were like the wind blowing away a storm cloud and letting the sun shine. Hruodland's past — whatever it was — dissolved.

Hruodland took Alda's arm again and led her to the hall. "Before we go inside," he said, "there is something you should know."

"What?" *Is there a bastard child he has not told me about?*

"My grandmother, the marriage to the Breton was her idea, and she may be angry that her plan will not come to pass."

"Oh," Alda sighed. "You already told me that."

"You see," Hruodland said, "she doted on me when I was a child. My nurse told me that my father carried out his duties after my mother died. But he seemed hollow, as if his heart had died with her."

"When we were in Geneva you told me that your grandmother had sent for you."

"My nurse called it a happy coincidence," Hruodland said. "Of course, the message had Grandfather's seal."

King Pepin, Alda reminded herself.

"But everyone knew it was Grandmother who dictated it," Hruodland continued.

Queen Mother Bertrada, Alda translated in her own mind.

"My nurse was right. It was a happy coincidence," he said. "I knew without my nurse telling me that my father had little interest in me."

Alda gasped. "How could he not care for you? You are his firstborn son."

"When I heard your mother say that your father doted on you and Alfihar, I envied you both."

"Oh," she said looking down, feeling almost guilty for her father's devotion.

"You should rejoice in your father's affection." He squeezed her hand. "Do not be unhappy on my account."

"What is your father like?" she asked tentatively.

"I have little memory of my early years," he said, "except that he was distant even when he visited me during the spring assemblies. When my father remarried, Grandmother Bertrada sent me back to the March of Brittany. I shall never forget that day. Grandmother had tears in her eyes while I wailed and kicked. I think I screamed for two days. My poor nurse. I was not princely at all."

"In Geneva, you told me you had seen but four or five winters," Alda said. "Why did the queen mother send you to Rennes?"

"It was the right thing to do. She wanted to remind my father of his firstborn, especially if he begat other sons."

"So you would have your rightful place with Gerard," Alda concluded.

"And she wanted me to learn the language and customs of the land I would inherit. Grandmother has always had my best interests at heart. She thought marriage to the Breton was in my best interest."

Alda nodded.

"And so," he said, "I need you to use your best manners with my grandmother. She will be sorely disappointed."

"Of course, I will use my best manners," Alda chided. "I am not a child."

As they entered the hall, Alda watched the queen mother embrace King Charles. She took Karl in her arms, kissed him, and cooed about how much he had grown. Prince Pepin sulked. Setting Karl down, Bertrada tousled Pepin's hair.

"Mother," Charles said, "in a few months, you will have another grandchild."

"Praise God and His Merciful Mother!" Bertrada cried, taking both of Hildegard's hands.

Hruodland and Alda approached the queen mother. Bertrada kissed Hruodland on the cheek and embraced him. "We must get you into a bath," she said.

Her gaze turned to Alda. The queen mother smiled, leaned toward Alda, and took her hand. Alda returned the smile.

"And you, young lady, I have seen you before," Bertrada said. "What is your name?"

"Alda of Drachenhaus," Hruodland answered, trying to sound casual. "She is my wife, Grandmother."

Bertrada drew herself up to her full height, and her smile disappeared. Composing herself, she let go of Alda's hand. "Welcome to Aachen. Charles," she said sharply, "I thought we had agreed that Hruodland would marry the daughter of the Breton duke."

"Now, Mother," the king said calmly, "you and Milo agreed to that. I never gave it my blessing. With those foreigners, the sword is better than nuptials. The Lombards understand might, so do the Bretons."

Alda watched helplessly as mother and son continued their discussion. The queen mother's voice shook with anger, but the king patiently listened and argued without raising his voice that a marriage to a woman with a generous dowry was better for Hruodland and for Francia than another disastrous union with a foreigner.

Alda turned to Hruodland and whispered, "I did as you said, but she is still offended."

"She is accustomed to having her way," he said. "I thought she would see how well-mannered you were..."

"I never had the chance," Alda interjected. "As soon as you said 'wife,' she and your uncle started quarreling."

* * * * *

The next day, the king established his court. There was much business to attend to. Bishops, abbots, and abbesses had died over the past year, and the king had to appoint new people to watch over those properties.

Over the passing days and weeks, Alda watched nobles arrive at the villa and ask the king to name one of their kin a bishop or an abbess. They had brought ox-carts laden with gifts for the royal family and the courtiers.

"This gossip is vicious," Alda told Hruodland one morning after prime Mass as they walked in one of the gardens. She pulled her skirt away from the thorns of a rose bush. "These courtiers are like wolves circling a wounded deer, except wolves show more civility."

"I forget how new this is to you," he said. "Rumor-mongering has no limits here."

"But the tales they tell," Alda said, her eyes wide. "Why, just last night, I heard..."

"Wife, you are not to take part in any of this," Hruodland interrupted. "I will decide the alliances we make."

"Do not use that tone of voice with me," Alda retorted. "I am not one of your soldiers. A good wife listens to gossip. How else am I to learn of the important families? Even if I had no desire to hear it, I cannot avoid it. The courtiers seek me out."

"Of course, they would. They cannot tell Uncle Charles directly, so they will tell anyone who listens, even an innocent new to the court. You are not to repeat any of these rumors."

"I am a grown woman, I can decide..."

"You have a sweet mouth," he said, tracing her lips with his finger. "I do not want it polluted with lies."

"I *must* listen to rumors," she said, stroking the stubble on his chin. "Other wives *will* tell their husbands about the gossip, and it might sway them. I cannot do my duty as a wife if I do not know what is said. Don't you want me to be a good wife?"

"I am trying to protect you. The courtiers are wolves, and you are a lamb. Listen to their stories, if you must, but do not repeat them."

Alda kissed him. "Except to you. You can sort truth from a lie. But," she added, trying to sound meek, "is there a harmless thing I can disclose to encourage people to talk to me? I can make it sound valuable like my mother and I do when we trade pottery with the merchants."

Hruodland laughed. "Tell them how I got my latest scar. A Lombard warrior twice your size charged at me on horseback..."

As Hruodland continued his story, Alda considered telling him what she had heard about Judith of Bordeaux, who was now a widow, but decided against it.

That night, while Hruodland and Alda sat side by side near the hearth and listened to the musicians, Judith approached them. She reeked of imported sandalwood perfume, and the firelight flickered on a ruby girdle along with her bracelets, rings, necklaces, and a jeweled headdress that secured her silk veil. Envying Judith's plump figure, ivory skin, and sky-blue eyes, Alda reached for Hruodland's hand and held it tightly. Hruodland patted Alda's hand.

Alda heard Judith say something to Hruodland in Roman. Hruodland answered with one word, and Alda felt her jealousy sink deeper. *Not only is she beautiful, she can also speak his language.*

Chapter 13

Judith spoke again in Roman. But Alda relaxed when she heard Hruodland answer with the Roman word for "no" — that much she had learned on the journey between Drachenhaus and Aachen. Hruodland added in Frankish, "I shall be neutral in this. It is my uncle's decision."

When Judith started speaking again in Roman, Hruodland interrupted in Frankish, "We are at the court, Countess. We should speak its language."

Judith pouted and cast a worried look at Alda.

"She is my wife, as you have no doubt heard by now," Hruodland said. "Anything you say to me can be said to her."

"I was telling Hruodland, now that my beloved husband is gone and left me childless, I wish to devote my life and my dowry to the Church," Judith said with an Aquitanian accent.

Alda's jaw dropped. Hruodland was barely suppressing a laugh.

"The affection you show your husband *after* his death is touching," Alda said. "Surely, you do not need my husband's help to join a cloister."

"Not just any cloister," Hruodland said, managing a serious look. "She wishes to lead the Abbey of Saint Stephen."

That explains why she has been the target of all those rumors, Alda thought.

Judith took a seat to Hruodland's left, while Alda remained at his right and tightened her grip on his hand.

"Hruodland," Judith said, her voice sweet as honey, her hand caressing his shoulder, "I could return the favor when your brother seeks a bishopric."

Alda turned to face Judith. "Begone!" she yelled. "Away from my husband, or I will repeat everything I have heard about you."

Other nobles in the room turned toward them. Alda immediately regretted her outburst. *I have embarrassed Hruodland,* she thought, wincing. *But I will not let her steal him right before my eyes.* She stiffened and then glared at Judith.

"Wife, hold your tongue!" Hruodland barked.

"Yes, Husband," Alda whimpered, staring at her knees.

"You must forgive my wife," Hruodland said. "She is new to the ways of the court."

Alda nodded numbly, still looking down. *Wait. Is this the way for a daughter of Drachenhaus to act?* she asked herself. She grabbed her iron dragon with her free hand and straightened her spine. She narrowed her eyes and leveled an angry gaze straight at Judith. Judith's hand shrank from Hruodland's shoulder.

"What is your will, *Husband*?" Alda asked.

"My will is that you remain discreet while I consider what Judith has said."

"Very well." Alda did not take her eyes from Judith.

"Judith," Hruodland said, "my wife and I must discuss a private matter."

Judith rose from the bench. As she walked away, she called over her shoulder, "Hruodland, I have yet to take the veil."

Frowning, Hruodland turned toward Alda. His dark eyes scorched her.

"I apologize," Alda murmured, swallowing angry tears, hoping to stave off the scolding she was to receive. "That outburst will not happen again."

"No," Hruodland said coldly, "it will not. You are so willful."

"Willful?" Alda blinked and then looked up at him. "But a few moments ago, I asked you for your will, and I will obey. I will not repeat all the rumors unless you tell me otherwise."

"What have you heard?"

"You said you hate gossip."

"I do," he said, turning toward her. "But this is an exception."

"Before a fever claimed him last winter, Judith's husband, he was an aged man?"

"He was old even in my early years at the court. He was old enough to be Judith's grandsire."

"What I heard is that he could not do his duty as a husband and that she met with many men while he was alive."

"Is that all?"

"I could tell you the names."

"What you have heard is nothing new." He shrugged. "Perhaps, it is fortunate Judith knows that you have heard rumors. It will allow me to remain neutral about the abbacy she seeks. The brothel is more apt than the convent for her, but I do not wish to make her family my enemy. Our family will need allies once a bishopric in the March of Brittany has need of a bishop. But you should have been more discreet. Now Judith's rivals will seek you out and wish to know what you have heard."

"They are the ones who told me the stories." She gave him a sly smile. "But if they wish to tell me more, I will listen, so I can tell my husband, if it is your will."

"You tell only me," he said sternly.

"Who else would I tell — besides Veronica?"

"You are not to divulge anything to your servant," he ordered. "Gossip among servants is even more rampant than the courtiers."

"Veronica is my foster sister." Alda bristled. "I never withhold anything from her."

"Make an exception when it comes to matters of the court."

"What I say to my foster sister is not your concern," Alda said defiantly.

"You are my wife. Everything you do is my concern."

"Yes, Husband." Alda was tired of arguing. She would do what every other wife had done. Defy her husband's will and hold her tongue about it. *Not tell Veronica what I hear? That is absolute nonsense.*

Hruodland stared at her, his brow furrowed, but he said nothing more about the matter. In fact, he barely spoke to her the rest of the night.

The Cross and the Dragon

* * * * *

A week later, Hruodland accompanied his uncle to the hall after prime Mass. The queen and Alda walked ahead of them, whispering and giggling. He thought he heard Judith's name.

Judith got her abbey, and they still gossip about her, Hruodland thought and shrugged. He had more important matters to consider.

"Uncle," Hruodland said, "I have a request. My men and I need your leave so that we can return home before winter and make sure the Bretons have not caused mischief in our absence."

"You have my leave," Charles answered. "I will send you word of where to meet in the spring.

"We will need tribute from the Bretons and gifts from the March of Brittany to help us with our campaign against the Saxons next spring. Damned heathens! Burning churches while we were defending Rome!"

* * * * *

The next morning, Alda and Gerard were helping Hruodland into his armor, a leather jerkin with small overlapping metal plates. With a smaller party, he had said last night, the armor was necessary to deter any brigands in the forest.

Wearing rust-stained woolen padding, Hruodland bent at the waist. Alda's arms strained just from holding her half of the armor, the left side. Alda and Gerard held the neck and arm holes open as Hruodland wriggled into his metal skin. *How can he wear this?* she wondered, amazed at how gracefully he bore the armor's weight, about as much as a large hunting dog.

Alda could not stop staring at him as he rubbed his neck and shrugged. After menservants strapped leg guards to his thighs, he donned his belt and hooked on his sword and seax. He slung his shield across his back, then pushed back his hair and put on a crested iron helmet. Alda laid her hand over her heart, admiring her powerful husband.

"If that doesn't frighten bandits," she said, "nothing will."

* * * * *

With Alda, Hruodland, and Gerard at the front of the procession, the party set off for Nantes, one of the cities in the March of Brittany. The language of the villages and cities changed as the travelers wove their way west among trees and brambles, around hills, through dust and mud. People did not speak the Frankish Alda grew up with. They, like the soldiers Hruodland led, spoke Roman, a musical language, sounding close to Latin. Alda had learned only a few vulgar words of Roman and hoped her Roman could be as good as Gerard's stilted Frankish.

After weeks of travel, they reached Angers. At the bishop's residence, Hruodland dictated a message in Roman to the clerk, who was transcribing it into Latin.

"Who is the message for?" Alda asked, warming herself by the fire.

"Two messages," Hruodland replied, "one for Uncle Guillaume — he is the bishop of Nantes — and one for my father."

"What do they say?" she asked as Gerard stepped to the fire and warmed his hands.

"By the grace of the Good Lord, we have victory in Lombardy and have secured Rome."

"It seems like you said more than that."

"Oh, there were the usual courtesies."

Gerard added, "And he say all of us well and king is well."

"Have you told him you are married?" she asked.

"He will learn in Nantes," Hruodland answered.

Gerard said something in Roman. Hruodland replied in the same language. Gerard said something again, more sharply.

"Have you no manners?" Alda asked, vexed with both Gerard and Hruodland. "If you are going to argue about me, do so in a tongue I understand."

Hruodland put his arm around Alda's shoulders and kissed her on the cheek. "Dearling, it is not worth understanding. Gerard speaks foolishness."

Gerard glowered at him.

"What were you saying?" Alda asked.

"You are a good wife," Hruodland said, "and Father will approve of you."

"You are, uh, good wife," Gerard said. "But," he paused, thinking of the words. "Hruodland marry you, uh, how do you say..." He said a word in Roman.

"Alliance," Hruodland translated.

"Alliance with Bretons..." He paused. "Not possible." He said something to Hruodland in Roman.

"Until I learn Roman," Alda said, "speak in a tongue I can understand. If it concerns me or my husband, it is fit for my ears."

"Pay no mind to Gerard, dearling," Hruodland said. "He speaks foolishness. Father knows I never would have married the Breton. Uncle Charles approves of you. So will Father."

"I hope so," Alda said, not hiding her uncertainty. "I will do my best. But I wish you had told him you are married when you sent the message."

"That what I told." Gerard smiled as if he had just won a prize. He shook his finger at Hruodland. "See? I am not fool here."

"I am a grown man and can decide for myself whom to marry. And he did not tell me he married a third time until after I returned home from Uncle Charles's court three years ago. All of a sudden, we had a new mother who is younger than me."

Gerard's jaw dropped. He looked at Alda and then Hruodland. "You not tell Father about Alda because you angry about his new marriage?" he asked in Frankish. "My mother dead a year then. You expect him to be monk? You are a fool."

"He does not care about me anyway," Hruodland said bitterly. "Let him find out about my bride the way I found out about his."

* * * * *

Three days later, the travelers again entered the forest and followed the Loire. After another week, they entered a clearing, and Alda first saw the stone walls to the city of Nantes extending all the way to the river. Her jaw dropped when she beheld the church's cylindrical tower and its soaring arches rising above the walls.

As she felt the moisture in the air, Alda heard the call of the horn from the city gate. Hruodland blew a call in response on his own bone white horn. The call was clear, a tenor voice, a victorious voice. The bells cried with ecstasy: the men have come home!

The gates opened. Hruodland, still on horseback, leaned toward one of the guards, pointed to Alda, and shouted something drowned out by the bells.

"What did you say to him?" Alda shouted.

He said in her ear, "I told him 'See this lady with the pale face and soft hands? Treat her well. She will be the next countess of the March of Brittany.'"

Alda looked about as they passed through the gates. Twig and thatch huts had an uncertain footing on the banks of the Loire, part of which was being diverted, and Alda wondered if they would collapse into the river during a spring rain. Hruodland drew his sword and held it aloft, leading his party toward the market square and the tavern and the church and Alda's in-laws.

Old men and young boys tending their gardens dropped their hoes and rushed through the streets, disturbing stray ducks, pigs, and cattle. Women with babies and toddlers left their huts. The hooves of horses and oxen stirred dust from the road. Everyone in the city crowded into the market square, where weeds struggled for a foothold in the cracks between pavers surrounded by the church, the count's manor, the brothel, and the tavern.

The church, a stone square building, sat at the highest point in the city, dominating the landscape with its wooden tower and series of arches. Beggars and pilgrims took shelter at its door, eyes unfocused, using crutches to drag useless legs, walking on blistered, bare feet. Pigeons strutted among the crowd, ready to dive for a dropped morsel.

The scene of reunion repeated itself. It was the same as it had been at Drachenhaus, Bonn, Cologne, Aachen, all the cities, towns, and villages. Only the language had changed. Mothers kissed sons. Wives embraced husbands. A handful of mothers and wives wept for the boys and men who did not return.

Hruodland helped Alda dismount near the church. Holding hands, they walked to the church steps, where the nobles awaited, staring at Alda. Hruodland and Gerard embraced the bishop and their father near a carved scene of heaven during the Last Judgment.

Alda could tell who they were by their age and clothes. The count, Hruodland's father, tall and thin with silver hair, had the look of a man who had seen many battles. He had a white, jagged scar on his cheek, a faint scar on his right hand and, Alda suspected, countless others beneath his clothes. His cheeks were hollow from the loss of teeth. He wore a gold circlet, an embroidered green tunic, and a blue cloak.

Next to him was the bishop, holding a crosier. In the sunlight, the bishop's robe and pointed linen helmet were a blinding white. The long faced man had an average build and was half a head taller than the count. He appeared to have seen almost as many winters as the count. Alda squinted, trying to guess how many. *Fifty?* she ventured.

When the bells exhausted their ringing, one of the soldiers blew a hunting horn. The crowd became quiet.

Hruodland wrapped his arm around Alda's waist and made a speech in Roman. Alda had learned a few words during the journey. She could pick out "death," "faith," "with God," "wife," and then her name. The crowd cheered. Alda smiled. She hoped they were welcoming her. Alda looked toward the man she would call Father. He did not smile. The count and the bishop stared at Hruodland, eyes wide and jaws dropped.

Soldiers went home, taking their carts with them to make the land again give wheat and onions. Finally, Hruodland introduced Alda to her new family: his uncle Guillaume the bishop, the countess who could not have been much older than Alda, and his father, Milo, prefect of the March of Brittany.

Milo blinked back his surprise and frowned. He said something to Alda in Roman. Alda searched his face for meaning. His eyes, the same dark brown as Hruodland's, were as cold as stone. Alda looked at her husband.

"He said, 'Welcome to Nantes,'" Hruodland translated.

Alda cringed. *It means 'welcome.' I should have known that word,* she thought, and then remembered how nobles in the cities the travelers had visited had used that word with a smile and open arms. Alda managed a smile and tried to hide her embarrassment in the Roman word for "thank you."

"You do not speak Roman?" Milo asked. His Roman accent did not mask the hostility in his voice.

"I... I shall learn, my lord," she stammered.

She looked at Hruodland again. He was glaring at his father.

The countess cleared her throat, timidly touched her husband's shoulder, and said something in Roman. Milo nodded.

The nobles descended the church steps. Alda was vexed with both Hruodland and her father-by-marriage: Hruodland for failing to tell his father about her and Milo for publicly pointing out that she didn't speak the language.

"What did she say?" Alda hissed to her husband. "They all know I do not speak the language — yet."

"We are going to the baths," Hruodland said. He slid his arm from her waist and held her hand.

"You should have told him about me."

Milo, who was ahead of them, turned toward the conversation. He wore a tight-lipped smile. "Yes, Hruodland, you should have told me about her," he said in Frankish. "It is good to see you have chosen someone with sense."

Guillaume frowned and said something in Roman to Milo. All Alda could pick out were "husband" and "Berthe," the name of Hruodland's mother.

Milo smiled and looked at Alda. For the first time, Alda thought she saw a glimmer of warmth in his expression. When he spoke to Guillaume, she understood, "...Berthe... good wife."

Guillaume flushed and snarled out something. Milo shouted back.

"What do they speak of?" Alda whispered to Hruodland.

"They are oblivious to anyone else whenever they bicker about my mother," he muttered.

"They have done this before?"

"I should have warned you about my family. I was too eager to make you my bride."

"He not want to scare you off," Gerard said with a grin. Hruodland glared at him.

Milo slammed his fist into his hand. The countess jumped. The count and bishop kept on arguing.

"Why do they quarrel about her?" Alda asked.

Hruodland stared intently at his father and his uncle.

Gerard hesitated then spoke slowly, as if carefully choosing his words, "My father and my uncle have... not same memories of Princess Berthe."

"But why quarrel now after... what? Twenty years?" Alda asked.

"More than that," Gerard replied. "I know not. I ask same question."

"Hold your tongue, both of you," Hruodland snapped.

When she saw how intently he was watching Milo and Guillaume, Alda tempered her usual urge to rebuke him. She watched his face. His eyebrows drew together. His frown deepened.

Guillaume said something to Milo. Hruodland yelled something in Roman. Whatever it was stunned both Milo and Guillaume into silence. Guillaume replied to Hruodland. Alda tried to discern his tone of voice. Conciliatory, perhaps?

Hruodland's dark eyes seemed to be on fire. He barked out something to Guillaume. Alda picked out the word "wife."

Hruodland stalked toward the castle. Alda followed him. "What troubles you so?"

"You are always asking questions."

"What did your uncle say about me?"

Hruodland stopped and pulled her close to him. He slid his hand under her veil and stroked her hair. "I do not wish to talk about it."

"I am your wife. If you are troubled, I am troubled." She kissed him.

"I am not troubled now."

"Yes, you are." She stamped her foot, barely missing his. "Tell me."

"All I will say is that you remind them of my mother. My father was very fond of her. When he realizes how clever you are, he will accept you as a daughter."

"And your uncle?"

"Not important."

Alda stroked her dragon and thought of her own family. Yes, they argued over the household and the harvest, but they didn't nurse grudges for decades. She momentarily envied the nuns who lived on Nonnenwerth Island in the Rhine. *Just prayers at the bells, no family squabbles over a woman who is long dead.*

Chapter 14

ven though Alda constantly asked questions to learn the language of her new home, she soon realized she had to learn more than the words — the food for one thing. The castle at Nantes had livestock and hunting grounds, but every few days, fishermen brought in their catch, which included the fruits of the sea.

Alda didn't know if Frankish words existed for the sea creatures. Some looked like larger and differently colored versions of the mussels she'd seen on the bank of the Rhine. Others resembled enormous insects with pinchers and hard shells.

At the table, she would watch the others eat the fruits of the sea before she made an attempt — and hoped her efforts didn't seem too awkward. To her surprise, she liked the delicate taste of these strange creatures. She hoped she would remember what they were called when she became countess.

The men from Rennes and Vannes had been sent home to help their families slaughter livestock before winter, but Hruodland and Alda stayed with his family in Nantes for a month. Milo softened toward Alda, especially when he learned of her dowry and the king's approval of the marriage, and smiled at her occasionally, but Bishop Guillaume acted as if she didn't exist.

After All Saints Day, Milo and his wife led the procession headed toward Rennes. Hruodland, Alda, and Gerard followed.

Guards trailed after them and protected the baggage train, where Veronica and other servants rode. Alda was glad to leave Guillaume behind in Nantes.

A crumbling stone road led into the forest. More sunlight poured though the bare tree branches, but evening came earlier. The horses' hooves crunched the layer of beech and oak leaves on the ground.

"Stay close to me," Hruodland said to Alda. "We are on the frontier."

"There are enough men to deter any bandits." She stared into the forest, still thick despite the loss of leaves.

"It is not only the bandits. We are in Breton country. Yes, they pay tribute — for now, and they claim to be Christians. But these are people who sleep in the forest and marry their own sisters. Lord knows what they would do to a Frankish lady."

Occasionally, the travelers had to stop their progress. Milo was bent over, coughing, struggling for air. He spat on the ground. Blood. Alda's eyes widened. She made the sign of the cross.

"Why did you make the sign of the cross?" Hruodland asked.

"Your father... I had seen six winters at the time, but I shall never forget it. My younger sister, God rest her soul, when she spat blood like that..." Her voice trailed off.

Alda remembered how she and her family had knelt by the cradle and prayed for her sister, who had seen but five months at the time. The baby's skin burned, and she had coughed and coughed and coughed. Alda winced at the memory.

"Your sister what?" Hruodland asked, raising his voice and bringing Alda back to the present.

"Hush!" Alda whispered. "This is for your ears only."

"What is it?" he muttered.

"When my sister coughed and spat blood like that," Alda shuddered, "she was not long for this world."

"No," he said, his voice barely audible. "No, it cannot be. He has survived so many battles."

Milo again was racked by a coughing fit so bad he had to stop his horse.

Mother of God, please let me be wrong. Making the sign of the cross, Alda mouthed, "*Ave Maria, gratia plena.*"

* * * * *

After five days of travel, Alda saw the glimmer of the sun on water through the leafless trees. She pointed ahead and asked her husband, "What is that river yonder?" In the chill morning air, her words smoked in front of her.

"The Vilaine," Hruodland answered. "We are near Rennes."

"What is Rennes like?"

"It is larger than Nantes. With the Bretons so close, we have fortified the defenses."

Suddenly, Milo had to stop his horse as he doubled over in another coughing fit. When the fit passed, the travelers started riding again. The forest thinned, and Alda saw the first sign of civilization: swineherds using crops and crooks to keep their charges near. The plump and sleek swine foraged through dried, brown leaves for acorns and beechnuts, and Alda thought they would make many fine dinners when most of them would be slaughtered later this month.

She saw the city ahead, just past the wooden bridge over the river. The red brick wall put the guards at the same level as the trees. The horses' hooves and ox-drawn carts clattered on the planks of the bridge over the Vilaine, which the fall sun made a glittering gold. Guards within the city walls pulled the great wooden gates open to admit the count and his family.

Alda gasped when she beheld the church at the heart of the city. The church and its bell tower were made with beige stone and dwarfed the wooden count's manor and the tavern flanking it.

"The church is beautiful," Alda murmured.

"One of my great-uncles had it built two centuries ago," Hruodland said. "My nurse told me stories about the church when I was but a child and had just returned to Rennes." He squinted as if he were thinking back over the years. "She said her grandmother told her that my uncle spared no expense. He wanted that church to be a proper home for a saint."

"Which saint?"

"Saint Melaine. His relics attract pilgrims from many leagues. The church and abbey are built around his tomb. Is there any place more worthy of the man who brought the True Faith here?"

Luc, the bishop of Rennes and younger brother of the count, stood on the church steps. He was a short, pudgy man, but he stood out in his white bishop's robe and pointed linen helmet. Above him, carved into the church, Christ made His Final

Judgment. Alda laid her hand on her cross, filled with joy to be so close to such a legendary saint.

* * * * *

Milo's cough worsened over the next few weeks as cold winds blew through bare trees and seeped into his manor. His spells would last for minutes, to the point where he had to take rattling breaths as he coughed. He spat blood on the floor. He insisted that he was well, even though his fits interrupted his judgment of a dispute between neighbors or his punishment of a thief. His coughs became more frequent during Mass and during meals while his family sat in awkward silence.

Before dawn one morning, Alda awakened in the solar to hear Hruodland and a maidservant speaking Roman with a note of urgency. Hruodland sat up immediately, dragging the furs and blankets from Alda's body. Shivering, Alda reached for her shift.

"What is it?" she asked while she and Hruodland hurriedly dressed.

"My father," he mumbled, pulling on his boots. "Something is wrong."

He threw his fur-lined, woolen cloak on his shoulders and followed the servant. Her teeth chattering, Alda felt for her cloak and wrapped it around her shoulders. She rubbed her hands vigorously to keep warm before putting on her gloves.

Hurrying to Milo's bed, she saw servants bringing candles to the solar and lighting them, filling the room with the smell of tallow. The countess, who was already dressed, was babbling to Hruodland and Gerard in Roman. Tears streaked her face. With the bed curtains drawn back, Alda could see the count lying on his side, his face white as bone. He struggled for breath, as if it hurt to take air into his lungs. Buried under blankets and furs, he was sweating, yet he shivered as if he lay on ice.

Alda made the sign of the cross. She heard Veronica whisper her name behind her.

"What is happening?" Alda whispered in Frankish.

"I do not know exactly," Veronica answered. "I heard the countess call out. Her maids came to her, and then all this chaos."

The physician, a young, sickly looking monk, bounded up the stairs and said something in Roman. A servant used a candle to light Saint John's wort twigs sitting in a small pot nearby. The wood gave more smoke than heat, and Milo coughed even more.

As the darkness lightened to gray, the bell tolled, calling the faithful to sunrise Mass.

"Come, Veronica," Alda whispered in Frankish, even though she knew most of the people in the room would not understand her. "Let us go to the church and pray. We are no help here."

* * * * *

Hruodland did not notice Alda and Veronica leave the solar. His eyes were on his father. He watched the physician feel Milo's hands.

"Have him sit up," the physician said. "I need to examine what he coughs up."

As menservants lifted Milo, the blanket fell away, revealing a cross and medal of Saint Sebastian, patron saint of soldiers, on his bare, pale, scarred chest. Milo had another coughing fit, and the physician held a bowl under the old count's lips. When the fit subsided, he collapsed against the pillows. The physician examined the bowl in the candlelight.

"Blood," he said. "His humors are unbalanced. He needs to be bled."

Hruodland and Gerard nodded numbly as their father doubled over in another coughing fit. A manservant who often assisted the physician stepped forward and drew his knife. The monk restrained Milo while his assistant made the incision in the count's arm. When enough blood had been drained, the physician crushed garlic on the wound and used a stained, brown rag to bind it. The blood seeped through the rag, then stopped.

Light from the morning sun shone into the solar through windows covered with resin-coated parchment. Milo still coughed, sweated, and shivered despite the extra blanket one of the servants placed on his bed. Hruodland heard footsteps on the stairs and turned toward the sound. He saw Alda and Veronica followed by his uncle Luc, wearing a brown wool cloak over his robe.

Hruodland's eyes brightened when Alda reached for his hand and squeezed it.

"Veronica and I went to church to pray for him," she whispered. "I could not think of anything else that we could do, other than telling your uncle."

"Thank you," he murmured.

He did not take his eyes off his father while Luc asked the physician, "How is he?"

"I am going to try a purgative," said the physician, his hand on his chin. "That will rid his body of bad humors."

The physician had the servants prop Milo up again and awaken him. The physician gave the count a purgative of dill and sour milk. Milo vomited into a basin and then lay on his side, clutching his belly.

"Am I dying, Brother?" he rasped to the physician.

"I don't know," he answered.

* * * * *

As the days shortened and the wind became even colder, Milo did not get better. He slept most of the time. When he was awake, he saw things no one else could see. He often gazed at a small, wooden carving of the Blessed Mother.

Hruodland had never felt so helpless. He could fight off Ganelon. He could smite Aquitanians, Lombards, and Saxons in battle. But he could do nothing about his father's illness except stand there and watch.

"Is there nothing more you can do?" Hruodland asked the physician, his voice cracking.

"Nothing I do works."

"Is he..." Hruodland could not bear to finish the question.

"Yes," the physician said softly. "I am sorry."

Alda put her hand to her mouth and then wrapped her arms around her husband. Hruodland held her tightly, as if she were the only thing he had left. He regretted every unkind thought and word and deed toward his father.

With Gerard fated for the clergy, Hruodland would be the count soon. He had trained his whole life to be a good warrior and lead men into battle and had watched his father judge quarrels between peasants and bring in the harvest.

But he wished it wasn't happening now. He had thought there would be time to better his relationship with the man who had sired him. And now that time was gone.

Hruodland swallowed his tears and kissed his wife. If he was going to inherit the March of Brittany soon, he had better act like the count.

"I must send messengers to Uncle Guillaume and Uncle Charles," he murmured.

* * * * * *

A vigil formed at the count's manor. Hruodland was numb. He visited his father but did not know what to say to him. He often muttered the Pater Noster, hoping Jesus would heal the old man and give father and son another chance. *My inheritance can wait.*

Propped on pillows, Milo opened his eyes a crack. Hruodland's heart rose for a moment. *Have my prayers been answered?* he wondered.

"I am dying," the old count murmured. "Luc, please pray for my soul. Hruodland, be a good count. I bequeath my sword and seax to you. May they serve you or your son well in battle."

Hruodland could stand no more. After the land, the blades were the greatest gifts from his father. Hruodland turned his back on the sickbed, went to one of the windows, and stared at the frost on the parchment. His shoulders heaved as he wept soundlessly. He felt Alda's hand on his back. He tried to wipe his eyes with his hand.

"There is no need," Alda whispered. "I am your wife."

"Why does God do this?" Hruodland sobbed. "He takes everyone I love."

"Everyone dies," Alda said gently. "Your father had a long life. Take comfort in that."

* * * * *

Alda did not tell Hruodland her own worries, which seemed so petty. Soon, she would be a countess, what she was born to be, but this was happening too soon. *I don't know the servants' names or their families or who is quarreling with whom. How am I ever going to give orders when I can barely speak the language?*

She heard a gurgle from the bed, the same noise her baby sister had made hours before her death. Eyes wide, Alda turned toward the sound. His voice weak, Milo was speaking to Luc. The bishop dabbed his fingers with chrism oil. Chanting in Latin, he made the sign of the cross several times on the dying man's body.

Last rites, Alda thought, bowing her head.

Luc gestured for the family to come to the bedside, where everyone knelt. As Milo wheezed and gurgled, Luc led the Pater Noster and prayers to the Blessed Mother and Saint Michael the Archangel to protect Milo's soul from the demons gathered around the bed, like a pack of wolves circling a deer, ready to rip it to shreds.

Shortly after matins, Milo fell silent.

* * * * *

After the body was washed, rubbed with a clove perfume, and dressed, the family knelt and made the sign of the cross while Luc placed the Host in the dead count's mouth. A servant bound Milo's jaw shut with a strip of linen. Alda left the solar with the now dowager countess. They had their own duties to the late count.

Grabbing a servant's arm, Alda said in heavily accented Roman, "Go church. Ring bell. Run!"

The bell would tell the city their count had died. Its song would scare away the demons and help Milo's soul see the path to heaven. The servants were already awake, waiting for this moment. They tried not to weep. If Milo's soul saw a tear, he would have a difficult time leaving this world.

Alda caught up with the dowager countess in the kitchen and listened to her mother-by-marriage order a feast fit for a warrior returning home. Alda recognized the Roman words for "bread" and "swine."

I am lady of this house now, she thought. *I must learn this language.*

Alda and the dowager countess returned to the hall as the bell started to clang wildly. They watched servants carry Milo's body down the stairs to the hall and lay him on an embroidered shroud, near the coffin they had just built. The servants placed coins on his eyes and put tiny, yellow buttons of tansy flowers in his hands along with his silver cross. They wrapped the shroud around the old count, placed him in the coffin, and packed tansy around his body, releasing a smell like pine, mint, and smoke. With the rest of the family, Alda knelt beside the coffin while Luc led prayers for the dead.

When the prime bells rang, four menservants picked up the coffin and carried it, leading a procession to the church. As the faithful crowded into the sanctuary, Milo's coffin was placed on a stand at the altar. With incense burning, Bishop Luc celebrated a funeral Mass for his brother and announced that Hruodland was the prefect of the March of Brittany.

Hruodland gave bread, beer, and alms to the beggars outside the church on behalf of his father. The commoners set up their party in the square and had their wake the same time the nobles had their feast. The eating, dancing, laughing, and storytelling lasted all day and all night. The next morning, the coffin was shut, sealed with pitch, and wrapped in leather. Menservants took Milo to the family crypt under the sanctuary and laid him with his deceased wives.

* * * * *

On a clear morning three weeks later, the dowager countess spoke to Alda in Frankish as they returned to the manor after prime Mass. Her accent was so heavy Alda asked her to repeat it.

"I return father house," the dowager countess stammered.

"You welcome here," Alda said in stilted Roman. She was not merely being polite. The dowager countess had helped her learn the language as well as the servants' names and characters.

"I bore Count Milo no children," the young widow said slowly in Roman. "My womanly courses started this morning. Now that I am certain there is no child in my belly, I wish to return home."

The keys to the castle jangled on a thick ring at Alda's hip. Now, it was Alda's duty to command the servants, make sure the meals were cooked, the castle was kept clean, the laundry was washed, chinks in the walls were fixed, baths were drawn every Saturday. She forced her mind to think in Roman and not to slip back into Frankish.

"God be with you," Alda said in Roman.

"And also with you," the dowager countess replied. She looked over her shoulder and spoke in a low voice. "Be wary of my late husband's brothers. They hate strong, clever women, and you are both."

Chapter 15

March 777
Rennes

Alda checked the carts a final time before the journey to the spring assembly. The leather-lined carts for beer and wine were full. Others had enough bread, salted and pickled beef and pork, and dried apples, pears, and apricots to sustain them until they could reach an abbey and bake more bread and buy more beer. She lifted a leather cover and inspected the tribute exacted from the Bretons as the price for peace with the Frankish king: furs, gold, bolts of linen and wool, and kegs of fine white wine. After she made sure the gold and jewels from the March of Brittany were secure, Alda dropped the cover and nodded to the guard.

She looked over her shoulder at the livestock. The cattle the Bretons had given mingled with the cattle from the March of Brittany.

Without bending down, she patted the sleek, black head of the year-old mastiff she and Hruodland would give the king. "You will make a fine hunter and a good sire."

Ignoring the doxies who were going to trail the baggage train, she walked past the foot soldiers to the front of the procession. She stroked a filly and patted a colt, both of which she and Hruodland planned to give to the king. She looked over the colt's mane and tail and called to one of the grooms.

"When you comb him tonight, make sure you get this tangle from his mane," she said in Roman.

Hruodland, wearing armor, helped Alda onto her mare and mounted his stallion beside her.

"Everything in order?" he asked.

Gerard was mounted on his steed. Veronica rode pillion with a huntsman.

"Yes," Alda replied, pulling her marten-fur-lined cloak closer to ward off the chill in the spring morning air.

Hruodland raised his sword and signaled for the procession to move forward. The road east briefly ran parallel to the Vilaine, now swollen and muddy with spring rains and melted snow.

Hruodland returned his sword to its sheath and donned a pair of leather gloves. The rain started to fall again as they entered the forest. Buds of leaves and flowers were forming on the trees, and the earth was turning green with the awakening of spring flowers. Alda shivered and pulled her cloak closer to her body with her free hand.

"I cannot believe we are traveling to a Saxon city," Alda told Hruodland.

"It is Paderborn," Hruodland said. "It has taken several years, but we have finally pacified the Saxons. Uncle Charles wants to show the world his victory by having his spring assembly there."

Alda no longer translated Uncle Charles into King Charles. After three years, she had become accustomed to her husband's manner with the royal family.

"I thought the Saxons could never be pacified," she said, grinning. "All my life, I have feared those heathens."

"They are Christians now, and many of their leaders will be at the assembly. Of course," he added, patting his sword hilt, "we'll watch them and make sure they keep their oaths."

"The Bretons say they are Christians, too."

"They are Bretons." Hruodland spat on the ground. "They are Christian in name only."

"That's what I think of the Saxons. Why should we trust them now? They have broken their oaths before, and their rat of an overlord is still free."

"If you call exile in Nordmannia free."

"I hope Widukind rots there, but what's to stop him from coming back?"

"Our might — the same way it pacifies the Aquitanians, the Lombards, the Bretons, and the Gascons. The Saxons will see that our God is stronger than their devils."

The party traveled until twilight and made camp. After a priest celebrated vespers Mass, Hruodland shed his armor with the help of menservants, and soldiers began unloading blankets and bread. Some searched for twigs and logs dry enough to burn. Alda looked over her shoulder and was glad no one was watching her. She reached into a saddlebag and withdrew a small pouch. Although she was shivering, she took off her gloves and tucked them into her girdle. She undid the cord of the pouch and withdrew a dried leaf. She closed the pouch again and returned it to the saddlebag. She looked about again. The men were still busy. Veronica was coming toward her with wine, bread, and a plate of pickled beef and dried apricots.

Alda crushed the leaf between her palms, rubbed them together, cupped her hands, put them to her face, and drew in a breath.

"What are you doing?" Veronica asked.

Despite herself, Alda was startled. She looked around again. Everyone was still busy with blankets and fires.

"I am inhaling the fumes of catnip," Alda said in a low voice. "The wise woman in Rennes said it will open my womb."

Veronica took a sip of wine and offered it to Alda. Alda took a drink.

"I wonder if this curse is the vengeance Ganelon promised when he learned I was going to marry Hruodland," she whispered to Veronica.

"I do not think Ganelon is intelligent enough to think of such a thing, and even if he did, he would not disobey the Church's prohibition on sorcery. He would seem to be more pleased with throttling someone with his bare hands." Veronica cringed.

Alda nodded. Veronica's words were strangely comforting.

Alda had first become alarmed that she and Hruodland had not conceived a child when they were spending their second Nativity together. *How could this be?* she had asked Saint Mary, Mother of God, after the Mass to celebrate Jesus's birth. She had knelt before a carved, painted, wooden statue of the Blessed

Mother and the infant Jesus. *How could I be barren? Why would God curse me this way? Please, give me a child.*

In the months that followed, Alda gave bread and blankets to pilgrims and beggars who had come to the churches at Rennes, Nantes, and Vannes. She gave coins to the Church so it could care for and school the foundlings left on its steps. She had hoped her gifts would atone for her sins and lift this curse.

Still, she did not conceive. She looked for hope in every little ache in her belly, every little feeling of nausea, every time she felt a premature tenderness in her breasts, every time she gained weight. Disappointment had come every month.

* * * * *

The travelers continued their journey east. As the days grew longer and warmer, the green shoots on the forest floor metamorphosed into flowers. The buds on the trees burst into blossoms and leaves. The spring rains continued, feeding the rivers and streams and turning the dirt on the road into muck.

At each city and town — Le Mans, Paris, Reims, Aachen, Cologne — their numbers increased. It was much like the journey to Geneva, although no war was planned this year.

They went north by horseback, foot, and cart to Lippeham, where they crossed the Rhine. In a thick forest in full leaf and bloom, they followed the Lippe River east for nine days, crossing it on a bridge close to the ruins of a Roman fortress. They arrived at the Pader, one of the Lippe's tributaries, and followed it south.

At midday, Alda beheld her first sight of the city: stumps of what were once large trees just outside the city's great gate, under which the river flowed. When they passed through the gate, the peasants stopped what they were doing in the fields and watched the procession. Unlike Frankish men, the Saxons wore their hair and beards long. They had sheepskin cloaks that laced at the right shoulder, knee-length wool tunics, and loose breeches bound with garters. Like the Saxon men, the women wore sheepskin cloaks. Unlike Alda's gowns, the Saxons' loose-fitting woolen dresses had no sleeves. Many wore colorful, voluminous veils.

"This is not what I expected at all," she said.

"What did you expect?" Hruodland asked.

"I thought Saxon land would have the mark of the Devil — gnarled trees, a wall shaped like fangs, fire burning from the earth, the stink of brimstone," she said. "This is so... ordinary."

"Good," Hruodland said. "It means we succeeded."

The travelers rode through the city and entered the palace's walled courtyard. Beside what must have been hundreds of springs, a new palace and church had been built with mortared, flat, gray and beige stones. A familiar and welcome face drew Alda's attention.

"Alfihar!" she called out.

She jumped down from her horse and ran toward him, heedless of the mud on her leather boots or the hem of her skirt.

Alfihar approached her, carrying a boy who had just seen his second winter. His wife, Gundrada, walked beside him, and the boy's nurse followed, carrying her own child.

"This must be Werinbert!" Alda said between breaths when she joined her brother. "Oh, Alfihar, you did not do your son justice in your messages. He bears an exact semblance to you. Look at those green eyes. He has the mark of the dragon. Oh, Werinbert," she said, kissing his cheek, "how good to finally see you!"

Alfihar laughed and shifted the child in his arms. "You are just as indulgent as Mother," he said to Alda.

The boy wore only a tunic and cloak. He put a fist in his mouth and stared at Alda. "This is your Auntie Alda," Alfihar said, his voice tender. "Say hello."

The toddler buried his face against his father's chest and then furtively turned toward his aunt. Alda waved. Werinbert waved back.

"How does Mother fare?" Alda asked her brother.

"She is well. She takes every opportunity to fatten Werinbert with cakes," Alfihar said as he again shifted his son's weight.

Alda laughed and then felt Hruodland's hand on her shoulder.

"Alfihar, you have a fine son," he said.

"In another year, he will get his first wooden sword and learn to ride a horse," Alfihar said.

"He will be a great warrior, just like his father," Hruodland said, tousling Werinbert's brown curls. Hruodland waved toward the hall. "Wife, we should go inside. We must greet our uncle."

As Alda, Hruodland, and their kin entered the hall, Alda noticed the doorways were tall enough for the king to pass through without stooping. Inside, servants were assembling trestle tables. Queen Hildegard and Queen Mother Bertrada rushed to greet them. *Saints be praised, Hildegard is still healthy after the birth,* Alda thought, remembering the king's message about her being with child.

Hildegard hugged Hruodland, Alda, and Gerard. Bertrada embraced Hruodland and clasped hand with Gerard, then Alda. When the queen mother's gaze flicked to Alda's still-flat belly, Alda braced herself. To her surprise, the older woman patted her hand before releasing it.

"Welcome to Paderborn," Hildegard said. "You must use our spring-fed baths and join us at the table."

"Thank you," Hruodland replied. "It's good to see you. You both look well."

Hildegard and Bertrada thanked him and returned the compliment.

"And how do the children fare?" Alda asked.

"They are all well," Hildegard gushed. "Carloman was born over a month ago, and the Good Lord has made him healthy and hungry. And I can't wait for you to see my Karl. What a little warrior! He so enjoys his wooden sword. And my lovely little Hruodtrude, just a toddling babe and already charming the courtiers."

"And Pepin is learning the Psalter," Bertrada added.

"Praise God and His Merciful Mother." Alda fought back a twinge of envy. *If I could bear but one healthy son.*

"We shall accept your invitation to the baths once I speak to Uncle Charles," Hruodland said.

Hildegard pointed to a dais to their right. Next to the queen's empty seat, the king slouched in his throne, leaning against one hand and drumming the fingers of the other against the arm of his chair. Standing before him were Ganelon and an older man, the bishop of Worms, whom Alda remembered from her journey to Geneva.

"What is happening?" Alda whispered to her brother.

Alfihar put his son on the floor beside his foster brother. The nurse gave a wooden ball to Werinbert. Holding it in both hands, he shrieked with joy then threw it. His foster brother chased the toy.

Alfihar leaned toward Alda and muttered, "Do you remember my message about Ganelon marrying a daughter of the bishop of Worms?"

"Yes," Alda said, remembering her relief when the clerk had read the news.

"When I arrived here, I learned that his wife had died," Alfihar said.

"When? How?" Alda's mouth went dry.

"I don't know. Listen."

"...Her dowry should be mine," Ganelon told the king. "She died after she had given birth. The babe lived but a day."

"I have lost a daughter and a granddaughter," the bishop of Worms said, his voice ragged. "That dowry was for one of them, not you. Was the babe baptized?"

"Yes, of course," Ganelon stammered. His voice became surer. "The priest who gave my wife last rites baptized the child."

"And what was my granddaughter's name?" the bishop asked, his voice the tone of an accusation.

"She was named after her mother," Ganelon said calmly.

"Where is she buried?"

"In the churchyard, of course, with her babe." Ganelon cleared his throat.

"Your Excellency, the dowry was for my daughter or her children — surviving children," the bishop of Worms insisted, clenching his fists.

"We have heard enough," the king said looking first at Ganelon and then the bishop of Worms. "Francia has much more pressing needs than this. Since no children survive the union of the houses of Dormagen and Worms, the dowry must be returned to Worms, and the bride price must be returned to Dormagen."

Both men started to protest the decision, but the king held up his hand. "Silence!" he barked. "We will hear no more. We have other important matters to attend."

"Poor Ganelon," Gundrada said.

Stiffening, Alda turned to her sister-by-marriage. "How can you be moved to pity him? His last words to me were, 'I will be avenged.'"

"That fool does not have the courage for vengeance," Hruodland said. "If he did, he would have challenged me to a duel years ago."

"But he married another, a lady from a good family," Gundrada said. "A pity the Lord called both her and their child."

Alda bit her lip and stroked her dragon. *If it was the Lord,* she thought with a shudder. She did not know why she was suspicious of Ganelon. There was something in his manner, no matter how gracious, that made Alda think he was not telling the complete truth. But it was a matter between the bishop of Worms and Ganelon, not her concern.

"I am certain Ganelon has long forgotten his plans of vengeance," Alda heard her uncle Beringar say behind her.

Alda spun around. "Uncle Beringar! Uncle Leonhard!" she cried, embracing them.

"Alda, let me look at you," Leonhard said, taking a step back. "Hruodland has taken good care of you. You have gained weight."

She smiled and blushed, glad he had noticed. She felt a twinge of envy as she glanced at Gundrada. She was still not as plump as her sister-by-marriage.

"I must agree with my brother about Ganelon," Leonhard said. "Those words were spoken in a moment of anger."

"It seemed more like hatred to me," Alda muttered.

"He has shown nothing but good graces to our family."

Alda was tired of talking about Ganelon and decided to change the subject. She turned toward Hruodland and asked, "What did our uncle mean about 'other important matters'?"

"I have yet to speak with him," he said.

"He means he will soon receive guests from Hispania," Leonhard said.

"Guests from Hispania?" Alda asked. "But that is so far away, beyond the Pyrenees."

"Come, dearling, my uncle is summoning us," Hruodland said.

* * * * *

With Gerard trailing them, Alda and her husband crossed the stone floor and greeted the king.

"What do you think of Paderborn, Nephew?" Charles asked, spreading his arms.

"The palace is a triumph," Hruodland said, gazing at the plastered walls covered with murals of Saint Georg slaying a dragon, the Blessed Mother and Child, the Last Judgment, and an inscription in Latin. Through the windows, he saw newly planted gardens of vegetables, roses, and herbs. "What is this I hear about guests from Hispania?"

"A delegation of emirs, in fact," the king replied. "Sulaiman Yaqzan ibn al-Arabi, his son Yusuf, and his son-by-marriage. They sent a message asking for my aid."

"What is an emir?" Alda asked.

"An Islamic nobleman," Gerard answered.

"Why are they asking for the aid of a Christian king?" Hruodland asked.

"I replied that I would listen to their plea. I promised nothing." The king's bright eyes gleamed. "They must know of our strength."

* * * * *

Dinner was lively, full of music and gossip. When Alda and the other guests rose from the benches at the end of the meal, Alda noticed the queen mother approaching her and Hruodland.

"Countess Alda," Bertrada said, "we have lovely gardens here. Let me show them to you."

"That's kind of you, Grandmother," Hruodland replied. "Alda will enjoy it."

Why is Bertrada being this friendly? Alda thought. She had not forgotten that the queen mother had wanted a different bride for Hruodland and was expecting the same cold civility she had received at Aachen. Yet Bertrada had been warm and charming since their arrival in Paderborn.

Forcing a smile to hide her confusion, Alda accompanied Bertrada outside. As they passed roses about to burst into bloom, Alda stole nervous glances up at the queen mother. The older woman's face was impassive.

"I have something to give you," Bertrada said. Halting her steps, she reached into an embroidered pouch on her girdle and withdrew a small gold disk on a chain. "It is a medal of Saint

Andrew. I did not conceive for the first three years I was married, but after I prayed to him, Charles quickened inside me."

"I... I... thank you," Alda stammered.

Alda gazed at the medal in her hand. It showed an image of a haloed, bearded man with an odd-looking cross in the background. She picked out the Latin words for "saint" and "pray" in the inscription along the edges. She kissed the medal.

"You have been a good wife to Hruodland," the queen mother said, "and I pray that his seed takes hold in your womb. But if God does not answer our prayers, perhaps He is calling you to a vocation. Taking the veil would be honorable and richly rewarded."

Alda's cheeks burned and her spine stiffened. *Should I not bear a son, she wants to free Hruodland for another marriage by offering me an abbey.* Alda chose her words carefully. "I thank you for the medal and your prayers. I will heed God's will, whatever it may be."

Closing her fingers around the medal, she tried to push aside the doubts creeping into her mind. *Is Hruodland trying to set me aside?*

* * * * *

Through the rest of the day and the next morning, Alda's doubts cast a shadow over her, even as she clutched her medal and murmured the Latin prayer to Saint Andrew as best she could. Again, she left coins on the altar, hoping it would please God enough to open her womb. She watched Hruodland intently, searching for signs that he wanted to marry someone else. Yet his manner toward her was as affectionate as ever. He seemed unaware that Bertrada had done anything more than give her the saint's medal, and her doubts almost quieted as she stood beside him while talking with the courtiers, usually about the delegation from Hispania. What did they look like? How did they dress? Was it true the emirs did not eat swine?

The answers came when the delegation — three emirs and their followers — arrived between prime Mass and dinner on their fourth day in Paderborn. Their servants blew brass horns, beat drums, and waved standards to announce their arrival. They rode on horses and strange beasts Alda had never seen before — with humps and long necks and shaggy beige hair.

The men, too, were unlike any Alda had seen before. Their skin was varying hues of an olive complexion, their eyes were dark, and their hair and beards were black. They wore black, white, dark yellow, and azure fabric wrapped around their heads, tunics that fell below their knees, and tall leather boots. The emirs wore long, embroidered robes of scarlet, sky blue, and gold. One of them held his garments close and shivered, although to Alda it was a warm day.

Dripping with jewels and dressed in fine clothes, Queen Hildegard came to the courtyard to receive the guests, and a Jew employed by the king made introductions and translated the invitation to bathe in the spring-fed pools and enjoy the feast to follow. At dinner, Alda was amazed the table could hold all the cooks' creations for the first course — the roasts, stews, loaves of bread, and countless other dishes. Yet there was no pork.

The king wore a diadem of gold and gems and special clothes for the occasion — a tunic embroidered with gold thread and fringed with silk, an embroidered woolen cloak that fastened with a gold brooch, and jeweled shoes. At his hip was a jeweled sword. Even with her widow's veil, Queen Mother Bertrada wore many jewels and clothes of the finest wool and silk.

The emirs spoke a tongue Alda had never heard before. After dinner, Sulaiman said to the king through the Jew, "Let us present you with our tribute of riches from our land."

As servants cleared plates and cups from the tables, the king climbed the stone steps to his throne, carved with patterns of flowers and leaves. His chamberlain brought him a scepter and orb. Queen Hildegard pressed her hands together, bowed to her husband, and sat on a smaller throne beside him. After bowing to her son, Queen Mother Bertrada sat in her ornate chair. The royal children follow suit and gathered around their grandmother. The emirs bowed deeply before the king. The Frankish nobility, along with many Saxon leaders, formed a half-circle around them.

Alda's eyes grew wide as the emirs' servants led horses and the strange beasts with harnesses of gold, saddles, and embroidered blankets on their backs. They brought in gold cups, silver coins, linen and silk pillows and tapestries, ivory statuettes shaped like horses, glass bottles with narrow necks and round bases and strips crisscrossed all around, earthenware with elaborate designs, spices, incense, and perfumes. The king nodded and his servants presented the emirs with jewels, gold, two hunting dogs, a falcon, tapestries, furs, and three cups from which he had drunk.

"We thank you for your gracious gifts," the king said in Frankish as the seneschal directed servants to secure the goods. "Now, tell me your request."

After the translator spoke the strange tongue, Sulaiman spoke while the others nodded. The translator said: "We seek your aid in ridding ourselves of the ruler of Cordoba."

"Why do you ask for aid from a Christian king?" Charles asked, his tone polite but stern. "Is he not a follower of Muhammad like you?"

The translator again spoke the strange tongue. Sulaiman spoke the same strange tongue, and the translator said: "The ruler of Cordoba is an Umayyad."

"Explain this to my son's court," Bertrada commanded.

After hearing the translation, the three emirs blinked back their surprise and whispered among themselves. Sulaiman spoke to the translator, who said: "We are Abbasid, descendants of the uncle of Prophet Muhammad, peace be upon him. The Umayyad is a descendant of Prophet Muhammad's archenemy. He is the last of an ungodly and corrupt family who have imprisoned and tortured holy men. His subjects would prefer a godly Christian king in his stead.

"God has granted you invincibility. Word has spread about how you have conquered every foe who has risen against you."

The king's lips curled into a smile.

"The Umayyad will fall easily if we form an alliance," the emir continued through the Jew. "Pamplona is a Christian city and would welcome a Christian king. I am governor of Barcelona and have influence north of the Ebro. With my force of Berbers from Africa, the city of Zaragoza will easily fall. As I said, the Muslims would prefer a godly Christian king to the corrupt, ungodly Umayyad, who is preparing to expand his realm beyond the Pyrenees."

The king thought for a moment, shifted in his seat, and asked, "How much iron do the hills in Hispania hold?"

As the emirs stared at each other, Alda realized they did not know how important iron was to Francia for weapons and armor. Nor did they know, she suspected, that the king himself owned iron mines.

Yusuf shrugged and spoke, and the translator said, "The hills are rich with iron."

Alfihar broke from the semicircle, bowed to the king, and said, "May it please Your Excellence, I am curious about the trade routes."

"What of the trade routes?" he asked his guests.

The emirs all spoke at once. The translator put up both hands and said something, and the emirs spoke one at a time. "I cannot translate directly," the Jew said. "They spoke of trade routes by land and sea to many places: Damascus, Jerusalem, Alexandria, Persia, to name a few."

The king nodded to his chamberlain, who took the orb and scepter. To the assembled Frankish nobility, he said, "You have heard our guests from Hispania. Any thoughts?"

"Is this truly our fight?" Leonhard asked. "We will have to cross the Pyrenees and take men away from their farms. If it was the Holy Father asking for aid, I would beseech you not to hesitate, but this seems to be a feud among Islamic factions."

"The Holy Father may not be making the appeal," Bertrada said, "but we should consider the Church in Hispania, which is under Islamic domination."

"And there are Christian cities under Islamic rule," Ganelon cried. "Surely, you cannot let that be, or worse, allow the infidels to enter Francia. Christians deserve a Christian king."

"And the emirs themselves said they would prefer a godly king, even a follower of Christ," Hruodland said. "Have we not conquered every foe who has risen against us?"

"It has been God's will," Hildegard said.

Alda bit her lip and tried to ignore a twinge in her belly. It went against all reason, but the emirs' request gave her a bad feeling. She envied Hildegard and Bertrada. Queens were the only women who could speak at the assemblies. Yet even if Alda could voice her worries, she dared not contradict her husband in public.

Alfihar said, "We have much to gain from an alliance with our guests. Look at the riches Hispania will offer — the horses, the spices, and they said the hills are rich in iron."

Alda closed her eyes and shook her head as more nobles spoke in favor of a conquest against the ruler of Cordoba.

* * * * *

Alone with Hruodland in bed that night, Alda rested her head against his bare chest. Her finger traced a scar he had gotten in the last war with the Saxons.

"Husband," she whispered, "I am afraid."

"What has Ganelon done?" he asked, his muscles tensing.

"No, not Ganelon. He has done nothing, not even a hard look."

"Oh," he said, relaxing. "What frightens you, dearling?"

"Going to war in Hispania. It gives me a bad feeling."

"Why?" His hand stroked her bare shoulder.

"I do not know. Maybe because it is a foreign land beyond the Pyrenees."

"We have crossed another mountain range to a foreign land — twice."

"But the wars in Lombardy were different," Alda said. "The Holy Father himself asked for our aid both times. How could God not grant us victory?"

"Would God not wish for us to give aid to the Church in Hispania?"

"Well, yes, but…"

"God has always sided with us. Uncle Charles is planning the biggest army ever for this conquest. How could we fail?" He kissed her.

Alda tried to swallow her fears. *Yes, God has always sided with us. So why can't I shake this premonition?*

Chapter 16

August 777
Rennes

Hruodland and his kin returned to Rennes during an unusually hot spate of days. He and Alda had spent much of the spring and part of the summer at the palace in Paderborn, where King Charles and the Frankish counts planned the invasion of Hispania, which would start next spring after the Feast of the Resurrection.

At prime Mass the day after their return, Hruodland pushed his hair off his forehead and fanned himself. A drop of sweat crept down his back.

When Mass ended, Alda touched Hruodland's arm. "I must return to the house and see what Veronica has learned about what has happened here during our absence."

"I am surprised you waited a day to learn the gossip." He chuckled.

"Veronica needed time to talk to the servants."

"Very well. Tell me if you learn anything important."

Alda gave him a quick kiss. "I always do."

He watched as she and Veronica chatted excitedly on their way back to the manor. "Women," he said to Gerard.

"It's their nature," Gerard said.

Their uncle Luc, the bishop of Rennes, tapped Hruodland on the shoulder. "I need a word with you," he said.

Hruodland nodded.

"Not here," Luc muttered, his gaze following Alda. "In my study."

Gerard took a step toward the stairs.

"I need to speak to Hruodland alone," Luc insisted.

Gerard and Hruodland glanced at each other; both of their faces had puzzled looks.

"I shall return to the house, then," Gerard said, "and hear the women gossip while I try to read. You are lucky to have Alda to sort through the nonsense."

Luc scowled at Gerard. When the bishop turned, Hruodland showed Gerard an exaggerated shrug before following his uncle up the winding stairs to the study above the sanctuary. The crucifix loomed over a room with a Bible and several other wood-and-leather-bound books from which Hruodland could read only a few words. Hruodland welcomed the breeze that came in through the open windows. He absently picked up and put down the half melted candles near the Bible.

"What is so important?" Hruodland asked, again pushing his hair from his eyes. He wore his lightest garments but was still hot.

With sweat dripping down his pudgy face and wetting the fringe of hair on the back of his head, Luc scanned the space outside the door before closing it. He gazed outside the window as he pushed back the long sleeves of his robe and fanned himself. Hruodland looked outside too and saw the usual beggars and pilgrims on the church steps and in the market below.

"Perhaps it is time you married a woman who can produce heirs," Luc finally said.

"What?"

"You have been married for three years, and Alda's belly is still flat. People will start to question your potency." Luc folded his hands and rested his chin on his short, fat fingers.

"Not with the way she screams." Hruodland was glad to see Luc blush.

"But we need heirs in this family," Luc continued. "I or your uncle Guillaume could easily annul your marriage. We could manage to keep a portion of her dowry. We could tell her family that since she has lived with us for three years…"

"Repudiate Alda?" Hruodland felt his face get even hotter. His fists clenched. "You are mad."

"You are besotted with her," Luc shot back. "It is a sin to be so besotted with any woman. You should adore God only."

"You think I am guided by fancy?" Hruodland spat. "Alda has been a good wife."

"Alda is not a good wife; why can't you see that?" Luc pounded his fist on his writing desk. "A good wife is like a dog — meek, loyal, and obedient. She is headstrong and has been a curse to this family. Your father died shortly after she came here."

"My father was already ill," Hruodland said evenly. He gripped the window frame so that he would not lunge at the short, pudgy man and throttle him. "I will have no more of this nonsense, Uncle."

"Perhaps, it is better that she is barren." Luc's squinty eyes shifted. "She will not be able to pass a bastard off as yours."

"My wife is an honest woman." Hruodland's voice was tight with anger.

"Can you be certain?" Luc licked his thin, almost colorless lips. "Would a woman who is so enthusiastic about lying with her husband be able to remain virtuous while he is away?"

"That proves nothing!"

"Women are weak. Eve could not resist temptation. Alda's humor would make her weak in the presence of a handsome man, especially if her husband was away and he would never know."

Hruodland thought back to the summer at Drachenhaus when he and Alda were betrothed. Alda was eager to lie with him, almost too eager. Could she succumb to another man's charms?

"There have been rumors," Luc said. "And I myself saw her with other men while you were away at war last year. She greatly enjoyed their company. And your uncle Guillaume told me he saw her acting like a coquette with a handsome, young merchant." He pursed his lips and looked down. "He said her clothes were rumpled as if she had lain with him."

"What is his name?"

"I do not know. He was a merchant. And it does not matter, since she is barren."

"No!" Hruodland yelled. "I will hear no more of this."

He strode past Luc and slammed the door. He shook his head as he ran down the stairs. *No, it cannot be,* he thought. But he could not stop other ideas from creeping into his mind. *Alda is a clever woman. And she did not bleed when I first met with her. If she was not chaste then...*

* * * * *

When she saw her husband come into the hall of the count's manor, Alda forgot what she was telling Gerard and stopped in midsentence. Something had infuriated Hruodland. She could see it in his face.

"I must attend to my husband," she whispered to Gerard in Frankish.

Alda approached him. She would have feared any other man with such a look of rage. But this was Hruodland, and he had never raised a hand against her. Before she could ask what troubled him, he grabbed her by the elbow and pulled her close.

"What have you been doing in my absence?" he yelled in Roman, his voice ragged.

Alda tried to pull herself away, but his grip was too strong. She looked around and saw the servants were listening. "Back to work!" she shouted in Roman.

Hruodland looked around and loosened his grip. Alda stepped back and gave him a puzzled look. "I fail to see why my getting news from Veronica — or answering Gerard's question — would trouble you," she said irritably.

"Who was he, Wife?" Hruodland demanded.

Alda looked around at the servants again. They had paused in their duties. "I said back to work," she commanded. "The first to stop working again will feel my wrath." The servants returned to their duties more quickly.

Alda turned back to her husband. She would have rather faced a charging stallion. His fists were clenched, and his dark eyes burned through her. She took another step back.

"What are you talking about?" she asked.

"Who have you betrayed me with?" he roared.

Gerard's jaw dropped. "Hruodland, this is nonsense," he called out.

"Gerard," Hruodland shouted back, "be quiet. This is not your concern."

"Gerard speaks the truth," she cried. "This is nonsense. I have been true to you!"

The servants stopped working again. Alda took a step toward a maid who was supposed to be sweeping the floor and directed her fury at her husband with a slap across the maid's face.

"I said to keep working," she barked, shaking her finger in the maid's face. "Disobey me again, and the punishment will be harsher." She approached Hruodland and hissed in Frankish, "Walk with me to the church. I have no wish to give the servants more fodder for gossip."

"Wife, we are going to the church," he said in Roman in a loud voice.

As they left the manor, Alda lifted her skirts to keep them from the dusty street. She felt her cheeks burn. She and Hruodland were barely outside the door when she said in Frankish between clenched teeth, "Why did you humiliate me in front of the servants? You could have spoken Frankish."

"Your sin of betrayal is much greater," he retorted in the same tongue.

Alda stopped walking. A chicken strutted in front of them.

"Why are you insisting on such nonsense?" she asked.

"I have on good authority that you have been a coquette with a merchant in my absence." Hruodland grabbed her elbow and led her toward the church.

"That is not betrayal." Alda yanked her elbow from his hand and quickened her pace.

"You do not deny it?" he asked. "You do not deny lying with a merchant?"

"A merchant?" She blinked back her disbelief. "You are accusing me of lying with a merchant? I have done nothing more than flatter them. If they think a countess desires them, they become more generous with their wares."

"Them? There has been more than one?" His expression was somewhere between shock and anger.

"Oh, Hruodland, for pity's sake," she snapped. "I complimented them on how their tunics became them and laughed at their bad jokes. There is no sin in that."

"But your clothes were rumpled," Hruodland insisted.

"I have lain with no one but you," Alda said as they approached the church steps. She let go of her skirts when they reached the door.

"You are lying, just like you lied when you said you were chaste before we married," Hruodland yelled.

Alda was too furious to answer. She clenched her teeth as dust clung to her sweaty skin. She yanked open the door and, without a word, stomped toward the altar. The summer sunlight streamed in on the oaken floor of the sanctuary, and lamps filled with walnut oil illuminated the penitents kneeling in prayer toward Saint Melaine's grave, which lay under the altar.

Alda stared at the wooden crucifix on the back wall and thought of Bertrada's offer and how much simpler a life in the cloister on the Rhine island of Nonnenwerth would be. *To be a bride of God and have a life of prayer. God would never accuse me of infidelity.*

Hruodland followed her toward the altar. "Do not be insolent with me!" he roared in Frankish.

Even though Hruodland and Alda were speaking a tongue most of them did not understand, the penitents turned toward the couple.

A thought stuck Alda and filled her with horror. She shivered despite the heat. She shouted in Frankish, "You are looking for an excuse to repudiate me because we have no heirs. You will not end this marriage by dishonoring me!"

"Quiet!" Hruodland barked.

"I will not be silenced. Not when you are inventing lies. I have tried everything to conceive. I have tried to be a good wife. And you... you..." Fury tied her tongue.

Trembling with rage, Alda pointed to a sidewall with a mural of the Crucifixion, where three women watched Christ at the moment of His death.

"Look at this," she demanded. "Look at the women. The women never forsake Christ. Remember their love for their Lord, Hruodland. Such has been my fidelity for you. May Saint Melaine strike me down if my words are not true!"

Hruodland stared at her, his jaw dropped.

"Well?" Alda asked, her voice dripping with fury. "Do you believe me now?"

Hruodland looked down, his cheeks coloring. Alda's chest was heaving. Her throat was tight. She let the silence hang in the air as heavily as the scent of incense.

Finally, he raised his head. "Yes, I believe you. Come, Wife. Let us return to the manor."

Alda stepped away from the altar, but she did not take the hand Hruodland held out for her. He grabbed her arm and hissed in Frankish, "You are not to embarrass me."

"The same way you embarrassed me?"

She looked at the penitents watching them. She did not want them to spread rumors. Despite her almost blinding anger, she gave her husband her arm.

As they left the church, Alda wondered if Bertrada had suggested divorce to Hruodland while they had been in Paderborn. *No, not in this way.* To keep the peace within her son's kingdom, Bertrada had been willing to make a bargain, what Alfihar would see as a fair trade to end the marriage and retain the family's honor.

It had to be somebody here. Picking up her skirts, Alda snarled: "Who is this perjurer who dishonored me? I want his right hand on a silver platter, and the rest of his body and his kin banished."

"He is beyond my justice," Hruodland said in a monotone.

"But the only people beyond your justice are..." The words caught in her throat for a moment. "Your kin." The full import of the words caused her to pause. "I have married into a nest of vipers."

"Do not say such things," Hruodland commanded.

"It is true. You wish to divorce me? Do it. I will take my dowry to Nonnenwerth, where it will be more welcome. And I will tell my brother and my uncles of your lies. Do you think your uncle Charles wishes for another blood feud in his realm? Do you want my brother to turn his back on you when you face the enemy?"

"Alda, peace," Hruodland said. "I have no intention of repudiating you. Without you, I would be lost."

Alda wiped a tear from her cheek with her free hand. Who could have told Hruodland that lie? Not Gerard, his face showed as much astonishment as she felt. Besides, he would inherit the March of Brittany if she and Hruodland had no children. The only other people beyond Hruodland's justice were his uncles.

Luc, she thought, remembering the warning from the old count's widow: *Be wary of my late husband's brothers.* For a moment, she wanted to flee from this serpent who called himself a bishop, despite the dishonor it would bring her own family. She wanted to flee to Nonnenwerth, where all she had to worry about were which prayers to say and not to be ever watchful of the most powerful man in the city. But she could not bear leaving Hruodland.

"You mean everything to me," she said softly. "If you were lost in Hispania next spring..."

"Lost in Hispania?" Hruodland said with a laugh. "Whatever made you think of such a thing?"

"I... I just keep having a feeling that a disaster will strike."

He kissed her. "It will be the largest army ever. It will include men from all over the realm, even some Lombards. There is nothing to worry about. The Christian cities will welcome a Christian king, and the Islamic cities, when they see our might, will likely surrender without a fight. We will be back by the hay-cutting month. If not then, in time for the harvest."

Alda wanted to believe him. But the premonition hung over her as oppressively as the summer heat.

* * * * *

The heat broke two days later, but Alda's premonition did not go away. It clung to her through the fall and winter and into the spring. She could not sleep on the eve that Hruodland would start his journey to Hispania.

This is the largest army ever, Alda told herself, *and God has always been on our side.*

Her eyes opened to blackness. The curtains on the bed had been closed to keep out the chill of the spring night. She lay in Hruodland's arms. They were both naked, having lain with each other one last time before he went away.

If only this could be the time I am with child, she thought.

She held him tighter. She could feel his breathing. Alda shuddered to think the March of Brittany would be left with only a few guards.

Suddenly, Hruodland's body stiffened. His throat made a noise like a muffled scream. His breathing changed from deep and slow to shallow and quick. He sweated. He gasped and rolled on his back. He sounded as if he was struggling to get enough air into his lungs.

"Dearling?" he whispered. His voice startled her.

"Yes, Husband," she said.

She could feel him turn toward her. She ran her fingers through his hair. She traced his ear, his neck, shoulder, chest. He held her tightly against his body, as if he was making sure she was real.

"Another nightmare?" she asked.

"It is but a dream."

Alda remained silent, knowing he would tell her if she did not prod him.

"I dreamt I watched a man barely out of boyhood die," Hruodland said, holding her closer. "He had perhaps seen fifteen winters. A Saxon arrow found him but did not land in his heart straight and true. And he screamed. He screamed for what seemed hours as the men tried to pull it out of him and stop the bleeding. And then I was that boy, screaming, and they could not stop the bleeding. That is when I awoke."

Despite herself, Alda gasped, wondering if Hruodland's nightmare was an omen.

As if he read her mind, he said, "It is but a dream. Something I saw during the war in Saxony. Nothing more." He touched her cheek. "I need you to be cheerful when we leave."

Alda swallowed. She decided not to tell him of her premonition again, but she could not just lie there and pretend to be cheerful. She had to do something to protect him, even if it meant leaving herself vulnerable to the Bretons or the thieves in the forest or Bishop Luc. What mattered most was that he came back.

"Husband, there is something I want you to take," Alda said.

She rose from the bed, letting the blankets fall from her body, and swung her feet over the edge. Shivering, she drew back the curtain. A thick night candle on a table next to the bed illuminated the solar and sleeping women. What she wanted lay next to the candle.

She picked up her iron dragon and retreated to the warmth of the blankets. The curtain was still drawn back and allowed candlelight to enter. She draped the chain that held the amulet on Hruodland's neck.

"This will protect you," she said.

Hruodland held it and stared at it in the candlelight. "But dearling," he stammered, "this is a gift from your father. I cannot take this from you."

"Husband, please," she insisted, pressing it into his hand. "It will ease my fears if you take it."

He gave her a tender smile. "I will give it back to you when I return."

"The stone comes from the mountain where Siegfried slew the dragon," she said.

The dragon's blood had made Siegfried invulnerable, almost, except for where the linden leaf fell on his shoulder.

Chapter 17

August 778
The Pyrenees

King Charles paced, waiting for the rear guard and baggage train to come to the rendezvous in the green foothills on Francia's side of the border. The Pyrenees mountain passes had forced the retreating Franks to march north in a long, narrow column, something they were not accustomed to. Since they had arrived at the rendezvous the previous day, they had waited all night and most of the day. Still was no sign.

"Where are they?" the king muttered as the light began to wane. "Something is wrong."

Gerard approached the king and bowed. Like the others, he had not bathed or shaved for weeks. "Your Excellence," he began in Latin, partly because he could speak it better than Frankish, partly because only a few counts understood Latin, "I have just heard rumors from the soldiers."

"And?" the king asked in Latin.

"Some soldiers have been talking of an ambush at twilight by men in light armor, an ambush so quick that no one could come to the rear guard's aid." Gerard's brow creased. "They might need medicine and prayers. If you appoint a scouting party, I would like

The Cross and the Dragon

for myself and my servants to be part of it. Hruodland is in the rear guard."

Halting his steps, Charles cursed under his breath. His frown deepened. "We need a scouting party. Count Beringar," the king called in Frankish, "you and your men will be part of a party to aid our rear guard and baggage train."

"I, too, would like to accompany the party with my servants," Leonhard said. "Our sister's son is in the rear guard with Hruodland. And I have a good physician with a cartload of potions and herbs."

Ganelon took a step toward the king and bowed. "May I and my men accompany the party?" he asked. "In case the rear guard needs more fighting men?"

The king looked at Beringar. Beringar shrugged his broad shoulders and nodded. "Count Ganelon's assistance is welcome."

"Very well," the king said. "While you find out what happened to the rear guard, we will take the army to Bordeaux and then go to Périgueux."

"We shall need to be quick," Leonhard said, "and we shall need horses instead of oxen."

"Borrow all the horses and carts you need," the king said.

Beringar selected the largest horses and the lightest carts for the steep mountain roads as narrow as paths. The men packed the carts with food and supplies.

Ganelon clapped his hands and called to his men, "Make haste, you dogs. The wounded will need our aid."

As the count of Dormagen gave profanity-laden orders, Gerard leaned toward Leonhard and said in Latin, "I wish Beringar had not agreed to let Ganelon join our party. He is as insufferable as ever."

"Can you not forget the feud for a moment?" Leonhard said. "We are all Franks here."

Gerard grudgingly admired Ganelon's efficiency as his men did indeed make haste. He couldn't tell whom the soldiers feared more: the enemy or their own pale-haired master.

* * * * *

After sunrise prayers, the scouting party started to retrace their steps from the retreat through the mountains. *A retreat that*

154

was barely more than a disgrace, Leonhard thought as they made their way along the narrow road among pines clawing the gray, stony, steep slopes and small flowers growing from the rocks. The horses strained to climb the terrain. Leonhard's alb, once white, was dingy from the dust of the road.

When they reached a clearing in the forest, Leonhard looked up. Like the Alps, some of the mountains were snow capped, even in summer. "This whole thing has been a disaster," he muttered to himself.

"Speaking such a thing is treason," Ganelon said with a look of incredulity.

"But it is true," Leonhard shot back. "I said at the assembly in Paderborn that this was not our fight, and unfortunately, I was right. Name one city that Francia has gained in this conquest."

"But every city and castle fell before us. We have gained much booty and many hostages."

"And destroyed one of the few Christian cities in Hispania."

"Pamplona was not a true Christian city." Ganelon clenched his free hand into a fist. "Damned Gascons! If they were true Christians, they would have cheered when they saw our king come to free them from the infidels. They preferred the infidels. They deserved their fate."

"Some of those infidels were our allies," Leonhard said.

"They lied to us! The Saracens in Zaragoza prefer their evil ruler to our godly king!"

"You are right about one thing, Leonhard," Gerard said in Frankish that was still not perfect. "We were right to, uh, leave Zaragoza. Zaragoza is not Pavia. This war was not for protection of His Holiness. It was not worth a long siege and having our men miss a harvest in addition to this one. Our king made right decision to come home."

Leonhard remembered how sickness and the summer heat at Zaragoza had crushed the soldiers in their heavy armor. The sun had burned and peeled their faces. Some of the men fainted. Some of them stripped off armor and helmet — their faces, hair, and tunics drenched. The pennyroyal oil to repel insects melted from their skin and mixed with the odor of sweat. Soldiers were arguing over the smallest things as their food and beer ran low. Leonhard had become worried about not having enough beer in that heat and had been glad when the Saracens' offer of gold, hostages, and a vow not to invade Francia convinced King Charles to withdraw, with the main army followed by the baggage train and the rear guard.

Ganelon's voice brought Leonhard back to the present, back to the narrow mountain passes in the Pyrenees, where he saw one of the goat-like animals run behind a beech in the forest.

"Did the Saracens decide to attack our retreating forces?" Ganelon wondered. "The rear guard surely would have made short work of them had they come from the south."

Leonhard pursed his parched lips. He wished he knew.

* * * * *

The party found their answer shortly after midday at the Pass of Roncevaux, in a forest so dense that only needles of sunlight broke through the leaves overhead. They smelled it before they saw it, a rotting stench in the thin air.

Descending into the valley, Leonhard gasped at what he beheld as large, bald-headed raptors flapped away. Bodies. Everywhere, bodies. All the soldiers in the rear guard and baggage train were dead, stabbed, beheaded, shot with arrows. The monks and a bishop shared the same fate as the soldiers. The soldiers' doxies lay with their dresses hiked above their hips, their throats slashed. The dogs' skulls had been crushed; some of the horses were pierced with arrows.

For a moment, the only sound was the buzzing of flies. Then, Leonhard heard Gerard vomit and one of the soldiers stifle a sob.

Leonhard could not stop staring. Along with the large birds, ravens, rats, and other beasts had eaten the bodies. Whoever attacked them looted the bodies of everything of value: shoes, boots, swords, armor, helmets, jewelry, cloaks. The carts from the baggage train were gone, and Leonhard suspected the attackers had stolen the surviving animals.

A wolfhound suddenly appeared in the midst of the carnage. He approached them trembling and whining, his tail between his legs.

"Dirty Saracens," Ganelon growled. "Broke their oath."

"It was not the Saracens," Beringar said. He dismounted and picked up a spearhead on a broken shaft. "This is not a Saracen weapon. It's Gascon." Beringar spat on the ground. "An ambush is just like the Gascons."

156

"Perhaps, this is the ambush you heard of, Lord Gerard," Leonhard said.

"The baggage train would have passed here at twilight," Beringar said. "In these thick woods, the Gascons would have been almost invisible. They could have attacked from the top of a nearby mountain."

Leonhard spotted a disembodied muscled arm with a short Gascon sleeve of light leather armor over a longer sleeve of wool. *Easy enough to run away.* A grim smile curled his lips. *Apparently, this one did not run fast enough.*

Beringar threw down the spearhead. "Between the Gascons' knowledge of their native land and our heavy armor, we stood no chance, especially with our men expecting an attack from the Saracens. They made perfect prey."

"Revenge!" Ganelon cried, raising a fist. "Cut them to a pulp!"

"How?" Leonhard asked. "We don't know where they went, and we are but a few. We will have vengeance later. Now we must give our men a Christian burial. Ganelon, Beringar, have your men bring the shovels and axes."

While the men retrieved wooden shovels and stone axes, Leonhard dismounted and prayed the Pater Noster, yet he thought, *Why, God, did You allow this to happen?*

Gerard dismounted. Staggering, he called out, "Hruodland!"

He tripped over a body, fell to his knees and buried his pale face in his hands. At that moment, Gerard looked small and vulnerable.

Leonhard swallowed, approached Gerard, and laid a hand on his shoulder. "Do not weep," he whispered in Latin. "The souls will linger in this world if they know people will miss them."

"My... my brother, he was ri-riding with this party." Gerard dried his eyes and stood and looked about.

"Alfihar was with them as well," Leonhard said, grimacing. "We must pray for them."

Leonhard saw the physician wander among the bodies and shake his head. The wolfhound strolled among the soldiers who had just arrived and nudged their hands to pet him. One of the soldiers, barely out of boyhood, gave the dog a morsel of meat.

Ganelon took three steps and slapped the boy, who was much shorter and thinner than his master. "Are you here to coddle a dog, you lazy worm?" he shouted.

"Ganelon!" Leonhard cried, his voice harsher than he intended. "The dog may be of some use."

"That is my man," he yelled, pointing to the cowering boy. "It is my duty to discipline him." Ganelon smacked the boy on the back of the head. "Get to work," he growled, and then called him an obscenity. Ganelon looked at the bodies and made the sign of the cross. "The sooner we are out of this grave, the better."

"On that, we agree," Leonhard said sadly.

As he heard Beringar call for Alfihar, Leonhard stepped over the bodies and found a flat spot near the road. His eyes scanned the ground, but Alfihar was not among them. Leonhard did not want to find his nephew. He did not want to believe that Alfihar was dead.

Do not tarry, he told himself. *You have a duty to the dead.*

Leonhard sprinkled holy water on the ground, removed his gold cross from his neck and placed it in the earth.

"I need four more crosses," he called, "so I can consecrate this ground for their graves."

Four men, including Gerard, handed him their crosses. Leonhard used his knife to dig through the hardened dirt and placed four crosses at the corners of the site. Then, he knelt in the dirt and prayed in Latin at each cross, asking God to bless the ground.

After his prayers, Leonhard used his knife to carve a circle in the ground around the site. He scratched the soil, leaves, beech twigs, stones, and tree roots. He wrote the names of God, Jehovah, Light of Lights, and symbols of Jesus and the saints — the cross, the fish, the eagle of Saint John, the dragon of Saint Georg, the lion of Saint Mark.

He carved the ground with the effort a butcher used to get through a bone. His right arm ached. Still, he clutched the knife, sawing at the ground, inscribing the holy symbols. The shifting shadows of the forest made it difficult for a man to see them, but the words and symbols were not meant for men's eyes. They were meant for those beings that wandered at dusk and midnight to prey on men's bodies and souls. No demon would cross the line of this circle, ever, as long as the circle was unbroken.

The smell of Leonhard's sweat mingled with the stench of rotting flesh, a stench that shoved its fingers up his nostrils, seeped into his hair and clothes and boots. He wondered if a bath would ever wash away this stink. He used his sleeve to wipe his forehead and left a smear of dirt. He heard the men hacking and digging at the hard ground, grunting as they used a large wooden stick to dislodge a heavy rock, trying to find some place among the tree roots and stones. It was slow work.

Leonhard finished his circle of protection as daylight started to fade. He sank to his knees near the shallow beginning of the mass grave. The men paused in their work and knelt with him. He said the vespers Mass at sunset and prayed for protection against demons, against bandits, against the Gascons.

"We commend Your soldiers to You," he prayed in Latin. "Let them be at peace. Amen."

He anointed himself and each man with holy water. Ganelon, like the other men covered with filth and gore, looked at the corpses and said, "Are you certain they will not harm us?"

Leonhard was surprised that Ganelon was more afraid of the dead than he. Ganelon was a muscular man, not as big as Beringar, but still strong enough to wield a sword and wear armor. "They know we are doing this for them," Leonhard replied. "They will not harm us."

The men moved the horses and carts into the circle. Their weapons were drawn. If the Gascons were going to ambush the party, this would be the ideal time. Someone familiar with the land would have just enough light to see, but a stranger would struggle.

Leonhard watched the trees and underbrush for motion and listened for rustling. He was weary but too afraid to sleep. He was hungry but had no desire to eat. He put a loaf of bread in a beech tree, out of reach of the dog, to appease restless spirits. The men lit fires to continue their work into the night. Leonhard found a thick fallen branch to use as a torch. He stroked his medals of Saint Peter and Saint Sebastian.

Leonhard approached the bodies outside the circle first, while daylight lingered. As he prayed over the bodies, he wished he had Hosts to put in their mouths. He recognized important men from Charles's court, Anselm, the count of the palace, Eggihard, the seneschal.

When he found Alfihar, what was left of his body, Leonhard had to walk away for a moment. He did not want to collapse, sobbing. He stumbled over something solid and looked down. It was Alfihar's dragon amulet. Picking it up, he saw the amulet's chain had broken.

Leonhard took a deep breath, swallowed, and returned to Alfihar, who had been stabbed in the back. The Gascons had taken everything except Alfihar's shirt. The strange birds and rats had eaten his flesh.

Alfihar needs prayers, Leonhard told himself. *Do not weep if you care about his soul.* Leonhard wiped his eyes with his hand. He slipped Alfihar's dragon into his own pouch. Perhaps, the amulet had fallen off Alfihar during the fight, and the Gascons did not notice it.

"I shall give it to your son," he managed to tell Alfihar, his voice cracking.

Most of the bodies were like Alfihar's — looted by the Gascons, pecked and partially eaten by carrion birds and beasts. Leonhard had to pause several times and pray for the strength not to weep.

The graying twilight thickened into an opaque black, and the air became cool. Leonhard almost dropped the torch when he stumbled over a tree root or a twig grabbed at his robes or hair. He was glad to see the firelight, glad to see living men. He called to his brother.

When Beringar approached him, Leonhard said softly, "I found Alfihar."

Beringar looked down and turned away from the fire. His immense shoulders shook with silent sobs. It was the first time Leonhard had seen any emotion in his older brother since they left the king's army. Leonhard closed his eyes and felt tears run down his cheeks and into the stubble on his chin. How was he going to tell Alda and Theodelinda?

Leonhard dried his eyes with his sleeve and threw the branch he had been using as a torch into the fire. He led the compline Mass and reminded the men that they were doing the Lord's work, that they should not be afraid.

Leonhard was beyond exhaustion. More than anything else, he wanted to leave this place. That desire drove him to go on, to say prayers for the dead, despite the howls of wolves, calls of insects, and rustling in the underbrush. Unable to find Hruodland after hours of searching, Gerard also knelt near the corpses and prayed for their souls. Leonhard noticed the hound had curled next to a body under a bush. He stumbled toward it and pushed back the brush.

"Hruodland," he whispered.

Hruodland's body had been untouched by ravens or rats. He looked like the living, a man who had been traveling for months — unshaven face, greasy, tangled dark hair, and skin coated with filth. Leonhard called to Gerard.

Gerard hurried through his prayer and staggered toward Leonhard. "Thank you," he said, his voice ragged.

His lower lip trembling, Gerard crouched beside Leonhard. As they had discovered with the others, Hruodland's sword and armor had been stolen. He was stripped to his leggings and a shirt stained with rust, blood, and dirt. Even his cross and medallion of Saint Sebastian were gone. Yet he still wore Alda's iron dragon amulet. Although the Gascons had been bold enough to loot a dead man of sword and armor, Leonhard guessed they thought the dragon was cursed and feared it too much to touch it.

"Leonhard," Gerard said softly in Latin, "tell me my eyes are not deceiving me. I think Hruodland is breathing."

Leonhard thought it must be a trick of the light and his own fatigue. He rubbed his eyes, smearing dust and sweat, and looked at Hruodland again. "No, your eyes do not deceive you," he said. "Hruodland *is* breathing."

"Saints be praised. He lives."

Leonhard then noticed odors of the living — sweat, urine, excrement. The stench of the corpses had masked it. *The Gascons must have left Hruodland for dead,* he thought, gazing at the large stain of dried blood on the shirt covering Hruodland's chest. *But they stabbed him one last time, just to be sure.*

Hruodland's left leg twisted at a strange angle. The dog licked Hruodland's face, but Hruodland neither moved nor flinched.

The hound must have kept the rats and birds away, Leonhard thought. He did not want to know what else the dog had eaten.

Gerard watched his brother breathe, then shook Hruodland's shoulder. "Hruodland! Hruodland!"

Hruodland did not awaken.

"Your brother," Leonhard stammered. He cleared his throat. "Your brother is not long for this world."

"No!" Gerard cried. "No! I will not believe it." He called to one of his servants in Roman and pointed at the closest campfire.

As Gerard and the servant carried Hruodland, Leonhard retrieved a vial of oil from his saddlebag. Returning the campfire, he knelt beside Gerard and Hruodland's prone body.

"We have a duty to Hruodland's soul," Leonhard said. "I must anoint him before it is too late."

After asking Hruodland for his confession, Leonhard traced the sign of the cross over Hruodland's eyes, ears, nose, mouth, hands, feet, and loins, each time praying, "Through this holy unction and His most tender mercy, may the Lord pardon you whatever sins and faults you have committed."

From the corner of his eye, Leonhard noticed that Ganelon was watching Hruodland intently. Leonhard tried to read Ganelon's icy blue eyes. Was it fear of the corpses or anger at his old rival?

* * * * *

While Leonhard spent the night praying for the dead, the men scraped the ground, dislodged stones, and hacked tree roots with axes. Gerard held his brother's head up as the physician, a monk who had seen perhaps forty years, trickled beer into Hruodland's mouth. Gerard watched the physician make a poultice of comfrey and garlic. He held up Hruodland's body as the monk lifted Hruodland's shirt, applied the poultice to the gash in Hruodland's chest, and wrapped the area in bandages.

The physician lowered the shirt, and Gerard gently laid Hruodland on the ground. Hruodland did not flinch when the physician removed the soiled leggings, set the broken bone in his leg, and applied the poultice and splint.

Perhaps, Leonhard is right, Gerard thought as his eyes began to fill with tears. He swallowed and wiped his eyes with his sleeve. *I shall be the count soon.* He pressed his lips tight and shook his head, rebuking himself for thinking of his inheritance at a time like this.

"I... I must say prayers for dead," he stammered to the physician in Frankish. He thought of his next words as he said them slowly, "I shall return to him, but if something changes, tell me."

Nodding, the physician draped a blanket over Hruodland. As Gerard approached one of the fallen soldiers, he spied Leonhard looking toward Hruodland and shaking his head. A flush burned Gerard's cheeks. Even if the effort was futile, the physician needed something to do, and someone needed to watch over Hruodland.

The men were sweating despite the chill in the night air. They finished digging the large, shallow grave, clawed and scraped and hacked among the trees, shortly before dawn. At sunrise, Leonhard said prime prayers. Afterward, the physician returned to Hruodland and gasped.

"Count Hruodland has opened his eyes," he called out.

"A miracle!" Gerard cried. "Hruodland!"

Hruodland said nothing. His eyes did not acknowledge Gerard.

As the day wore on, Hruodland's eyes did not follow Leonhard and Gerard moving from body to body, praying for the dead. His eyes did not follow the movement of men trying not to faint in the stench as they carried bodies and laid them in the grave. He did not flinch when the dog licked his face or nudged his arms.

Gerard returned to Hruodland as the physician trickled wine into Hruodland's mouth. No effect.

"This is like tending to a dead man," the physician muttered.

* * * * *

Leonhard and the other men spent the rest of the day placing bodies in the grave. He did not care that such work was beneath him. He wanted to leave Roncevaux. He wanted to return to Francia and a bath smelling of lavender and mint.

Beringar bade his men to strip armor from his body, broad as a tree trunk. "Armor did not help them," he told Leonhard. "Why are you carrying bodies?"

"I shall do anything to hasten our departure from this horrid place."

"So shall I," he said. He wiped his hand on his high forehead, which had been getting higher over the years, looked at the rust, and wiped his hand on his tunic. He held his sandy hair off his neck and fanned himself.

Ganelon, too, had his men remove his armor. The rust from his helmet left a line in his pale blond hair. Gerard, Beringar, and Ganelon joined Leonhard in carrying corpses to the grave while the physician attended to Hruodland. The men worked as quickly as they could, pausing only for beer or prayers. They spent the second night shoveling earth and piling rock, twigs, leaves — and anything else they could carry — into a mound over the dead. Leonhard again assured them the dead would do them no harm.

They finished when the sun, what Leonhard could see of it, was high in the sky the next day. He fashioned a larger cross from two fallen limbs of beech, and intoned a final prayer at the grave.

"Our work here is finished," Leonhard said. "Let us rejoin the king."

"What of Hruodland?" Ganelon asked, his voice sharp.

Gerard strode a few paces and knelt near his brother. Hruodland was staring at nothing again. "We take him with us," he said in Frankish.

"But he is not long for this world. Taking him with us will slow us down," Ganelon said matter of factly.

Gerard's dark eyes flashed as if a fire had ignited within them. He leapt to his feet and drew his eating knife, gesturing with it as he spoke. "I will not abandon him. If leaving him part of feud, you..." He let out a string of obscenities in Roman, Frankish, and Latin.

If Ganelon had been standing closer, Leonhard was certain Gerard would have stabbed him long past the point of death. Red-faced, Gerard had the look of a madman. Like everyone else here, he was filthy, and his clothes were stained with gore. His hair was greasy and unkempt. Even Ganelon's soldiers stepped back.

"If you want to end feud, I end it with you," Gerard said in Frankish, slashing the air with his knife.

Ganelon's men stared at their master, and Ganelon stared at Gerard. Leonhard saw the old hatred coming back into Ganelon's icy eyes as Ganelon's hand went for the hilt of his seax.

"Peace," Leonhard barked, his voice dripping with disgust for both of them. "We are on enemy land, and we shall not fight among ourselves. You two can cut each other to ribbons once we cross the border. But I have seen enough death among my countrymen to last a lifetime."

Ganelon took his hand off his seax. "You speak the truth, Bishop Leonhard," Ganelon said, his eyes boring into Gerard. "I cannot fight a man who is at a disadvantage."

Gerard muttered something in Roman as he thrust his knife back in its sheath. He wiped his brow with his sleeve. "We take Hruodland with us," he said in Frankish.

"We have no choice," Leonhard said calmly. "We cannot bury him, and we cannot leave him to die without a Christian burial."

Chapter 18

erard's servants carried Hruodland to one of the carts. To make enough room for him and the supplies, they placed him in a sitting position and propped him up with blankets.

There was not room enough for the servants to ride in the cart, and the party could go only as fast as the men who were walking. The dog sometimes walked with them, sometimes rode with Hruodland.

As they wound their way through the gray and green mountains, the smell of death still filled Gerard's nostrils, and he found it difficult to breathe in the dust. He looked at the other men. They were unshaven and filthy, and Gerard knew he did not look any better. They made camp at sunset. After vespers Mass, Leonhard insisted the men eat.

"I am not hungry," Gerard murmured in Latin.

"You must keep up your strength," Leonhard replied. "For your brother's sake."

Gerard took a few bites of moistened travel bread, although it had the texture of wet leather and was tasteless to him. Ganelon wolfed down his meal, while even his own men nibbled at their food.

How can he eat? Gerard wondered. *It is as if he saw nothing.*

Ganelon turned toward the physician. "How is the prefect of the March of Brittany?" he asked, his mouth full of salted pork.

"Nothing has changed," the physician said, shaking his head. "I have never seen anything like this before."

"What kind of potions do you have to help him?" Ganelon asked. He shoved the last of his food into his mouth and licked his fingers.

"I can show you," he answered, brightening as he picked up a fallen branch and dipped it in the fire.

Gerard pursed his lips. Strange. Only hours before, Ganelon had wanted to leave Hruodland behind. Why the sudden interest in medicine? Yet Gerard's own curiosity was piqued. "I would like to see as well," he said.

The physician led Ganelon and Gerard to the wagon and lifted the leather cover. "Of course, I have wine," he said, pointing to five clay jugs, "essential for any medicine. There's garlic for wounds, comfrey roots for broken bones." He held up another clay jug. "This is the linseed oil and pennyroyal we have been using to repel fleas and flies. I have gathered some herbs during our journey. This," he said, opening a small sack to reveal shiny green leaves and green berries, "is mistletoe."

"Isn't that poison?" Gerard asked, raising his brows.

"Many herbs are poisonous in large doses. But a little mistletoe quiets a seizure."

Ganelon held up a small clay jar. "What is in here?"

"I use the small jars for my most potent medicine," the physician said. "What you are holding is essence of wormwood, which makes whoever drinks it not care about pain, and this" he said holding up another small jar, "is hemlock."

"What do you use hemlock for?" Ganelon asked.

"To induce sleep," the physician answered, "but if I were to use more than a drop, my patient would never awaken."

"You will not give that to Hruodland," Gerard said slowly to make sure the physician understood his Frankish.

"No need, my lord," said the physician. "His problem is not lack of sleep."

* * * * *

The next day, the party reached the foothills on Francia's side of the mountain range. As they made their way toward the road near the ocean, Hruodland sometimes opened his dark eyes, and the physician gave him wine when he seemed awake.

"He is like a dead man," the physician muttered, "insensible to pain or hunger or thirst. But a dead man would not be sitting in his own waste."

Gerard looked at his brother. Hruodland's eyes were vacant, as if he did not comprehend the world around him. Gerard swallowed and draped his medal of Saint Peter around Hruodland's neck. Murmuring the Latin prayer to the saint, he thought, *End this. End his suffering.*

At sunset two days later, they saw the gray walls of Lapurdum. Sitting at the confluence of two rivers near the ocean, the fortified Gascon town accepted King Charles's rule as grudgingly as the Aquitanians to the north. Gerard welcomed the salty scent of the sea — anything other than the death stench that still clung to their clothes.

During their three-day stay to rest the animals and replenish supplies, Hruodland's condition did not change. When they returned to the road, the party traveled through the Landes forest, which was thick with pines. When they arrived at the marshes seven days later, they saw thousands of birds picking tiny fish from the small pools of water in the long grasses.

When the sun was at its zenith the next day, the party saw the Abbey of Saint Stephen, standing on a high spot of the marsh, walled with timber cut from a nearby forest. As he slapped at flies, Gerard's heart rose to see the abbey's tenants watching over their grazing cattle, goats, and other animals.

They reached the abbey after crossing a stream. A guard posted on the ramparts descended and ushered them through the gate. The porter, a shrill-voiced old woman residing in a small house near the gate, called out for a blessing, the same thing all porters asked of visitors. By her accent, Gerard knew they were in the southernmost part of Aquitaine.

Leonhard smiled. "*Dominus vobiscum.*"

"*Et cum spiritu tuo,*" she said. "We are expecting you. The king's army stayed here and left two days ago."

After translating the porter's words for his companions, Gerard looked about the abbey. It had a mill, livestock yards, gardens, an orchard cemetery, guesthouses for aristocrats and commoners, two houses for novices, and two dormitories for monks and nuns. The abbess's residence, connected to the church, was as splendid as any count's manor.

"Does this abbey have a hospital?" Gerard asked the porter.

"Yes."

"My brother needs care of sisters," Gerard said in Frankish. "I must attend to him."

He dismounted and handed the reins to a servant, who led the horse to the stables. A boy, apparently drawn by the noise near the gate, approached Gerard and his party. Gerard gave the child a coin and asked him to lead his party to the hospital. He ordered three of his menservants to accompany him as the cart carried his brother. They stopped in front of a door to a large, one-story wooden building with many windows.

Gerard's nose wrinkled at the smell of urine when the servants lifted his brother's shoulders and legs. Servants had washed Hruodland, his shirt and drawers, and the cart as best they could whenever they were near a stream or pond, but they could keep neither him nor the cart clean.

"You will clean this cart before we continue our journey — and see if you can pay a laundress to wash the blanket," Gerard told a servant, handing him some coins. "His clothes are ruined. Cut them off him and burn them."

Gerard gingerly removed the iron dragon from Hruodland's neck.

"Which hospital ward should we take him to, Count Gerard?" one of the servants asked, cutting off the soiled shirt.

Count Gerard. It echoed in Gerard's mind. He did not bother to correct the servant. Gerard stared at the dragon in the palm of his hand and swallowed. He gazed at his elder brother. Hruodland still had that empty look in his eyes, and he had become even thinner. Gerard shook his head, unable to believe what he was about to say.

"Take him to the ward for the dying," Gerard answered, his voice cracking.

* * * * *

The boy ran into the hospital. "Sister Elisabeth," he called in Roman with an Aquitanian accent Gerard could not place. "Some people are bringing a new patient."

A plump woman of about fifty years turned when the boy called to her. Although she wore the same black habit and veil as the other sisters, Gerard could tell she was the mistress of the hospital. Walking toward him, she had a regal bearing.

Sister Elisabeth brushed back a strand of silvered hair as she greeted Gerard at the door and bade him to follow her inside the ward, a small, clean room with five cots. Open windows let in the late summer light, and a sea breeze billowed the curtains covering a doorway at the far end. Sister Elisabeth's habit brushed the floor, which was covered with dried tansy, wormwood, and mint.

"Why doesn't he have any clothes?" she asked. She sounded like she was from Bordeaux.

Gerard blushed.

"Tell me." Her dark blue eyes met his gaze. "My work has been in this hospital for," she paused, thinking, "more years than you have walked about this earth. There is nothing I have not seen."

"He ruined his shirt, and he will ruin whatever cot my servants lay him on. He is unable to tell you when he must answer the call of nature."

"Put a sheet on the cot, Illuna," Sister Elisabeth said to another nun, a younger, taller woman. When that was done, she said to the menservants, "Lay him there, gently, and be careful of his leg." She put her hand to her chin. "He needs a bath and fresh dressing for his leg and chest. Illuna, fetch a tub and have another lay sister help you get some water from the stream."

"You are going to bathe him?" Gerard's blush became a deeper red.

"We have bathed men before. It is like bathing a child." Her face became somber as she touched Gerard's shoulder. "We will do our best to make him comfortable in his final days."

"Thank you," he murmured, staring at the iron dragon he still held in his hand.

"What happened to him?" she asked. "Did he fall from a horse and land on his head?"

"I do not know. We found him this way at Roncevaux. The Lord should have taken him on the battlefield, but his soul is lingering. He is a great hero. Will you watch over his body and give him a Christian burial?"

"Of course," Sister Elisabeth said gently. "It is why we are here. What is his name?"

The Cross and the Dragon

"He was my brother, Hruodland, prefect of the March of Brittany."

Two sisters brought in a wooden tub and placed it beside the bed. They fetched buckets and walked toward the stream.

"Speaking of baths," Sister Elisabeth said, "you should see the abbess. She no doubt will have ordered her servants to prepare baths for you and the nobles in your party. She always treats her noble guests well."

Gerard could not help but notice the bitterness in Sister Elisabeth's voice when she said "noble."

* * * * *

Gerard found Leonhard, Ganelon, Beringar, and the abbess chatting in front of her residence. It had been a few years since he had last seen her, but Gerard recognized her instantly.

"Judith," he murmured. "Judith of Bordeaux."

Judith, Gerard remembered, the woman who had bedded Hruodland and many others before her husband had died. The king had appointed her the abbess the summer after Lombardy was conquered. *Retired from the world?* Gerard thought. *She looks and acts like a queen.*

Judith reeked of sandalwood perfume from the Holy Land. Her clothes were pure white linen, the lack of dye her sole concession to humility, but even they were embroidered with blue. A tight bodice and a girdle of gold and sapphires showed off a plump figure any countess would envy. She wore a silk veil, secured with a sapphire headdress. Rings covered her pale, soft fingers, bracelets jangled on her wrists, her necklaces entwined with each other on her bosom.

"Lord Gerard?" Judith said in Frankish, her eyes widening. "I almost did not recognize you. Bishop Leonhard told me what happened at Roncevaux, God rest their souls," she added, bowing her head. "Is your brother comfortable?"

"Yes," he mumbled.

Gerard looked down and realized he had been holding the dragon amulet all this time. He slipped it into a pouch on his belt.

A servant whispered in Judith's ear. "The baths are ready," she said. "You and your party must rest here a few days. I shall have the laundresses wash your clothes — you may borrow some I lend to guests at my residence. After the baths, please join me at the table."

* * * * *

As he sat in the tub, Leonhard wondered if he would ever feel clean again, if he would ever stop smelling death.

"Your brother, how does he fare?" Ganelon asked Gerard. His tone reflected more eagerness than concern. He might as well have said, "Is he dead yet?"

Gerard sat up straight, and his cheeks colored. "His condition has not changed," he said slowly, then muttered something in Roman.

"What did you say?" Ganelon asked, scowling.

"What will it take to stop this foolish quarrel?" Leonhard said. He stepped out of the tub and reaching for a drying cloth a servant handed him. "Is the massacre of our kin not enough? Even if you disliked them in life, we should mourn their death."

His gaze darted to Ganelon's face and Gerard's. Something burned in both pairs of eyes, something that was extinguished in Leonhard when he saw Alfihar's body. He was tired, tired of death, tired of keeping a truce between two feuding families.

"We have more important concerns," he snapped.

As he donned borrowed clothes in the warming room, Leonhard hoped his brother could keep those two from each other's throats long enough to rejoin the main army. Beringar had seen – what? forty winters? – and had lost much of his hair, but he was a battle-hardened warrior and had the scars to prove it. If Beringar could not manage those two young idiots, no man could.

* * * * *

The smell of bread, roasted goose and pork, soups, stews, and other dishes greeted Gerard, Leonhard, Beringar, and Ganelon when they entered the abbess's dining room. Judith's jewelry glittered in the evening sun as her musicians played zithers and flutes and sang love songs.

"Those clothes suit you, Lord Gerard," Judith said, passing him a cup of wine.

"Thank you," he said. "I like to," he cleared his throat and corrected himself, "would like to buy them from you."

Judith looked at Gerard with wide sky-blue eyes.

"Abbess, I do not know if the bishop has apprised you of how grave my brother's condition is," he said. Determined not to show any sign of weakness, he spoke slowly, careful of his Frankish grammar. "He is dying, and I am his heir. If I am to be a count, I must look like a count. I have some money." He cleared his throat. "As for his care..." He fumbled in his pouch but found only a few coins and the dragon amulet.

"You need not worry about such things," said the abbess, putting a jeweled hand on Gerard's shoulder. "I remember Hruodland from court. What a pity. He was so charming. We shall attend to him. We are sisters of charity."

"I am of noble blood, like you. I need no charity," he replied. He paused. "I would like to give you our hound. He is a fine animal."

"He will have a special place among my dogs," she said. "I have fine kennels and servants to look after him."

"It's fitting the dog stay with Hruodland," Gerard said. "He kept the beasts away from his body."

They all were silent for a few minutes. Then Judith asked, "What will you tell the king about Hruodland?"

Leonhard and Beringar dropped their knives. Gerard dropped a piece of bread, and Ganelon froze in the middle of biting into a drumstick. The four noblemen looked at each other.

"We cannot tell the king that Hruodland lingered so," Leonhard said. "It would be too difficult for him. The deaths of his closest friends and his nephew will be hard enough. And Alda, if she knew he was here, no matter how faint the hope of seeing him alive, she would come here."

"Such a journey would be dangerous," Beringar said, "but that headstrong girl would have little regard for her own safety."

"We shall say Hruodland died in battle — he is dying as a result of the battle," Leonhard said. "And that his soul is commended to heaven — I gave him last rites, and Abbess, you will see that he has a Christian burial."

"Of course," Judith murmured.

Gerard and Beringar nodded numbly.

"So we are to make Hruodland a hero who fell on the battlefield?" Ganelon sneered.

"He is no less a hero for taking his last breath in a hospital," Judith snapped. "He gave his life fighting for the Lord's cause."

"Count Ganelon," Beringar barked, "you were the one who did not want to take Hruodland with us from Roncevaux because it would slow us down. Do you wish to take him with us now?"

Ganelon glared at Beringar.

"I thought so," Beringar continued. "Then we have no choice but to leave him here in the sisters' care. Do you want to tell the king his nephew is at the hospital and incur His Excellence's wrath for leaving Hruodland behind?"

"No," Ganelon muttered. He paused. "It's best to say he died at Roncevaux."

"That is what Hruodland would want," Gerard said. "By the time we meet the king, Hruodland will be dead regardless. There is no need to speak of his suffering in the hospital. He would not want the king to know. Nor would he want Alda to endanger herself."

* * * * *

After matins prayers, Sister Elisabeth knew she would not be able to sleep for a while. With the passing of her womanly courses, sleep did not come easily most nights.

Instead of going to the sisters' dormitories, she walked to the ward for the dying to check on her patients. Although clouds obscured the moonlight, she knew her way. As she approached the hospital, she saw the flicker of the night candles in the windows.

When she entered the ward for the dying, she was surprised to see a man bending over a patient — what was his name? Oh yes, Hruodland of the March of Brittany. The stranger looked up at her. He was a handsome man in his twenties with pale blond hair. In the candlelight, his eyes looked like ice. Elisabeth recognized the blond as one of the abbess's noble guests. She could tell from his build that he was a warrior, but he was not as broad as the other warrior, an older man with thinning hair. He held a wineskin. He seemed startled, then his look became accusing, as if to ask her what she was doing here.

Elisabeth's brows drew together and her mind flooded with questions.

"I am Sister Elisabeth," she said loudly and clearly in Roman. She thrust out her chin and drew herself to her full height, such as it was. "And from whom do I have the pleasure of this visit to the sick at this strange hour?"

He gave her a blank look. She repeated the question in Latin. Still, a blank stare. Elisabeth rubbed her temples. She knew little Frankish. She asked one of the few questions she did know in that language, "What is your name?"

"Beringar of Bonn," the blond answered. He said something else quickly in Frankish.

Now, it was Elisabeth's turn to give the blank stare.

"Wine for him," he said slowly in Frankish, pointing to the inert body on the cot.

Elisabeth smiled. Of course, giving wine to his friend. "Kind act," she replied in Frankish.

She patted the stranger's hand and looked into his icy blue eyes. She wished she knew enough words of Frankish to say something of comfort. She turned her back on the blond to attend to the ward's other patient, a man who had spent most of his life at the abbey.

The warrior must be a dear friend, she thought, *for him to come here in the middle of the night.*

Chapter 19

erard visited the hospital's ward for the dying one last time before the scouting party resumed its journey. He knelt beside the cot and held Hruodland's hand. He admired how the nuns had cleaned up his brother. They had shaved off his beard, closely cut his greasy, tangled locks, and washed what hair was left. Hruodland lay between the sheets, wearing only the medal of Saint Peter. The flesh on his scarred chest had started to waste away.

Hruodland's eyes were closed, and he smelled of urine again. Lay sisters scurried behind Gerard to fill a tub with water.

"I did everything I could," he said. Gerard bowed his head and murmured the Pater Noster. *Please, Jesus, call him home.* He made the sign of the cross. "Go with God."

Releasing Hruodland's hand, Gerard rose to his feet and regarded his brother. Hruodland lay very still, and his breathing was slow and deep.

Sister Elisabeth entered the ward for the dying through a curtained doorway from another ward and approached Gerard. She watched the lay sisters bring water to the tub.

"We will take care of him," she said.

"Your sisters can do better than my servants," he said, reminding himself of why he was leaving Hruodland behind. "He looks more peaceful than I have ever seen him. The orchard cemetery is a better resting place than the wayside."

"His suffering will end soon," Elisabeth said.

Gerard thanked Sister Elisabeth and left the hospital. He took in the sea breezes and wished he could enjoy them. He straightened his shoulders and held up his chin. If he was going to be the count, he had better act like one. He joined the party at the entrance to the abbey and mounted his horse.

"How does your brother fare?" Ganelon asked, again in a tone that eagerly said, "Is he dead yet?"

Gerard narrowed his eyes. "His condition is declining. Sister Elisabeth says he will enter heaven soon."

Ganelon looked down and smiled.

"My brother is dying because of battlefield!" Anger made Gerard's Frankish stilted and his Roman accent heavy. "He was brave man, unlike..."

"Stop it!" Leonhard barked. "Both of you!"

Beringar's sword sang as he withdrew it from its sheath. "You boys can continue your bickering once we join the main army. But there will be no bloodshed here. Act like men!"

Gerard and Ganelon glared at each other like two fighting tomcats that had had water thrown on them. Leonhard and Beringar looked at each other and shook their heads.

As Beringar sheathed his sword, the great gate to the abbey opened and the scouting party rode out. Leonhard and Beringar rode side by side between Ganelon and Gerard. The soldiers and carts of supplies followed. The road through the marsh was solid, and the sky was overcast.

The noblemen rode at a canter at the head of the group. To make haste, they had decided to replenish the supplies to last only until they arrived at the next city, Bordeaux. The lightened load allowed the horses towing the carts to trot.

For a moment, all that could be heard was the rhythm of the horses' hooves, the jostling of the jars, axes, and other items in the carts, and the sea birds' calls.

"You know, Leonhard," Beringar said, "Alda is free to marry again. She is still young and has a generous dowry."

"My brother not even dead yet, and you talk of Alda marrying again?" Gerard asked angrily in stilted Frankish.

Leonhard, Beringar, and Ganelon turned toward him. They all had puzzled looks.

"Hruodland very well could be dead by now," Leonhard said. "He will certainly be dead by the time we tell the king. Or am I mistaken?"

"No mistake," Gerard muttered. "It too soon to be talking remarriage for Alda."

"Too soon?" Ganelon snorted. "You are already assuming the title of count even before your brother is in the grave."

Gerard's lips drew into a taut line.

"You have no claim on Alda," Ganelon added.

"Neither do you," Gerard shot back.

As Ganelon frowned, Gerard smiled, glad to see his barb hit its mark.

If circumstances were different, Gerard thought, *I would ask for her hand myself. She was a good wife with a good dowry. What a shame she could not have children.* He shook his head at the irony. The fact that Alda could not conceive was the very reason he had encouraged Hruodland to stay married to her. Gerard had never wanted to take the vow and join the Church, even if it did almost assure him a bishopric. He had wanted to rule the March of Brittany, and now he had his inheritance. *But I wish it had not happened like this.*

"I could have a claim on Alda," Ganelon mused. "I have been looking for a wife."

"You need Alda's consent," Gerard retorted. "You think she consent to you?"

"Alda's future is our concern, not yours," Leonhard snapped.

* * * * *

After three days of travel, the scouting party met the king's army at Bordeaux. Dark clouds were gathering as Leonhard and the other noblemen were immediately led to Charles. Standing beside the king, a panting messenger was leaning against a sweaty horse. Charles was holding a parchment. As he read it, he scowled, and his face and thick neck turned crimson.

"Damned Saxons!" he spat, crushing the parchment in his hands.

Leonhard felt the blood leave his face.

"The Saxons have broken their oath of loyalty," the king growled. "Widukind, that God-cursed scum, came out of his hole in Nordmannia and roused the tribes. Not only did they destroy the palace in Paderborn; they are burning churches again and advancing toward the Rhine." The king threw the parchment on the ground. "I shall send aid now to drive them off, but come next spring, the heathens will know my full wrath. Bishop Leonhard, what news do you have?"

"Sad news," he answered, looking down. "The rear guard and the baggage train were slaughtered by the Gascons."

"Who survived?" the king asked.

"No one," Leonhard said quietly.

"No one?" the king echoed, his voice cracked. "No one? Not Anselm, not Eggihard, not... Hruodland?"

"They all perished," Leonhard said, as the other three noblemen looked down. All four made the sign of the cross. "And they all received Christian burials." *If Hruodland is not in his grave now, he soon will be.*

"This cannot be. First the Saxons and now this." Kicking at the ground, he screamed a litany of obscenities.

"Someday, we will establish a march between Francia and Hispania," he continued, "but now we must prepare for another war with the Saxons. Filthy heathens." He spat on the ground. "They cannot face us like real men. Instead, they wait until our backs are turned and slaughter women and children and missionaries. They will pay in blood."

* * * * *

An hour before dawn, Gerard was awakened by the sound of many feet running. He rose, threw on a tunic and boots, and left his tent and the whore who had made him forget Roncevaux and feel alive for a few hours. A group had gathered around the tent where Beringar and Leonhard slept. Rubbing his eyes, he walked toward the commotion and peeked through the tent flaps. Leonhard's physician was shaking Beringar's massive shoulders as Leonhard screamed Beringar's name.

Beringar stared at nothing. His broad chest was still.

"What is happening?" Gerard whispered to one of the soldiers in Frankish.

"His servants said he clutched at his chest, yelled 'Mother of God, help me!' and now he is as you see him," the soldier whispered back.

"Beringar! Beringar! Answer me!" Leonhard shouted.

Ganelon stole past Gerard. Standing behind Leonhard, he laid his hand on the bishop's shoulder. "The sight at Roncevaux must have been too much for Beringar's heart."

"This cannot be. This cannot be. He was perfectly well this morning." Leonhard turned away, his shoulders heaving with sobs.

Gerard stuck out his lower lip. Something was amiss about Beringar's death. Although no longer young, Beringar had been strong — in body and mind. He had seen death on the battlefield before. So why should the carnage at Roncevaux be too much to bear?

As Gerard watched Leonhard give last rites to his brother, two other questions repeated themselves in his mind: *Is Hruodland at peace now? What shall I tell Alda?*

* * * * *

Alda stared at Gerard as if he had spoken a foreign tongue beyond her comprehension. She was standing on the church steps on a fall morning, frozen in the light of the slanting sun. The sobs and keening from the inhabitants of Nantes sounded distant to her.

"No," she whispered. "No."

Gerard spoke again. His lips moved, but only a few words reached her ears. Ambush. All slain.

"No," Alda said vehemently, shaking her head as if she could will this away. "No."

The townsfolk's keening grew louder.

"Not Hruodland," Alda moaned, laying her hand over her heart. "I would know."

Gerard reached into a pouch on his belt and pressed an object into her hand. She knew it by touch but had to look at it. She was holding the iron dragon that was supposed to keep Hruodland from harm.

Alda fell silent. She became an empty shell like the ones that washed up on the banks of the Rhine, all the life devoured and only a hollow body remaining.

* * * * *

Grief clouded Alda's vision as she sat by the fire at the wake for Hruodland. She was only vaguely aware of the meal the household had just eaten and songs the musicians were playing.

Prime Mass that morning seemed to be centuries ago. Alda barely remembered Gerard telling her about Roncevaux. She had no memory of ordering the servants to make preparations for the wake.

He's dead. He's dead. He's dead. The thought repeated itself in Alda's mind until the words themselves were no longer words but a rhythm that grew into a fog. And yet she could not believe it. She stared at the dragon she held in her hand.

Veronica pressed the cup of wine into Alda's free hand. "Drink this. Please."

Alda blinked, but she could not see through the fog. Although Veronica sat beside her, her foster sister's voice seemed to come from leagues away. To placate Veronica, Alda took a sip — the wine was tasteless to her — and passed the cup back.

"Alda, I am worried," Veronica said. "You are like a statue. You did not eat at dinner. You barely speak. You do not weep."

"I cannot weep at a wake," Alda said tonelessly.

"At least, I would know you are... well. All you do is stare at that ring that Hruodland gave to you and the amulet. Drink some more wine. Perhaps, it will revive you."

"The dead cannot be revived." Alda caressed her dragon.

"Only a part of your life is gone. You are still alive."

Gerard sat down on the other side of Alda and put his arm around her shoulders. Alda barely felt his hand. "How are you faring?" he asked.

Slowly, Alda met Gerard's gaze. She did not know what to say. The whole world had gone.

She did not resist as he drew her closer and kissed her. Although the taste of wine was strong on his breath, Alda closed her eyes and yielded to him for a moment. Then, she burst into tears.

"What is wrong?" Gerard asked, startled.

"You are not Hruodland," she sobbed, pulling away from him. She dropped the dragon in her lap and buried her face in her hands.

"Of course, I am not Hruodland," he said irritably, dropping his arm from her shoulder.

Alda wiped her tears with her sleeve. "I loved your brother."

"Yes, I know."

"I have lain with no one but him."

"It is no concern of mine," Gerard grumbled.

Alda buried her face in her hands again. Her body was racked with sobs. Veronica pulled Alda into an embrace.

"Hruodland will forgive you for weeping," Veronica whispered.

Sitting nearby, Bishop Guillaume snorted. "She is as faithless to her husband in death as she was when he was alive."

Alda pulled herself from Veronica, sat up straight, and wiped her wet face. Anger burned in the pit of her gut as the word "faithless" pierced through the fog of grief and rang through her mind.

"I never betrayed Hruodland," she snapped. "Never. Call me willful. Call me proud. Call me ugly and ill mannered. But never call me faithless."

* * * * *

Alda lay awake in the solar as the lauds bells rang. She sat up and drew back the bed curtain, admitting the light of the night candle.

"Hruodland," she murmured, staring at the dragon amulet, "you said you would return. This should have kept you from harm. Why did it not protect you?"

She kissed the ring Hruodland had given her. "You cannot be dead. Why can't I feel in my heart that you are dead?"

She lay against the pillow, waiting to awaken from this nightmare.

* * * * *

Alda's empty shell of a body went to prime Mass the next morning and said prayers and then came home to give orders to the servants before it retreated to a bench near the fire with its knees drawn up to its chin.

"I do not care if you are the lord of this castle," she heard Veronica say from afar. "You are not to disturb my sister."

"Veronica," Gerard said sternly, "I have no wish to strike you, but I will not tolerate insolence."

"I am Alda's servant, not yours," she shot back.

"Peace, Veronica," Alda said tonelessly. She put her feet on the floor and turned toward the voices behind her. "What is your will, my lord?"

"You seem ill," Gerard said.

"I am well," Alda said. Her body was well.

"Veronica, find the cupbearer to fetch your lady some wine," Gerard said.

Veronica nodded numbly and left to do as she was bid.

Alda turned toward the flames. She did not need wine. Without Hruodland, she needed a place that was solid under her feet. Drachenhaus.

"By your leave, my lord," Alda said, "I will instruct my servants to prepare for my journey home."

"No. This is your home."

"What did you say?" She squinted.

"This is your home," he repeated.

"Your uncle has made it obvious that I am not welcome here."

"I am welcoming you here," Gerard cried.

"It is not enough," she said softly.

"But I love you," he blurted.

Alda's hands dropped to her side. She stared at him. He seemed perfectly sober. She steadied herself on the bench. Veronica came with a cup full of wine. Taking the cup, Gerard approached Alda, took hold of her wrist, raised her arm, and pushed the cup into her hand.

Alda took a gulp of wine before answering, "Gerard, I love you as I would love my brother."

"That is what I meant."

"Despite my affection for you, I cannot stay here. I bore Hruodland no children, and I am not going to stay in a place where I am called faithless."

"You would have an honored place in my household," he pleaded. "I will protect you."

"I have an honored place at Drachenhaus and the protection of my brother."

His eyes pained, Gerard sat down beside her and held her hand. "Your home will not be the same as when you left it."

"Alfihar has a wife and son, but I am still his sister."

Gerard stared at her. He opened his mouth, but the words seemed to catch in his throat.

"What is it, Gerard?" she asked. "What are you not telling me?"

"Roncevaux... it claimed Alfihar, and the strain was too much for your uncle Beringar."

"No," she whispered, "not them, too." She gasped for air as the horror overwhelmed her. She could feel in her heart that *they* were dead. "Why... why didn't you tell me?"

"I saw your heart break when I told you Hruodland died. I..." His voice trailed off.

"I must go home," Alda said, her voice urgent. "My family needs me."

"But..."

"My mother is old, my nephew is very young, and my sister-by-marriage is not clever."

"But..."

"There is no place for me here," Alda said. "You will marry, and your wife will be mistress of this house. And I cannot stay in a place where the bishops blacken my name."

"What are you speaking of?"

"Bishop Luc lied to my husband a year ago. Don't you remember Hruodland storming into the manor at Rennes, accusing me of adultery?"

"How could I forget? He comes in all enraged and leaves with you. Then you both come back, and it is like normal." Gerard shrugged. "I thought it was a fit of my brother's jealousy that you managed to calm. What does Uncle Luc have to do with it?"

"He is the one who told Hruodland that lie," Alda said emphatically.

"Uncle Luc? Why would he do such a thing?"

"Isn't it obvious? I bore Hruodland no children, and he wanted Hruodland to divorce me and free himself for another marriage."

"If the law of consanguinity did not forbid marriage between spiritual brothers and sisters," Gerard said, "I would ask for your hand. You were a good wife to my brother."

"You are the only one I would have consented to marry." *If only I could bear children*, she mused.

The guilt she felt about Gerard's kiss made her wince. Despite what Gerard had said yesterday, she could not believe Hruodland was dead. She looked toward the entrance to the manor as if Hruodland could come in any minute.

"What I do not understand is why Bishop Guillaume would blacken my name after my husband has died," she said. "It serves no purpose now."

"Perhaps, he feared you would entice me to sin."

All the more reason to leave, Alda thought. "I am returning to my father's house, with or without your leave, as soon as the servants gather my dowry. My mother and nephew need me." *And I need to ask the mountain why it failed me.*

"You have my leave," he murmured. He straightened his spine. "But you should wait until spring. The Saxons were advancing toward the Rhine this summer."

Alda gasped.

"Do not fear for your kin," Gerard said hastily. "Our king sent troops."

"Then our soldiers will have cut the Saxons down by now. I must go home with all haste. Werinbert has seen but three winters and lost his father, and my mother has lost her son."

"There is something else you should know."

"What is it?"

"When I was still with the main army, I saw Ganelon speaking to the prefect of Koblenz."

"Gundrada's father?"

"Ganelon was asking him if Gundrada was interested in marrying again."

"No," Alda cried. "This cannot be. My sister does not even know she is a widow, and her family is thinking of binding her to that beast? I must not tarry." She let go of Gerard's hand and rose from the bench.

"Wait until spring," Gerard pleaded. "Ganelon will be back in Dormagen by then."

"With my sister as his wife — either beaten like a slave or dead. If I stay here and do nothing, her death will be on my soul."

"There is nothing you can do."

Alda started pacing. "I must speak to her, tell her to refuse her consent, even if it means a beating from her father. If I leave now, perhaps it will not be too late."

"But I can protect you here," Gerard protested. "I cannot protect you from Ganelon if he comes to Drachenhaus."

"That is a risk I must take," Alda said.

"I will send some guards along to protect you on your journey," he said, his shoulders slumping.

"I will send them back with the bride price Hruodland gave my family."

"Hruodland's dower is yours. I read his will after prime Mass this morning. He left me his lands and castles. He bequeathed the bride price to you if he were to die childless."

Alda touched her cross. *Mother of God, give me strength,* she prayed. She bit her lip and tried to suppress the tears, but they welled in her eyes. Hruodland had no obligation to provide for her after his death, yet he did anyway. "He did love me," she sobbed.

"Yes," Gerard said gravely, "he did."

Chapter 20

Sister Elisabeth made her rounds in the hospital at the Abbey of Saint Stephen. She enjoyed the late morning autumnal sun and sea breezes after a rare night in which she was able to fall asleep after matins prayers. She watched lay sisters bring oatmeal porridge and wine to the patients so they could break their fast.

"How does Denis fare?" asked one of the lay sisters, who was handing a bowl of porridge to a patient in the ward for women.

Sister Elisabeth stared in the direction of the ward for the dying. "When I saw him before vespers, he had not changed."

The sister shook her head. The patient asked, "Who is Denis?"

Sister Elisabeth cocked her head. How could she describe Denis to someone who hadn't met him? "Denis has lived at this cloister for as long as I or anyone else can remember. He has the mind of a child, yet he was — is — the kindest soul and our most loyal servant. A strange illness has afflicted him." She looked down for a moment. "Denis was helping us carry a large patient to the bath and he cried out, 'My head, my head,' and collapsed. He still breathed, and we tried to revive him. But the left side of his body does not move. He is a patient in the ward for the dying."

Elisabeth bowed her head and swallowed back the frustration from her argument with the abbess over where Denis should be buried. "Thank you for asking about him," she said to the lay sister. "Denis will be pleased."

Elisabeth's wooden shoes crushed the dried tansy, wormwood, and mint on the floor as she walked to the ward for the sick. After making her rounds there, she drew back the curtain and entered the ward for the dying. A new lay sister, young enough to be Elisabeth's granddaughter, dumped a bucket of water into a tub beside Hruodland's cot, picked up the two empty buckets, and left the ward to fetch more from the stream.

Denis was propped up on pillows, and Illuna, one of the experienced lay sisters, was feeding him porridge. Like Hruodland, who was lying on a nearby cot, Denis was naked under the sheet. He wore a wooden cross. It was difficult to guess his age, other than old. His skin was like leather, and his closely cropped hair was white. He had few teeth left. Half of Denis' face smiled when he saw Elisabeth.

Elisabeth's gaze fell on Hruodland. He was young enough to be Denis's son, perhaps even his grandson, yet the prince was more helpless than Denis. For a month, he had not moved at all, as if his rest had been induced by the strongest of sleeping draughts. His eyes were now open but vacant. *A pity,* she thought, *to die so young like this.*

Illuna, whom Elisabeth had known for well over a decade, looked up from Denis and met Elisabeth's gaze. Illuna was starting to show signs of age. Fine lines were etching their way into the tall, thin woman's face, and a few streaks of gray had snuck into her dark hair.

"Have you talked to the abbess about where Denis will be buried?" Illuna asked.

Elisabeth tucked a stray silvered lock of hair behind her ear. She walked to a far corner and gestured for Illuna to follow. Illuna patted Denis' hand, rose, and joined Elisabeth.

"I do not want Denis to hear this," Elisabeth whispered. "Yes, I spoke to the abbess. Again."

"She still will not allow Denis to be buried next to Sister Richarde in the orchard?"

"I told her, 'Richarde was like a mother to Denis. His devotion to this cloister was surpassed only by the full brothers' and sisters' — most of them.' And her reply?" Elisabeth's eyes widened. "Her reply was, 'Denis was a commoner and a dunce and should be buried with the other commoners. The orchard cemetery is only for sisters and brothers of noble blood.'"

Elisabeth looked toward Denis. To her relief, he had fallen asleep.

Illuna muttered, "So that Frankish prince of hers — who never took the vow — will not be buried in the orchard cemetery either?"

"Oh, he is different," Elisabeth said bitterly. "That Frank is a noble who was wounded doing God's work."

"I do not care if he is a prince," Illuna said through clenched teeth. "Denis has been serving Our Lord for all his life — and he is one of us."

Denis stirred and opened his eyes a crack. Illuna and Elisabeth rushed to his side. "I am going to see Auntie Richarde soon," he slurred, his voice barely audible.

"Yes," Sister Elisabeth said to Denis, "you will see Sister Richarde in heaven."

The young lay sister returned with two buckets full of water and emptied them into the tub. Elisabeth looked at Hruodland and pitied him, despite her anger over where Denis would be buried.

Hruodland was curled on his side like a newborn without swaddling. Illuna pulled back the top sheet, releasing the odor of urine on the bottom sheet.

"Should we fetch a lay brother?" the young lay sister asked.

"He has lost so much weight, we can easily carry him to the bath," Illuna answered. "I'll take his shoulders, you take his feet. On the count of three..."

They carried him to a tub of cold water. Elisabeth held him up in the tub while the lay sisters changed his bed sheets.

Elisabeth looked down at her patient. His leg had healed, and the wound on his chest had turned into a scar. But his muscles had given way to bone.

The lay sisters returned to Hruodland and bathed him. They lifted him from the tub, dried him and laid him on the bed.

"He has bedsores," Illuna said. She handed the young lay sister a jar. "Rub them with this poultice of garlic and agrimony."

After they applied the poultice and covered Hruodland with a sheet, the two lay sisters propped him up on pillows. Elisabeth knelt beside Hruodland and trickled wine then milk into his mouth. The terce bell rang. The sisters settled Hruodland on the cot and went to church to chant and pray.

After the prayers, Abbess Judith approached Elisabeth.

What does she want now? Elisabeth thought as the sun made the gems in her niece's headdress, necklace, and girdle sparkle against a gown and veil of blinding white.

"How does your patient fare?" Judith asked.

"Which patient? We have many."

"Hruodland of the March of Brittany."

"The same," Elisabeth replied curtly. "I must attend to *all* my patients." She turned her back on the abbess and walked away.

Elisabeth seethed as she returned to the ward. She found Denis asleep, and Illuna had pulled back Hruodland's sheet to rub more of the poultice on his sores.

Elisabeth's eyes widened at what she saw. Hruodland's right hand was clenched into an obscene gesture.

"Illuna, look!"

The gesture remained for a few minutes. Then the fingers relaxed and the light in his eyes left. The nuns looked at each other and made the sign of the cross.

"W-what does this mean?" Illuna stammered.

"The bishop gave him last rites, but..."

"Could this be the work of a demon?"

"Stay calm," Elisabeth ordered, although her pulse throbbed in her ears. "We cannot help him if we give in to fear. Let us cross his arms in prayer."

Illuna nodded and crossed Hruodland's arms. Elisabeth was ashamed of her anger against the abbess and mouthed a short prayer for forgiveness.

Elisabeth knelt near the bed. "We must pray to Saint Michael the Archangel to watch over his soul."

* * * * *

Elisabeth could not sleep after matins prayers and visited the ward for the dying. Denis lay on his back, eyes open.

"Denis?" she whispered.

Something did not seem right. She kept staring at him and finally realized what it was. He was still, too still. His chest did not rise or fall.

"Denis?" she asked again. She held her hand under his nose, hoping to feel a breath. Nothing.

By the light of a single candle, she closed Denis's eyes, bowed her head, and made the sign of the cross.

"You, of all the souls I have known, deserve to go to heaven," she whispered.

Elisabeth awakened Illuna and the other lay sister who worked in the ward for the dying, two lay brothers, and the priest. While Elisabeth and the lay sisters washed and dressed the body, the lay brothers fetched a coffin. After the priest placed a Host in Denis's mouth, Elisabeth tied his jaw shut with a band of cloth. She made sure his wooden cross lay over his heart before the lay sisters wrapped him in a coarse linen shroud. Elisabeth stayed up all night and prayed, with the help of her lay sisters.

Prime prayers became a funeral Mass. Word of Denis's death must have spread. Tenants stood elbow to elbow in the back with the monks and nuns, almost like the Feast of the Resurrection. Denis was buried in hallowed ground but not the orchard cemetery, where Sister Richarde was. After prayers over the grave, Elisabeth and her lay sisters returned to the hospital.

"You should rest," Illuna said.

Elisabeth shook her head. "The patients need me, need us."

At the hospital, Elisabeth made her rounds, supervising the lay sisters and speaking with the patients. When she came to the ward for the dying, she saw Illuna had laid Hruodland's arms to his side and propped him on pillows. She was kneeling beside him as she trickled beef broth down his throat.

He sputtered.

Elisabeth gasped and put her hand to her mouth. Illuna's eyes grew wide as she pulled the bowl away and kept staring at Hruodland.

A light appeared in his eyes, as if his soul was reconnecting to his body. The eyes looked about the room, the beds, the herbs on the floor, the tub. For the first time, the eyes had an expression: terror.

Illuna backed away from Hruodland. "C-could this be a demon?"

"Fetch the Host," Elisabeth whispered.

The prince's eyes followed Illuna as she ran through the ward, out the door, and toward the church. His eyes met Elisabeth's. They were piercing brown eyes, human, as far as Elisabeth could tell. *But Satan's servants are deceptive.*

Hruodland slurred something in a voice that sounded like the rustle of pages in the wind. Elisabeth was not sure what language he spoke.

"Repeat that," Elisabeth said loudly in Roman, hoping he spoke her language. "I do not understand you."

"Where... am... I?" His voice strained over those whispered, slurred words.

"You are in a hospital of the Abbey of Saint Stephen," she said, clenching her fists, never taking her eyes off him. "And who are you?"

"Hruodland of the March of Brittany," he said, his voice barely above a breath, trying to separate each word.

Illuna rushed back into the room with the Host and gave it to Elisabeth.

Elisabeth drew herself to her full height and stuck out her chin, determined not to show fear. "Open your mouth," she commanded.

He complied. She held up the Host and said, *"Corpus Christi."*

"Amen," he answered.

She placed it on his tongue and watched his face. A demon would resist the presence of Christ, howl in pain. But he ate it.

"Bring some porridge," she told Illuna. Turning toward her patient, she smiled and said, "We are going to feed you, Prince Hruodland."

"Feed me?" He gave Elisabeth a quizzical look and then gazed down at his ribs, his skeletal hands. His nose wrinkled at the smell of his own mess in the bed. His right hand rose briefly and fell.

"What happened to me?" he struggled to rasp.

Illuna returned to the room with porridge and started to feed him as Elisabeth explained, "You were injured at Roncevaux. I was told there was an ambush by the Gascons. They killed every man except you."

"All dead?" His eyes filled with tears. "Alfihar? Anselm? Eggihard?"

"We were told that you are the only survivor," she said gently.

He closed his eyes hard. Tears trickled into the stubble on his chin. "I have no memory of the battle." A stylus scratching on parchment would have been louder. He wept.

"We heard you were quite valiant," Illuna said. "The others were buried in consecrated ground, and so will…"

Elisabeth gave her a look that cut her off.

Tears kept sliding down his face. Elisabeth took two steps to the cot and wiped his tears with the frayed edge of her sleeve. She regretted telling him about Roncevaux. She was afraid his grief would crush what little strength he had.

"Prince Hruodland, your friends are in heaven now," she said. "They are happy that you survived. You will trouble their spirits if you keep weeping."

He calmed himself. He closed his eyes. Elisabeth wiped the last of the tears that hung on his eyelashes. She was worried.

"Surely, someone waits for you at home," she said, trying to give him a reason to hang on.

"Alda," he whispered, opening his eyes.

Illuna resumed feeding him. He stared at his protruding ribs again. Elisabeth realized that he might have never known hunger as the peasants had nor seen his own body waste away.

"You have slept for a month," Elisabeth said. She knew "slept" was not the right word, but she knew no better description. "You have not eaten. Let Illuna finish feeding you. Rest your voice now. It is unaccustomed to speaking."

After he ate, he blushed when Elisabeth told him the sisters would bathe him.

"We have been bathing you for a month," Elisabeth said with a laugh.

Two sisters bathed Hruodland and changed his sheets. Illuna finished dressing his bedsores as the terce bells rang. After prayers, Judith asked about the patient.

"Abbess," Elisabeth replied, "we might be witnessing a miracle."

Chapter 21

Three days later, Alda was ready for her journey. As she made a final check of the carts, Gerard asked: "Are you certain? It is such a long journey. Why not wait until spring?"

"I need my home," she said, "and I need to leave now."

Of all things, this was her one certainty. At Drachenhaus, she would be welcome, and no one would dare to call her faithless or tell lies about her. Alda prayed that she would arrive in time and could convince Gundrada to refuse her consent to nuptials with Ganelon.

"Alda, please," Gerard said, "can you stay until I do marry?"

"The bishops will find someone to tend to affairs of the home," she said. "Have you started negotiations?"

"The count of Orleans has a daughter. My uncles wish for me to marry soon."

"I must not tarry any longer," she said quickly. "God be with you."

"And also with you."

* * * * *

All through the six-week journey to Bonn, questions that had no answers repeated themselves in Alda's mind. Why did God allow the disaster at Roncevaux to happen? Why could she not believe that Hruodland was dead, when she knew Alfihar and Beringar were? What would she say to her mother? What would she say to her little nephew? And how could three women raise this boy and protect a village?

As they arrived at Bonn's city gates, Alda's legs and back ached, and mud splattered her boots and cloak. She smelled of sweat and horses. At the city walls, she sent a servant to let the bishop know of her arrival.

Riding toward the church, Alda remembered the ecstasy of the summer she married Hruodland, the absolute joy of triumph and reunion. She wondered what homecoming had been like this year. Alda stopped her musing when her uncle Leonhard greeted her in the courtyard of his residence. She dismounted.

"Why didn't you send a messenger a few days ago?" he asked, embracing her.

"I do not have enough guards for both myself and a messenger," Alda answered.

"Surely, Gerard could have..." He stopped himself and shook his head. "No, he could not."

"There are not enough young men," Alda finished for him.

"It was a nightmare." He shook his head as if to shake off a memory.

"I know. Every city we visited — even the ones whose young men had not died at Roncevaux — has a sadness about it. No one speaks of it, but the sadness hangs in the air as if a giant fist has crushed their hearts. When I go to Mass, I always have the same question: why did God let this happen?"

"My dear, do not lose faith. I don't know why this happened, but there must be a reason."

"Some of the bishops have said it was to punish us for sin," Alda said. "But what sin? We were fighting for the Lord. If we had won, I would understand the deaths as the price for victory. But nothing was gained from this conquest. Hispania is still under Saracen rule."

"I have asked the same question myself, and I have no answer." Leonhard put his arm around Alda's shoulders. "I am glad to see you. The servants are drawing baths as we speak, and then dinner will be ready."

* * * * *

At dinner, Leonhard told Alda nothing Gerard had not already said, except that Ganelon had been a great help in giving the men a Christian burial. She was surprised by how favorably he spoke of Ganelon, yet she could see that it pained him to see those bodies again in his memory.

"But Alda," he said, "take comfort. You are still young."

"What do you mean?"

"I am seeking another husband for you. With your dowry..."

"Did anyone ask me if I want to marry again?" she snapped.

Veronica looked down and said nothing.

"You do not want to marry again?" asked Leonhard.

"There is a man I might have consented to marry, but a union with him is impossible, even if I could bear children."

"How do you know you cannot produce heirs?"

"Is it not obvious? I bore Hruodland no children," she said flatly.

Leonhard thought for a moment. "How many winters had Hruodland seen when he married you?"

"Two and twenty, maybe three and twenty."

"I do not remember hearing of any bastards."

"No, he had no bastards," she murmured, looking down. "Why does it matter?"

"If he did not have bastards at three and twenty winters, he might not have been able to engender children. That is what I will tell any suitors," he said casually, as if he were talking about the weather.

"I will not have you blacken my husband's name," Alda said as evenly as she could manage.

"My point is that many men would desire to marry you." He patted her hand. "You are still young, you have a generous dowry..."

"No," Alda cut him off. "I do not wish to remarry. I have more than I need. Hruodland left me the bride price in his will. Besides, my mother did not remarry."

"Your mother is no longer young."

"And she would not consent to marrying another." Alda vaguely remembered her mother dictating a message to Beringar

The Cross and the Dragon

and Leonhard that it was Alfihar's will that she remain at Drachenhaus. Not that it was Alfihar's decision.

"She refused to leave you and Alfihar, and like Hruodland, her husband had been generous to her in his will." Leonhard shook his head. "And you are just as stubborn as she is."

"Hruodland was a good husband. He was a gift from God. I do not want to take my chances of being bound to a man who would push me down the stairs over the slightest thing to displease him."

"Are you telling me you will let your gifts go to waste?" Leonhard asked. "We have our choice of men who will make a solid alliance. You need not consider Ganelon of Dormagen, even though he has expressed an interest."

"Gerard told me Ganelon is seeking Gundrada's hand."

"I received a message from your mother yesterday. They are betrothed."

Alda grimaced as her hand flew to her dragon amulet. *Too late. Too late.* A betrothal could not be broken. *Unless...* "Uncle Leonhard, is there anything you can do to stop the nuptials?"

"I will do nothing." Leonhard crossed his arms. "Unlike you, Gundrada is showing some sense and obeying her family."

"But, Uncle, Ganelon is a dangerous man. My sister is in harm's way."

"What concern is it of yours? Gundrada has consented to the marriage. According to your mother, she did so readily."

"Then, she is readily going to her death."

* * * * *

Alda stayed with Leonhard for five days, more than enough time to rest her animals. To her relief, he did not bring up the subject of remarriage again, and he sent a message to Theodelinda at Drachenhaus. After two days of travel, Alda and her followers arrived at the Drachenhaus village at sunset. She heard the call of a horn.

Although she was tired when she arrived, Alda was glad to see the village and castle. It was as if she was seeing an old friend. The castle, made with rocks once drenched in the dragon's blood, was silhouetted against a deep pink sky. Alda looked down at her amulet. *Why did this fail?*

198

Villagers stood and called out words of comfort as Alda passed them. Alda waved and thanked them. She hurried the party along. Sunset was a perfect time for the kobolds and dwarves of the forest to work their mischief. Shadows lengthened and darkened as the party climbed the forest trail up the mountain. Alda saw movement in the underbrush, now bare of leaves. A hare paused in its nighttime foraging, and a stag peered at them among the near dark of the trees. At the top of the mountain, guards pulled the gate open.

Alda was barely inside the courtyard when she heard her mother call her name. Theodelinda ran to her. Alda had just dismounted when her mother held her in a fierce embrace.

"You have come home. I knew you would," Theodelinda sobbed.

Alda realized she, too, was weeping. "I needed to come home. I needed to be with you and Werinbert."

Theodelinda pulled back from Alda. Her face had more wrinkles and the hair that peeked from her veil was streaked with more gray. "Werinbert," Theodelinda called, "come see your Aunt Alda."

Aunt Alda, Alda mused. *No child will ever call me Mother.*

Werinbert looked up from the folds of his nurse's skirt.

"He has Alfihar's eyes," Alda said. "I am glad to see him wearing the dragon amulet."

Gundrada came out of the manor, and Alda immediately sensed the tension between her mother and sister-by-marriage. Gundrada walked toward Alda and stopped halfway.

"Was there no place for you in the March of Brittany?" Gundrada asked.

Alda's hand flew to the dragon amulet. Gundrada might as well have asked why Alda was intruding. Alda seethed.

"This is Alda's home," Theodelinda spat. "She is more a part of this place than you will ever be. The people know it, and the servants know it."

Alda gasped, pitying Gundrada.

"Surely, they would have looked after you," Gundrada said to Alda.

Alda's pity burned to ashes. "I needed to come home. To think."

"About what?" Gundrada said, eyes widening.

Interesting question from one who has never thought about anything. "Hruodland's death, Alfihar's death, Uncle Beringar's death," Alda replied.

"I stayed where I was," Gundrada said with a sniff. "But, of course, I have a son. Too bad God did not bless you with children. But then again, it makes it easier to travel."

"Of course." Alda narrowed her eyes.

"You are free to leave whenever you wish, Gundrada," Theodelinda said. "I can arrange for travel to Koblenz in an instant."

"I shall be traveling to Koblenz two days hence and then to Dormagen."

"So I have heard," said Alda.

"Alfihar's body is still warm, and she will marry another," said Theodelinda.

"Alfihar's body is cold in the ground," Gundrada retorted.

Alda looked down and blushed, remembering how she let Gerard kiss her the night after she was told of Hruodland's death. She cleared her throat. "Gundrada, I understand why you would want to marry another. You are still young. But Ganelon? Why would you consent to marry him? Already one woman in his care has died."

"It was her time." Gundrada shrugged.

"Are you certain of that?"

"Ganelon was so charming, so gentle when he was here," Gundrada replied.

"He was here?" Alda asked.

"He brought us the news," Gundrada said.

"He was well mannered — I will grant you that," Theodelinda grumbled. "But to ask for your hand right after telling you of Alfihar's and Beringar's deaths?"

Alda's jaw dropped.

"He was on his way to finish negotiations with my father in Koblenz. He wanted my consent." Gundrada looked into the distance. "He is perfect. He is pious along with being wealthy and handsome."

Alda shut her eyes tight and clenched her fists and teeth. *Mother of God, what a fool! How can Mother suffer her?*

"Ganelon's piety is twisted. In his piety," Alda snapped, making the word "piety" sound like a jab, "he would have beaten me because I gave bread to one of his servants. If it were not for Hruodland..." Her voice trailed off. She swallowed back the tears at the mention of Hruodland's name.

"You simply angered Ganelon. As long as I am a good wife, he will treat me well. I am so fortunate that he and my father completed negotiations so soon. Ganelon has offered a generous bride price." Gundrada put her hands on her hips. "Alda, your jealousy of my betrothal does not befit a noble."

"Jealous?" Alda laughed bitterly. "My brother was negotiating with Ganelon years ago, and I refused to consent to a union. Why would I be jealous now?"

She shuddered. All sorts of possibilities entered her mind. Beaten to death. Sealed in a barrel and drowned on trumped up charges of witchcraft. Driven to murder.

"And what will become of Werinbert?" Alda asked.

"Werinbert will stay here," Gundrada said. "He is the count now, and I am leaving a portion of my dowry with him. He has good men to advise him, and Ganelon will send a trusted steward to Drachenhaus."

"What a steward?" Werinbert asked his grandmother.

"A man who would take control of *your* land away," Theodelinda spat.

Werinbert burst into tears. "I the count," he bawled. "I the count."

Theodelinda approached her grandson and knelt. He ran into her arms, still crying. "There, there, my little count," she said, stroking his hair. "Of course, you are the count. Your mother's new husband will *not* send a steward, unless he wants his servant to have boiling oil poured upon him at our gate. Come with Grandmother, dearling, and she will give you some cakes."

Taking Werinbert's hand, Theodelinda led him inside. Gundrada opened her mouth as if to say something and then closed it. Alda ordered her own followers to bring her belongings inside.

As Alda passed her sister-by-marriage, Gundrada muttered, "It is not my fault that the Lord has struck you barren."

"I would rather be barren than to have given Ganelon ten sons," Alda hissed.

The Cross and the Dragon

* * * * *

When Alda entered the hall, a fire was blazing in the hearth, and servants were setting up a table and benches. Veronica followed Alda, and Gundrada came in shortly.

Gundrada slapped a manservant. "Why are you setting up the table? I gave no such order."

The servant looked nervously from Gundrada to Alda, bowed his head, and mumbled, "The dowager countess ordered us to do so."

"I am the dowager countess," Gundrada snarled, slapping him again. "I give the orders."

Alda shoved Gundrada. "I have had enough. That servant did not deserve to be slapped."

"Who asked you to come here?" Gundrada snarled.

The servants hurried about their tasks, pretending not to notice.

"I want her here." Theodelinda's voice reverberated through the room. "Alda, Veronica, come to the table. You must be hungry."

* * * * *

The women retired to the solar after the matins bells rang. Alda noticed a new bed and pointed at it.

"It's a gift from Alfihar," Theodelinda said, her eyes filling with tears.

Theodelinda wiped her cheek with her hand and removed her veil. As Alda took off her own circlet and veil, she beheld just how much grayer her mother's hair had become.

The tapestry of Saint Mary cradling her infant Son caught Alda's eye. It was half hidden in candlelight, yet Alda knelt before the tapestry and laid her hand on her cross. *Blessed Mother, why did God show His mercy to Ganelon and not my husband? Why did He allow Hruodland to die without heirs? Please come to my aid.*

As Alda rose, she felt her mother's hand on her shoulder. "I am glad you are home," she said. "Losing Alfihar has been like having my heart torn from my bosom. It is a comfort to have you here."

"Does the pain ever leave?" Alda asked in a small voice.

Werinbert's nurse undressed him and put him in the bed with his mother. The nurse and her own son slept on two cots pushed together. Gundrada drew the bed curtains.

"I will be glad when she leaves," Theodelinda muttered, looking toward the bed where Gundrada lay. "She has been insufferable."

"She is a fool, but she does not deserve her fate," Alda whispered. She found a strange comfort in Gundrada's foolishness. Even if she had arrived in time, it would not have changed anything.

* * * * *

Two days later, Alda and Theodelinda stood in the courtyard and watched Gundrada leave. Gundrada called over her shoulder, "Ganelon and I shall return about two weeks hence."

After the last of the carts departed from the castle, Alda turned to her mother. "Ganelon is coming here?"

"We are simply providing shelter and a chance to rest their animals for three days," she said, waving Alda's words away.

"But his parting words to me were..."

"I will watch him," Theodelinda interrupted, "but with Alfihar and Hruodland dead, how can the old grudges possibly matter? This is an opportunity to make peace between our families, and the fewer enemies Werinbert has, the better."

"But just yesterday, you were angry with Gundrada for marrying Ganelon," Alda protested.

"I am angry with her for consenting to another marriage the same day she learned that Alfihar died, not for marrying Ganelon."

Alda shuddered, already dreading Ganelon's visit. She was certain of one thing: the passage of time and the deaths of her loved ones would scarcely quench Ganelon's thirst for vengeance.

"You do have tasters for Werinbert?" Alda asked, clutching her iron dragon.

"The same ones Alfihar had," Theodelinda said. "Honestly, Alda, do you think Ganelon would try to poison a child?"

"I would put nothing past him."

Chapter 22

ach time Hruodland woke up, he found himself in a strange place, lying on a cot in a room bright with candles and a fire from the hearth, smelling of tansy, mint, and wormwood. In a panic, he called out, "Where am I?" and was surprised by the slur in his own voice.

A nun rushed in with a chamber pot. "For the — I have lost count of how many times. You are at the Abbey of Saint Stephen." He knew she was an Aquitanian named Illuna but did not know how he knew.

And then he remembered. They had told him his rear guard and baggage train had been attacked by the Gascons, and he was the sole survivor. He mourned for the loss of his friends all over again.

Illuna whipped back the sheet and blanket. Hruodland saw that he was naked and stared at his ribs.

"I need help to lift him," Illuna called. "He has gained weight."

Another Aquitanian nun old enough to be his mother — somehow, he knew her name was Elisabeth — helped Illuna lift him onto the chamber pot. He blushed. How did they know he needed to answer the call of nature?

"This is not necessary," he slurred. "I do not need help."

"He says this every time," she said, rolling her eyes.

"Patience, Illuna," Elisabeth said gently. "It is better than having him lie in his own waste. Only two months ago, we thought he was dying."

After Hruodland relieved himself, Illuna took the chamber pot to the privies. Elisabeth covered Hruodland again with the sheet.

Hruodland wanted to get out of bed and get dressed. He wanted to go home to Alda and the March of Brittany. He could not recall ever having an illness, except for a few childhood fevers. He tried to get out of bed and found himself exhausted with the effort of sitting up.

Elisabeth propped him up against pillows and told a young lay sister to fetch some bread and lentils.

"How did you know I was hungry?" Hruodland slurred.

"You are always hungry when you awaken," Elisabeth said.

Hruodland tried to remember the attack. Where did the nuns say it was? Oh yes, Roncevaux. He closed his eyes hard, but he could not remember, no matter how hard he concentrated.

"Why am I speaking like a drunkard?" he asked.

"I do not know."

The lay sister came with a steaming bowl of lentil soup and small loaf of barley bread and gave it to Elisabeth. Sister Illuna returned from the privies. Elisabeth broke the bread and gave it to Hruodland along with the bowl.

"Why are you giving me peasant food?" he asked.

"Because that is what the cooks make in the kitchen," Elisabeth said curtly. "Try to feed yourself."

Hruodland glared at the nuns. Of course, he could feed himself. Did they think he was a cretin? But his arms felt heavy as if someone had tied stones to his wrists. He concentrated on dipping the bread into the bowl and eating it.

"Very good," Elisabeth said as if praising a dog.

"I have seen... twenty-seven winters? I can feed myself."

"You could not do that a month ago," Elisabeth said, her usual patience returning.

"Where is Durendal?"

"Durendal?" Elisabeth asked.

"His sword," Illuna said, tossing her head. "He is always asking about his sword. Again, we have no idea what happened to your sword or your horse or your clothes or your armor or the dragon amulet you keep asking about. Your brother brought you here with nothing but the medal of Saint Peter. We gave you the cross."

"It's my brother's medal," he said, looking down at his bare chest.

"Your brother gave it to you to assure your passage to heaven."

"And where did my brother go?"

"He and the others went to rejoin the king and his army."

"And we have no news of your wife or your brother or the king," Illuna interjected.

"How did you know I was going to ask?" Hruodland said.

"You always ask."

* * * * *

That night, Hruodland woke up screaming. He raised himself on his elbows and looked around but could see nothing but the night candle, a low burning fire, and empty cots. He was sweating, and his pulse was pounding. He fell back on the cot, feeling foolish, and was relieved he was alone. Then, he heard familiar footsteps. Elisabeth drew back the curtain.

"My lord, are you well?" she asked.

"It's nothing but a dream," he slurred.

The candlelight flickered on a lock of her silvered hair and blue eyes. For the first time, he noticed that she looked exhausted. Although the night air was chilly, she was sweating and fanning herself.

"What are you doing here?" he said slowly, trying to control his speech. "It must be after compline."

"It is after matins," she said. "I cannot sleep — again."

"Why do you not take a sleeping draught?"

"Sometimes I do, but it often leaves me with a pain in my head at prime Mass. What is this dream you speak of?"

"It is nothing. Strange, though. I was dreaming about an old adversary. I have never been afraid of him, and I do not understand why I would fear him now."

"Perhaps the dream is a message," she prompted. "Please tell me. Anything that troubles your soul concerns me."

"You are like my wife," he said.

"Is she old enough to be your mother as well?" Elisabeth raised her silvered eyebrows.

"No, she is young, almost twenty winters, I think. She is as insistent as you are. Why is she not here?" The thought had suddenly occurred to him. He had been here for several weeks, and there had been no word from her.

"I do not know. Perhaps she waits for you at home."

"That is unlike her," Hruodland said, propping himself up on his elbows. "She is the kind of woman who would come here and pray over my body, even during my long sleep."

"Perhaps, she prays for you at church," Elisabeth said, placing pillows behind him.

Remembering that she had prayed for his father, he could see Alda kneeling before a wooden statue of the Blessed Mother in Nantes or praying to Saint Melaine's relics in Rennes. Then, his brow furrowed.

"She would send a message. I know she would." He sank against the pillows. "What shall I tell her about the dragon?"

"Is that the amulet you keep asking about?" Elisabeth adjusted Hruodland's blanket.

"Yes. She will be most vexed. She gave it to me for protection. It was her most precious possession, a gift from her father, and I lost it. I do not remember how. It was an iron amulet with a stone from Drachenfels Mountain."

Elisabeth put her hand to her mouth.

"Do you know something?" Hruodland asked.

"I cannot believe I had forgotten. Your brother, he was holding the dragon amulet when he brought you here."

"Why would he do that?" he slurred.

"I did not ask. I did not know whose amulet it was."

"He would have given it to her." He frowned. "Why no word from her?"

"I do not know. Now tell me about your dream."

Hruodland sank against the pillows. Already, he was tired. Why did little tasks like sitting up and trying to speak clearly exhaust him? He knew Elisabeth would not be satisfied until he told her, even as his words became more slurred.

"I was lying in the dust," he began, "unable to move, unable to raise my littlest finger, and my blood enemy was standing over me. He bent over. I saw a flash and then felt a sharp pain in my chest."

Elisabeth flinched.

"That is not the worst of it," Hruodland said.

"It isn't?" Elisabeth's eyes widened. She removed her cloak and fanned herself.

"The next thing I remember is lying in the dark, still unable to move. Ganelon — that is my blood enemy's name — was again standing over me, and he forced wine so strong it burned down my throat. Then his face was close to mine." Hruodland translated the Frankish to Roman. "He said, 'I do not know why you keep living, but God has given me the opportunity to have my vengeance and smite you. There is enough hemlock in this wine to finish you off. The bishop gave you last rites, but I know where your soul is going. You are going to hell. You stole her from me and never did penance.'"

"Her?" Elisabeth asked.

"It's a long tale. Suffice it to say he was suitor for my wife's hand, but she never would have consented to marry him."

"Is that why you are blood enemies?"

"No. My father is responsible for that. That, too, is a long tale." His eyes fluttered shut.

"Is that all of your dream?" Elisabeth asked.

Hruodland opened his eyes, although his eyelids felt heavy. "The last thing he said in the dream was, 'When you arrive in hell, tell the Devil that Ganelon of Dormagen sent you.'"

Elisabeth gasped. "What a twisted mind!"

"Yes," he murmured, "twisted. That is why my wife refused him."

Hruodland yawned and closed his eyes. Elisabeth moved the pillows so that he lay on the bed and pulled the sheets over Hruodland's chest.

"It appears she made the right choice," Elisabeth said. "As for your dream... Are you still awake?"

Hruodland nodded.

"As for your dream," she continued, "perhaps it is a message that your blood enemy is not as harmless as you think."

Hruodland nodded, too tired to talk or even open his eyes again. If he but had the strength, he would have said he never called Ganelon harmless, just too cowardly to fight anyone who could fight back.

* * * * *

Hruodland was awakened by the prime bells. As gray light seeped through the crack between the shutters, he realized he was in the hospital of the Abbey of Saint Stephen. He had to answer the call of nature and struggled to sit up. He managed to put his feet on the floor and sit on the edge of the cot.

But he could not stand. He was too weak. He collapsed on the cot, knowing the sisters would find him like this. *Why can't I will my body to do what I want?* he wondered, unable to lift his feet and put them back on the cot. *Is this going to be my life?*

Hruodland did not know how long he had lain on the bed when he saw Sister Illuna enter the room. He called out to her, expecting her to rebuke him the way she always did.

"Do you think you can make it to the privies?" she asked. Surprisingly, there was no irritation in her voice this time.

"No," he mumbled.

She grabbed a chamber pot, ran to him, and held it as he relieved himself. She helped him lie down on the cot and took the chamber pot to the privies.

As Hruodland waited for Illuna, Sister Elisabeth entered through the curtained doorway. She blinked back her surprise.

"You are awake," she said.

Hruodland nodded, too weary to speak. He looked at Sister Elisabeth. She had dark circles under her eyes. She should be lying in the cot, not him. All he ever did was sleep. So why was he so tired and weak all the time? He had to speak, even if it took all of his strength.

"Why... is... God doing this to me?" he asked, laboring over each word.

Elisabeth stared at him, mouth open. Did she not understand him? He thought his words were mostly clear.

Sister Illuna entered the ward through the door to the outside. "Sister Elisabeth," she cried, putting the empty chamber pot back in its place. "Prince Hruodland, you should tell her."

"Tell her what?" he struggled to say.

"Sister Elisabeth, his feet were on the floor when I came in!" Illuna said.

"How wonderful! Praise God!" Sister Elisabeth beamed, like a mother proud of her baby taking his first step.

They were happy because he could put his feet on the floor? "I wish I were dead," he muttered.

Sister Elisabeth's smile turned into a scowl. "You will say no such thing. God gave you your life back. Do not belittle His gift."

"But," he said, propping himself on his elbows, "I am so weak."

"You are gaining strength. Two months ago, you could not sit up." Elisabeth set pillows behind him.

"Is this going to be my life?" he slurred out. "I cannot walk. My speech is like a drunkard's."

"I do not know what will come to pass," she said, using the tone of a mother to her son. "In all my years in the hospital, I have never seen anything like this. We must take hope wherever we can find it. Do you understand?"

Hruodland swallowed and nodded.

"Illuna, fetch some porridge for Hruodland." Elisabeth met Hruodland's gaze. "Now, Hruodland, after you break your fast, the lay sisters will help you bathe and shave."

"Must they?"

"It is like bathing a child."

Hruodland blushed. "It is humiliating, no matter what you say."

"I would have had them wait a couple of days, but the abbess insisted on visiting you today. Apparently, she is an old friend from the court."

"Who is she?" he asked, sitting up from the pillows.

"Judith of Bordeaux, my brother's daughter."

Hruodland rolled his eyes and sank back into the pillows.

"Why did you just give me that look?"

"It is not you," he struggled to say without slurring. "You have been kind. All the sisters have been kind, even Sister Illuna."

"She will be glad to hear that. But why that look at the mention of Judith's name?"

Hruodland gave Sister Elisabeth a pleading look. He remembered his last encounter with Judith a few summers ago at Aachen and Alda's outburst — a threat to spread rumors if Judith did not leave Hruodland alone. Hruodland did not dislike Judith, but he did not like her much, either. She had satisfied his lust once — well, a few times, but there had been no affection between them. It would take so much effort to explain this situation without insult in normal circumstances, and he did not have the strength.

"Why that look?" Elisabeth asked.

"I do not want her to see me like this," he said, too tired not to slur his words. That, too, was true. He hated the sight of his own body wasted away.

"It is your pride." Elisabeth patted his hand.

Hruodland nodded. *Let her think it is pride.*

"I tried to tell her. I tried to tell her you had lost much flesh. I tried to tell her it was a great effort for you to speak." She threw up her hands. "All for naught. I might as well have been speaking to the wall. It was all I could do to have her visit after you were bathed."

She sank down and sat on the cot beside Hruodland. She rested her elbow on her knee and propped her head against her hand.

"You should rest," he murmured.

"I wish I could." Elisabeth rose as Sister Illuna entered, carrying bean porridge. "I shall return when Judith comes to visit."

"Thank you," Hruodland slurred.

After Hruodland ate his porridge, the sisters filled the tub, and Illuna fetched a lay brother. Hruodland sat up and managed to put his feet on the floor. He would have fallen back on the cot, if Sister Illuna and the lay brother, a burly fellow, had not held him up.

"Lean on us, Prince Hruodland," she said. "On the count of three..."

He concentrated on standing as the sister and brother helped him. He looked down. He was standing! He was actually standing!

"Good," Illuna said.

"I cannot stand on my own," he said, terrified.

"Just a few steps," Illuna coaxed.

He concentrated. Lift left foot. Move forward. Lift right foot. Move forward.

"Big step now," Illuna said.

He stepped into the tub, which smelled of lavender and mint. Illuna and the lay brother gently lowered him. He was exhausted, and his legs felt like water, and the bed seemed impossibly far away. His shoulders sank.

"Why are you troubled?" Sister Illuna asked. "That was wonderful."

"It was all I could do," he said, splashing his face and chest.

"You are doing more than you could do a month ago," she replied. "You could not even wash yourself a month ago."

He could barely wash himself now. As he sat in the tub, Illuna gave him a comb. He made a few swipes through his short, dark hair, and then the comb slipped from his fingers. He could do no more.

"You have many scars," the lay brother said. "How many battles have you seen?"

"More than I can count," he replied, flattered and then saddened because he could not even hold a sword now.

"You have not asked me where you are," Illuna said as she finished combing his hair.

"I am in the Abbey of Saint Stephen," he replied.

Illuna dropped the comb. "Saints be praised," she said as she retrieved it.

After Illuna and the lay brother managed to dry him and return him to the bed, Hruodland fell into a doze, wondering why it exhausted him to do such simple tasks.

* * * * *

Hruodland awoke to the sound of voices. His limbs, even his eyelids, felt too heavy to move.

"What have you done to him?" he heard Judith's outraged voice say.

"I told you," Sister Elisabeth said, a tremor in her voice, "he lost weight while he was sleeping. A sleeping man cannot eat."

"But he used to be so muscular," Judith retorted. "And what have you done to his hair?"

"He was barely alive two months ago, and you are asking me about his hair?" Elisabeth's voice became angrier and louder. "It will grow back."

Hruodland opened his eyes a crack. Judith stood before him in all her glory. Under a wool cloak, an embroidered woolen gown flattered a plump figure. Convent life had not caused her to abstain from jewels — headdress, girdle, rings, necklaces.

"Hruodland, you are awake," Judith said, smiling.

God's wounds! Hruodland thought. *I should have pretended to be asleep.*

Hruodland opened his eyes all the way and struggled to prop himself on his elbows. Sister Elisabeth rushed toward him with pillows and helped him settle against them. She adjusted the sheet and blankets so that they hid most of his body.

"How are you feeling?" Judith asked.

Hruodland closed his eyes. He did not know how to answer. He felt weak, too tired to speak. But he had to try.

"The sisters have been kind," he said, concentrating on his speech.

"Have they treated you well?" Judith asked in Frankish.

A puzzled look on his face, Hruodland nodded. Why was she speaking Frankish? The sisters here spoke Aquitanian-accented Roman.

"You can tell me the truth," she said in Frankish. "They do not understand Frankish."

"It is true," he said in Frankish, sinking into the pillows. Shocked by her distrust in her own sisters, he wished he could sit upright and tell her more, but he was exhausted.

Judith covered her mouth and ran out of the ward.

"What did you tell her?" Elisabeth asked in Roman, her voice cross.

"I said you treated me well," he slurred. "I swear by the saints."

"I wonder what upset her," Elisabeth said half to herself.

"Sister," Hruodland said, again struggling with his speech, "could you ask her to send a message to my wife?"

"Yes, I will ask her. You wouldn't know," she muttered.

"Would not know what?" Hruodland asked.

"Suffice it to say that I am not the abbess's favorite sister, even though we are kin," she said with a grim smile.

"I guessed as much." Hruodland shrugged. "If I could, I would dress and walk out there..."

"I said I would ask," she said irritably. "What should the message to your wife say?"

"'Come here. Your husband needs you.'"

* * * * *

Elisabeth leveled a gaze at the door, drew herself to her full height, and squared her shoulders. Gritting her teeth, she suspected Hruodland still did not understand how she loathed speaking to her niece about anything. She was still seething about the location of Denis's grave.

Elisabeth strode out the door in search of the abbess. After asking a few lay sisters and servants, she found the abbess in her residence, slumped by the hearth. Elisabeth fought back her anger and sat down beside Judith.

"What has caused you such distress?" Elisabeth asked as gently as she could manage.

Judith looked up, her eyes red and swollen. "You could never understand."

"What could I not understand?" Elisabeth asked, barely keeping her anger in check.

"You have been in the convent since you were a child. You did not see Hruodland in his prime. He was so muscular, so handsome, and now he is..." Her lower lip trembled before she could finish the sentence.

"Just because I have been in a convent all my life does not mean I cannot appreciate a man's beauty," Elisabeth snapped. "But you are right about one thing. I have only known him since his brother brought him here, when his eyes were open but saw nothing. To me, he looks much better."

"What?"

"He is getting flesh back on his bones, his color is returning, and he no longer stares at nothing. Sister Illuna told me he took a few steps today."

Elisabeth felt hot, unbearably hot. She rose and took a step away from the fire. She threw back her veil, tugged at her habit, and fanned herself. "I do not care if the Lord never gives him back his looks. He has already given back Prince Hruodland's life."

"What kind of a life is it?" Tears streamed on Judith's cheeks.

"I do not know what will come to pass. But I know how you can help him."

Judith looked up and wiped her face with her hands. "How?"

"You can send a message to his wife and tell her that her husband wants her to come here. Surely, she would be eager for news of him."

"Invite her to my abbey?" Judith asked indignantly.

"I thought you said Hruodland is a friend."

"Hruodland is. His wife is not."

"Then I am sure Hruodland will be all the more grateful when you do invite her."

"What makes you think I am going to invite that little shrew here?" Judith stood up, her frown deepening, all vestiges of tears dry.

Elisabeth swallowed back her frustration. She thought a message to Hruodland's wife would be a simple favor, a piece of parchment or a wax tablet to be sent with the next merchant. Why could nothing be easy with Judith? She suppressed the urge to scream, *Think of someone other than yourself.* Instead, she said, "Because such an invitation would help Prince Hruodland."

"It would help him to hear I sent a message to his wife?"

"Yes."

"Very well. Tell him I will send a message."

"Thank you, Abbess." Elisabeth bowed.

As her anger seeped out, Elisabeth felt the weight of her nights without sleep. Leaving the abbess's residence, she thought about getting some rest, but she had one more thing to do. She pulled her veil back over her head and strode to the ward for the dying. To her surprise, Hruodland was awake, propped on pillows.

"The abbess will do as you ask," Elisabeth said.

The smile on Hruodland's face made Elisabeth glad she had spoken to the abbess. It was the happiest she had seen him. But she wondered how much to reveal to Hruodland.

"Did you know your wife and the abbess are acquainted with each other?" she asked.

"You put it delicately," Hruodland said with a laugh. "It all seems so silly now. Surely, Judith realizes my wife was barely out of girlhood at the time. She doesn't harbor any ill will, does she?"

Elisabeth hesitated for a moment, pondering what to say. "The abbess wishes to help you."

"Do you think my wife will receive the message in time to travel here? Winter will come soon, and travel will be too dangerous."

Elisabeth pulled her cloak closer to her. Now that the spell of heat had passed, she was cold again. The trees were bare, and the days had become shorter.

"I do not know when the message will reach her," she answered. "She will receive it in time to travel this spring."

Hruodland nodded and smiled. "She will come. It is simply a matter of when."

* * * * *

In the middle of the night, Hruodland woke up screaming again. He looked about in the light of the night candle and small fire in the hearth. He saw nothing but cots — no Ganelon, no knife, no wine. Although he shivered in the chill of late autumn, he was sweating. He felt his chest, which was heaving, and found the medal of Saint Peter, the wooden cross, and the scars.

I am still alive. Why do I keep having this dream of Ganelon?

Hruodland searched his memories. Ganelon would never have challenged him to a duel. He never fought any worthy opponent. On the battlefield, Ganelon always sought out the youth who was seeing his first battle and shaking so hard he could barely hold his sword. Off the battlefield, Ganelon always abused those who could not fight back.

"Alda," Hruodland whispered.

A panic seized him. That was the meaning of the dream! Ganelon was going to fulfill his vow of vengeance on Alda while Hruodland was absent.

Hruodland had to leave. Now. While there was still time to travel home. He had to protect Alda.

He sat up, put his feet on the floor and clenched his fists. *Stand!* he commanded his body. *Stand!*

He rose slowly, unsteadily, to his feet. *Walk! Walk!* He lifted one foot, wobbled, and then collapsed. He lay beside the cot, weeping. He could not protect Alda. He could not even take a step on his own. A husband was supposed to protect his wife, and he had failed.

"Alda, Alda," he cried out. "Will you ever forgive me?"

Chapter 23

Alda felt the weight of her grief lighten a little as she settled into life at Drachenhaus. Like her mother, she often gave cakes to Werinbert. She liked the way his eyes lit at the mention of the treat. And he was curious, like all children who had seen three winters. Alda loved his curiosity. He wanted to know about everything.

"Why sun rise, Auntie?" he asked one morning as they walked to prime Mass.

"Because God makes it rise," Alda answered.

"Why He make it rise?"

"Because it is His will."

"Why it His will?"

Alda laughed and bent to kiss her nephew's forehead. "Because it is. Come, child," she said, holding his hand, "let us not tarry and be late for Mass."

Even with Werinbert to distract her, a fear gnawed at a corner of Alda's mind: Ganelon was coming to Drachenhaus.

* * * * *

Two weeks after Gundrada had left for Koblenz, Alda heard the call of the horn from the tower and felt a chill run through her body, despite her marten-fur-lined wool cloak. *He is here. Ganelon is here.* She pulled out her eating knife, sharpened just this morning, and sheathed it again.

Alda and Theodelinda entered the courtyard just as Ganelon and Gundrada came through the castle gates with their guards and a few servants. Alda noticed Ganelon's guards were well fed but his servants were as thin as ever. The Drachenhaus nurse brought Werinbert and his foster brother to the courtyard.

"Mother!" Werinbert cried. He let go of his nurse's hand and ran to her.

Gundrada cast a fearful look at Ganelon, dismounted, and bent to embrace her son. She tousled his hair and cooed, "My child, my sweet, sweet child. How I missed you!"

Ganelon glowered at them. Alda swallowed as her hand flew to her dragon.

"Welcome to Drachenhaus," Theodelinda called.

Ganelon dismounted. His expression was now pleasant — so much of a change from a moment ago that Alda wondered if his look of anger had been her fancy. Holding her son's hand, Gundrada followed Ganelon, her shoulders hunched and her eyes downcast, like a dog that had just been beaten.

"Countess," Ganelon said, taking Theodelinda's hand, "I thank you for your hospitality. Leave my wife's things in the hall instead of the solar," he told the servants. "If it is not too much trouble, Countess. Since we shall stay only three days, it would be easier on the servants."

Alda was so surprised at his concern for the servants' welfare that she barely noticed Gundrada look up at her husband before looking down again.

"It's no trouble," Theodelinda replied. "But where are your carts?"

"I sent the carts ahead and decided to use packhorses." He looked at the cloudy sky. "Winter is fast approaching, and we must make haste. Unfortunately, our stay will be brief, and the carts would be nothing but a burden. We came with a few servants and guards and some clothes."

"Well, the baths are ready," Theodelinda said. "I told the servants to put extra logs on the fires in the warming rooms."

"Lady Alda," Ganelon said warmly, "what a pleasant surprise to see you again."

Alda blinked back her astonishment. Was this the same Ganelon who had threatened to make her virtuous with his fists?

"It's a pleasure to see you as well," she stammered.

* * * * *

As the women undressed before a roaring fire in the warming room on their side of the bathhouse, Alda noticed Gundrada still had a plump figure but she had bruises on her thighs and arms.

"It's nothing but a fall," Gundrada snapped.

"Gundrada, I can send a message to your father to come to your aid," Alda said, careful to keep her voice low. She heard Werinbert's nurse laugh as he and his foster brother splashed in a tub in the room with the baths.

"I will not bring dishonor on my family," she hissed. "Maybe you care nothing for causing a feud..."

"I caused no feud," Alda cried. Lowering her voice, she added. "It existed before I was born. Gundrada, if he is beating you after but two weeks..."

"It is not your concern," she insisted, stiffening.

Alda shook her head but held her tongue. Nothing she could say could convince Gundrada that no wife could placate this beast.

* * * * *

To Alda's surprise, the next three days were pleasant. Although his wife and servants seemed to fear him, Ganelon was such a gracious guest that Alda barely recognized him.

But on the first night, one thing disturbed Alda. After Werinbert was sent to the solar, Ganelon took his wife's hand, and they withdrew to the darkness of the hall. Alda guessed they were going to lie on a couple of pallets. Alda's conversation with her mother was interrupted by the sound of a hard slap.

"You care more for Alfihar's son than your husband," Ganelon snarled.

"My lord, he is my son," Gundrada whimpered.

"You are my wife. I will show you who is important."

"My lord, no," Gundrada pleaded, "you are hurting me."

Then, Gundrada was too quiet. She said nothing, no moans, no sighs. Alda grimaced as she heard Ganelon grunt.

"This is not our concern," Theodelinda whispered. "Let us retire."

As the women climbed the stairs to the solar, Alda could not help but pity Gundrada.

* * * * *

On the night before Ganelon and Gundrada were to depart, Theodelinda, Alda, and Veronica retired to the solar as usual, where Werinbert already slept. As usual, Gundrada remained in the hall below with her husband.

Alda and Veronica undressed and climbed into the new bed, where they would use each other's warmth to ward off the chill of the near-winter air. The flame of a thick night candle cast a flickering light on the maids sleeping in the solar. Alda grasped the edge of the bed curtains and watched her mother climb into the bed where Werinbert slept.

Alda closed her own bed curtains and sank in the warm darkness of the wool blankets and rabbit pelts. Tomorrow, Ganelon would leave, and she would no longer have to trouble herself about him. Although Veronica squirmed restlessly beside her, Alda laid her hand on her cross and dragon and fell asleep.

Alda awoke to a draft of freezing air. Lying on her back, her eyes still closed, she groped at Veronica's side of the bed. Empty. It was unlike Veronica to be careless and leave the bed curtains open. More asleep than awake, Alda moved to close the curtains.

A hand clamped over her mouth. Alda opened her eyes as her arms and legs flailed. Her scream choked in her throat. *Ganelon!*

He bent over her like a spider drinking blood from a moth. Raising her hands again, she felt something cold and hard and moist against her throat.

"Be still," Ganelon hissed. "Utter one word or make one move, and I will slit your throat."

Alda's arms fell to her side. As Ganelon withdrew his hand from her mouth, she could hear her heart pounding in her ears. *What has he done to Werinbert? To Mother? To Veronica?*

"I am your lord now," he taunted, his face close to hers.

Alda tried to still her trembling hands. *Show no fear*, she told herself. She looked straight into Ganelon's cold, cold eyes, icy and full of malice, like a fiend's.

"Push back the blankets slowly, very slowly," he said, his voice low. "Any false move, and you will share the fate of the guard at the foot of the stairs."

Alda fought back a wave of nausea. If she could but scream, a host of servants and guards would come to her aid. She could not even call to the maids who were sleeping nearby. She could do nothing, nothing, except obey his command, his hateful, hateful command. Still, she hesitated, trying to find some way to avoid...

"Do as I tell you," Ganelon growled, pressing the knife closer to her throat.

Alda pushed back the blankets and furs and stopped when they reached her waist.

"Push them down all the way," Ganelon commanded. "I want to see all of you. You are going to do my will now, just like you should have when we first met."

Alda looked for a weapon. *My knife!* It was on a small table just out of reach.

"What are you looking at?" Ganelon's eyes narrowed like a snake ready to strike.

"Nothing," Alda whimpered.

But Ganelon's eyes followed her gaze and fell on the knife. He chuckled. "You think you could stop me with that?" he sneered.

Never taking his eyes off Alda, he reached with his free hand and silently moved the knife into the shadows. "Now do my bidding," he barked. "Remove the blankets."

With the edge of his knife against her throat, Alda pushed the blankets aside. *Mother of God, help me!*

With his free hand, Ganelon tore off her cross and dragon and threw them. Alda closed her eyes as she heard them thunk against the floor. Now she had nothing, nothing to protect her.

"Where is the other who shares this bed?" he asked.

"No one shares this bed," Alda said, her voice barely above a whisper.

Despite herself, tears filled Alda's eyes. Ganelon's lips curved into a smile.

"This is a sin, Ganelon," she gasped.

"Silence," he snarled. "Or your next words will be your last. God has granted me an opportunity for vengeance, and I am taking what is rightfully mine."

Blood drained from Alda's face as Ganelon shifted his weight to his free hand and climbed on top of her, his knife still close to her throat. Feeling his bare thighs straddle her hips, she flinched. His weight smothered her.

"I will fill you with my seed," he jeered, "and you will bear Drachenhaus's true heir."

The spider now had the moth exactly where he wanted her. The moth was paralyzed and trapped, and all the spider had to do now was drink his fill.

Suddenly, several men's hands grabbed Ganelon, and Alda felt his weight jerked from her body. She sat up, grabbing a blanket to cover herself, and blinked back the blur of tears. Guards surrounded Ganelon, their weapons drawn. Theodelinda, wrapped in a bear pelt, stood in the guards' midst.

"Take him to a cell," Theodelinda commanded the guards. "He will be punished at dawn and pay dearly. I want all to see what happens to those who betray Drachenhaus." Theodelinda growled in Ganelon's ear, "You will be deprived of your manhood, your lying tongue, and your eyes."

Ganelon broke from the guards, his tunic and cloak tearing. He raced for the window, threw open the thick shutters, and leapt. The guards dropped the rags in their hands and ran downstairs. The women rushed to the window. They heard something snap. Ganelon screamed, let out a stream of obscenities, and called to his guards. Alda heard a tramp of feet and horses' hooves leaving the courtyard.

"That cur!" Theodelinda cried. "He had his guards in the courtyard. He had planned to leave in the middle of the night after..." She grabbed Alda and held her in a fierce embrace. Alda felt her mother tremble with fury. "How could I be so foolish to endanger you? When I heard a man's voice in the solar, I wanted to scream and choke him with my bare hands, but reason told me to be quiet and summon the guards."

Alda heard the beat of horses' hooves in the courtyard and knew Ganelon and his followers were descending the mountain and escaping justice.

"Mother," Alda said, still shaking, "if you had not summoned the guards, he would have succeeded. No woman could have fought him off."

Alda heard a moan behind her and turned toward the sound. Veronica stood near the top of the stairway. "I should have never left your side," she wailed. "How will you ever forgive me? If I was not restless and wandering in the hall..."

"He would have killed you," Alda said softly.

Alda heard Werinbert sleepily call for his grandmother.

"Saints be praised," Alda sighed, "he is unharmed. Mother, you should attend to him."

As Theodelinda soothed her grandson, Alda shivered as the cold draft blew against her bare feet. Her knees felt like water. She gathered her cross and dragon off the floor and held them to her heart.

"Hush, my dearling," her mother said. "Grandmother is here. That wicked man is gone now."

"Why he here?"

"He is not here. He will never return. We will kill him if he does."

"Why?" the boy asked.

Alda listened as she stood near the candle and fumbled to string her cross and dragon on a ribbon and tie it.

"Because he is wicked," Theodelinda said.

"Why he wicked?"

Alda slipped her cross and dragon over her head and then opened a chest. She let her blanket fall and pulled on her shift, wondering what her mother was going to tell Werinbert. Veronica stood and unfastened her cloak, which had covered her shift, and started to dress.

"He does wicked things," Theodelinda replied.

"Why?"

"I do not know," she said softly.

"Why, Grandmother?" Werinbert's voice revealed his frustration. "Why he do wicked thing?"

"He is swayed by the Devil," Theodelinda answered.

"Why?"

"My dearling, that I shall never know."

"Why do you not know?"

"Oh, child."

"Where Mother?"

Theodelinda was silent.

"Where Mother?" the boy repeated.

"I do not know," Theodelinda finally said. "Let us pray to the Mother of God to protect her and our family. You remember how it goes? *Ave Maria...*"

"...*gratia plena*," Alda murmured.

* * * * *

After Werinbert finally fell back to sleep, Alda, Theodelinda, and Veronica finished dressing and descended the stairs to the hall. Alda shuddered as she passed the dead guard at the foot of the stairs. Ganelon had stabbed him in the back.

Theodelinda ordered the servants to fetch the priest, fetch a coffin for the man, and throw another log on the fire. The women stared into the flames unable to say anything more.

Moments later, the captain of the guard approached Theodelinda, bowed, and said, "I regret to report that the count of Dormagen has escaped our justice."

Theodelinda nodded for him to continue.

"By the time we arrived at the courtyard," the guard said clenching his fists, "the gate was already open, and the guard at the gate was dead."

"How did he die?" Alda asked, wincing.

"Some worm slashed his throat," the captain growled. "We searched the grounds and found that all of Count Ganelon's possessions were gone, even his packhorses."

Theodelinda buried her face in her hands. "How could I have been so foolish?"

Although Alda's hands still trembled, she hated to see her mother racked with guilt. She touched Theodelinda's shoulder.

"Countess, he had been long in planning this," Veronica said. "Think about it. He was charming to you and Alda, but not his new wife. He had Gundrada's things placed in the hall and made it easier for his servants to leave in haste and do it quietly. He had his guards already in the courtyard when he came to the solar."

"Why did I not see this?" Theodelinda's eyes were filled with tears. "If Beringar were still alive, I would ask him to challenge Ganelon to a duel and avenge us, but Beringar's son is so young and inexperienced with the sword..." Her voice trailed off.

"I know, Mother." Alda studied her hands. "Ganelon would kill him. I have no desire to see more death among our kin."

"Perhaps, you can tell the king," Veronica said.

"Knowing Ganelon and his twisted piety, he would tell the king I tempted him," Alda said bitterly.

"That is the most ridiculous thing," Veronica spat.

"But would the king think so?" Alda asked. "Ganelon's fool of a wife would probably extol his virtues and fair looks and say I led him astray."

"The king might believe you," Veronica said. "Neither he nor the queen like Ganelon."

"Even with our allies at court," Theodelinda said, slumping, "the king needs his nobles to see him as a fair judge. To settle the matter, he would order a duel, and we already know the outcome of that."

"I was so worried about you and Werinbert, I thought he had..." Alda paused.

"You thought he had what?" Theodelinda asked.

"I thought he had killed you both, but... I think Werinbert is still alive because I am still alive."

"If Werinbert dies," Theodelinda whispered, "you would inherit Drachenhaus."

"Ganelon could not abide that. If Ganelon and I had wed and Alfihar died childless..."

"He would have been master of Drachenhaus. Is that why he is so vile? Does he think our house is rightfully his?"

"He said he was going to take what was rightfully his." Alda grimaced. "He said... he said he would engender Drachenhaus's true heir in me."

"If Ganelon had succeeded," Theodelinda murmured, "his son would become count if Werinbert died."

"I will never be free of that man," Alda said half to herself, shivering. "And if I die, there is nothing to stop him from murdering Werinbert."

"Daughter, I will have this castle under heavy guard," Theodelinda said. "No harm will come to you or to Werinbert."

"He will try again to stain my honor or kill me. If not by his own hand, perhaps by an assassin's."

Theodelinda bowed her head. Alda knew they were thinking the same thing: they knew Ganelon, but an assassin could take any guise, a merchant, a pilgrim, even a traveling priest. Not even a husband could protect Alda from that.

"The only way this family will ever be free of him is for me to disappear," Alda murmured.

* * * * *

For several days, Alda agonized over what to do. She had come all this way to her home, her birthplace, Drachenhaus. She wanted nothing more than to stay with her mother and nephew. Now she dared not remain where Ganelon could find her. But there was nowhere to go... except the abbey at Nonnenwerth. The more she thought about it, the more sense a retreat to Nonnenwerth made. She would be hidden but close to home.

Alda then wrestled with how she would tell her mother. Theodelinda had been through enough heartbreak. There would be no good time to tell her. Alda searched for her mother and found her in the kitchen planning dinner. Although it was smoky, Alda welcomed the warmth of the fires. Alda spoke as soon as Theodelinda was done ordering the servants.

"Mother, I wish to take orders at Nonnenwerth," she said softly.

"Are you certain? It will not be like the life you are accustomed to. And I have heard rumors about how strange the abbess is."

"Mother, I have already told you I shall not marry again. I would rather be a bride of God than take my chances with another man."

"But the abbess..."

"I have heard the same rumors. A strange mistress is better than being left to the mercy of Ganelon."

"A nun's life is not that of a countess," Theodelinda said. "And when you take the vows, you will not be able to inherit."

"I shall have a year before I must decide to take the vow. I shall not be far, and you and Werinbert can visit me from time to time.

Tell the world I am on a spiritual journey. Let them think it is a pilgrimage."

Theodelinda looked down.

"Even if I do take the vow," Alda said, "Ganelon will not know where I am or if I am alive or dead, and that will ensure Werinbert's safety."

Chapter 24

When a merchant boat arrived two days later, Alda bade farewell to Werinbert. He cried so much that Alda almost changed her mind. Almost.

She kissed him. "One day, I hope you will understand why I did this."

"No, Auntie, no," he wailed.

Alda swallowed back her own tears.

"You need not do this," Theodelinda said as she and Alda embraced. "There must be another way."

"There is not," Alda replied, "none that I want."

"Once you have taken the vow, you may never be able to leave the island." Theodelinda's hold tightened.

"Mother, I wish to be removed from the world," Alda said gently.

"It might not be the life you think it is. Please, Daughter, reconsider this."

"I have made my decision."

When Alda started to walk away, her mother clung to her hand. Alda looked down and wondered about her decision. She then straightened her shoulders and told herself to be strong. This was for the best. She gave her mother's hand a final squeeze before letting go.

As she rode down the mountain path accompanied by Veronica and a servant driving a cart, Alda looked over her shoulder. Her mother was hugging Werinbert. Alda turned away so that she would not start weeping.

At the bank of the river, the servant loaded tapestries, bolts of cloths, and a chest with coins and most of Alda's jewelry onto the boat. It was part of her dowry to the Church.

"There is no room for my horses, dogs, or hawks," Alda told Veronica. "Mother will have to send them over later. I shall have Mother sell my cattle."

Alda removed the necklaces and bracelets she was wearing, except for her cross and dragon, and pressed them into Veronica's hands. Alda took a breath. Leaving Veronica was like leaving a part of herself.

"This is for you," Alda said. "I shall have no need of them."

"Do not leave," Veronica said, her voice cracked. "How shall I live without you?"

"You have been with me all my life." She laid a hand on Veronica's shoulder. "But you should make a life of your own now. You know you will always have a home at Drachenhaus."

They lingered in an embrace before Alda stepped into the merchant boat. Alda gazed up at the tree-covered mountains that would forever loom over her. Most of the bare trees were brown and gray, punctuated by evergreens. She looked at the river, reflecting the gray of the clouds, a lifeline, a connection, bearer of goods from the kingdom and the rest of the world, and now the watery path to the abbey.

Alda looked behind her. Veronica stood on the shore. *Loyal as always.*

"Are you certain you want me to take you to Nonnenwerth?" the merchant asked.

Alda nodded and then looked up at Drachenhaus looming above as if it were in the clouds. She stroked the amulet.

The trip continued in silence as the merchant's slaves guided the boat to a dock at the abbey on Nonnenwerth. A bell tower at the center of the abbey rose above a wall of split trunks from the forest. The merchant's servants knocked on the door of the porter's quarters, adjacent to the great gate. All became silent as Alda heard shuffling from inside and the tap of a cane.

An old, bent woman opened the door a crack. She was so old, Alda could not even guess at her age, other than past sixty winters. She wore a woolen cloak, black wool habit, wooden shoes, and a belt with an eating knife. A gloved hand held the cane.

"Thanks be to God," the old woman said.

"Thanks be to God," Alda said.

"We have business with the abbess," the merchant added.

The porter gazed at them and then opened the door to let them into the gatehouse. The porter opened a second door to allow the guests to enter the abbey's grounds and then hobbled toward Alda. "Madam, you have the look of nobility, not a merchant's wife."

Alda waved to the merchants to go to the abbess while she spoke to the porter. "I am Alda, wife of Hruodland, the late prefect of the March of Brittany, and sis — aunt of the count of Drachenhaus, and I wish to speak with the abbess."

"About what?"

"I wish to join this order."

"Life here is very hard," the porter said. "We adhere closely to the Rule of Saint Benedict, and the path to God's love is not easy. Joining the cloister means giving up your body and your will. You will not have servants to wait on you. Your face will become wrinkled. Your hands will bleed and become calloused. Above all, you must obey. Is that what you want?"

"Are there no servants?" Alda asked.

"We have a few lay sisters and lay brothers. Until this last war, we had tenants to work the land, but we sent soldiers to war under the count's command."

"My kin gave their lives to the Lord," Alda retorted. The mention of her brother reopened a wound that had not completely healed. "My brother is not to blame for the abbey's loss."

"I do not know how we will get through winter. The abbess says to pray."

The porter stared past Alda as if the old woman could see into a few months from now, when loaves of bread would be smaller, when wine would barely cover the bottom of the cup.

"It will take more than prayer," Alda muttered, thinking the porter would not hear.

"That is bold, and Saint Benedict frowns on boldness," the porter replied. "Yet, some people would admire that, especially among the laity. You would make a better countess than a nun. Why do you wish to join?"

"I have no place left to go," Alda said. "Like you and your sisters, I suffered a terrible loss in the war, and I wish to withdraw from the world."

Alda gazed out through the open door of the porter's house. This walled community was the sisters' whole world, a world Alda had seen from the Drachenhaus tower, a world where all of the buildings were made with the trees cleared from this space, the little bit of civilization hacked from the forest. The church and its bell tower stood at the center of the complex.

"I shall take you to the abbess," the porter said.

Alda followed the porter, who leaned heavily on a cane as she led Alda to the abbess's house. In the hall, Alda shivered, pulled her cloak closer and stood by a small fire in the hearth as she waited for the porter to find the abbess. A moment later, Alda heard the tap of the porter's cane.

"The abbess will see you now in her reception room," the porter said. She led Alda down a dark corridor. "Through this door."

When Alda walked into the reception room, she was overwhelmed by the murals of sin and redemption. While the abbess and her prioress spoke to the merchant, Alda beheld the back wall, where candles illuminated Jesus crucified with the two thieves. To Alda's left, Adam and Eve departed the apple orchards of Eden, while an angel barred their way back. To Alda's right were the hearth and a mural of the Nativity.

Alda turned around. Framing the door to the room was the Final Judgment. Heaven, a land of blue sky and white clouds tinged with gold, was to the right of Jesus the judge. Ten times the size of the mortals, He wore a gold crown and blue robe as did His mother, Mary, Queen of Heaven, who sat beside Him and was almost His size. The righteous wore white robes and sang the praises of God with the angels. Sinners went naked to His left, to hell, a land of dark sky, gray-brown hills, and black pits. Sinners burned in the lake of fire. Devils were the same size as the men, tiny men. Proud princes hung by their ankles and were dipped in ice, then boiling water. A demon excreted gold and forced a greedy man to eat it, while a lazy man was prodded awake with knives. Alda could not take in all the tortures at one glance.

"You did not come all this way to admire the art," said a voice.

Alda turned, murmuring an apology. To her surprise, she found the abbess scowling at her prioress.

"Silence, Sister Plectrude," the abbess barked. "Those murals are meant to be seen and turn one's thoughts to God."

Despite herself, Alda smiled while Prioress Plectrude looked down.

"But Mother Radegunde," Plectrude protested, "she asked to see us and then..." A glare from the abbess cut her off.

Radegunde appeared to have seen forty or fifty winters — Alda could not tell — and wore a humble cloak and robe of black wool and a matching veil. A leather belt instead of a jeweled girdle cinched the waist of her thin figure. Radegunde's only jewelry was a gold crucifix and her abbess's ring. Holding a staff, she sat on an ornate chair resting on a dais three broad steps above the floor, like a throne.

Plectrude appeared to be at least a decade, perhaps two decades, younger. She wore a costume like the other sisters, black cloak, black veil and robe, sheepskin mittens, leather girdle with a purse and knife, and wooden shoes, but she had a regal bearing.

"Lady Alda asked to speak to me, not you," the abbess said. "Take the merchant and his party to the hall and attend to them there."

Alda stood up straight and tried to conceal her puzzlement while she watched the prioress. Plectrude folded her hands and bowed but not before Alda caught a slight frown. When Plectrude looked up at the abbess again, her face was blank.

As soon as the door closed behind Plectrude and the others, Radegunde said, "Sister Porter tells me you wish to join."

"I do," Alda replied, looking straight into the abbess's clear blue eyes.

"You have eyes like a wild thing in the forest," the abbess said. "How can I be assured of your humility?"

A wild thing? How dare she? Alda's cheeks burned crimson. "I fail to see what having green eyes has to do with anything."

"You have not answered my question. You have given me reason to believe you will be proud and bold. You have told Sister Porter it will take more than prayer to get through the winter."

"My mother managed to have the harvest brought in." Alda clenched her fists by her side, determined not to lose her temper. "Perhaps, she could give you grain as alms or as part of my dowry."

"Was it brought in by men who worked on the Sabbath?" The abbess leaned forward.

"Knowing Mother, yes."

"We cannot use it." The abbess sank back into her chair.

"What?"

"It would be a sin."

Alda shook her head, not comprehending.

"When your mother had the men work on the Lord's Day," the abbess said, "she risked their souls as well as her own."

"Surely, God understood. The men were away fighting His war. He did not let us starve when they were in Lombardy."

"You are presuming the will of God. Your mother's faith is not strong enough."

"My mother is a good, Christian woman," Alda shot back. "It is a greater sin to let people starve." *Hruodland, why did you die and leave me vulnerable to Ganelon? I have no choice but to join this order run by a woman mad with piety.*

"You are terribly bold. Saint Benedict would not approve of you. I might not be able to let you join this order."

"But my dowry is a generous gift," Alda blurted.

"Do you think you can buy your way in?"

"It is not a bribe. It is my gift when I join."

"If you join," the abbess admonished.

"You know I am right about the harvest."

"We must not fear hunger. It is but a weakness of the flesh. A temptation Satan used against Christ and now uses against us."

Alda had fasted during Lent and Advent but never knew of a time when she could not break that fast. She had seen true hunger in the skeletal beggars at the church. They stalked those who might have something to eat, dug through refuse for a scrap of moldy bread, and fought for that scrap.

"Perhaps, Abbess, you have the strength to face hunger," Alda said, "but think of your tenants. A hard winter might shake their faith. They have already lost their sons in the war to spread God's truth, as I have lost my husband, brother, and an uncle. You could accept the grain, and the tenants could survive winter and praise God. Or they could starve and think that God has abandoned them." *As I have often wondered.*

"It is their weakness. God tests us constantly, and we must still obey His commandments, not follow only the ones we find convenient."

"Would Christ or one of His saints not intercede for us?"

"Christ still wants us to follow God's laws." Abbess Radegunde looked Alda up and down and smiled. "I like your wit. You will make an interesting pupil and later a good abbess, if you stay, if you can endure the hardships on the path to God's love. You are welcome to stay in the guesthouse for a couple of days, and if you still wish to join, you will reside in the novitiate. You may join us for prayers at vespers tonight. I would invite you to dine afterward, but I am fasting in hopes of a vision from the Mother of God."

"The answer is here," Alda muttered. "You simply do not like it."

* * * * *

After three days in the guesthouse, Alda moved to the novices' convent, where she was told to exchange her fine clothes and jewelry for humble, black garments. Alda half expected Veronica to help her dress before realizing she was not here. It was the first time in years Alda had not felt the weight of a jeweled girdle on her waist.

After sext prayers, Radegunde pointed to the ring Alda still wore, Hruodland's morning gift to her. "You were told to divest yourself of all finery, and that includes that ring and that amulet. I see you must learn humility and obedience."

Alda cupped her hand around the dragon amulet. "This finery, as you call it, is all I have left of my husband and my kin."

"You must renounce the world, including those," Radegunde ordered.

"They are but trinkets," Alda protested.

"Perhaps. But if I allow you to wear jewelry that turns one's thoughts to the world, the other sisters will pester me about satisfying their vanity, and it will not be in remembrance of a husband."

"Very well, Abbess. I will put them with my jewels for safekeeping."

Alda found her chest of jewels in the treasury and fished out two ribbons. She strung the amulet on one and Hruodland's ring on the other. She gazed at them a long time before she kissed them and tucked them both under her shift. They would be near her heart, where she could touch them and remember her loved ones. Putting away the ring and the dragon would be like giving up Hruodland, and she could not give up Hruodland, not yet.

* * * * *

Hruodland woke to the bell calling the inhabitants of the Abbey of Saint Stephen to prime prayers. Through a crack in the shutters, he could see a sliver of gray light. He made the sign of the cross and clutched his small wooden cross. He murmured the Pater Noster and silently added his own wish, *Give me strength.*

Shivering, Hruodland sat up and felt the cold morning air, unaffected by the embers burning low in the hearth. His breath smoking in front of him, he blew on his hands and rubbed them together, then reached for a tunic that lay near his bed and pulled it on. Judith had given him the tunic and leggings a week ago. It felt good to wear clothes again.

Hruodland turned and put his feet on the floor. The cold shot up through his bones. He reached for his crutches, held them upright, and used them to help himself stand. He did not know why, but he wanted to see the sky, and he did not want to wait for a lay brother or sister to open the shutters, which would only show light through resin coated parchment. The sisters did not want him to use the crutches when they were not there, but he had to see the sky.

He looked at his arms. The bruises he had gotten a month ago when he rose from bed and tried to go home had disappeared. He tried to return to the bed that night but could not. His arms were not strong enough to lift his body.

When Sister Illuna found him the next morning, she helped him get off the floor and into the bed.

"What happened?" she asked.

"I fell," he answered.

"I can see that," she said irritably. "Are you hurt?"

"No."

"Can you move your arms? Show me. Bend your legs. Just a few bruises," she said. "What were you doing on the floor?"

"I do not know." He did not want to admit that he had tried to go home.

As Illuna went outside and opened the shutters to allow daylight, everything he had thought the previous night seemed so foolish. He had been without clothes, horse, and sword, and he did not even have the strength to hold a weapon. Yet he had tried to rescue Alda. From what? He still could not shake the feeling that she was in danger and agonized over his helplessness.

A chill draft from under the door brought Hruodland back to the matter at hand. His crutches thunked against the wooden floor as he shuffled toward the door. This tunic hung loosely on his shoulders. Before Roncevaux, it would have stretched across his chest, if he could have worn it at all. The sisters had told him he was gaining weight. Day by day, he could see his bones sinking back into his flesh but not quickly enough.

His arms and legs were starting to strain when he reached the door. He opened the door a crack and used a crutch to keep it open. The sky was a slate gray, and a cold wind blew. Winter had arrived.

Hruodland let the door close and shuffled back to the nearest cot, sank down on it, and waited for a lay sister or brother who would come to the door and help him to the privies.

As he stared at the embers, another thought occurred to him. If merchants came today and delivered the message to Alda, it would take at least a month, maybe two, to reach the March of Brittany. Alda might try to travel, even in the dead of winter.

Hruodland's eyes widened at the thought of Alda subjecting herself to the danger of freezing to death in a sudden snowstorm or extreme cold.

But something did not make sense. Surely by now, four months after the ambush at Roncevaux, Gerard would have told her he was here, and she would need no invitation to come to him. Why was she not here? Was she with child? Was she ill? But if she was ill or with child, Gerard would send a message.

His mind flooded with other questions: Who was protecting his people from the Bretons? What was Gerard doing? Why was there no word at all from home or from the court?

Hruodland watched Illuna open the door, followed by a burly lay brother carrying wood. Illuna greeted Hruodland with a look of surprise.

"You are dressed," she said. "How did you..." Her voice trailed off as she beheld the crutches against the cot. Illuna shook her head and sighed. "You are stubborn. You could have waited until I arrived."

He wanted to tell Sister Illuna how much he hated his weakness and dependence on other people, but he did not have time to argue. He had a more urgent matter at hand.

As the lay brother placed the wood on the glowing embers, Hruodland said, "Brother, I require your assistance."

Illuna reached for a pair of wooden shoes and a cloak and handed them to Hruodland. "It's cold outside," she said.

Saying nothing, Hruodland slipped his feet into the shoes and wrapped the cloak around his shoulders.

"I do not want you to be bruised again," Illuna said.

"They were but bruises," Hruodland snapped. "I am a grown man, not a babe." Leaning on the brother's shoulder, he used a crutch to stand.

"The abbess rebuked Sister Elisabeth for the bruises," Illuna said, looking down.

"What foolishness! Tell Judith if I am to learn to walk again and ride a horse again and hold a sword again, I am going to be bruised. I would much rather be bruised than live like a cripple."

"I agree," Illuna said, her tall, thin frame straightening. "But I also wish to protect Sister Elisabeth."

* * * * *

As Hruodland was returning from the privies, he and the lay brother both stopped walking for a moment. Hruodland's eyes were attracted to a movement at the gate.

"Are those merchant carts?" Hruodland asked.

"Could be." The lay brother squinted into the distance.

Merchants, Hruodland thought, *finally. A chance to send a message to Alda.*

Hruodland wanted to quicken his steps and cursed under his breath when he found his feet were already going as fast as they could.

"What troubles you?" the brother asked.

"I must make haste. I must go to the ward, make myself presentable, and then speak to Judith."

"I am sure the abbess will wish to speak to you as well." He rolled his eyes. "She probably wishes to bestow another gift on you."

"The only favor I want is to send a message home," Hruodland said. "I am not some kind of a pet."

"Of course," the lay brother murmured.

The hospital room was warmer when Hruodland returned with the lay brother, who helped him settle on a bench close to the hearth. Hruodland washed his hands and face in a basin of cold water. Illuna handed him salted pork, bean soup, and bread. As Hruodland tore at the meat, Sister Elisabeth entered the ward through the door to the outside.

"Once you have finished breaking your fast," she said, "the abbess will wish to see you."

Hruodland nodded and licked his fingers before breaking off a piece of bread and digging into the soup. "I wish to speak to her about sending a message to my wife," he slurred. "I hope she has not forgotten."

Elisabeth unsuccessfully tried to stifle a laugh. "How could she when you ask her about it every time she comes to see you? But this time, she will see you in the ward for the sick."

Hruodland looked at her questioningly.

"It appears that the Good Lord has decided you should live," Elisabeth answered. "This is a ward for the dying. You should be in the ward for those who will live."

When he was done eating, Hruodland again steadied his crutches and stood, and Sister Elisabeth led him through the curtained doorway. The ward for the sick had five pallets, each of which could sleep two men and give the patients the warmth of each other's bodies at night. It was just as clean as the ward for the dying, and it, too, smelled of tansy, mint, wormwood, and sickness. Five men sat on the benches near the hearth.

Hruodland's feet and crutches crunched the dried herbs as he walked to a stool. When he sat down, a lay sister shaved the stubble from his chin.

Judith came to the hospital after sext prayers while Hruodland was learning how to braid a leather harness and will his hands to do the task. He was glad for the interruption and for an excuse to put the leather aside. His fingers ached, but he did not want to admit it.

Behind Judith, a servant held a wolfhound on a leash. The wolfhound looked familiar, but Hruodland could not remember when or where he had seen him. The dog saw Hruodland and began shifting his feet, whining, and wagging his tail.

"You cannot bring a dog, especially one of that size, in here," Elisabeth scolded.

"This hound is for Hruodland," Judith said indignantly. "And if I say he can have a dog in here, he can."

"Let the hound come to me," Hruodland said slowly.

The servant took off the leash, and the dog trotted to Hruodland and nudged his arm.

"The dog saved your life," Judith said. "He was there when they found you."

Hruodland scratched the dog behind the ears. "This hound deserves a name. What is Latin for 'loyal'?"

"Fidelis," Elisabeth said curtly.

"Fidelis," Hruodland echoed. He cleared his throat. "I see merchants are here."

"Would you like me to buy you anything?" Judith asked.

"I only want them to deliver a message to my wife," he said deliberately. "In the message, you must tell her I insist that she not endanger herself. I insist that she wait until spring before she comes here."

"The merchants are traveling to Toulouse," Judith said, sticking out her lower lip.

Hruodland frowned. They were traveling in the opposite direction from what he needed. Toulouse was south and east of here. The March of Brittany was far to the north. A hopeful thought entered his mind, and the frown disappeared. If the merchants came from the north...

"Do they have any message from my wife or brother or Uncle Charles?" Hruodland asked.

Judith shook her head.

Why haven't they sent a message? Hruodland scowled.

"They do have some news from the court," Judith said cheerfully.

"What did they say?" Hruodland sat up straighter.

"The queen delivered twin boys last summer. Alas, one lived only a few days, but the other is strong and healthy."

"Did they tell you his name?"

"Louis."

"And is everyone else in the royal family well?"

"Yes, they are well. Oh, Hruodland, the merchants have wonderful things. I could buy some otter furs for a vest. Would you like that?"

"I will repay you someday."

"That is not necessary." She laid a jeweled hand on Hruodland's shoulder.

Hruodland patted Judith's hand and looked up at her. She was lovely. He then gazed into the fire. What he wanted most of all she could not give him. He wanted a message from Alda. Any message.

Chapter 25

Life on Nonnenwerth was different than Alda had expected. She had expected to pray when the bell rang every three hours. She had expected to fast from time to time. She had not expected to be thinking about food and sleep all the time.

Alda craved meat, yet the sisters ate peasant food, which rumbled through her belly after she ate: coarse, dark rye bread with a stew of beans, onions, and carrots. Some nuns removed their mittens and warmed their hands over the steaming stew before eating it. Alda was glad the abbess ate — or fasted — alone in her own house. Alda did not care for yet another show of how Abbess Radegunde was superior in resisting the pleasures of the flesh. In whispers with other sisters, Alda had learned that Radegunde wore a hair shirt under her clothes and whipped herself with sticks.

And then there was kitchen duty.

"Why are we here?" Alda asked one morning, yawning and rubbing her eyes as the group stood in the kitchen.

"Saint Benedict says that all novices must have kitchen duty," said the nun who led the novices.

"Must we?" Alda asked.

Alda had no idea what to do. She had planned feasts and wakes, but she had never cooked or cleaned.

"Yes. The abbess is strict about following the rule of Saint Benedict."

As Alda followed the lay sisters' instructions and hauled wood and water into the kitchen, she wished Veronica were here to help her, although Veronica never had worked in a kitchen either.

As she cleaned pots, Alda watched her white lady's hands become filthy. Crescents of dirt formed under her fingernails, which broke and became ragged.

Alda's heart lifted when the bell rang and broke the drudgery. It meant she could go to the church to pray and chant.

When she crawled into bed between compline and matins, she was too tired to cry for her loss or relive Ganelon's attack. But she thought of both when the bell woke her.

* * * * *

The abbess sent for Alda after a week of kitchen duty. As Alda left the warmth and smoke of the kitchen, the cold air hit her face and stung her lungs. She saw a few snowflakes drifting in the air and held her cloak close to her as she walked on snow-covered frozen mud. She was still shivering when she met Radegunde in her reception room.

"You have worked in the kitchen long enough," Radegunde said. "Do you wish to learn to read and write?"

"Yes." *To be able to read*, Alda thought almost in rapture.

"My successor must be able to read and write," Radegunde said. "I do not want our sisterhood to depend on men for more than we must."

My successor. Alda repeated the words in her mind, hardly able to believe her luck, *my successor*. She would have to find a way to keep the appointment secret from Ganelon, but if she could be mistress of this abbey, life would not be so harsh.

* * * * *

When Epiphany came, there was less food at dinner. The stew the lay sisters had made was watery, and the loaves of bread were smaller.

Hunger gnawed at Alda constantly. She and the other sisters stared at the empty baskets as if their gaze would make more food appear.

Alda tried to silence her longing for meat. But at night, she dreamt she was plump and dining with Hruodland at a table groaning under the weight of roast ducks, swine, and venison, and she woke sobbing that it was only a dream.

After nones prayers one afternoon, Alda and Nanthild, a young novice also learning to read and write, walked back to their class, past fields of winter wheat, where green shoots poked through the snow, half as much as she had seen at Drachenhaus. *It will be a meager harvest,* she thought.

"I heard the stores of grain are already half empty," Nanthild said to Alda in a low voice. "How will we feed ourselves?"

"I told the abbess my mother would give us grain," Alda replied. "She refused."

"Why?" Nanthild asked.

"Mother had the peasants work on the Lord's Day."

"What does that have to do with it?"

"Abbess Radegunde said God would punish us — that accepting the wheat would be the same as breaking His commandment ourselves."

Nanthild gasped. "She would let us starve for that?"

Alda nodded.

"We could do penance," Nanthild said. "I would rather ask for God's forgiveness than starve."

"Somehow, I must tell my mother to send us some of her wheat," Alda said in a hushed tone. "If she knew of our need, she would not let us starve."

Alda heard someone behind her sneeze. She turned and saw Prioress Plectrude. She stared at Plectrude with wide eyes. *What did she hear? And what will she tell the abbess?*

* * * * *

Two days after Epiphany, Alda was leaving the church after sext prayers and saw the door in the porter's house swing open in the cold, wet mid-morning fog. Alda stood still as she watched who was coming through.

"Mother!" she called, lifting her skirt, ready to run through the snow.

Alda felt an icy, claw-like hand on her forearm and turned. Radegunde glowered at her.

"What are you doing?" Radegunde said, her voice as chilled as the wind.

"My mother is here," Alda said, beaming. "And she has brought my nephew."

"Did they ask me for permission?"

"Permission? Permission for what?"

"Any visitor needs my permission," the abbess said, her spine stiffening.

Alda opened her mouth to argue that she needed no one's permission to see her kin but decided it would be simpler to get this formality done with. "Very well. Mother Radegunde, may I have permission to visit my kin?"

"No. No novice may have visitors. It is too much temptation."

"Temptation of what?" Alda asked, stamping her wooden shoe into the snow. "They are my kin, and it has been weeks since I saw them last. Please. Let me speak to them for but a few minutes."

"No," Radegunde said, her voice stronger.

Alda yanked her arm away from the abbess and ran toward Theodelinda. "Mother!"

"Alda!" Theodelinda smiled, but her eyes had a look of horror.

"I missed you," she whispered, holding her mother in a fierce embrace.

"I missed you," Theodelinda said as they pulled away from each other. As Alda bent to embrace Werinbert, she heard her mother say, "Daughter, come home."

Alda stood and felt a cold hand on her shoulder. She turned and faced Plectrude.

"How dare you defy the abbess's will!" the prioress spat.

"They are my kin." Alda snorted, the breath from her nose like a dragon's flame.

"Madam," Plectrude said over Alda's head, "if you do not wish for your daughter to receive the stripes, you will tell her to rejoin her sisters now."

"She is coming home." Theodelinda's eyes flashed. "It is obvious she does not have enough to eat here."

Alda swallowed. Had she lost that much weight?

"Alda," Theodelinda pleaded, "come home. I will have you well guarded."

Alda remembered the night Ganelon had tried to rape her. She closed her eyes against the fear. Again, she felt the edge of the cold knife on her throat, her nakedness as he straddled her, her helplessness. She shuddered.

Alda opened her eyes. She was standing in the snow outside the porter's house, wearing a black habit and wooden shoes. If she had to leave her mother, it was better than the terror of that night. Anything was better.

"We had guards that night," Alda said. "No number of guards could stay Ganelon's hand. I shall remain with my sisters. May I have a moment alone with my mother, Sister Prioress?"

"No," Plectrude said coldly, "you will return now."

Alda shoulders slumped as she returned to the group. If only she could have spoken to her mother but for a moment. If only she could have said two more words, "Need wheat." Why would Plectrude do this? Did she not know she was condemning herself to hunger as well?

* * * * *

Seven days later, Radegunde, her face gaunt, announced after sext prayers that she had a vision from Jesus. "We are to fast and pray until Candlemas."

The novices all flinched, and some of them groaned.

"Think of the temptation Jesus went through for us," the abbess scolded. "Forty days with neither food nor drink. Is two weeks without food too much to ask?"

The abbess paused as several sisters looked at their feet. Alda stared at her.

"The Lord is punishing all of us for the lack of faith of at least two sisters," Radegunde said. "Alda, Nanthild, come forward."

They obeyed. Alda looked Radegunde straight in the eyes. Nanthild stared at her feet, trembling.

"Alda, did you tell Sister Nanthild that I should have accepted wheat harvested by men who worked on the Lord's Day?"

"I did," Alda said, still looking Radegunde in the eye.

"Do you repent that utterance?" she asked, gripping her staff.

"No. I should have lied," Alda said defiantly. "I should have told you my mother forbade them to work on the Lord's Day. Then, we would have enough to eat."

"You will be given the stripes for your sins."

"It was not a sin," Alda shot back. "I am of noble blood. I shall not be beaten like a common slave."

"If you wish to join this order, you will submit to discipline. You have committed a sin."

"What sin? I told you the day we met that you should accept wheat from my mother. I have not lied."

"You have committed the sin of pride, the deadliest of all."

Alda seethed but held her tongue. She still hoped to be the abbess's heir. But she could not help thinking, *I have committed the sin of pride? Who has all but boasted about how she could fast the longest and mortify her flesh the most?*

"And Nanthild," Radegunde continued, "did you tell Alda that you agreed with her, that God would forgive us if we violated His rule?"

"No," Nanthild almost screamed, "Never." She was shaking, almost in tears. Alda glared at her.

"You lie," Radegunde spat. "You will be given double the stripes of Alda for your double sin."

"It was not a sin," Alda protested as one of the sisters opened a trap door Alda had not noticed in the candlelight.

Six sisters, staring straight ahead, dragged Alda and Nanthild down the steps to a room beneath the sanctuary. The others followed slowly, not daring to look up. The damp basement had a dirt floor and was lit by only one torch, just enough to see the steps and the post and ropes.

The abbess handed a small whip to one of the stouter sisters. Alda and Nanthild were stripped of everything but their shoes. Alda shivered and her teeth chattered. She heard gasps and looked down at herself, pale skin stretched over bones, ribs. *The others must wonder if they look this bad.* Alda could not see her sisters, except for Nanthild.

"Why do you carry those worldly symbols?" Radegunde scolded, ripping away Hruodland's ring and the dragon amulet.

"They are worth nothing to you," Alda said, her voice tight.

"Your disobedience shall cost you three more stripes," Radegunde's voice boomed from the shadows.

Alda and Nanthild were tied to the post. The rope hurt Alda's wrists.

"Alda, you will be given seven stripes for the sin of pride and three for disobedience," Radegunde said.

Nanthild was sobbing. Alda was having a hard time keeping her face in check. *I shall not cry. I shall not scream.*

The leather smacked Alda's back. She grimaced, clenched her fists, clamped her teeth together, pulled against the tight knots on her wrists, and bottled the scream in her throat. The sister paused between each lash.

Nanthild screamed when the strap hit her back, screams from the bottom of the gut, screams that Alda had refused to let loose.

"Let this serve as an example for those who defy God's will," Radegunde said.

* * * * *

Alda shivered and tugged at the knots that bound her wrists. In the dark, she heard the abbess and the sisters climb up the steps. Alda thought she heard at least one sister stifle a sob.

"Sister Prioress," she heard Radegunde scold, "where have you been?"

"I thought I heard a merchant boat outside," Plectrude said, panting. "But it was the wind."

"Why must you insist on attending to worldly matters before spiritual ones?"

"If it were a merchant vessel, he might have had incense for the church," Plectrude replied. "I only thought I was doing your will. You were occupied, Mother Radegunde. What are those objects in your hand?"

"Worldly symbols of Sister Alda's," Radegunde snapped.

"Let me put them away for you, so that you can return to your residence and pray."

"Where are you going, Sister Prioress?" the abbess growled.

"To the cellar, to see the example you made of the faithless sisters."

Holding a candle, Plectrude descended the steps. In a pool of flickering light, the prioress's head was cocked as if listening to the footsteps above.

Plectrude stepped toward Alda and Nanthild and undid the knots. Her breath smoked in front of her as she shouted, "The abbess was merciful. If it were my will, I would have given you three-fold the stripes."

Alda rubbed her arms and wrists as Plectrude pointed to where the habits lay. Alda and Nanthild ran to them. Alda beheld the welts on Nanthild's back. They were bright red, but the skin had not been broken. Alda wished she could awaken from this nightmare of facing a slow painful death if she stayed on Nonnenwerth or rape and torture if she left.

"Do you know what you have done?" Alda hissed to the prioress as her numb fingers picked up her shift. "You have condemned us to starve."

Plectrude paused, her head cocked again as if listening, and let out a giddy laugh. "We will live. Because of you, we will live through the winter."

"How?" Alda asked, tears studding her eyes as she pulled on her shift, heedless of the sting of the fabric against her own welts. "Through prayer?"

"That and the wheat your mother sent us." Plectrude beamed.

Alda froze and dropped her habit. Plectrude seized Alda's hand and pressed the ring and amulet into it. Countless questions flooded Alda's mind. She opened her mouth, but words failed her.

"It worked," Plectrude sighed. "Saints be praised, it worked."

"What worked?" Alda asked as she retied the ribbons and slipped her ring and dragon under her shift.

"When you rejoined your sisters," Plectrude replied. "I gave your mother a letter and told her it was from you."

"You lied to my mother? How could you?" Alda asked, tugging on her habit.

"Was it a lie? Did you not want to say, 'Dearest Mother, we need grain'? Did you not want to instruct her on how she could give it to us without the abbess's notice? Did you not want to say, 'Seven days hence, after the prime bells toll on Nonnenwerth, send boats with as many sacks of grain as you can spare'?"

"Of course, but…"

"Fortunately, I can write," Plectrude said. "When I saw Drachenhaus's boats at our dock, I bade the men to stay until they heard the sext bells. I then made all haste to the abbess and told her of your conversation with Nanthild. I knew the news would send her into a rage. I begged her not to punish you, knowing my words would have the exact opposite effect."

"Why?" Nanthild snapped. "What wrong did we do to you?"

"The abbess had to be distracted," Plectrude said, shifting her weight from foot to foot. "Discipline in this cellar was the perfect way to keep her unaware of what went on above."

"While we were whipped," Alda said slowly, "you were directing the men to fill our stores. That is why you were out of breath."

"You both suffered for us all," Plectrude said. "I ask your forgiveness, but I knew no other way."

"You are forgiven. The stripes are a small price to pay for not starving. They will heal," Alda said even though the welts still burned. "But why did you not tell me?"

"Alda, I needed you to be your willful self," Plectrude said. "It gave me more time. And the abbess might have become suspicious if you were humble and obedient and might have tried to beat the information out of you, and then she would scatter our grain to the birds."

"She wouldn't!" Nanthild's eyes widened.

"She would," Plectrude said. "I have known this woman longer than either of you. When she has an idea, nothing will change her mind. She did not listen to me when I told her the Good Lord Himself plucked grain on the Sabbath and said, 'Sabbath was made for man, not man for the Sabbath' and therefore it is no sin to harvest on the Sabbath in a time of need. As far as she is concerned, she will obey the commandment, 'Remember the Sabbath and keep it holy,' and all else fades."

Plectrude gestured for the novices to accompany her up the steps. As Alda followed, she stammered, "I do not know how to thank you for returning my things. They are all I have left of my husband."

When they all ascended the steps, Plectrude stared at the images of Christ and the Blessed Mother above the altar, but instead of the fear she had seen in Radegunde's face, Plectrude's eyes had the look of love like a daughter would have for her father.

"Sister Prioress," Alda asked, "why does Mother Radegunde treat you so?"

"What do you mean?"

"She always rebukes you, even when you do her will."

Plectrude gazed upon Christ. "She knows I do not believe her teachings. I do not see inflicting pain on the body as the path to God's love. Christ took our pain and sin to save us. I believe He wants us to relieve the suffering of others — feeding the hungry, clothing the poor, schooling the children, sheltering travelers, tending the sick and crippled.

"And I remind her of her uncle's sin. Even though my father acknowledged and dowered me, she still will not believe that I am the daughter of a bishop. She will never forgive that my mother was a commoner."

"But you said your father acknowledged you."

"She thinks he was tricked." Plectrude rolled her eyes. "She thought her uncle could do no wrong until my birth told her otherwise. She hates me for that, and she hates me for keeping her and the abbey alive."

"Keeping her alive?"

"Do you think the sisters would allow the abbess to starve them? Merchants have told me of well-timed accidents befalling harsh mistresses."

Alda and Nanthild both gasped.

"The only reason the sisters have not fled this abbey is that I assured them we would have enough food to survive the winter, and I always keep my word," Plectrude said. "I was not about to see the sisters or the tenants reduced to eating rats."

"You have defied the abbess's will before?" Alda asked.

"For the good of this abbey. In Radegunde's heart," the prioress said, looking at her hands, "she knows I subvert her will and that she needs me to subvert her will, although she believes my fate should be that of a fatherless whore."

"But the sin is your father's, not yours."

"I have thought so as well, but she will not forgive me for not repenting that I am a natural child."

"You have nothing to repent," Alda said.

Plectrude shrugged. "I have long learned to ignore the abbess when she calls me a bastard or tells me that she allows me to stay here only as a favor to her favorite uncle."

"Why do you stay?"

"This is the only life I have known. What would I do outside the abbey?"

"You could find a kinder mistress at a different abbey," Nanthild said.

"Or a crueler one," Plectrude replied. "Someone who takes joy in inflicting pain. Radegunde is cruel because she thinks it will save souls."

"But why do you protect the abbess?" Alda asked.

"She is a kinswoman. Family is still family. Perhaps, she is my penance." The prioress gestured for the novices to follow her to the altar. "Let us pray. When the abbess comes here at nones, I would advise you to throw yourself at her feet and tell her you repent. The abbess will say you are forgiven, and the matter will be closed."

"I have done nothing wrong," Alda said bitterly. "And you said what I did was not a sin."

"Simply say you repent, do not say for what sin," Plectrude said. "There must be some sin."

Kneeling on the cold wooden floor, Alda could think of something to repent: wanting to take Plectrude's inheritance. Plectrude was more worthy to succeed Radegunde. Plectrude could have left this place years ago, but she endured Radegunde because she loved Christ and this abbey. With a twinge of guilt, Alda realized she did not feel this passion. Alda loved Christ the way the laity loved Him — as one who loves her king or country.

Alda looked up at the painting of Christ in His majesty with His Mother beside Him. Heaven. To no longer feel hunger or pain or loss. She put her hand over her heart and pressed the ring and amulet to her flesh. *Hruodland.* She swallowed back the tears. It had been how long? Five months since he had died, and yet the sadness always returned. *Hruodland, I should have never loved you. Then I would not miss you so.*

Chapter 26

The Nativity and Epiphany were lonely for Hruodland, even though he was surrounded by people. For four years, he had spent those holy days with Alda. As winter went on at the Abbey of Saint Stephen, he had one goal: return home.

He drove himself to walk normally, without crutches or wobbling steps. He did not care how many times he fell. He had to be ready for the journey home this spring. He had to silence those dreams of Ganelon hovering over him. He was torn between kissing Alda at their reunion and slapping her for not sending him a message. He was irritated with Gerard and Charles as well. Why were there no tidings of home or court?

Two weeks after Epiphany, Hruodland went to prime Mass at the church. It felt good to be in a church again amid prayers, candles, and incense. *Why did God allow the Roncevaux massacre to happen?* he asked Saint Sebastian. *Why did He spare me?*

"Hruodland," Judith called after the Mass, "the otter vest becomes you."

"Thank you. Any word from my home?" he asked.

Judith shook her head. "You no longer need the hospital. Would you like to stay at my residence? You would be an honored guest."

She was right. He did not need lay sisters tending to his every need. His speech was still somewhat slurred, but he was able to walk on his own and dress himself and use the privies without help. Still, he was not as strong as he had been.

"I accept your kind offer," he said.

* * * * *

After dinner in the abbess's residence, Hruodland asked Judith for a horse.

"You are not planning to travel in the middle of the winter, are you?"

"If I am to go home, I need to learn how to ride a horse again."

"Of course," she murmured, "let one of my servants help you."

"As I have been telling your good sisters," Hruodland said irritably, "I must do this without help."

In midafternoon, a groom led the horse into an open courtyard. Hruodland suspected Judith had ordered the servant to bring the most docile animal he could find. Fidelis the wolfhound watched his master as Hruodland sized up the horse. It was a sleepy-looking brown mare whose shoulder was as tall as Hruodland's neck. His first task: mount the horse.

So why was he hesitating? Hadn't he been riding horses for as long as he could remember? Riding had become as natural as walking, so natural that he would leap onto the saddle. But right now, leaping onto anything seemed impossible.

It is only a horse. He placed his hand on the pommel and tried to pull himself up, but his grip was too weak. He fell backward and landed in the icy mud.

As Hruodland cursed, Fidelis whined and licked his master's face. Hruodland heard a stifled laugh. He looked up and saw the groom. He got to his feet and fixed his eyes on the servant, who was no older than twenty winters.

"Have you slain a Saxon charging at you on horseback?" Hruodland said, using the tone in which he spoke to the Bretons.

The young man stopped laughing. His eyes grew wide as Hruodland raised his hand to let a sleeve fall and expose a scar.

"I will speak slowly so you can understand me," Hruodland continued. "I am a warrior. I have more scars than this from the Gascons, the Saxons, and the Lombards. I survived the massacre at Roncevaux, slaying many Gascons. I shall become strong again, and I shall remember how I was treated."

The groom looked down, silent. Hruodland smiled. He still had the gift of command, the gift that had made the Bretons give him tribute for the king, the gift that had made his men follow him into battle. What this groom did not know was that Hruodland still could not remember the Roncevaux attack. Judith kept telling him how valiant he had been, and he believed her. The evidence he had of it was a thick scar near his heart.

* * * * *

As Lent approached, Hruodland pushed himself to relearn his old ways, to regain the muscle he had lost. He sparred with the guards of the monastery and practiced riding in the marshes outside the abbey's walls.

The days lengthened and became warmer. Hruodland became angrier as Lent began and he still had no word from Alda or Gerard or Charles. He was going to start his journey home soon. Spring was returning. The grass in the marshes was sending up green shoots among the spring flowers, and the stream beside the abbey was swollen with rain.

After dinner one temperate day, he and Judith walked through the orchard cemetery, where buds of leaves and flowers were studding the trees and birds were building nests. Fidelis followed them, leaving paw prints in the moist earth. Hruodland had another favor to ask of Judith and felt guilty. Already, she had been so kind, although it bothered him that she was a coquette and looked at him longingly.

"When I return home, I shall send gifts to you and your order," he said.

"We have no need for gifts," she said. "We are sisters of charity."

"I am a noble, not a beggar."

"The Gascons took everything they could find. You needed our help. We gave it to you."

"And I shall repay you." He cleared his throat. "In two days hence, I will begin my journey home."

"Stay here," the abbess interrupted, touching his hand. "You are safe here. I could make you very happy. The March of Brittany will go on without you."

"The March of Brittany is my home."

Judith looked down, hurt.

Hruodland could not understand her reaction. Yes, they had lain with each other, but that was years ago. He had been nothing but a plaything to her.

"You are beautiful," he said. "But you are an abbess, and I have a wife, whom I love, and she is waiting for me."

Hruodland gritted his teeth, wondering about that last thought. Alda had a lot of explaining to do. How could she be so cruel as not to send a message?

"Th-there is something I have not told you," Judith stammered. "When the scouting party brought you here, we... we all thought the Lord would take you any day."

"So I heard," Hruodland said, reaching down to scratch the dog behind the ears.

"We were trying to spare your family some grief," she blurted. "We had the best of intentions."

"What are you talking about?" Hruodland stopped petting the dog.

"The nobles decided to tell the world you were slain at Roncevaux."

"They told the world I was dead, and you allowed this?" He felt as if he had been punched in the chest.

"We... we thought you were dying. Bishop Leonhard had given you last rites, and we were waiting to give you a Christian burial. We... they... did not want your uncle to think you had suffered."

"So they left me here to die and lied about it." Fury rose from the pit of his gut.

"You were dying — we thought you were dying — from your injuries at Roncevaux," Judith pleaded. "If you had died here, to say you were slain there would not be a lie. They needed to join the king's army. They brought you here to assure your journey to heaven. We would have buried you in the hallowed ground of our orchard, held Mass for you, said prayers for you. Would you have preferred to be buried at the side of the road?"

"But I did not die." Hruodland forced the words through clenched teeth.

"You still breathed. Your heart still beat. But you did not move for a month. Your eyes were open, but they did not see. Perhaps, it is because they left you in our care that you have recovered."

"You did not send a message to the king or my wife when it became apparent the Lord would spare me, did you?"

"I cannot write."

"You have a clerk," Hruodland spat, his word slurring.

Judith looked down but said nothing.

Staring at a grave, Hruodland was too angry to speak. *The world thinks I am dead. Alda thinks I am dead.*

"Say something, Hruodland," Judith begged. "I find your silence difficult to bear."

"Leave me alone," he snarled.

Weeping, Judith rushed out of the orchard. Hruodland did not care if she was in tears. He wanted to be alone among the graves, where he should have been but for the grace of God.

Hruodland wandered among the apple and pear trees of the orchard. For a long time, fury clouded his thoughts. *Why did she not send a message to somebody, anybody — even my wife?*

He leaned against an apple tree, petting his dog and staring at the seedlings covering the sodden graves. Outside these walls, the world thought he was dead. It was like he was a ghost.

Should he stay here as Judith asked? His grave would be in sanctified ground, in an orchard, forever watching the trees bloom in the spring and the fruit ripen in the fall. Alda thought he was dead. Judith had some affection for him. He could pretend to have tender feelings for Judith and be in her favor.

He grimaced as if he had just bitten into a rotten apple. Why was he even thinking such a thing? Surely, God did not spare his life to corrupt an abbess or himself. He could not stay here. That much was certain.

But what did God want him to do? Join a monastery? Perhaps, that was it, even though he was born to fight, trained to fight since he could hold a wooden sword when he had seen three winters. Gerard was the count now and intelligent and capable enough to govern the March of Brittany.

And what about Alda? She thought he was dead. Rage jolted through him. If Alda thought he was dead, she must have married another by now. She was still young — and wealthy. What cur of a man had she married? How dare she marry again when he had provided for her in his will?

He pressed his palms to his temples to silence the voices of wrath. He had no idea. Perhaps, Alda was true. But how was that possible? Surely, her family would be urging her to marry, even if she did not want to. He slammed his fist into his hand. Was she lying with another man at this moment even as he stood in the orchard?

He had to return to Rennes, pray to the relics of Saint Melaine for answers, and reclaim his wife. That much was certain.

* * * * *

Hruodland drew himself to his full height and threw back his head as he entered the abbess's residence. He felt not even a trace of guilt about what he was going to ask her. She owed him this. He found Judith warming herself by the fire.

"I am leaving for the March of Brittany two days hence," Hruodland said.

"I see," she said, looking down at her hands.

"I shall need a horse and a cart and a sword and..."

"We cannot spare them," she interjected.

Hruodland blinked back his surprise.

"My order and my tenants need all those things," she said. "Have you any idea how difficult it is to acquire horses and the few weapons we have?"

"No more lies," Hruodland roared. "You have ruined my life. If you think you can trap me here, you are mistaken. God did not spare my life so that I could become your plaything."

"You ingrate," she spat, her face flushing. "Leave. Leave now."

"Very well, I will leave," he said evenly. He strode to the door. Fidelis followed him.

"You cannot take that dog," Judith shouted.

Too angry to speak, Hruodland shrugged and kept walking. He ignored the questions buzzing through his mind. How was he going to eat? How was he to protect himself from bandits? Was he truly going to walk all the way to Rennes? As he slammed the door, he noticed the dog ignored Judith as well.

Hruodland marched toward the gate, wondering why Judith was not following him and begging for his forgiveness. Once outside the abbey, he told himself, *This is foolhardy. Go back to the Abbey of Saint Stephen. No, I cannot go back. I will not humble myself to her.*

He made his way through the marshes, barely noticing the long-legged birds fishing in the pools in the high grass and the seagulls flying overhead. He paid no heed to the music of birdcalls and cries.

By dusk, Hruodland had entered the forest and was looking for shelter. Although the days were warmer, nights were still cold. Most of the trees were still bare, and the ground was damp. He spotted an old tree with a hollow near its roots. He crouched on wet leaves and wrapped the cloak around himself and the dog. Through the tree branches, Hruodland could see the full moon on the horizon to his left. He fell asleep listening to frogs call for their mates, wolves howling to one another, and hares and deer foraging in the brush.

* * * * *

Hruodland awoke from a dream of Ganelon forcing strong wine and hemlock down his throat. He did not know for how long he had slept. Among frog calls and wolf howls, he heard the creak of wheels and the clop of horses' hooves against the stone in the road.

The moon was high in the sky as he stood and drew his eating knife. It was no defense unless he could convince whoever it was that he was seeing a ghost. Fidelis, too, stood. Hruodland expected the dog to bare his teeth and growl. Instead, he was wagging his tail. What sorcery had afflicted the hound?

If whoever it was intended to rob him, he was not making any haste. In the moonlight, Hruodland saw the silhouette of a mule and rider, a riderless horse, and a horse-drawn cart.

"Hruodland?" a woman's voice called.

"Sister Elisabeth, what are you doing here?" Hruodland sheathed his knife.

"Saints be praised, you are well," Elisabeth said, dismounting. "When I watched you storm out of the abbey, I thought at any moment you would come to your senses and return. I underestimated your pride."

"I shall *not* return to the abbey," Hruodland said.

"I am not on an errand for the abbess. Illuna and I are going on a pilgrimage, and we need the protection of a man."

"But your hospital..."

"It is in good hands with the lay sisters. No doubt the abbess will find sisters to replace us." Sister Elisabeth looked over her shoulder and then back at Hruodland. "I wish to pray to the relics of Saint Melaine at Rennes and then visit Rome. I am an old woman, and if I am going to make this pilgrimage, now is the time."

"But a pilgrimage is not safe for a woman."

"Neither of us is young," Sister Elisabeth said with a laugh. "But we sought you out for your protection."

"If a thin man with no sword is protection. I am still not as strong as I once was."

Illuna stepped down from the cart and beckoned Hruodland. She lifted a blanket, revealing a sword in a leather sheath, a throwing ax, and a leather-covered wooden shield.

"These will help you protect us," she said.

Hruodland picked up the sword and drew it. It was not as high quality as Durendal or his father's weapon, but it was adequate. The sword felt heavy in his hand. If he held it too long, it would make his arm ache. Still, he could practice with it and regain his strength.

He sheathed the sword and lifted the ax. Few warriors used these anymore, but this one was sturdy. Weighing the ax's head in his left hand, he nodded his approval. After tucking the ax into his belt, he strapped the shield on his back.

"Where did you get these?" he asked.

"One of the guards used them. Elisabeth and I believe weapons that belong to the abbey should protect its sisters within and without its walls."

"I will do my best."

As Elisabeth approached him, Hruodland could make out a sly expression on her face.

"Why are you leaving for a pilgrimage in the middle of the night?" he asked.

"As I said, I am not on an errand for the abbess. Since she often sleeps through matins prayers, she will not likely find out we are gone until after prime."

Hruodland peered inside the cart. It had a barrel of beer, several loaves of bread, a basket of greens, another basket with salted pork, a pot, and a locked chest.

"The abbess is providing the means for our pilgrimage," Elisabeth said. "I was on a walk when I heard what she told you in the orchard." She snorted. "Illuna and I didn't fight to bring you back into the world only for her to deny it to you."

"So Judith wishes to atone for her guilt by providing for us?" Hruodland asked.

But that did not make sense. If the abbess wished to atone, Illuna and Elisabeth would not leave at such a strange hour. Some piece of this riddle was missing.

"What is in the chest?" Hruodland asked.

"The abbess's jewels," Elisabeth replied, proud as a cat ready to drop the mouse at her master's feet.

"You stole them?" He tried to force his face into a stern expression, only to find himself laughing.

"It is a pious fraud," Elisabeth said, brushing back a lock of silvered hair. "I took enough to equal my dowry. She owes us all a debt — you, me, Illuna, Denis, a most beloved lay brother — and will provide for our pilgrimage and your journey home."

"She will be displeased," Illuna said.

"I hope she is displeased," Elisabeth said. "She will not feel half the anger I felt when she refused to let Denis be buried in the orchard cemetery or when I learned she let the world think Prince Hruodland was dead."

"Nor mine," Hruodland said. "But if anyone asks, your protector is named Sebastian."

Elisabeth and Illuna gave him quizzical looks.

"The world thinks Hruodland, prefect of the March of Brittany, died at Roncevaux," he said, answering the question on their faces. "Now is not the time to undeceive them. Hruodland, nephew of the king, should not be traveling like this. Hruodland will make his return to the world like a noble, with a sword drawn and raised above his head. Until then, I am Sebastian, making a pilgrimage to Saint Melaine at Rennes. And I can induce more fear in brigands if they think they are facing a ghost, an enemy they cannot kill."

After helping Elisabeth onto her mule, Hruodland mounted the horse that had been riderless. His steed was obviously a farm animal, not one trained for battle, but it was obedient to the rein.

"We should put as many leagues as possible between us and the abbey," he said. "The abbess will send her guards after you as soon as she learns both her jewels and two of her sisters are missing."

Elisabeth and Illuna giggled.

"What did you do?" Hruodland asked.

"Their morning beer will seem more intoxicating than normal," Elisabeth said, "especially with the sleeping potion I slipped in."

This time, Hruodland gave her a look of horror. How much had he corrupted the sisters, first stealing, now poisoning?

"It isn't enough to cause harm," Elisabeth said. "They simply will be too sleepy to follow us until about nones tomorrow. And then they will feel pain in their heads as if they had drunk too much wine. By the next morning, they will be as if nothing had happened."

"That gives us an extra day," Hruodland said, "but it will not take long for Judith's guards to overtake us."

"Not if they think we're traveling to Toulouse," Illuna replied.

"The opposite direction. Why would she think we're going to Toulouse?" he asked.

"I asked lay brothers to help us prepare for our pilgrimage," Illuna said, chuckling, "and I kept saying things like, 'That should be enough beer for a journey to Toulouse' and 'It is warmer in Toulouse, but we might need those blankets at night.'"

"And you spoke the literal truth," Elisabeth said. "You never actually said we were going to Toulouse."

"So how will word that we are going to Toulouse reach Judith's ears?" Hruodland asked.

"Those lay brothers are the worst gossips in the abbey," Illuna said. "They could not hold their tongues about anything if their very lives depended on it."

"By the time Judith realizes we have not gone to Toulouse," Elisabeth added, "we will be in Bordeaux and under the protection of my brother, the archbishop, well beyond her reach. He is not at all fond of Judith or her father."

* * * * *

After prime Mass, Alda lingered in the church and gazed at the mural of Christ and His Mother in majesty. She drew her damp, black cloak closer to her.

Yesterday, a sister had read the Rule of Saint Benedict to her in Latin. She understood a word here and there but found most of it beyond her comprehension. The language was close to Roman but not close enough.

The nun who read the Rule said something in Latin. Alda just stared.

Another sister nudged Alda and translated, "Here is the Rule under which you will fight. Do you accept it?"

"I do," Alda said, having no idea what she was accepting, only that it was important. She wished someone had translated the Rule into Frankish. But even if she could understand it, she simply had no choice. If she did not stay here on Nonnenwerth, she would endanger herself and Werinbert.

"Your novitiate will continue," Abbess Radegunde had said. "In two months' time, the Rule will be read to you again, and two weeks later, you will take the vow."

Alone in the church now, Alda knelt before the altar and pressed her amulet and Hruodland's ring to her heart. Outside, nature itself seemed to anticipate the Feast of the Resurrection. Maples were setting flower buds, and flowers awoke under the trees in the orchard. The wheat grew again, the kale sent up yellow flowers, and the lettuce was young and tender. Birds were returning. Life was returning.

The night before, Alda had dreamt she and Hruodland were in a garden, talking as if he were still alive. When the prime bell had awakened her, it took all her effort not to weep during prayers, mourning that it had been only a dream. Alda was startled from her thoughts when she heard Plectrude open the church door.

"Alda, are you well?"

"I was thinking of my husband," she said. "Just when I think my heart has healed, I dream of him again."

"What did he say to you?"

"That he did not die. That he was testing my fidelity."

"Perhaps he is telling you not to take the vow. Once you do, you will cut yourself off from the world forever and never be able to leave here."

"Or he is telling me to take the vow. He would not be jealous if I became a bride of God."

"But you have doubts?" Plectrude asked.

"Hruodland and I last saw each other about this time a year ago. After all this time, I still cannot believe he is dead. I cannot feel it in my heart. I keep thinking he is going to come back. But that's nonsense, isn't it?"

Chapter 27

our days after they had set out from the Abbey of Saint Stephen, Hruodland and the sisters arrived at the gates of Bordeaux, a walled city surrounded by vineyards on marshy ground near the Garonne River. Inside the gates, they passed gigantic Roman pillars and made their way to the church. The beggars and pilgrims at the church doors ignored Hruodland. At Rennes, they had gathered around him, asking for alms.

Hruodland patted his sword hilt, just in case. Among the truly blind and lame were frauds and pickpockets. He and the sisters went to the archbishop's residence near the church. The archbishop's home was as magnificent as any of the king's villas, with its turrets, murals, and hearths.

As he stood in the hall and gazed at a mural of Saint Michael the Archangel slaying the dragon, Hruodland wondered if the archbishop might recognize him. The army had stopped in Bordeaux on the way to Hispania over a year ago, and Hruodland had been one of his many guests.

When the archbishop greeted his sister and her companions, he stared at Hruodland, who had been introduced as Sebastian, an abbey tenant.

"Sebastian, you look familiar." The archbishop shook his head. "Must be a fancy."

After dinner, Hruodland sat by the fire with the sisters as the archbishop's musician tuned his harp.

"What can you tell me about the family who rules the March of Brittany?" Elisabeth asked her brother. "I have heard little of important families during my stay at the abbey and would like to know something about my hosts in Rennes."

Wishing he could thank Elisabeth outright, Hruodland smiled at her.

"The family has experienced a great loss," the archbishop replied, bowing his head. "Count Hruodland fell at the Pass of Roncevaux. What a tragedy! He was the nephew of the king and a great warrior. His brother, Gerard, rules there now. He passed through here, an intelligent man, but not a warrior like his brother."

"Was Hruodland married?"

"Yes, to a wealthy Rhinelander, a strong-willed woman, I hear. I don't know what became of her. Your host might be married by now. The merchants tell me he was starting negotiations with... I forget the name."

Hruodland wondered what Alda was doing right now. A chill went through him as he remembered the nightmare that followed him on the road. Had Ganelon tried to harm her? Had she married again, seeking the protection of another man? Hruodland was torn between jealousy over the new husband and anger at himself for failing to protect her.

Elisabeth's next question drew his attention. "Have you heard news of the court?"

"The queen is with child again," the archbishop replied.

Hruodland smiled. Charles was lucky to have such a fertile wife. Whenever Alda heard such news, he remembered, she would say it was wonderful, yet her hand would stray to her belly. How he wished God had let a child grow inside her!

"The children and the queen mother, are they well?" Hruodland asked instead. "And how does the king fare?"

"All are well," the archbishop said, raising his brows. "The king is preparing for another war with the Saxons and is gathering his forces at Düren."

"So the Saxons broke their promise of peace," Hruodland said bitterly.

"You truly have been removed from the world," the archbishop said to Hruodland. "While our men were fighting the infidels in Hispania, the heathens attacked our churches."

Hruodland glowered. If it were not for the attack at Roncevaux, Charles might have summoned him to fight alongside Alfihar. He swallowed back his sadness as he remembered that Alfihar was dead.

A few notes on the harp stirred Hruodland from his thoughts.

"This song is about a hero in our time, a man you spoke of a little while ago," the singer began. "I speak of Hruodland, prefect of the March of Brittany and nephew of the king. His story is the ultimate tale of loyalty, courage, and sacrifice."

Hruodland stared into the flames. He was not sure if he wanted to hear this about himself. He took a gulp of wine from a cup and passed it to Illuna, who patted his hand.

The man sang about the Saracens massing on the field, breaking their promise of peace with the Franks. Hruodland and other nobles in the rear guard stayed behind. Then the singer described how Hruodland sliced ribs off his enemies' bodies and burst their eyeballs. Although defeat was imminent, Hruodland was proud and refused to blow on his horn, until almost everyone around him was dead and needed a Christian burial.

Hruodland walked away from the fire for a moment. He still had no memory of Roncevaux, except that he and the other soldiers were marching through densely wooded, narrow mountain passes, but a gut feeling told him the battle did not happen like this. For one thing, if he were facing thousands of Saracens — or any other foe — on the battlefield as the song described, sounding the horn would be the first thing he would have done to summon help and perhaps scare the enemy.

From what the nuns told him about the ambush by the Gascons, there had been no glory, not the way the singer was portraying it. Hruodland mourned for Alfihar and the others all over again. Anger burned in his belly. His friends and kinsmen had been slaughtered, and here was this fool who had obviously never seen battle making it into a song.

When Hruodland turned toward the fire, Elisabeth was staring at him, and Illuna was wringing her hands.

"Were you there?" Hruodland asked the singer. He made no effort to disguise his ire.

"I would be dead if I was. I first heard about what happened at Roncevaux when the king was here, and the song just came to me."

"I doubt the prefect of the March of Brittany would be that stupid," Hruodland growled.

"He was a gifted warrior," the singer said, "but he was proud."

"Not to the point of idiocy!"

Elisabeth coughed to disguise a laugh, and he knew what she was thinking. He had left the safety of the abbey with only a knife, a dog, and the clothes on his back. He had taken neither horse nor food nor even a wineskin.

"Not to the point of needlessly endangering others," Hruodland added, looking directly at Elisabeth.

"Did you know Hruodland?" the singer asked.

Elisabeth and Illuna nervously glanced at each other.

"My father is from the March of Brittany," Hruodland answered. "Hruodland was a good warrior and proud of his scars, but he was not so proud that he would allow the slaughter of his fellows without calling for aid. And the people who attacked the rear guard were the Gascons, not the Saracens."

"I don't care who it was. The Saracens are infidels and followers of Muhammad, and our king was there because they threatened the Church."

"We were there..." Hruodland stopped himself, partly because he did not want to reveal himself, partly because he could not make sense of the war against the ruler of Cordoba.

* * * * *

After a three day stay in Bordeaux, Hruodland and the sisters found six other pilgrims, four men and two women, traveling to Rennes. The slow pace of the journey frustrated him, but he knew it was safer to travel with more people, even if one of the men was old and another was frail.

When they entered the forest again, Hruodland felt the hairs on the back of his neck rise. The group had only a sword, an ax, a few knives and cudgels, and a handful of arrows to fend off bandits or demons or kobolds or whatever else hid in the green darkness, resenting their presence.

On the third day in the forest, Hruodland heard a whistle that did not sound like any birdcall he knew. Walking beside his master, Fidelis perked his ears. Hruodland stopped his horse and listened for a moment but did not hear it again. He grimaced at the memory of pilgrims' bodies being brought to Rennes in carts, their throats slashed, their skulls crushed. He leaned toward Sister Elisabeth.

"Remember, if we are attacked, you and Sister Illuna must take cover behind the cart," he muttered.

"Did you see something?" Elisabeth asked, straightening her spine.

"Heard something."

Drawing his throwing ax, he sat erect in the saddle, watching, listening, hoping his horse would not be spooked.

Turning, he called behind him: "Draw your weapons."

Slowly, the group moved forward. Nothing seemed out of the ordinary. Birds flitted among the trees. Rabbits scurried into the underbrush. Perhaps the whistle he had heard truly was a birdcall. He lowered his ax.

Again, the strange whistle. Before Hruodland could raise his hand, an arrow whizzed by his nose, and another thunked into the shield on his back. There was a shout of pain behind him. Beneath him, his horse tensed and trembled like animal about to bolt.

Rage surged through Hruodland and gave him strength. To his right, he saw movement in the shrubs. He hurled his ax, swung his legs over the stiff horse's side, and slid down from the saddle. His flying ax cut through the twigs and smacked into flesh. Despite the arrows sailing over him, Fidelis dashed toward the shrubs and pounced on a man-sized shadow.

Two more arrows soared toward Hruodland's neck. As the horse galloped away, Hruodland dropped to one knee and whipped his shield off his back. Holding the shield in front of him, he stood and unsheathed his sword. With a battle cry, he raised his weapon and charged at the nearest spot where he saw motion, barely hearing the screams around him. At a narrow opening between the shrubs, a thief stood up and shot his arrow straight at Hruodland's chest.

The arrow dove into the shield, causing it to vibrate, yet the shield held. Hruodland kept running. The bandit dropped his bow and picked up a large ax. The thief lunged at Hruodland, intent on splitting his foe's skull. Blocking the blow with his shield, Hruodland heard it crack. His pulse pounding, Hruodland twisted and hacked into the thief's neck, almost beheading him in a burst of blood. Hruodland yanked the sword out of the corpse as the bandit's body tumbled to the ground. Tightening his grip with a blood-slick hand, he held the sword aloft again.

"You have roused the wrath of Hruodland of the March of Brittany!" he roared.

"He's a ghost," a thief screeched. "Flee! Flee!"

Six bandits dashed away from their hiding places and disappeared into the trees.

"Sebastian!" Elisabeth yelled. "Do not give chase! We need you here to protect us."

Hruodland stopped, his teeth clenched, his chest heaving. He wanted to smite every last one of them.

"Mother!" a young man wailed.

Turning toward the sound, Hruodland saw one of the pilgrims, an old woman, lying face down in a spreading pool of blood. A burning kindled in Hruodland's gut. *Hanging is too good for them!*

The young man and the nuns rushed to the old woman. Sister Elisabeth asked for her confession. Hruodland leapt over a thief's body and ran to help, with Fidelis at his heels. The young man lifted his mother's limp body. An arrow was buried in her blood-soaked chest.

"We must get her to a church with all haste so she can be buried in hallowed ground," Elisabeth ordered with a tremor in her voice.

Cradling his mother, the young man wept.

"Sebastian, how far is..." Elisabeth gasped when she looked at Hruodland. "Are you hurt?"

He looked down. The thief's blood covered his right arm and chest.

"No," he said, setting the ruined shield aside. He wiped his sword on his cloak. "You were asking about the next city?"

Staring at him with wide eyes, Elisabeth nodded. Illuna was pale and trembling.

"We are a day's journey from Saintes," he said.

Another pilgrim, a pockmarked man, groaned. Blood trickled through the fingers of his left hand pressed against his right arm. With some color returning to her face, Illuna told the man to stay still while she fetched bandages. As Illuna tended to the pilgrim, Hruodland hurriedly retrieved his throwing ax, and the other men rushed to gather their weapons. Thinking of the attack again, he scowled. *Damned thieves! Killing an old woman!* He again wanted to hunt them down, but helping the woman's soul go to heaven was far more important. Behind him, he heard the horse trotting back. *Cowardly beast!*

As the excitement of the battle waned and his pulse slowed, Hruodland felt a weariness settle on him. He would have to leave justice to the count of Saintes. As Hruodland had done in the March of Brittany, the count would send well-equipped men on good horses to pursue the bandits.

He took in his companions' situation with a glance. Thankfully, no other pilgrim was injured, but only he and one other man were fit for fighting. Four of the thieves had been slain. If the thieves did not claim their own dead, the count's men would bury them in shallow graves at the side of the road.

"God curse them," Hruodland muttered.

* * * * *

With help from Elisabeth, Hruodland bought a new shield in Saintes. During the next two months of travel, he was ever alert to the smallest noise during the day and made sure a man kept watch at night. The pilgrims had some difficulties: they broke a wheel, and one of the men succumbed to his illness. But they did not encounter brigands again. When the pilgrims arrived at Nantes about an hour before sunset, Hruodland's spirits rose. Seeing the tower and its arches rise above the city walls was like seeing snowdrop flowers rise through the snow and bloom. He was home, and he was not sure of what to do. A boy on the verge of manhood stood at the platform on top of the city walls, almost the same height as the trees.

"Who goes there?" the boy called down.

"Fetch your father," a pilgrim said.

"My father died at Roncevaux."

Hruodland looked down as he heard the boy tell other guards to let the pilgrims into the city. He was thinking of the men who had not returned. He knew them all. They were his men, and he could not save them. *Why, Lord, did You allow them to die? Why did You spare me?*

As Hruodland dismounted, the boy turned pale and made the sign of the cross. *I cannot be that changed,* Hruodland thought, reaching down to scratch his dog behind the ears. He was thinner, and his dark hair reached only the base of his neck. He had not shaved during the two months of the pilgrimage to Rennes and now had a beard.

"Young man," Hruodland asked, speaking slowly, "is Countess Alda here in Nantes or in Rennes?"

"C-countess Alda left the March of Brittany shortly after she learned of h-her husband's death," the boy stammered, bowing his head.

A knot formed in Hruodland's gut. "Where did she go? Did she marry another?"

"I don't know," he answered, staring at his wooden shoes and shifting from foot to foot. "I heard sh-she returned to her home."

"And Lord, uh, Count Gerard, where is he?"

"H-he is in Rennes." The boy's voice was barely audible.

Hruodland reached into his purse and tossed a coin — part of the profits of the jewels Elisabeth had sold. The boy caught the coin and thanked him but still did not look up.

Hruodland stood in the paved street, wet from a recent rain. Children were playing and begging. A child swineherd chased an errant pig. Women and old farmers haggled in the marketplace, some speaking Brythonic, others speaking Roman. Peasants who did notice Hruodland made the sign of the cross.

The evening sun made the church look like it was made of gold, a heavenly refuge from the mud and dung on the streets. Hruodland and the sisters arrived at the church steps under a carving of the Last Judgment. Hruodland pondered what to do next. He decided against walking directly to the manor. He had no wish to frighten the servants. Instead, he would see his uncle Guillaume, but not during Mass, not in public.

"Tend to my horse and Fidelis," he said to Elisabeth. "Once I speak to my uncle, I shall send for you."

Hruodland walked into the church and climbed the spiraling stairs to the bishop's study. It was almost time for vespers prayers, and he knew his uncle would want to read Scripture before Mass. Hruodland tried the door and found it was locked. He leaned against the wall and waited in the dark.

A light appeared at the end of the hall. Hruodland stood and tapped his left foot nervously. It had been so long since he had seen a kinsman. The point of light came closer, a candle held by a clerk. Hruodland called to Guillaume from the shadows. The bishop and the clerk both started. The clerk almost dropped the candle.

"Who is there?" the bishop asked, making the sign of the cross.

"It is Hruodland." He spoke very slowly, pronouncing each syllable, so it came out clearly.

The bishop's face and hands became pale. The clerk's knuckles whitened as he tightened his grip on the candle in his shaking hand. Guillaume fainted, his tall, gaunt frame falling into his clerk. The clerk lost his balance, and the candle flew out of his hand and landed at Hruodland's feet. Hruodland retrieved it and stamped out the tiny fire on the floor. He heard steps running away. Hruodland looked up. The clerk had fled.

"Wait!" Hruodland cried.

Guillaume moaned. He had red bump on his forehead. Hruodland knelt beside his uncle and carefully placed the candle on the floor. Guillaume opened his eyes and looked up into Hruodland's face. He gasped and sat up. He backed away from Hruodland, clutching his gold cross.

"What disturbs your peace?" Guillaume whispered, his eyes bulging.

"Somebody help me," a young man, probably the clerk, called out.

"Over here!" Hruodland slurred. "I will not hurt you."

Guillaume's face turned crimson. He brushed Hruodland away as he staggered to his feet. Hruodland rose.

"You are no ghost," Guillaume growled. His eyes raked Hruodland up and down. "My nephew did not look or speak thus. I shall not have him mocked. You will be flogged." He called to the clerk, "Come here. This man is a mere drunkard."

"I *am* your nephew," Hruodland said. "Do you not recognize me?"

"My nephew died at Roncevaux. He is in heaven. Both I and my brother said prayers to assure that."

"I did not die. Look at me."

"You bear an uncanny semblance to him, but my nephew was a warrior. You are no warrior."

The clerk returned and retrieved the candle. He stared at Hruodland.

Hruodland pushed back a sleeve. "Would a mere drunkard have battle scars?" he growled.

The bishop hesitantly touched a white, ropey scar. "Hruodland?"

"Yes. Hruodland," he said impatiently.

"It can't be," he murmured. He shook his head and looked dazed. "It can't be. Gerard, he... he told me that you fell at Roncevaux."

"They tell me I was near dead."

"Who?" Guillaume fumbled for a key on his belt.

"Sister Elisabeth and Sister Illuna. They are the ones who brought me back from the dead."

Guillaume's hand trembled as he tried to fit the key in the lock. He succeeded on the third attempt.

Stepping into the study, Hruodland explained, "I awoke at a hospital in the care of the nuns at Abbey of Saint Stephen. The sisters told me everyone was lost except me, and they thought I would die."

"Your Eminence," the clerk said, "we are expected at prayers."

"Tell them I am indisposed. And have the servants draw a bath and find some clothes worthy of a count."

"Ask them to draw baths for women as well," Hruodland added. "I have been traveling with Sister Elisabeth and Sister Illuna."

The bells rang. Hruodland and Guillaume bowed their heads and mouthed the Pater Noster.

As the ringing subsided, Hruodland asked, "Where did Alda go?"

"She went back to the Rhineland shortly after she heard of your..."

"Death," Hruodland finished for him. "I cannot believe she left."

"What did you expect? She failed to bear you children."

"You could have encouraged her to stay." Hruodland scowled.

"And let her tempt Gerard as well?"

"Tempt Gerard into what?"

"Into sin. The night she was told that you had fallen at Roncevaux that faithless woman was kissing your brother. I saw it with my own eyes."

"Alda would not do that."

"She did," the bishop insisted. "How can you be so blind to her?"

"She was — is — a good wife." Hruodland started pacing. "After I woke up from my long sleep, the only thing that pulled me through was the thought of coming back to Alda. If Gerard had not lied, she would still be here. Have you heard any word of her? Is she well? Has she married again?"

"What concern is it of mine?"

"I must find out what happened to her." Hruodland stopped pacing and stared out the window at the darkening sky.

"Why do you care? She never produced any children for you. You should be glad to be rid of her."

"What if she is in danger?"

"She left." Guillaume threw up his hands. "She is no longer your responsibility, and you are free to marry a fruitful woman."

"Alda is my wife. Do you expect me to abandon her, without knowing if she is alive or dead or married to another?"

"I expect you to serve your kinsmen and your king."

"And I shall," Hruodland said, "after I learn what happened to Alda."

"I do not understand why you would go through so much trouble for a barren woman."

"Alda was not barren," Hruodland retorted.

"Alda was a bad wife," Guillaume continued. "She was untrue to you. She was barren. She was disobedient. You should have repudiated her years ago. You no longer need to fear the wrath of her brother. You have another chance."

"I will hear no more of this nonsense."

Still, a trickle of doubt ran through his mind. Maybe, Guillaume spoke the truth — that Alda was barren. Perhaps he should forget about his love for his wife and marry a lady who could produce heirs. He was called away from his thoughts when a servant told his uncle the baths were ready.

As he and Guillaume walked to the men's bathhouse, Guillaume asked, "What happened at Roncevaux?"

"I don't know," Hruodland replied. "All I remember is climbing up a narrow path in the Pyrenees and then awakening in the hospital where Gerard had left me."

"Gerard. That liar. I will..."

"Peace, Uncle. Justice is mine."

"W-what will you do?" Guillaume stammered.

"I shall not harm him, if that is what you fear. He is still my brother. But he will account for his sin."

"Do not be too harsh. He has begotten an heir."

"Gerard is married?"

"Yes, he was married this winter. His wife is with child," Guillaume said, "and he has engendered a child in his concubine."

"That's good to hear," Hruodland muttered.

During their baths, Guillaume told Hruodland other news about the March of Brittany, but Hruodland only half listened. His mind was too full of worry for Alda. After the baths, Hruodland could not savor the fresh clothes smelling of wormwood. He could not enjoy the texture of the fine linen tunic and silk leggings or the feel of a smooth chin after his beard was shaved off. He wanted his wife.

Chapter 28

ruodland did not tarry in Nantes. He wanted to pray to the relics of Saint Melaine and talk to his brother. Gerard would know what had happened to Alda.

He and the sisters reached Rennes a week later, after a rainy, two-day journey through thick forest. The sun shone as they rode through the streets. Seeing more people make the sign of the cross, Hruodland wondered if a public announcement that he survived would have been better. He had decided to let the world think he was dead for a little while longer.

"I will meet you and Sister Illuna at the church," Hruodland told Elisabeth.

"Whither shall you go?" she asked.

"The count's manor. I have a matter to settle with my brother."

"Have mercy on him," Elisabeth pleaded. "He was distraught when he thought you were dying."

"He is just as much a part of this lie as Judith," Hruodland snapped. "And he will be punished. This is between me and him."

Hruodland marched into the count's manor. Fidelis followed at his heels. The guard, too terrified not to comply, let Hruodland into the castle and then ran away. As Hruodland entered the hall, a maidservant screamed, fell to her knees, and begged for mercy.

"Where is Gerard?" Hruodland said slowly, steadying his words.

"In the garden."

"Is he alone?"

"Yes," she whimpered.

Hruodland strode past her to the garden, where the late spring sun shone on plants in full leaf and flower. Gerard stood next to a rose bush laden with buds ready to burst into bloom.

"Gerard!" Hruodland bellowed.

The color left Gerard's face as he turned. "W-what t-troubles your soul?" he stammered.

"Why did you try to seduce my wife?" Hruodland roared.

"You are haunting me over a kiss?"

"I am alive!" he slurred.

"You are alive?" Gerard gasped, stumbling forward a step. "And there is the dog who protected you at Roncevaux!"

"I want an answer, Gerard. Why did you try to seduce my wife?"

"You are alive! I take your lands, and you are angry over a little kiss." Gerard laughed uncontrollably.

"I do not find this amusing."

"Very well. Here is your answer. When I kissed Alda, I was drunk, and I thought you were in the grave. When we left you at the abbey, I thought you had but one or two days left in this world." His eyes fell to the medal of Saint Peter on Hruodland's chest. "That is why I gave you the medal. If you could have but seen yourself... and we were trying to protect Alda."

"So you could seduce her?"

"As soon as I kissed her, she started weeping that I was not you."

Hruodland blinked and smiled. How could he have doubted her? His smile faded. "How were you protecting Alda by lying to her?" he asked sharply.

"She would have traveled all the way to the abbey, regardless of the danger. She would have risked rape, murder, or both — for what? A dead man? She could have prayed for your soul here in the March of Brittany. I thought you would want us to keep her safe."

Hruodland remembered his fight with the bandits and the old woman who had died. He shuddered at the thought of what might have happened to Alda during such an encounter.

"I have a feeling she is in danger," Hruodland said.

"Have you tidings of her?" Gerard asked eagerly.

"I was going to ask you the same question."

"She safely returned to Drachenhaus — my guards made sure of that. But the merchants say she left again. I don't know anything else." He shook his head. "If I could have but persuaded her to remain here. She would not heed me." Gerard stared at his hands and looked up at Hruodland again. "You say she is in danger?"

"It's a foreboding that follows me like a shadow. Perhaps her new husband is not so kind."

"Why do you allow your jealousy to lead you?"

"Do you not question your wife's fidelity?"

"My wife is too pious to be unfaithful," Gerard muttered.

"Too pious?" Hruodland arched a brow. "How can a woman be too pious?"

"When she uses Church teachings to refuse me. I might as well be married to a nun. She takes no pleasure in coupling with me, despite my best efforts." He shrugged. "At least, she is dutiful. My concubine is less virtuous than my wife, but she enjoys lying with me."

"No wonder you took a concubine."

"But it's difficult to keep two women happy. They are both demanding, especially now that they are both with child."

"They both know you are anxious for your unborn children and are acting accordingly." Hruodland chuckled. "They know you will do whatever you can to please them. For a man who claims to know the ways of women, you can be naïve."

"As can you," Gerard retorted. "As for Alda, I doubt she married again. She said I am the only one she would have consented to wed." His eyes widened as soon as he uttered the words.

"What?" Hruodland spat.

"When I told her you were dead, I thought I was speaking the truth. And if circumstances were different, I would have asked for her hand. She would have made a good wife."

They stared at each other in silence for a moment.

"So will you claim the March of Brittany and pretend the past year has not happened?" Gerard asked.

"I don't know what I shall do. I am torn between my duty to my family and my wife. I am going to the church to pray for guidance."

"If you need anything for a journey, say the word, and I will provide it, regardless of the expense. I owe you a great debt."

"That you do," Hruodland said bitterly.

"I thought I spoke the truth when I said you were dead. Why did I not get a message that you were alive?"

"Abbess Judith did not send any message despite my frequent requests. She lied to me as well, Gerard. Lies beget lies."

* * * * *

Hruodland hurried to the church. It was a work of art at the center of the city, towering over the stench of the streets and shells of huts, reaching toward heaven. Beggars crowded the steps where the carved Last Judgment loomed overhead. Although they trembled, the beggars still asked for alms. Hruodland grabbed a fistful of coins, threw them into the crowd, and entered the church.

He strode toward the altar, kissed the slab marking Saint Melaine's tomb, and knelt before him. Hruodland looked for his companions. To his right, Illuna was deep in prayer. Beside her, Elisabeth wept, her hand on the slab.

Hruodland closed his eyes and bowed his head. *What shall I do?* he asked the saint. *Did God spare my life so I could return home and serve the king? Maybe He let this happen so Alda would leave and I would be free to marry a woman who will give me heirs.*

He was ashamed of that last sentiment. *But why else would one get married?*

He felt a longing for Alda. Hruodland looked to his left and stared at the mural of the Crucifixion scene. The sorrow of the women watching from afar caught his eye.

Look at this, a voice told him. *Look at the women. The women never forsake Christ. Remember their love for their Lord,*

Hruodland. Such has been my fidelity for you. May Saint Melaine strike me down if my words are not true!

"Alda," Hruodland whispered. He could see her again, her emerald eyes blazing with a fire from within, her chest heaving, as if at any moment she would transform into a dragon and start breathing fire.

And Hruodland knew what the saint was telling him: Alda was his true bride, and he was to spare nothing in finding her.

* * * * *

When Hruodland told his brother of his intent to travel to Drachenhaus, Gerard was more than true to his word. He gave Hruodland their father's sword and seax. Hruodland unsheathed the sword and beheld the blade bequeathed to him by his father. A better weapon than the one from the abbey, the hilt felt as if it had been made for his hand.

Gerard told Hruodland to take the finest horse and handed him a sack full of coins. Hruodland planned to ride with five guards and some packhorses, changing horses instead of resting the animals. He did not know what had become of Alda, but his dreams of Ganelon had become more frequent.

Yet saying farewell to Sisters Elisabeth and Illuna was difficult.

"I must leave," he said. "The saint is instructing me to find Alda and to do so with all haste. I have ordered one my best men to guard you on your journey."

"Thank you for the protection. Illuna and I shall join pilgrims going to Rome. God be with you."

"And also with you," Hruodland replied. "And thank you for not forsaking me when I was in your care." He gave her the medal of Saint Peter. "A token of my gratitude."

Fidelis followed Hruodland as he mounted his horse. "Come along," Hruodland said as if the wolfhound would do anything else.

The forest swallowed Hruodland and his party. The trees and underbrush dressed richly in full leaf. The days were warm and longer. At the cities and abbeys, Hruodland again assumed the name Sebastian and told his hosts he was a natural son of Milo. He had a feeling it was to his advantage to let the world think

Hruodland of the March of Brittany was dead, just for a little while longer.

* * * * *

At Nonnenwerth, Plectrude again read the Rule of Saint Benedict to Alda during nones prayers. Alda understood more Latin words and phrases this time but not sentences.

Again, Plectrude posed a question to Alda in Latin. Alda, understanding only "Rule" and "fight," answered, "Yes."

"Very good," Radegunde said. "Two weeks hence, you shall take the vow."

"But Mother Radegunde," Plectrude protested, "a novitiate should last a year, not several months. So says the Rule of Saint Benedict."

"Alda is ready..." Radegunde's words were cut off by a coughing fit. Alda and the other sisters waited in silence.

Radegunde has been coughing much lately, Alda thought, *much as Hruodland's father did before...* She bowed her head and made the sign of the cross.

When Radegunde caught her breath, she said, "I have had a vision from the Mother of God that Alda should take the vow in two weeks' time."

"I still think it is unwise," Plectrude argued. "Saint Benedict had a reason to require novices to wait a year. He wants us to come to God of our own free will."

Radegunde again started coughing. "You come to God of your own free will, do you not, Alda?" she asked between rattling breaths.

Alda nodded numbly.

"So Sister Prioress, you wish to defy the will of the Blessed Mother?"

"No," Plectrude mumbled, her face turning crimson.

"Then, Alda will take the vow in two weeks," Radegunde said.

As the abbess and the others filed out of the church, Alda lingered and knelt before the altar, gazing at Christ and His Mother in Their majesty. In her heart, Alda knew Plectrude should be the next abbess, but what support did the prioress have among the nobility? Plectrude's mother was a commoner, and her father was dead. It would be better if Alda was abbess and could let Plectrude manage the abbey as she saw fit rather than have some stranger here who would do God only knew what.

Why did doubt still gnaw at her mind? *Mother of God, what shall I do?*

"I think Mother Radegunde's vision is of her own death," Plectrude muttered, startling Alda. "She should not defy the rule of Saint Benedict."

"I do not see how delaying the vow until late autumn would change anything."

Plectrude said something in Latin. Alda looked at her quizzically.

"Just as I thought," Plectrude said. "You have little idea of what I read to you at prayers."

"You told me you were taught Latin since you were a child. It is unfair to rebuke me for not completely comprehending a language I have studied for only a few months."

"I am not finding fault with you," she said. "But you cannot fight under a Rule you do not understand. What I told you translates like this: 'When she is to be received, she promises before all in the oratory stability, fidelity to the monastic life, and obedience. This promise she shall make before God and His saints, so that if she should ever act otherwise, she may know she will be condemned by Him whom she mocks.'"

"Oh," Alda said, looking down.

"You should leave now. As a novice, you are free."

Alda's thoughts strayed to Drachenhaus. How she missed Werinbert and her mother and Veronica. She pressed her iron dragon close to her heart. *When I become the abbess, we will all be allowed a visit from family.* The thought strengthened her resolve, but still, she longed to be home.

"If I could," Alda said, her voice barely audible, "but I have no place else to go. The outside world is dangerous for me, and if my enemy finds me, my nephew will be slain."

"But once you take the vow, you cannot leave, even to see your nephew."

"I know," she murmured, "but if I am hidden and removed from the world, my enemy will let him be."

Chapter 29

uring the two-week journey, two heartrending questions followed Hruodland as he rode through rain and shine and green shadows. Had Alda married again? Was she in danger?

When he arrived at the village near Drachenhaus, he was dirty, damp, and unshaven. Hruodland remembered how he had come to Alda in this state a few years ago, yet she had wanted him anyway.

As Hruodland and his party rode on the muddy path that led toward the mountain, the villagers paused in their chores to stare at him. Hruodland recognized a dark-haired woman on the path before him. She made the sign of the cross when she saw him and trembled when he dismounted.

He called her by name: "Veronica!"

Veronica became pale. She opened her mouth but no sound came out.

"Fear not," he said, laboring to keep his words clear, "I am no spirit. I mean you no harm."

"You are alive?" Veronica whispered.

"Yes, alive."

She drew a sharp breath, and her eyes opened wide. Then, a smile spread on her face. "Saints be praised. But how...?"

"I have come for Alda," Hruodland said.

"You have come for Alda," Veronica echoed. "You... have come... for Alda."

"Is she at Drachenhaus?"

Veronica shook her head, looking dazed.

"Has she married again?" he asked.

"No."

"Then where is she?"

"She... she is on Nonnenwerth."

"Take me there at once."

"If I could, my lord. But there is a river between us and Nonnenwerth. We need a boat, and the countess can provide you with one. She will be so glad. Come with me to the castle." She tugged at his hands.

They started to ascend the mountain trail. Hruodland led his horse as Veronica walked beside him. Fidelis and Hruodland's men followed. The trees on either side of them formed a green thicket so dense that Hruodland half-expected them to close behind him, the way the wall of fire closed behind Siegfried when he went to Brunhilde's castle and awakened her. For a few moments, the only sound was the horses' hooves hitting the ground.

"I have no idea how I shall tell the dowager countess that you are alive," Veronica said half to herself.

"Allow me to do so."

"I have no wish to frighten my lady," Veronica said.

At the gate, Veronica explained to the guard that Hruodland and his men were friends. "Wait here," she told Hruodland. "I will not tarry."

"It will be a shock, no matter who tells her," he said. He handed his horse's reins to one of his men and followed Veronica.

When they entered the hall, Theodelinda was ordering the servants to clean the hearth. Turning toward the sound at the door, she screamed, "Lord help us!"

Hruodland drew his sword and looked behind him for the intruder as Veronica ran toward Theodelinda.

"Countess, he is not a ghost," she cried. "He is alive."

Hruodland sheathed his sword. Theodelinda was gasping for air.

"I did not mean to frighten you, Mother," he said. He grabbed a servant's arm. "Have the cupbearer fetch some wine."

Theodelinda leaned on Veronica and staggered to a seat near the fire. "Welcome to the House of the Dragon," she mumbled. She stared at Hruodland as if she were awakening from a dream.

"Countess," Veronica whispered, "our prayers have been answered."

"More than answered," Theodelinda murmured, still staring at Hruodland.

The cupbearer came with a full cup, took a sip, then handed it to Theodelinda. Theodelinda swallowed a gulp of wine, watching Hruodland over the rim of the cup.

"I need a boat to take me to Nonnenwerth," Hruodland said, sitting across from Theodelinda.

"I shall have a fisherman take you there after prime prayers tomorrow, but only if you promise to take Alda home with you." Color was returning to Theodelinda's face.

"Of course, I will take Alda home with me. Why else would I go?"

"What happened to you?" Theodelinda asked. "We were told you and Alfihar fell at Roncevaux. Leonhard sent me Alfihar's amulet."

Hruodland looked down at the mention of Alfihar's name. He felt a pang in his heart. How he wished he could tell Theodelinda what had happened at that pass in the Pyrenees.

"I have no memory of the battle," he said. "I awoke in a hospital, barely able to move or speak. The sisters healed my body, but my tongue is still slow."

"Why didn't you send a message to Alda?" Theodelinda asked bitterly. "Or did you no longer want to give her your protection?"

"Lies kept me from my wife. I will fetch Alda from Nonnenwerth at this moment, if you would but lend me a boat."

"If I had one available now, you could use it, but the fishermen are all out on the river." She looked Hruodland up and down. "And you need a bath unless you wish to present yourself to your wife as a slovenly beggar."

"You are right, Mother." Hruodland laughed. "I should look like a prince, not a ruffian. What tidings do you have of Alda?"

"I saw her at Epiphany, and..." Theodelinda paused. "She was thin. The prioress handed me a message from her. She was asking for all the grain I could spare. So I sent wheat."

"Have you gotten any other message from her?"

"The message last winter was the only one," Veronica said.

"But," Theodelinda interjected, "the merchants told me they saw bread on the tables at Nonnenwerth. One of them talked about a novice who drew her veil over her face as soon as he entered the abbess's reception room. He said the novice flattered him and engaged him in bargaining. Then, the abbess rebuked her for enjoying the worldliness of trade."

"That's Alda," Hruodland said with a smile. "Why would she hide her face?"

"If it were not for..." Theodelinda and Veronica exchanged a look.

"For what?" Hruodland asked. What were they not telling him? Had she become disfigured from smallpox?

"It is for Alda to tell you," Theodelinda said. "Once she knows she has your protection again, she will leave that hateful island."

* * * * *

Alda donned the clothes from her old life. Today was the day: she was going to take the vow.

She thought of the ring and the dragon amulet she had hidden under her pillow. She had given her property to the monastery, even her girdles, necklaces, bracelets, circlets, and rings. After today, she would give up control of her own body. She remembered how Radegunde had translated Saint Benedict's words: "Reserving nothing at all for herself." *But my ring and amulet are not worth much*, Alda reasoned. *The Church can have them after my death.*

She had dreamt of Hruodland two nights ago. She dreamt she was making love to him. *Is this the right path?* she had asked the Blessed Virgin yesterday as she knelt in the church before the image of Christ and Mary in heaven. There must be some reason God had not taken her when He took Hruodland. There must be some reason she remained in this world.

As she entered the church, she thought, *No turning back.*

She walked past the images of martyrdom, toward the altar. The sun illuminated the image of Christ and Mary. The image filled Alda's mind. Her arms opened as if to embrace the Savior and His Mother. The sisters stood in a circle. Alda was in the middle. She fell to her knees and took the vow of stability, fidelity to monastic life, and obedience.

A clerk wrote a document as Alda spoke, and Alda scrawled her name at the bottom. She placed the document and her hand upon the altar and sang in Latin, concentrating on the pronunciation. The sisters responded in Latin.

Alda lay on the floor, prostrating herself at her sisters' feet. This was difficult for her, but Saint Benedict wanted humility, not pride. The sisters prayed over her. She was a Sister of the Sacred Blood now, a bride of God. She would stay with the sisters forever.

The prayers ended. One of the sisters took her blue silk veil. Another cut Alda's hair close to her scalp. The sisters removed her old clothes, her old life, embroidered gown, leather boots. They dressed her in the garb of a sister, black wool habit and rude linen veil, wooden shoes, a scrap of leather for a belt.

The sisters, her sisters, smiled. Radegunde was smiling. Alda managed a smile, but she was troubled. She should have felt joy at this moment. But a nameless doubt still gnawed at the corner of her mind.

Chapter 30

A cold rain soaked Hruodland as he set foot on the dock at Nonnenwerth the next morning. The fisherman who had rowed the boat followed him. Hruodland rapped on the door of the gatehouse. After a moment, he heard the tapping of a cane and the shuffling of wooden shoes against a floor. An old woman, so wizened that Hruodland could not even begin to guess her age, opened the door. After he said his business was with the abbess, the porter walked with him through the rain and mud to the abbess's residence, a two-story building made of the wood from the forest. Hruodland welcomed the solid wood under his feet as he stepped into the hall, illuminated by gray light seeping through the windows and the glowing hearth at its center.

"Who should I say is here to see her?" the porter asked.

"Hruodland, prefect of the March of Brittany."

"It is not kind to joke like that, sir. I can make out enough details to see that you are a nobleman, but your noble blood does not excuse you from mocking the dead. Hruodland was a kinsman of the abbess and the husband of one of our sisters. He died at Roncevaux doing the work of our Lord. Show some respect."

"I meant no mockery," Hruodland said slowly, pushing his wet hair from his eyes. "I survived the slaughter at Roncevaux. I am Hruodland. Tell the abbess one of her kinsmen is here to see her."

The porter hobbled off and returned minutes later. She said, "They will see you now."

"They?"

"The abbess and her prioress."

Hruodland offered his arm to the porter. Her gnarled hands were icy. She already seemed exhausted from her errand.

Hruodland entered the room in which the abbess received guests. The porter left. The abbess looked down at Hruodland from an ornate chair, a mural of the Crucifixion behind her, candles blazed on either side of her. The abbess sat erect, chin up. The prioress stood to the abbess's right, half in the shadows.

Another pair of candles burned to Hruodland's left and right, lighting the scene from the Final Judgment, brightening the golden white of heaven, adding more flames to hell. Radegunde's face betrayed no emotion. Her talon-like hand gripped the staff tightly.

"What is your errand?" Radegunde growled.

She wastes no time on formality or politeness. "I have come here for my wife," he answered.

The abbess had a coughing fit. When she caught her breath again, she frowned.

Why does she act so? She is not glad that I survived Roncevaux? "Is Alda here?" Hruodland asked irritably.

"Yes, she is here," the abbess said.

A long silence.

Hruodland cleared his throat. "I have come to take her home."

"This is her home. She took the vow yesterday. She is one of us."

"But she is my wife."

"Marriage is an arrangement between men. Alda has made a vow to God. Do you expect your wife to break a sacred promise? Do you want your wife to leave the monastery if it means mocking God and damning her soul?" She looked at the mural above Hruodland's head, at the Christ larger than life, at the small naked figure before Him.

"But I love her," Hruodland said. "Surely, God will understand."

"You presume the will of God."

"So do you," Hruodland said, not disguising that his patience was wearing thin.

"The writings of Saint Benedict say once a woman takes the vow she cannot leave the monastery. Alda took the vow of her own free will."

"Saint Melaine told me to come for Alda," Hruodland said emphatically. "I prayed before his relics. He spoke to me in Alda's voice."

"Allow me to pray on this," Radegunde said, staring at the Final Judgment. "Sister Prioress, take him to the hall." She dismissed Hruodland with a wave of her hand.

Hruodland swallowed his anger at being treated like a servant and followed the prioress out of the room. *Do whatever you must to bring Alda home.*

The prioress led him to the hall. "We will wait here."

"You can wait here," Hruodland snapped. "I am going to the church. I, too, wish to pray."

He turned his back on the prioress and left before she had a chance to reply. Outside, the rain had become a drizzle. He walked through the mud to the church, where a candle was burning at the altar before a mural of Christ and His Mother. He strode to the altar and lit a second candle. A glint of metal on the floor caught his eye. He bent toward the object and picked it up. It was a ring.

He held it in the light of a candle. It was Alda's ring, his morning gift to her.

* * * * *

Alda slowly walked toward the church, her eyes scanning the mud. She hoped her ring had not sunk into it. She had kept it on a ribbon under her habit and had discovered during her class that the ribbon had broken.

Alda had excused herself to go to the privy. Outside the classroom, she tied the broken ends of the ribbon together. Mud oozed around her wooden shoes and splattered her habit.

It is a sin to search for the ring. It is worldly. Return to class this instant, she told herself as she continued to scan the mud. *It is God's will you lose the ring.*

Alda drew her cloak closer to her as the drizzle wetted her face. She kept searching for a glimmer of gold or the wink of a ruby in the mud. She was shivering when she arrived at the church. *Mother of God, please let it be in there.*

Entering the church, she noticed a second candle was burning at the altar and saw the silhouette of a tall man. As he turned toward the door, she beheld his face. She gasped.

"Hruodland?"

"Alda?"

At first, she walked toward him. Then, her steps quickened to a run. Her shoes clattered against the wooden floor.

She and Hruodland embraced. Alda was struck speechless, weeping. He kissed her. She kissed him. He felt so real, so warm, like he was alive.

"I missed you," she whispered.

Hruodland, too, was crying. "You are the only one to have no fear of me."

What happened to his speech? The angels must serve wine. "Why would I fear you?" she said. "I love you."

"I love you, Alda." He held her face in his hands. "I have longed for you."

As she caressed him, her desire was reawakened.

"What troubles your soul?" she asked, noticing that he was thinner than she remembered. "What brings you here?"

"I have come to take you home."

"I have prayed for this for so long."

Alda had thought death would be painful, a crushing of the heart, a stiffness of the body, the soul forced through the mouth. Yet she had not noticed it. She wondered where her body was. She did not see it in the church. *It must be lying in the mud outside. No matter. I no longer need it.*

"When did I die?" she asked.

His jaw dropped, then his eyes searched her face. "You are alive," he said.

"Then, this is another dream?" She looked down, disappointed.

"It is not a dream."

Alda shook her head, confused.

"Alda, my dearling, I am not dead, either. I survived the attack at Roncevaux."

If Hruodland had not been holding her, Alda was sure she would have swooned. They staggered to a bench along the wall and held each other for a long time in silence. *It did work,* she thought. *The amulet did protect him.*

"Hruodland, I thought, your brother himself told me..."

"We were both deceived. When Gerard told you I was dead, he believed it. I had been gravely wounded on the battlefield, and he and his men had taken me to an abbey to await a Christian burial."

"If I had known, I would have gone to you."

"I know."

Alda leaned against Hruodland's shoulder. She wanted to hold him, make sure he was real.

"I prayed for you every day," she finally said.

Hruodland kissed her. "Why did you come here instead of remaining at Drachenhaus?"

Alda trembled and bit her lip. She looked up at him, tears studding her eyes. Again, she felt Ganelon's weight and the cold iron against her throat.

"Ganelon," she managed to say before her sobs overwhelmed her. She felt Hruodland's torso and arms stiffen.

"What did he do?" Hruodland's voice echoed in the church.

"He... he tried to... tried to..." She buried her face in her hands.

"He tried to rape you?"

"My virtue is intact," she said in a choked voice. She glanced up at her husband. His eyes blazed; his jaw was rigid.

"He will never trouble you again." Hruodland's voice was even but carried an undercurrent of rage. "But now gather your things, and we shall go to Drachenhaus."

The mention of Alda's birthplace stirred memories of a hot bath smelling of rosemary and lavender. A bathhouse warming room with a bright fire. Imported, spicy perfume. Roasted pork. Wine sweetened with honey and woodruff. Ribbons and bracelets and girdles. Linen and silk. Everything she had done without. Everything she had sworn to forsake.

"When I took the vow, I thought you were lost to me."

"I am here now," he replied. "We can start anew."

"No. I lost you by my own hand, by taking the vow. I am married to God. I cannot go back with you." She remembered what Plectrude had told her: if she left, she would be condemned for mocking God. "I still love you. I shall always love you. But I took the vow with God."

"God will understand," Hruodland said. "One of His saints sent me here to find you. I heard him speaking to me in your voice."

Alda brightened. "Did he say for me to come with you?"

"Not explicitly. He was talking about the women who were with Christ when He died, the way you were when you swore your fidelity to me."

They both heard the church door creak open and turned toward the sound as Plectrude entered.

"The abbess will see you," she said.

Leaving the church, Hruodland and Alda held hands and walked through the mist to the abbess's residence.

"The abbess will speak to Alda first," Plectrude said.

Alda kissed Hruodland before she followed Plectrude into the abbess's reception room. Although it was summer, Alda felt as if she were stepping on ice when she entered through the doorway below Christ judging the dead. Alda drew her damp veil and cloak close to her.

"I apologize for the wait," Alda said. "I was in the church."

"Do you pine for your old life?" Radegunde asked, her face and voice stern.

"I know my husband is alive, Mother Radegunde."

Alda looked at Christ crucified in the mural behind the abbess, the supreme sacrifice, this death so the faithful could live. *Which saint should I heed?* she asked Him. *What is Your will?*

Radegunde had another coughing fit. "Your vow to Our Lord is more sacred than an arrangement between your husband and your kin."

"I know," Alda said softly. "But..." She could not say any more.

"Mother," Plectrude interjected, "perhaps the Lord did send Hruodland."

Radegunde cut Plectrude off with a glare and dismissed the prioress with a wave of her hand.

"But..." Plectrude protested.

"Go," Radegunde barked, before coughing again.

Plectrude hesitated and then obeyed.

When Plectrude left the room, Radegunde laid her staff aside. She rose from her chair, descended the steps and touched Alda's sleeve. "The love of Our Lord is more glorious than that of any man," she said.

"Can I not love both the Lord and my husband?" Alda asked, her voice cracked.

"Your husband might say he loves you, but…"

"I know he loves me," Alda interrupted, drawing her arm away from Radegunde. "I have given him reason to have the marriage annulled. No doubt his uncles would oblige. To come all this way for a woman who did not bear him children, why else would he be here?"

"Perhaps on an errand from the Devil to tempt your soul from the path to heaven."

"My husband is a good man." She squared her shoulders. "He would never…"

The abbess doubled over as she coughed again. She took a rattling breath. "Perhaps, this man is not your husband," Radegunde rasped.

"I know he is," Alda insisted.

"The Devil is very clever. He knows your weakness."

"But Hruodland was in the church. A devil would not step foot into a church. A devil would not wear a cross."

"Then, perhaps, he is an agent of the Devil — an unintentional one."

"I don't understand."

"Did he tell you that Saint Melaine sent him?"

"Yes."

"Perhaps, it was not Saint Melaine, but the Devil."

"How could that be? The relics would protect him."

"The Devil is very clever, child," the abbess said, guiding Alda to her adjoining study with one arm and taking a candle in her free hand. "But we have the Word of God as a defense. We have the Rule of Saint Benedict." The abbess lit the candles in her study. "You can read."

"A little," Alda replied. The language of the church was still foreign to her.

"Read Saint Benedict for yourself," Radegunde said.

The abbess picked a leather-and-wood-bound volume from a shelf and held it by the edges in both hands, almost afraid her touch would spoil it. She laid the book on the desk next to a small

Pieta and turned the parchment, each page crafted with letters and illuminations. She pointed out the passage.

Alda bent over the book and read. She struggled over the curves of the letters and tried stringing them into words, translating them to Frankish, piecing the translation into a sentence.

"I cannot comprehend this," she confessed.

"Saint Benedict is clear," the abbess said. "It translates like this. 'When she is to be received, she promises before all in the oratory stability, fidelity to the monastic life, and obedience. This promise she shall make before God and His saints, so that if she should ever act otherwise, she may know she will be condemned by Him whom she mocks.'"

Must this be Your will, Lord? Alda prayed, gazing at the Pieta. It was as if a pack of wolves grabbed her heart and left nothing but a smudge of blood. Alda stared at the words, wishing she could will them to change, to make an exception. She knew Radegunde was watching her, yet she could not look up at her.

Radegunde coughed and spat on the ground. Blood.

"What is your choice, child?" she croaked.

As if I had a choice. "I shall follow God's will, Mother," Alda murmured, looking down.

"Good. Return to your class."

"What shall I tell Hruodland?"

"Nothing. I shall speak to him."

"Allow me to see him one last time," Alda pleaded.

"You have had enough temptation. Return to your class."

"But this will break his heart. He ought to hear it from me. I am his wife. He deserves that. He ought to know it is God's will, not mine."

"You owe him nothing. He already is sabotaging your journey to heaven by bringing back your willfulness. Return to your class. Now."

"Please," Alda begged.

She felt the iron dragon amulet against her heart. It used to give her courage, boldness, like the boldness Siegfried needed to face the dragon.

Now it was a mere remembrance of an old life. She wanted to give it to Hruodland so he would remember her, even as he found another wife. She wanted him to remember that she never stopped loving him.

"No," the abbess said harshly. "Need I remind you of your vow to obey? Return to your class. And leave here by a back door. I do not want you to see him."

Radegunde followed Alda to the door of the reception room. Alda turned toward the hall, where Hruodland was.

"You are to go through that door," Radegunde ordered, pointing the opposite way.

Alda's gaze met the abbess's.

Radegunde shuddered. "I see the Devil's malice in your eyes. Obey me, or God will punish you."

Alda pressed her lips together holding back the curses she wanted to yell. She obeyed the abbess's command. Her eyes stung as she left the abbess's residence. She hated the abbess and hoped her death would be bitter and painful. *I have just cut myself off forever from my husband.*

* * * * *

Hruodland entered the abbess's reception room. She sat on her throne, framed by the Crucifixion. She stared past Hruodland at the Christ over the doorway, the Christ judging a small naked soul, hearing at this moment whether she would wear white and go to the golden, rosy clouds or be thrown naked to the tortures of demons.

"Where is Alda?" Hruodland asked.

"She has chosen to follow the path to God," Radegunde replied as if the Christ above the doorway asked the question.

"What do you mean?"

"She will remain at the abbey."

Hruodland was silent for a moment. "She is my wife," he said.

The abbess tightened her grip on her staff. With her free hand, she fingered her crucifix. Still staring at Christ, she said, "She is no longer yours. Her vow to God is sacred." Her hand swallowed the crucifix. Her voice trembled. "There is no love greater than what Christ gives to us. I shall not let you break it. I shall not let you condemn her soul."

The Cross and the Dragon

She wants Alda's wealth, Hruodland thought, his wife's gaunt face fresh in his mind. *I must get Alda to leave this madwoman, no matter what price, or she will die.* "If she returns with me," he said, "I shall let you keep her dowry."

"What does a dowry mean to God?" Radegunde snapped. "She is a sister, and we shall not forsake her."

"I shall have the king remove you from your abbey."

Radegunde's frown deepened. Then she started coughing, the way his father had before he died. When the fit passed, the abbess's spine straightened. Her eyes dropped from Christ to Hruodland and pierced him. The fist around the crucifix tightened.

"You will not threaten me," she snarled. "Begone."

"I almost died for Our Lord," Hruodland roared.

The abbess stood and drove her staff to the floor beside her. "I said begone. If you do not leave, I shall have you removed."

"By whom?" Hruodland mocked. "That lame, blind, old woman? Do you think I did not notice you want for young men among your tenants?"

Hruodland was going to take Alda back by force. No one could stop him. To his satisfaction, he saw the abbess was quaking. "Very well," he said slowly. "I shall leave your residence."

He walked to the church and waited in the cold mist. When the terce bell rang, he saw the women coming for prayers. Hruodland spotted Alda. Her eyes were red. Her face was flushed. She froze as he approached her. Other nuns turned to look at him.

He took two steps toward her and seized her arm. "You will come with me."

"Husband, I cannot," she said, looking toward the abbess.

Hruodland glared at the abbess. How dare she fill Alda's head with such ideas! If it were not for Ganelon, Alda would never have met this madwoman. She would be at Drachenhaus, well fed and bargaining with the merchants.

"You are my wife," he commanded. "You will do as I say."

"Please do not make this more difficult. If you could but read the words of Saint Benedict..."

"And what does Saint Benedict say?"

"He says my soul will be damned if I leave the abbey."

Hruodland was too stunned to speak. Alda would be damned? Alda? She had done nothing wrong, only sought refuge from Ganelon. Ganelon, that cur, was the one who should be damned. And if he were standing here, Hruodland would run a sword through him and send him to hell, where he belonged.

"I do not know why Saint Melaine sent you here," Alda finally said. "Perhaps it is for me to release you so that you can marry a woman who will give you children."

"You took a vow with me," he growled, his grip tightening, "and I do not release you from it."

Alda could no longer hold back the tears. She pulled her arm away from his grasp and reached for a ribbon under her clothes. She brought out the iron dragon amulet with the stone from Drachenfels and untied the ribbon. Pressing the amulet into his hand, she kissed him.

"Remember me," she said. "Remember my love for you."

She slipped a ring off his little finger. His morning gift to her.

"I shall not forget you," she whispered.

She ran to her sisters. The abbess put her arm around Alda's shoulders. Hruodland could see by the slump of Alda's shoulders that she was crying. Her sisters gathered around her.

Hruodland knew he could carry her off, but he would not do so if it meant endangering her soul. Hruodland stared at the amulet. No one could have stopped him from taking her back. No one except her.

Fury clouded Hruodland's eyes. Fury with Ganelon for such a low act. Fury with himself for failing to protect his wife. His blood enemy had won. Ganelon had failed to steal Alda's honor, but he had done much worse. Because of Ganelon, Hruodland and Alda could no longer be together as man and wife.

"I will be avenged," Hruodland muttered to the dragon. "We both will be."

Chapter 31

ruodland had one thought as the boat took him back to Drachenhaus's riverbank: vengeance.

He looked toward the castle and found that clouds shrouded the mountain the way rage shrouded his heart. As he rode up the mountain, he brooded: Alda was forever lost to him, and it was Ganelon who caused it.

As soon as he stepped foot into the hall at Drachenhaus, his grief deepened. Servants had polished the table and chairs with linseed oil and lemon balm. The floor had been scrubbed and covered with fresh rushes, and a fire blazed in the hearth.

Theodelinda and Werinbert ran toward him. The smile on the dowager countess's lips faded. "Where's Alda?" she demanded.

"Alda cannot leave the abbey," Hruodland growled.

Werinbert burst into tears. "Why?"

Theodelinda bent to comfort her grandson. "But she is still a novice. I thought novices could leave of their own free will."

"That madwoman convinced her to take the vow early." Fury burned in Hruodland's dark eyes. "I tried to take her back by force, but she said she will be damned if she leaves the island."

"Ask my brother about that," Theodelinda said. "He is a learned man, and he owes me a debt. It is because of his lie that Alda is on that island."

"His and my brother's," Hruodland muttered. "Well intentioned lies. But it is not the lies that put Alda there. It is Ganelon."

"Is he the wicked man?" Werinbert asked, looking up at his grandmother.

"Very wicked," Hruodland said.

"She told you," Theodelinda whispered.

"That cur will pay for his sin," Hruodland snarled. "Alda's honor will be avenged."

"What is avenge?" Werinbert asked.

"It means to right a wrong, dearling." She stood and turned toward Hruodland. "I cannot thank you enough. Ask me for what you will need, and I will provide it."

"Where is Ganelon? Did he go to battle the Saxons this year?"

"The merchants told me he remains at Dormagen, although his leg has healed." Theodelinda smiled grimly. "Ganelon leapt out the window from the solar to avoid our justice. I had hoped the fall would cripple him."

"Why did he stay behind?" Hruodland asked.

"I suspect he lied about his leg — and how it was injured."

Hruodland knew his next move. Even if Alda couldn't leave the abbey, he was going to make certain that Ganelon could never threaten her again. And the only way to do that was to kill him.

The next morning, Hruodland set out for Dormagen by horse with his guards and a servant who drove a well-provisioned cart drawn by a mule. Unbidden, Fidelis trotted alongside Hruodland.

Hruodland smiled and threw a piece of salted meat to the wolfhound. The dog wagged his tail and relished the treat.

"Fidelis, you have no idea of the evil we shall face," he said.

* * * * *

Ever since Hruodland had left Nonnenwerth two days before, Alda did nothing but kneel and pray in the church before the image of Christ and the Blessed Mother in majesty.

"Why?" she whispered, clutching her cross.

She stared at the ring on her finger and kissed it. She didn't care if Radegunde would have her beaten for wearing it. She didn't care about anything now that Hruodland was gone. She felt like a shell with the life sucked out of it. How much worse could hell be than this?

She barely noticed the bell tolling for nones prayers. She stood as the other sisters entered. Radegunde came in, coughing. The abbess was shivering, and her face was sickly pale.

Good, Alda thought, *let her suffer. Oh God, forgive me.*

While Alda and the other sisters chanted, Radegunde mumbled and could barely keep her eyes open. In the middle of a song, the abbess swooned. Alda stood still as a statue as the sisters tried to revive her.

"Mother Radegunde, Mother Radegunde," one of them yelled, shaking the abbess's shoulder.

Radegunde opened her eyes a slit and groaned.

"Take her to a cot in the infirmary," Prioress Plectrude ordered.

Radegunde had a look of horror as two sisters lifted her.

"Don't worry, Mother Radegunde," Plectrude said sarcastically. "God will forgive you if we make you comfortable in your final hours."

"No," Radegunde moaned. "Die... bed of ashes."

"Take her to a cot. Now!" Plectrude shouted. "All of you accompany her and pray for her soul. I will come soon to read from Revelation."

Alda stayed behind while the other sisters left. Soon, she and Plectrude were alone in the church.

"What troubles you, Alda? For two days, I have seen you here at the altar. You do not go to class or eat or sleep."

Alda swallowed back the tears. "Mother Radegunde says if I rejoin my husband I shall be condemned, yet I cannot stop thinking of him."

"Mother Radegunde is mortal."

"That has become painfully clear," Alda said bitterly.

Plectrude looked at the door through which Radegunde had left and scowled. She turned toward Alda. "You will not be condemned if you go to your husband."

"But Saint Benedict says..."

"I only told you that so you would leave before you bound yourself to a Rule that you did not understand. And you still do not understand it," Plectrude snapped. "You do not want to be a nun. You *never* wanted to be a nun."

"But I am a nun, and I will be damned if I leave. Radegunde said so."

"Radegunde twisted the truth," Plectrude said, "so that you would stay here — so that you, not her bastard cousin, would succeed her as abbess. I am more worthy to lead this abbey, despite my low birth. You know that. You know that in your heart."

"It was Radegunde's scheme, not mine," Alda retorted. "And now I am trapped, too."

"You are not trapped. I should have told you this two days ago. If I but had the courage to argue with Radegunde openly — no matter now. Radegunde is dying, and I can tell you the whole truth, not just what Radegunde wanted you to hear. You can leave. You have a place with your husband."

"How?" Alda pleaded. "How can I leave here without being damned?"

Plectrude walked toward a lectern upon which a Bible rested, its parchment pages open. "Mother Radegunde first broke the Rule of Saint Benedict by pressing you to take the vow before a year had expired. Saint Benedict wants a woman to deliberate for a full year before making a decision to stay in the monastery forever. Saint Benedict and the Lord Himself would hold you blameless."

Plectrude stooped over the Bible in a sphere of candlelight and flipped the pages. "Here are the words of Our Lord from the Gospel of Saint Mark. It translates into this: 'But from the beginning of the creation God made them male and female. For this cause, shall a man leave his father and mother and cleave to his wife. And the twain shall be one flesh. What therefore God has joined together, let not man put asunder.'" She looked up. "Because your husband lives, you need his permission to join this order."

The last sentence Plectrude had read echoed in Alda's mind. *What therefore God has joined together, let not man put asunder.* The words of Jesus Himself.

Alda trembled and covered her mouth. She looked at the prioress, who was gazing over her shoulder at Christ. Again, Alda saw adoration on Plectrude's face.

Was there a way to persuade the king to appoint Plectrude as the abbess? Plectrude knew the Bible and Saint Benedict's Rule, and like Alda, she wanted to make life better for the sisters. Above all, Plectrude had a vocation — something Alda lacked.

Plectrude turned her gaze toward Alda.

"I must join my husband." Alda smiled as if a boulder had been lifted from her chest. "He said he did not release me from the vow I made to him. We are of one flesh. It is God's will I be with him, isn't it?"

"Yes, it's God's will."

"How can I ever thank you?"

"Extol my virtues to the king when he seeks a successor to Radegunde and send him gifts on my behalf," Plectrude answered. "When I am abbess, such a case as yours will not happen again. Sisters will understand the Rule under which they shall live and serve — and take a full year to deliberate."

"You have my word," Alda replied, "and my promise to provide for the sisters in times of need."

The sun was shining as Alda and Plectrude left the church.

"Come with me to the treasury," Plectrude said under her breath.

"Why?" Alda asked as she hurriedly following the prioress.

Plectrude's keys clanked at her hip.

"That is where we have kept your dowry. The Lord has given us an opportunity. If you leave now, you will not be missed. Gather your things and leave as soon as a boat arrives, and fare well."

"God be with you," Alda said.

"And also with you."

* * * * *

Because the ceremony for Alda to take the vow had been rushed, Alda found that her old clothes were still in the novices' wardrobes. Plectrude had told her Saint Benedict said to keep them in case a woman would ever leave the monastery. Alda reminded herself of Jesus' words: *What therefore God has joined together, let not man put asunder.*

As the words echoed in her mind, she felt joy for the first time in more than a year. She loved God, adored Him, would do anything, sacrifice anything for Him, now that He had set her free.

She realized fear had kept her at Nonnenwerth. It was not love for God, she thought, weeping. She had not felt this adoration until moments ago, when Plectrude told her she could leave. For months, she had felt fear, fear of Ganelon, then of God, the same way Radegunde did. Radegunde knew only God's rule, not God's love.

Radegunde, Alda thought, frowning, and then pushed the thought from her mind. She was not about to let anger taint her euphoria, this elixir stronger than wine.

Now, she knew that her calling was to be Hruodland's wife, not a nun. She had no vocation.

Yet God forgave her, she thought wiping her face, and He loved her despite that. He *loved* her. And she adored Him more than she ever had. She *could* love both her husband and God.

She laughed giddily as she donned her clothes, still intact despite a couple of holes eaten by moths and a musty smell. She was glad the veil hid her shorn hair and the gown covered her thin frame.

She could not stop smiling. Soon, she would see Veronica, her mother, Werinbert, and Hruodland. She kissed the ring. She giggled, anticipating the look on Hruodland's face.

As she stepped outside, she welcomed the breeze from the Rhine. The mountains were a patchwork of green, and the sun shone golden on the river. She pushed and dragged the chests of coins and jewels through the mud, heedless of the dirt on her dress and boots. At the church, she grabbed two fistfuls of coins and laid them on the steps, her gift to God, a token of her gratitude.

"Thank you, Lord," she whispered. "Thank you. Thank you. Thank you."

She struggled to shove the chests to the dock on Nonnenwerth and waited for a fisherman's boat to arrive.

She paced as the hours passed. The sun was on the verge of dipping below the mountains when a boat finally came. After the man unloaded his catch on the dock, Alda offered him enough silver coins to overcome his fear of night terrors and take her and her dowry to Drachenhaus at this late hour.

As she seated herself in the boat, Alda looked up at her birthplace. Drachenhaus loomed overhead.

The guard at the house by the river was startled by Alda's arrival. After the fisherman unloaded the chests, the guard blew on a horn.

"Welcome home, Lady Alda," he stammered. "Boy," he called to a young passer-by, "go to Drachenhaus and fetch a horse."

Alda waited and beamed in anticipation of seeing Hruodland again. After a few moments, she directed her gaze toward the castle at the top of the hill, now a silhouette in the evening light. She watched as four figures approached her: a boy leading a horse, Theodelinda mounted on a second horse, Veronica on foot, and a manservant driving an empty cart. *Where is Hruodland?*

Theodelinda dismounted, ran toward Alda, and embraced her.

"Daughter, you have come home," Theodelinda said, her face a mix of joy and alarm. "I will have the cooks prepare a meal with all haste."

"Hruodland told us that..." Veronica began.

"Prioress Plectrude showed me the truth," Alda interrupted as she let go of her mother and embraced Veronica. "The Good Lord Himself said 'What therefore God has joined together, let not man put asunder.'"

"Saints be praised," Veronica said. "We were so worried about you."

"Why were you worried?"

"We had not heard from you," Veronica answered.

As the guard helped Alda mount her horse and the manservant loaded the chests into the cart, she asked, "Where is Hruodland? Is he ill?"

Theodelinda and Veronica looked at each other as they headed for the mountain path, where the tree branches knit together in a canopy.

"No, he is not ill," Theodelinda said. "Come. I will explain during the evening meal."

Alda pouted. She knew it would be useless to press her mother. They were keeping something from her. Alda reasoned that Hruodland was doing something that would make her angry with him. Perhaps he had gone to seek solace with the village slut. Alda shook her head. She loathed the thought of him lying with another woman but blamed herself. She had released him from his vow with her. Still she wished he had not sought a whore so soon.

A shadow fell on her heart. Did Hruodland already set off for the March of Brittany so that he could annul their marriage? Why was it her fate to arrive too late, always too late? Perhaps she was not following the will of God as she had thought.

Alda was pulled from her thoughts when she heard her mother say half to herself, "I should have sent more wheat."

"Mother, the wheat you sent staved off starvation," Alda said.

"You have lost much flesh."

"Don't you think I know that?" Alda said, gazing at her bony hands.

"Some things never change," Veronica said.

As they approached the castle, Alda noticed the gates had been thrown open and servants had assembled in the muddy courtyard.

Alda heard a sharp cry as she rode into the courtyard and dismounted. "Auntie!"

Werinbert ran toward her, splashing mud in his wake.

Alda embraced the boy. "My dearling nephew, how you resemble your father more day by day. And you have a wooden sword, how wonderful! You shall make a fine warrior."

"Look at what Uncle Hruodland taught me last night." He stepped back and brandished the sword.

"Where is your uncle?" Alda asked.

"He set off for Dormagen," Werinbert said and then looked behind him.

Alda whirled around toward her mother and Veronica, who stared at Werinbert with wide eyes.

"Dormagen?" Alda asked. "The abode of Ganelon?"

"We will tell you about it during the evening meal," Theodelinda said. "You must eat before you do anything else."

"You will tell me about it now," Alda demanded. She and the others walked through the twilight shadows toward the light and warmth of the hall, where servants were setting the table.

"Hruodland is going to avenge us," Theodelinda said, smiling.

"And you let him?" Alda asked.

"You want vengeance, don't you?"

"Of course, I want vengeance," Alda said. "But not at the price of my husband's life."

"Hruodland is a practiced warrior," Theodelinda said.

"Ganelon is not an honorable man," Alda snapped. "He will not face Hruodland man to man in a duel. He will call for his guards, and even the most gifted warrior is no match for ten or twenty guards."

"Even if I asked him not to go, do you think I could have stopped him?"

"No," Alda said softly. Her hand flew to where the dragon used to be. When she felt only her cross, she asked, "Does he have the dragon amulet?"

"Yes."

"When did he leave?"

"This morning, after prime prayers."

"I must follow him," Alda said.

"You will do no such thing," Theodelinda cried. "You have endangered yourself enough. Wait for him here and grow plump."

"I shall not lose him a third time," Alda said defiantly. "Do not try to stop me."

"I am not going to lose you again, either."

Mother and daughter stared at each other while the servants scurried about their duties and pretended not to notice.

Alda spoke first, "Did he tell you he would return to Drachenhaus?"

"No," Theodelinda said.

"He does not know I have left Nonnenwerth," Alda said, again grabbing her cross. "What is there to stop him from returning to the March of Brittany and annulling our marriage?"

"I shall send a messenger."

"I am going to him. He will believe me only. I will go to him with or without your leave. Danger does not matter to me."

"You are so willful," Theodelinda said, exasperated.

They stared at each other in silence again.

"Very well," Theodelinda said, gritting her teeth. "Allow me to send guards with you, and promise me you will not put yourself in harm's way."

"I shall watch for my safety." She held her cross tightly.

"You should. Your husband will not be cheered if he finds you dead at the side of the road."

* * * * *

Because it was already late, Theodelinda persuaded Alda to eat and stay at Drachenhaus rather than risking travel overnight. After prime prayers the next morning, Alda set out for Dormagen with five guards. To make haste, she decided not to use a cart and had minimal provisions carried by five packhorses.

The men can eat salted pork for a few days, she thought. *I survived on less for a whole winter.*

She had to stop this duel at any cost. *Vengeance can wait. I cannot let him die.*

Chapter 32

R age burned in Hruodland's eyes during the five days it took to travel to the town of Dormagen. Now that Alda was lost to him, vengeance was all he cared about. If he died in the attempt, he could at least blind or maim his blood enemy.

He and his followers arrived at the edge of the town in the late afternoon. Rather than take the road through the town where they would be seen, they slowly made their way through the forest, Ganelon's hunting grounds. Sometimes, they had to stop and push the cart over a large tree root or cut through brush. Close to sunset, they arrived at the edge of the forest, where shrubs and trees hid them, but they still had a clear view of the castle's great gate.

Hruodland dismounted and told his guards and the servant with the cart to tarry. They watched and waited. As twilight approached, the postern, a man-sized door near the great gate, opened, and ten men left through it, walking toward the town. Already full of drink, the men laughed, sang, and talked loudly.

"Who are they?" one of the guards whispered.

"Ganelon's guards," Hruodland answered, keeping his voice low. "About half of them, I believe."

"Why are they leaving at such a late hour?"

"Seeking pleasure, I guess. Perhaps, they wish to get to the brothel before dark and stay for the night."

As soon as Ganelon's guards were out of sight and earshot, Hruodland handed the reins of his horse to one of his men. It was now twilight, an in-between time, not yet the end of day or the beginning of night, when restless spirits came to earth.

"The Lord has given us an opportunity," he said. "But I must go alone from here."

"Why?" the guard asked. His face had a look of horror. "Don't you want every fighting man?"

"We are too few to storm the castle."

"Then how will we get in?"

"*I* will get in through the guards' own fear," Hruodland replied. "Terror is my greatest weapon. A ghost has no need for guards."

"Will they recognize you?"

"If not, I shall tell them. They know who Hruodland of the March of Brittany is — just as you know of the enmity between us and Dormagen."

He strode toward the castle with Fidelis trailing him. He glanced over his shoulder and saw his men frowning and looking down. Looking ahead again, he reached the postern and pounded on the heavy door. A small window in the door opened, allowing Hruodland to see the guard's face. He looked vaguely familiar, but Hruodland could not remember when or where he had seen him.

"I am Hruodland of the March of Brittany," he shouted. "Your master has disturbed my peace."

The guard blanched and made the sign of the cross. "Please, have mercy," he begged.

"I have come for Ganelon. Open this door," Hruodland ordered, "and no harm will come to you."

To Hruodland's surprise, the guard did as he was bidden. Hruodland suppressed a smile. He did not have to lie. Simply let the guard think that he was dealing with a ghost and be too terrified of a spirit's wrath to disobey or even ask questions.

With Fidelis at his heels, Hruodland marched across the courtyard toward the hall. As he entered, he noticed servants, some of whom he recognized, shrinking away and making the sign of the cross. Even the guards cowered. The servants were living skeletons, their eyes sunken, cheeks hollow. Perhaps that was why none stood in his way, but merely stepped back and whispered, "That is the master's blood enemy, who fell at Roncevaux."

"Ganelon," Hruodland roared, "it is I, Hruodland of the March of Brittany. Show yourself."

Hruodland heard a woman pleading, "But I am faithful. I am faithful. The child is yours."

Hruodland looked about, trying to find the source of the sound.

He heard a slap, and then Ganelon shouted, "I will not suffer a bastard in this house."

"My lord, no!" the woman screamed.

Hruodland heard a crash and turned toward the sound. In the firelight at the foot of the stairs, he saw a woman heavy with child and ran to her.

"Fetch a physician and a midwife," he barked to the nearest maid.

He knelt near the woman and turned her face toward him. He gasped. "Gundrada."

He barely recognized her. Except for the swelling of her belly, her beautiful plump figure had wasted away. Her drawn face was scratched as if from a ring.

"Am I dying?" she whimpered.

Hruodland held her hand. "Do not give up hope. Help is coming."

Blood stained the floor beneath her hips.

One of the maids clutched the cross at her bosom with a trembling hand and hesitantly approached Gundrada. "Sh-she is my lady," the woman stammered.

"Then tend to her," Hruodland snapped.

The maid lifted her lady's gown, ripped cloth from her own skirt, and tried to staunch the blood. "It's no use," the woman cried. "The baby is lost."

"The child was his," Gundrada mumbled. "He did not believe me. He said I was untrue — like his first wife. But I *was* faithful."

"Of course, you were true," Hruodland said. Not that it mattered. No one deserved this fate.

"Pray for me," Gundrada murmured, closing her eyes. Her hand went limp.

"Gundrada? Gundrada," he yelled.

The Cross and the Dragon

No response.

Hruodland bowed his head and made the sign of the cross. As he rose, he looked up and saw a pair of icy blue eyes staring at him from the top of the stairs.

"Ganelon," Hruodland shouted, "ravisher and murderer of women and children, come down here."

Ganelon withdrew into the shadows. Hruodland waited for a few moments for Ganelon to descend to the hall. He heard guards shuffling toward him as it became clear Ganelon was not going to answer his challenge.

Hruodland let out a stream of obscenities, all in Frankish to make sure Ganelon understood. From the corner of his eye, he saw the servants shrink back further and the guards hesitate in their approach. One hissed, "That's Hruodland's shade. Only he would call the master such vile names."

"If you cannot face me like a man," Hruodland bellowed, "I will come up there." He turned to the wolfhound. "Fidelis, stay."

Hruodland bounded up the stairs. The solar was illuminated by candles and reeked of dank rushes on the floor. Ganelon was kneeling before a tapestry of the Mother of God and her Child.

"What want you from me?" Ganelon blubbered.

"Justice," Hruodland answered coldly. "Gird yourself with a weapon. I shall not slay an unarmed man."

"Hruodland, have mercy," Ganelon begged.

"What mercy did you show my wife, you dung-eating cur?"

"She tempted me."

"Do not lie," Hruodland spat.

As he lunged toward his enemy, he tripped over a large rat scurrying through the rushes. He stumbled and cursed under his breath.

"A ghost would not stumble. You are alive!" Leaping to his feet, he snarled, "What black arts did you use? I stabbed you at Roncevaux, and you live. I put hemlock in your wine at Saint Stephen's, and you live. I should have used mistletoe, but I needed all there was to slay a big man like Count Beringar."

Hruodland swallowed back his bile, remembering the nightmares, the scrape of metal and the pain in his chest, the burning in his throat, his own paralysis. *It wasn't a mere dream!* "One of us will die now," he growled, drawing his sword.

Ganelon looked Hruodland up and down as he backed toward a table. "You are not so strong now, and my leg has healed," he said, reaching for and drawing his sword. "I shall take great joy in smiting you."

"Smite me?" Hruodland said, as he and Ganelon circled each other. "I doubt you even know how to fight a man who can strike back. You're so cowardly you stab a cripple lying on the battlefield. I am not a cripple now. I've earned my scars."

"Earn this," Ganelon hissed. He rushed toward Hruodland, aiming his sword at his heart.

Hruodland parried the blow and then struck for Ganelon's neck. Ganelon blocked Hruodland's attempt with his weapon.

Sword clashed on sword, and the two rivals were heedless of what went on below.

* * * * *

Riding toward Ganelon's castle, Alda heard a man calling, "Princess Alda! Princess Alda!"

Alda started and turned toward the voice. It sounded like one of the guards from the March of Brittany. She gasped when five guards emerged from the forest on horseback. Their faces wore looks of astonishment.

"Where is your lord?" she asked in Roman between breaths.

"He told us to wait out here, Princess," one of the guards answered with a scowl. "He said a ghost would have no need of guards or servants."

"Ghost or not, he has need of his wife. Come with me if you want him to live."

"Thank you," the guard said, beckoning the others to follow. "We are at your service."

"Whatever happens, do not let Ganelon's guards come to his master's aid," Alda said, first in Frankish, then in Roman.

Alda's mind raced as she and her companions hurried to the postern. She had to think of a way to get inside with all these men. *A ghost would have no need of guards or servants.*

She dismounted and told the guards to do the same. "Watch the horses and our belongings," she said to the servant who drove the cart.

She pounded on the postern. When the shutter was drawn back, she recognized the castle guard from Ganelon's visit to Drachenhaus. She stood on her toes to block his view of the men behind her.

"I am Alda, wife of Hruodland, the late prefect of the March of Brittany," she said, masking her own terror. "Admit me, and Hruodland will haunt you no more."

The guard was pale and trembling. "Are you a sorceress? Did you summon him here?"

"Yes. He is here to avenge the stain on my honor," Alda spat. "Ganelon and those who helped him will pay."

"Have mercy," the guard cried. "I only did as I was ordered."

"You will open the door at once," she barked, "or I shall make your manhood shrivel and fall off."

"No," the guard wailed, "please, lady, I beg you..."

"Do as I say, or..."

Before Alda could finish the thought, the guard ducked and she heard the bar being lifted. Alda quickly stepped back and gestured to her warriors, mouthing "Now." When the door opened a crack, her men thrust against it and forced it open. Alda rushed in behind them.

"Remember your promise," Ganelon's guard called after her.

Alda spat on him. The guard, shaking from head to toe, shrieked as if she had just sprayed venom.

"That is for your complicity in your master's crime," she growled. "If he had not escaped justice at Drachenhaus, my husband would not be here." To one of her guards, she muttered, "Watch him."

Alda and the guards from Drachenhaus and the March of Brittany barreled across the courtyard to the hall, whose door was wide open. Servants clothed in rags huddled against the walls. Ganelon's guards, their backs to her, stood in front of a wolfhound, who bared his fangs and growled, barring the way up the stairs. She heard the scuffling of feet and metal scraping metal above her in the solar. She was too late. Always, always too late. But she had to try.

Ganelon's bone-thin servants simply listened to the fight overhead and made no attempt to get past the dog and help their master. *The price of Ganelon's cruelty,* Alda thought. She turned her attention to the guards in front of her.

Kim Rendfeld

One of Ganelon's guards pointed to the wolfhound. "I tell you that is a hound from hell," he said. "No living dog would obey a ghost. Try to slay him and your arm will fall off."

"Sp-sp-spear it," another guard sputtered. "I-it's an ordinary dog."

"Then *you* try to spear it," a third man said, handing the weapon to the second man. "But it will be no use. You can't kill it."

The guards shifted their feet as if unable to decide if the snarling wolfhound before them came from this world or another.

A cry of pain came from the solar, and Alda's heart rose. *Ganelon! Hruodland slew Ganelon!*

"Guards! Come here!" Ganelon bellowed.

Before Ganelon's guards could rush up the stairs, Alda's men raced past her and attacked them. One hacked his enemy through the neck. Another ran a sword through one of Ganelon's guards as he was starting to turn. The dog leapt into the fray, knocking down the man holding the spear, and stood on the man's chest, growling and snapping at his face. The remainder of Ganelon's men fought back but could not get to the stairs.

Alda sidled around the fighting men. Her attention was so fixed on the battle above, she hardly saw the bleeding woman she stepped over or the weeping maid. She hurried up the stairs.

Chapter 33

Surprised Ganelon would cry out over a flesh wound and torn sleeve, Hruodland did not see the dagger in Ganelon's left hand until his enemy slashed at him. Hruodland jumped back, but the dagger skimmed his flesh and cut his forehead. Hruodland blinked back the blood and sweat that stung his eyes and drew his own dagger with his left hand.

Grunting, Ganelon raised his sword above his head and aimed for the middle of Hruodland's skull. Hruodland blocked the blow with his sword and thrust his dagger at Ganelon's gut. Ganelon sprang back, reeking of sweat.

Where are your guards, coward? His heart pounding in his ears, Hruodland advanced, trying to hack his enemy's neck from his shoulders.

Ganelon parried and thrust his dagger at Hruodland's throat. Hruodland deflected the blow with his own weapon.

Baring his teeth, Ganelon raised his sword and again tried to split Hruodland's skull. Hruodland blocked the blow and stepped back from the dagger pointed at his heart. His heel caught on an uneven plank under the rushes. He slipped and fell on his back, slamming his head against the wooden floor and losing his grip on his sword. Before Hruodland could react, Ganelon took a step and kicked him in the ribs.

"Beg for mercy," his enemy sneered.

Hruodland gritted his teeth against the pain and rolled quickly onto his right side, the dagger in his left hand diving at Ganelon's foot.

Ganelon stepped back and slashed at Hruodland's wrist. Hruodland pulled his hand close to his chest as the sword sliced through the air.

Still holding the dagger in his left hand, Hruodland shifted his weight and reached for his sword with his right. Ganelon took a side step and tried to chop Hruodland's hand. Hruodland pulled his right hand back and aimed to skewer Ganelon's foot with the dagger in his left. Ganelon yelped and retreated out of Hruodland's reach before the blow could connect.

Ganelon drew himself to his full height, turned, and raised his sword, aiming for Hruodland's feet. "Go to hell in pieces!"

An unearthly shriek tore through the air. "No!"

"Alda!" Hruodland whispered.

Wearing the garb of a countess, she was standing at the top of the stairs screaming like an undead spirit. Ganelon's head whipped toward the noise.

Calling Ganelon the vilest of names, Alda grabbed her eating knife and threw it straight at his heart, forcing him to lower his sword and duck. The knife sailed just over his head.

Hruodland tightened his grip on his dagger. He had to protect Alda at all costs. *If I die now, Ganelon will...* He didn't dare finish the thought. Taking advantage of Ganelon's distraction, he rolled out of his enemy's reach. As Hruodland struggled to his feet, Ganelon looked back toward him.

"You sack of dung!" Ganelon shouted. He turned toward Hruodland and raised his sword again. "Your whore fights for you!"

"Muck-eating worm!" Hruodland spat, switching his dagger from his left hand to his right.

Screaming, Alda ran and grabbed the first object within reach, a candlestick with a burning candle, and hurled it. It hit Ganelon in the chest as he turned toward her.

"Bitch!" Ganelon yelled, looking toward her.

"Alda, get out!" Hruodland roared.

Hruodland lunged. Ganelon lunged as well, trying to impale Hruodland with his sword. Hruodland twisted to avoid his enemy's weapon, but Ganelon's sword ripped through his sleeve and bit into his left shoulder.

Barely feeling the pain, Hruodland saw only his enemy's outstretched neck. "Yes!" he yelled. He plunged his dagger into Ganelon's throat.

Blood burst from Ganelon's great veins. Ganelon pitched forward, bearing Hruodland with him. They both crashed to the floor.

Alda raced to the fallen men. "Hruodland! Hruodland!" she screamed.

Hruodland pushed Ganelon aside and sat up, laughing giddily. "Alda, my dearling, my disobedient wife, did you think I was going to make you a widow?"

Alda knelt, kissed him, and held him close. "Don't joke like that," she sobbed. "I thought I was too late, I thought I was going to lose you again."

"Don't weep," Hruodland said softly, holding her. She felt fragile. "I am here. I am well."

"But you are bleeding."

Hruodland looked at his shoulders and chest. He was covered with blood — Ganelon's blood. He laughed again. "It isn't my blood."

He felt a trickle on his forehead and wiped it with his sleeve. The gash on his shoulder was not deep. He looked at Ganelon, lying face down in a spreading pool of blood. "I am better off than him. These are only flesh wounds, dearling."

He had countless questions for Alda, but they could wait. A more urgent matter was at hand. He did not want to await the return of the guards who had left Ganelon's castle earlier. They might decide to avenge their master's death, and Hruodland was no match for all of them, even if he had his full strength.

"Let us leave the house of our enemy," he said, as he and Alda rose to their feet.

Alda nodded numbly.

Retrieving his weapons, Hruodland realized he had another problem — how to get himself and Alda past the guards who had remained in Ganelon's castle. When he had thought Alda was lost to him, he had cared only about getting into Ganelon's castle and fighting him. He hadn't planned an escape.

How in the world did Alda get past Ganelon's men? There must have been ten of them downstairs.

Alda crept to the top of the stairs and listened for noises in the hall below their feet. It was eerily quiet.

Hruodland drew his sword and joined his wife.

"I don't think that will be needed," Alda said.

"Alda, if I cannot convince Ganelon's men I am..."

"Our men might have already done away with Ganelon's guards," she interrupted.

"Our men?" he asked.

"You don't think I came to Dormagen alone, do you?"

"I should have known. How many men did you bring?"

"Five — save one at the gate, along with your five."

"They would be evenly matched with Ganelon's guards."

"And they would prevent Ganelon's men from answering their master's summons." Her eyes narrowed as she looked at Ganelon's body. "I knew he wouldn't fight fairly."

One of Alda's guards called to her from the foot of the stairs, where the bleeding woman still lay in the shadows and a maid sat listlessly beside her.

"I am well," Alda replied. "Hruodland is..." She looked at her husband.

"I am well and am coming down with my lady," Hruodland called. "How many of Ganelon's men are left?"

"None, save the one at the entrance."

Hruodland sheathed his sword. They descended the steps to the hall.

"She's lost!" the maid moaned.

Hruodland shook his head at the body at the foot of the stairs. "If I had but arrived earlier I might have been able to save her life as well as avenge your honor."

"Who is she?" Alda asked.

Hruodland's jaw dropped. Then he realized he might not have recognized her either in the candlelight.

"Gundrada."

"We must pray for her," Alda murmured, making the sign of the cross.

"And her baby," Hruodland said sadly.

"Her baby? What kind of a man would kill his own baby?"

"What kind of a man would kill any baby? What kind of man would try to rape a widow? What kind of man would stab and then poison someone lying helpless?"

"A monster." Alda trembled. "A wicked, twisted monster."

"The monster is dead, dearling."

* * * * *

The servants stared at Hruodland and Alda. Most of Ganelon's guards lay near the foot of the stairs. The men from the March of Brittany and Drachenhaus were binding their wounds. The wolfhound, unhurt, stood and wagged his tail.

One of the servants, an old woman, stepped forward and asked: "Is our master dead?"

"Yes," Hruodland said grimly as he put his arm protectively around Alda's shoulders.

"Praise God!"

"Who is his heir?" Alda asked.

"His sister's son, completely unlike him," the old woman answered. "You have given us a kinder master."

"And what will you tell your new master?" Alda asked.

"As far as we know, the spirit of the prefect of the March of Brittany was restless, and he slew our master because of his cruelty to his servants."

"A wise decision," Hruodland said. "I would not like to hear that you've changed it."

Alda hesitated as Hruodland led her to the door.

"What is it?" he asked.

"We cannot leave all these people here unattended. They need a Christian burial, especially Gundrada. You," she said to the maid whom she now recognized as Gundrada's servant, "will you fetch a priest to see to the burial?"

"I will do it for my lady," the maid said, wiping her tears with her hand. "But if it were my will, I would have Count Ganelon and his men thrown to the rats."

* * * * *

The Cross and the Dragon

The guard at the castle gate fled through the postern when he saw Hruodland in the moonlight.

Once the group returned to their horses, Fidelis climbed into the cart and curled up for a nap. As the heat of battle wore off, Hruodland felt weary, and his sword arm and shoulder ached. His men looked tired as well, but they could not rest yet.

"I would rather risk the night terrors than stay another minute in this horrid place," he said as he helped Alda mount her horse.

As they rode, Hruodland finally asked her what had been on his mind since he first saw her in Ganelon's solar. "Is your soul in danger for leaving Nonnenwerth?"

"No." Smiling, she explained what Plectrude had told her. "It's God's will I be with you, wherever you go. Our Savior says that no man should break what God has joined together. I need your permission to join any cloister."

"The only permission I give you is to stay by my side." He reached for Alda's hand.

* * * * *

They continued their journey until what seemed to be matins and camped for the rest of the night. After the guards prepared a site, Hruodland and Alda slipped into a tent and quenched their long-denied desires. Alda had never been so hungry, nor so satisfied.

"Whither do we go now, Husband?" Alda asked, leaning against his bare chest.

"When I went to Dormagen, the thought of vengeance consumed me. I did not look beyond it. I thought all I had left of you was the dragon amulet."

"When I followed you, I had no thought but to prevent your death. The thought of losing you again..." Her voice trailed off as she held him more closely, inhaling his scent.

They were silent for a few moments.

"First, we must go to Bonn," Hruodland finally said. "I have a matter to settle with the bishop."

"You are to do no harm to my uncle." Alda rose slightly and leaned on her elbow.

"Are you not angry with him?" Hruodland asked, putting his hand on her bare shoulder.

330

"Very. But he is still my mother's brother."

"I have no intention of harming him," Hruodland said, drawing her close. "But I want him to know what he did. I want your uncle to know I am still alive, but I don't know if we should tell the world."

"Why not?"

"If the world thinks I am dead, Ganelon's kin will think a ghost slew him, and they cannot exact vengeance from Gerard and his children for the acts of a restless spirit."

Alda shuddered. She and Hruodland both knew of feuds that had ended in the slaughter of entire families.

"Gerard has children?" Alda asked.

"His wife and his concubine are expecting. The March of Brittany needs heirs. Maybe Ganelon's heir will be a kinder master, but I wish to end this blood feud. If the world thinks a ghost is protecting the March of Brittany, so much the better."

"Little Werinbert needs an uncle who will teach him the art of hunting game in the forest and holding a sword in battle," Alda mused, "and Drachenhaus needs a count, in deed if not in name."

"The child needs a mother as well, in deed if not in name," Hruodland said, his hand on Alda's hip. "I see much of myself in the boy. I felt lost when I was growing up. My mother had died, and my father had little to do with me. Perhaps, God means for us to care for Werinbert."

"I would like that," Alda said softly.

* * * * *

On the three-day journey to Bonn, Hruodland and Alda talked about all that had happened in the past year. At the gates to Bonn, Hruodland drew his hood low over his face. The guards admitted the travelers when Alda told them who she was.

Alda and Hruodland met Leonhard in the hall of his residence, and Hruodland drew back his hood. Bishop Leonhard quavered when he saw the anger on Hruodland's face and dropped the piece of parchment that he had been holding.

"You owe me a debt," Hruodland said, sitting on a bench near the hearth, in which a small fire burned.

"You owe us both a debt," Alda added, taking a seat near her husband. "You lied to me."

Leonhard looked at Alda with wide eyes as he picked up the parchment and stared at it. "Your mother's letter says that Hruodland is alive, you've left the cloister at Nonnenwerth, and a messenger told her that Abbess Radegunde is dead."

Alda bowed her head and made the sign of the cross. Leonhard staggered forward a step and sat down heavily on the bench across from Hruodland and Alda. He steadied himself as he stared into the flames.

"When I said Hruodland was dead, I thought I was merely altering the manner and place where he died." He closed his eyes and shook his head. "What have I done?"

"Uncle," Alda said gently, "you can repay the debt."

"How?"

"Write to my brother," Hruodland said. "Tell him our blood enemy is dead."

"Ganelon," Leonhard said, his voice barely audible. "You slew Ganelon."

"It was in a duel."

"So, Hruodland, I am to write to your brother that your blood enemy is slain and what else?"

"That he can govern in the March of Brittany as long as he is a good count," Hruodland said. "And that the world must think I am dead for the sake of his children. If Ganelon's family thinks it was a ghost who slew him, it will cool any thoughts of vengeance."

"I hear his heir had little affection for him," Leonhard said, "but honor is honor. No one would hold Gerard responsible for the acts of his brother's shade."

"Exactly."

"What of your uncle the king?" Leonhard asked, his voice tense.

A weight sank in Hruodland's heart. He missed Charles and Bertrada and had no doubt they had mourned him. "I would like nothing better than for my uncle and my grandmother to know I am alive," he said finally. "But if Uncle Charles knew the truth, I fear Gerard would be punished for lying to him."

"You owe a debt to both of us, Uncle," Alda interjected, gazing at the fire, "and it will take me some time to forgive you. But I do not want the king's retribution to fall upon you."

Leonhard relaxed a little.

Kim Rendfeld

"Write to him that Alda has married again," Hruodland said, squeezing Alda's hand.

"Hruodland..." Alda started to say.

"Hush, dearling." He put his finger to her lips. Turning to Leonhard, he continued, "Say that she has married Sebastian, a natural son of Milo, and he has an uncanny semblance to his brother Hruodland. Tell him you blessed this marriage and granted us a dispensation to the law of consanguinity because..."

"He was the only one I would consent to marry," Alda finished for him.

"And he offered her his protection and a generous dower and agreed to stay with her at Drachenhaus so that the young count will have an uncle to teach him the ways of men."

"You will need to stay away from the king for a couple of years," Leonhard said, "but in time, he will accept Sebastian. How else shall I pay the debt I owe you?"

Alda sat up straight. "You will write to the king extolling the virtues of Plectrude, the prioress who lives on Nonnenwerth and whose words reunited me with my husband. Both our houses will send gifts on her behalf. And..." Alda continued before Hruodland could speak. "...your finest pair of breeding horses, a Psalter, a clerk who will teach Werinbert to read when he has seen seven winters, and enough iron for a sword for Werinbert, when he is old enough to wield one."

"You ask for much," Leonhard said, studying his hands, "but if it will earn your forgiveness, all of it is yours."

* * * * *

After five days at Bonn, the party left for Drachenhaus. They approached the village two days later as the sun sank below the mountains. Alda smiled when she heard two blasts from the horn. Leonhard had sent a message of their homecoming ahead.

"I have something to give you," Hruodland said, gazing at the silhouette of Drachenfels across the river. He took the dragon amulet from his own neck and placed it on Alda's. "Now that I have you, I have no need for a reminder. It belongs to the House of the Dragon."

"Why?" she asked. "Why did you give up your land for my sake?"

"God gave me back my life. He gave you back to me, and He has given us a child. The land is a small price."

Kim Rendfeld

Ristorical Note

ny portrayal of Hruodland of the March of Brittany, the inspiration for *The Song of Roland* and other legends, is going to be fictitious. The only historical mention of him is part of a sentence. In Einhard's biography of King Charles (better known to us as Charlemagne), Hruodland (or Roland) is listed among the dead in the ambush at Roncevaux. I borrowed names from *The Song of Roland*, but the anonymous eleventh-century Old French epic should be interpreted for its artistic rather than historic value.

In legend, Hruodland is often portrayed as Charles's nephew, the son of the monarch's sister, a close relationship in medieval times. In fact, Charles's only sister to survive to adulthood, Gisela, was a nun. If Hruodland and Charles were kin, the exact relationship is unknown. However, they must have been allies, and Hruodland must have been important for Einhard to list him with two high-ranking court officials. Hruodland's parents, uncles, brother, and wife are all my invention.

For the royal family, the personal and political were intertwined, as illustrated by the early years of Charles's reign. On his deathbed in 768, King Pepin split his kingdom between his sons, Charles and Carloman, following Frankish tradition to divide the inheritance.

At the time, Charles was married to the Frankish noblewoman Himiltrude, a bride chosen for him by his father. Queen Mother

335

Bertrada thought she had a better idea and arranged for Charles to marry a Lombard princess, which meant he would divorce Himiltrude, the mother of his eldest son, Pepin. Hearing the rumor of the marriage to a Lombard, Pope Stephen, Hadrian's predecessor, wrote a strongly worded letter to both brothers against the idea.

Charles and Carloman did not get along, and Bertrada worked for peace between them. But Carloman died in December 771 at age twenty, and Charles wanted his lands, even though Carloman had sons. Out goes the Lombard princess. In comes Hildegard of Swabia, part of Carloman's realm. Charles apparently was a steadfast husband to her. Hildegard bore Charles nine children, three of whom died in infancy. After Hildegard's death in 783 in her mid-twenties, he married Fastrada, and after she passed away, Liutgard. After his fifth wife's passing in 800, he had four recognized mistresses.

The early decades of Charles's reign were dominated by wars, which usually lasted a summer — the men had to get back and harvest the crops. He did not always call for one freeman (as opposed to a slave) from each house in every city in the realm to go to war, but the Frankish armies that fought the Lombards and the ruler of Cordoba likely were particularly large.

At the beginning of his long reign, he crushed a rebellion in Aquitaine, and the pope asked him to come to his aid and fight the Lombards. The Franks were at war with the Saxons on and off from 772 to 785, then the mid-790s to 804, the year Saxons living beyond the Elbe River were deported into Francia. The pattern was the Franks would conquer, the Saxons would surrender, the Franks would turn their attention elsewhere, and the Saxons would rebel again, burning churches and slaughtering indiscriminately. Those wars became more and more brutal over the years. Perhaps the 782 massacre of 4,500 Saxon leaders in Verdun (if we are to believe the Royal Frankish Annals) was a manifestation of Charles's frustration.

In 777, Charles mistakenly thought the Saxons were "pacified" (beaten into submission) when he held his assembly at Paderborn, where a delegation of three emirs asked for Charles's help against the ruler of Cordoba. They may have told Charles the emir of Cordoba would encroach on his territories, as evidenced by a letter from Pope Hadrian referring to Charles's fear of invasion. In the campaign against Hispania the next year, the Basques (also called the Gascons) ambushed the rear guard and baggage train at

Roncevaux, and the Franks were slain "to a man," according to Einhard.

The challenge of writing fiction is this era is what to leave out for the sake of not bogging down the plot. One intriguing character I had to omit was Charles's first cousin Tassilo, duke of Bavaria, also married to a Lombard princess, Liutberga, daughter of Desiderius and sister of Charles's second wife. Charles and Tassilo had a thorny relationship. Nor did I mention that Desiderius was brought back to Francia as a prisoner or that he had yet another daughter married to a duke in Italy.

I also cheated a little by using Karl (the German form of Charles) as the name for the first son of Charles and Hildegard instead of Charles the Younger. Their second son was originally named Carloman, but his name was changed to Pepin in 781, when he was four. Yes, Charles had two sons named Pepin (also spelled Pippin). The eldest is often called Pepin the Hunchback.

History is silent on what happened to Carloman's widow, Gerberga, and her sons. That they were sent to the cloister is plausible. Gerberga did surrender voluntarily. In an age of punishment by blinding, drowning, beheading, and other brutality, sending one's political rivals to the cloister is an act of mercy. It happened repeatedly in Charles's reign: Desiderius, Tassilo, even his eldest son Pepin, who rebelled against him as an adult.

Those who have read the Royal Frankish Annals will note no mention of Charles visiting Aachen in 774. According to the annals, Charles spent Christmas and Easter in Quierzy in today's France. It's possible he spent time in Aachen in today's Germany. I had him going to Aachen because it is the site of the villa that became Aix-La-Chapelle. Built in the 790s, it was his most famous palace and one of his favorites. The Royal Frankish Annals also say Charles found out about the Saxons' 778 revolt in Auxerre, rather than Bordeaux as he does in this novel. At the time of this story, Charles's realm included today's France, Germany, Holland, Belgium, Luxembourg, and Switzerland, along with the lands he conquered in northern Italy. With that vast territory came several languages, including a form of German; Roman (also called the Romance language), a form of Latin whose pronunciation varied from place to place; and the Latin used at Mass and written down in official records. The Bretons and the Gascons spoke their own tongues.

As Charles expanded his kingdom even more, he had to figure out how to govern from afar and protect borderlands. Like his father, Charles established marches, or to use modern parlance, buffer zones, between Francia and foreign entities such as Brittany and Hispania. He would then appoint a count (or prefect) to govern the march. Hruodland was one of those counts.

Although not as bitter as the conflict with the Saxons, the tensions between the Franks and Bretons continued after Hruodland's death. In 786, Audulf the seneschal invaded Brittany and brought Breton leaders back as prisoners. In 799, Wido, then the prefect of the March of Brittany, led a force into Brittany and won.

The fate of Sulaiman, one of the Muslims who traveled to Paderborn to ask for Charles's aid, is unclear. One source says he was killed as a traitor to the Muslim cause. Another has him being brought back to Francia as a prisoner.

In addition to Hruodland, the other characters who are drawn from real life are Charles and his family, Widukind the leader of the Saxon rebels, Sulaiman and his fellow emirs, and Fulrad the archchaplain, along with Eggihard the seneschal, and Anselm, the count of the palace, both of whom also died at the Pass of Roncevaux. Ganelon is the antagonist in *The Song of Roland*, so I borrowed the name. The poem's author may have named his villain after Guenelon (also spelled Vénilon), a ninth-century bishop of Sens accused of betraying one of Charles's grandsons.

Most of the cities I named existed at the time of this story, but their leaders are my invention. Bonn was not a bishopric. Dormagen was not a county. Drachenhaus and its inhabitants are fictitious, as are the Abbey of Saint Stephen and the Sisters of the Sacred Blood. Convents have made their homes on Nonnenwerth, but the first one was established on the island in 1126.

The inspiration for this story is Rolandsbogen, the ruins of a castle on the Rhine, where I have placed Drachenhaus. One of the legends is that Roland built the castle for his bride and went off to fight the Saracens. The bride heard false news that he had died in battle and joined the cloister on Nonnenwerth. When Roland returned, he spent the rest of his days gazing out the castle window, hoping to catch a glimpse of her. In truth, Rolandsbogen was built in the eleventh century.

All that remains of this castle is an arch, which on a sunny day can be seen clearly from the castle ruins at Drachenfels, a small mountain across the Rhine from Rolandsbogen.

— Kim Rendfeld, New Castle, Indiana, 2012

Kim Rendfeld

A Conversation
with the Author

What inspired you to write *The Cross and the Dragon?*

I was on a family vacation in Germany and came across a story about the ruins at Rolandsbogen — an ivy-covered arch on a hill — in a guide book. There are variations, but the legend is that Roland (Hruodland) built the castle for his bride and then went off to war. His bride heard that he had died in Roncevaux and went to the convent on Nonnenwerth, where she took a vow of chastity. The news the bride heard was false. When Roland returned, he spent the rest of his days in the castle, looking at Nonnenwerth, trying to catch a glimpse of her as she went to and from prayers.

The legend is not true. Both the castle and convent are centuries after Roland, and the only thing we know of the historical Roland is that he died in Roncevaux. But the story would not leave me alone. On the flight back to the States, I wrote about it in my journal, and I kept wondering why someone would tell the bride this false news. The story grew from there.

339

The Cross and the Dragon

How much did you know about the Middle Ages when you started writing?

Very little. I had heard of Charlemagne, knights, and feudalism, and I enjoyed The Lord of the Rings series along with Arthurian legends and Grimm's fairy tales. However, I had to research historical events along with how people lived and thought. The former is much easier than the latter. I owe a lot to my friend and fellow novelist Roberta Gellis for correcting my errors and misconceptions and explaining why medieval people did what they did. (And I will echo the disclaimer of all historical novelists: mistakes in my book are mine and mine alone.)

It's a shame that many modern-day Americans know so little of the Middle Ages and the Carolingian period in particular. There are so many fascinating people and stories. The melding of the political and personal is fertile ground for a writer. Still, I would much rather write about the Middle Ages than live in that era. I like my microwave, cell phone, and Internet, not to mention women's right and modern health care. I also like that family scandals among today's leaders are fodder for the tabloids rather than cause for war.

Did all the wars in the story really take place?

Yes. Charles, as he was known then, went to war for much of his reign. In his later years, his son Charles the Younger (called Karl in The Cross and the Dragon) led the army. The authors of the Royal Frankish Annals even noted when there was no war a particular year.

One of my challenges was to portray the history and politics without bogging down the story.

You portray some real historic people such as Charles and his family in The Cross and the Dragon. Where did your information about them come from?

One of Charles's courtiers, Einhard, wrote a biography about him between 830 and 833, almost two decades after the emperor's death. The physical descriptions of Charles, including his voice, are based on this work. A coin he had minted also bears his image.

Kim Rendfeld

Those who are familiar with *The Song of Roland* know him as a hero who stubbornly refuses to use his horn to call for help. The poem portrays the battle and the brutal justice that follows in gory detail. Why did you take a different approach?

To use modern parlance, I suspect the poem was a propaganda piece for the Crusades. Although it has artistic merit, especially about courage and betrayal, any resemblance between it and what actually happened at the Pass of Roncevaux is purely coincidental. However, the copyright has long run out, and I did borrow some names.

I read the poem after I had encountered the love story, and I like the love story better. The Roland in the poem would be difficult for a 21st century audience, especially those of us who consider ourselves tolerant.

Your characters aren't tolerant.

Nor were most medieval people. For example, the Saxons' conversion to Christianity was at the point of a sword (not that the church-burning Saxons were innocent). If you expressed horror of forced conversions to eighth-century Franks, they would think you were crazy.

Being tolerant of differences, even celebrating them, is a modern concept. Another reason I am glad to live in my century.

Why do you make so many references to religion throughout the story?

Religion was a central part of medieval life, although church attendance interestingly spiked on Easter. This was an age that believed in divine intervention. During his first war in Lombardy, Charles did meet with the pope in Rome, probably seeking God's help to end the siege at Pavia, which has dragged on for months.

This example of seeking divine favor is not unique. Before his invasion of Avaria in 791, Charles participated in three days of litanies.

To ignore the role that faith played would be a major disservice to the reader.

Questions for Discussion

1. During the Middle Ages, magic and religion existed side by side. By wearing an amulet along with her cross, Alda is following a common practice. Is this contradictory? Discuss the pagan and Christian symbols that abound throughout the novel and how magic and religion shape the characters' lives.

2. The characters have varied concept of who God is, ranging from harsh judge to loving protector. How do these different visions of God affect and justify the characters' actions?

3. How do the characters use the supernatural to explain their world and what happens to them?

4. In many marriages during the Middle Ages and Renaissance, one of a noblewoman's most important duties was to bear her husband a healthy son and heir, and she was blamed if the couple could not conceive. Would Hruodland and Alda's marriage have survived if the attack at the Pass of Roncevaux had not happened?

5. The political and the personal were intertwined during this period. How did King Charles's decisions about his marriages affect his relations with his vassals and other rulers?

6. What do you think are the Muslim emirs' motives for asking for Charles's aid? Why did the Christian Gascons in Pamplona reject Charles as their ruler, despite their shared faith?
7. Charles's reign was marked by frequent wars. How do they affect the mindset of the characters?
8. When Hruodland was in a coma, did Gerard and Alda's uncles make the right decision to let her think he was dead, even in light of what they knew at the time? Is there ever a time when telling a lie or letting someone believe something that isn't true is the right thing to do?
9. How do Alda's and Gundrada's reactions to their widowhood differ? Which loyalty should prevail, the husband's memory or the family's need for an alliance? Was Hruodland right to put his wife's needs above everyone else's?
10. When seeking justice and protection for Alda, did Hruodland have any alternative to a duel with Ganelon?

About the Author

Kim Rendfeld

A former journalist and current copy editor for a university public relations office, Kim Rendfeld has a lifelong fascination with fairy tales and legends, which set her on her quest to write *The Cross and the Dragon*. She lives in Indiana with her husband, Randy, and their spoiled cats. They have a daughter and two granddaughters.

For more about Kim, visit www.kimrendfeld.com.

For the Finest in
Nautical and Historical
Fiction and Nonfiction
WWW.FIRESHIPPRESS.COM

Interesting • Informative • Authoritative

The Assassin's Wife
by
Moonyeen Blakey

Fireship Press
www.FireshipPress.com
Sales@ Fireshippress.com
ISBN-13: 978-1-61179-218-8 (paperback)
**Found in all leading Booksellers and on line eBook
distributers**

Winner of the Cornerstones "Wow Factor" Writing Competition

Second Sight is Dangerous

Nan's visions of two noble boys imprisoned in a tower frighten her village priest.
The penalty for witchcraft is death.
Despite his warnings, Nan's determination to the save these boys launches her on a nightmare journey. As fifteenth-century England teeters on the edge of civil war, her talent as a Seer draws powerful, ambitious people around her.
Not all of them are honourable.
Twists of fate bring her to a ghost-ridden house in Silver Street where she is entrusted with a secret which could destroy a dynasty.
Pursued by the unscrupulous Bishop Stillington, she finds refuge with a gypsy wisewoman, until a chance encounter takes her to Middleham Castle. Here she embarks on a passionate affair with Miles Forrest, the Duke of Gloucester's trusted henchman. But is her lover all he seems?

"...a vivid and visceral journey into the darkest hearts of men during the Wars of the Roses... An incredible, unforgettable story, surely made for the screen. Moonyeen Blakey is a major new talent to watch."

— Sally Spedding

THE ASTREYA TRILOGY
BY SEYMOUR HAMILTON

A tale of the sea, a mystery, and a love story from another time, and a different coast, where true-to-life adventures challenge believable characters.

"...a trilogy that will fascinate all those who have the sea in their blood and yearn for those days of sail. This is a sailor's yarn brilliantly told... I could not put this book down."
-- Commander David Newing, LVO, Royal Navy retired

BOOK I: THE VOYAGE SOUTH
BOOK II: THE MEN OF THE SEA
BOOK III: THE WANDERER'S CURSE

FOR MORE ABOUT ASTREYA'S WORLD, VISIT
ASTREYATRILOGY.COM

Available at:
Amazon.com and through leading bookstores and ebook sellers internationally. For the finest in nautical and historical fiction and non-fiction, visit:

www.Fireshippress.com

CPSIA information can be obtained at www.ICGtesting.com
Printed in the USA
LVOW041514260712

291582LV00003B/2/P